THE WATER TRADE

CLESS KAI

NANI PUBLISHING

❀ Created with Vellum

For Mom and Dad...

"I fear not the man who has practiced 10,000 kicks once, but I fear the man who had practiced one kick 10,000 times."

— **Bruce Lee**

My kid brother would create his own language—words and phrases we all understood. Responded to. Until the day, fifteen years ago, when he shouted, "Sugi-sugi-obake," and we didn't run. We didn't run, and now he was dead.

The guilt was relentless. I tried to outrun it, but the images continued to chase after me in step. It circled me, haunted me every day, sometimes every hour. So, I ran faster. My breathing strained, heart beating rapid against my chest.

A thin branch suddenly whipped across my face. Though I knew it would leave a mark, I didn't care. The branch was a quick reminder to not only *see* with the eyes, but to also *feel* with the senses.

Hell no, I wasn't a masochist. I hated pain.

If only everything in my life were that simple—no more over-thinking, no more overanalyzing, done with the exhaustion of living in a tireless loop, dissecting every fraction of time for cracks, places where I might have done things differently.

I welcomed misjudging the branch. For just a second, the incident vanished from my mind. No afterthought. No pondering my

error or misjudgment. Just whack—whipped across the face—
then it was over.

Once a star on the girl's track and basketball teams at Kaiser
High School, I was now twenty-one, unemployed, and broke.
With me standing at five-seven, my strides were long, quick, and
deliberate.

Dead branches from fallen trees raked at my legs like claws
reaching up from the damp ground. The wet, decaying leaves that
covered the forest floor made for slippery footing as I dodged and
twisted around trunks and vines and sinkholes, working to maintain my balance.

No novice hikers on this trail—a steep forty-five-degree
incline at the start, squeezing through densely packed *hau* bush,
jumping from boulder to boulder traversing mountain streams,
then tracing narrow trails cut into overgrown wild ferns that
snaked the edge of a cliff with a six-hundred-foot drop to the
bottom.

Although the terrain was *not* rhythmic, my breathing was.

I recalled how my father, Navy Lieutenant Colonel John
Hunter, would bark, "Keep your eyes moving, always scanning
for the next step."

I hurdled over dead stumps and ducked under fallen tree
limbs. I avoided loose rocks and slippery moss, or ledges that
could collapse under my weight. Never moving in a straight line,
I zigzagged and jumped from one solid footing to the next,
surveying ten to fifteen feet in front.

No time to study the best path, simply reacting on instincts.

At the end of the mountain trail, the finale, my father and I
would fist-bump, high-five, and give a guttural, "Hooyah!"

The damp forest, the crisp mountain air, the quiet, the physi-
cality—this was where I found solace. The serenity of being on
the top of the world freed my mind, helped me focus and elimi-
nate some, if not all, of the noise in my head.

But today was different. The image was still scribed like hieroglyphs on my brain, and no amount of running could erase what I'd found in the kitchen drawer lying atop a measuring spoon, a metal grater, and other cooking utensils.

My mind drifted as my trainers struck the muddy trail.

Once again came that tireless loop of asking my mother, "How does a mom abandon her child? Why did you leave me? Did you care that I was seventeen and alone in the emergency room, plastic tubing and a suction pump pulling the sleeping pills back up?"

I pushed harder at the last half-mile mark. My body was slick with sweat, and my breath plumed in the chilly air of the Koolau Mountain Range, a dormant volcano with a summit ridge spanning over two thousand feet above sea level.

"Hol-it! Hol-it!" came sudden screams from behind.

Fifty feet back, Lani glared with fire in her eyes. Her heavy breathing amplified within the quiet canopy of Norfolk pine. She choked, coughed, then held up a left palm like a traffic cop. With hands on knees, she signaled for me to give her a second.

Taking a deep breath, she gasped, "What da fuck, Gena! You said this would be fun!"

As sweat dripped off my brow, a tinge of guilt hit me at seeing my best friend collapse on a massive tree trunk that appeared to have been struck by lightning some time ago.

Catching my breath, I strolled back and stood in front of her. "But it's fun."

"The hell it is," Lani cried out, frowning as if I'd lost my marbles.

Her face sagged with exhaustion. She clutched the empty twenty-ounce water bottle as though squeezing the handle of a slot machine. From the bottom of her form-fitting red athletic shorts to the top of her white ankle socks, her legs were smeared with mud. Her right shoe appeared to have been dunked in a vat of molten chocolate, with more mud on her cheeks, chin, and forehead.

Lani Fernandez had been my closest friend since elementary school and throughout high school. She stood at five-foot-two, and her long, flowing black hair was pinned, bundled, and tucked under a Nike baseball cap. A local beauty to the core, she would say she was one-fifth Portuguese, one-fifth Chinese, one-fifth Filipino, one-fifth Japanese, and the final fifth rum and coke.

"Poi dog to the max," she'd say proudly.

I shuffled close and plopped down next to her. Cool moisture from the collapsed tree soaked through my camo-printed shorts. I pinched together the black, sleeveless, sweaty spandex top, then glanced out at the distant horizon.

The city of Honolulu was spread out below, the blue ocean water of the harbor at its edge. To the distant left was the iconic Diamond Head Crater with the densely packed Waikiki hotels in the foreground. This amazing panoramic view reminded me that only in Hawaii were we able to surf at six in the morning and hike to the top of a mountain in the same day.

I loved the silence of the forest. The only sounds were the wind blowing past my ears and the occasional singsong melody of chirping birds in the brush.

Though today, I hated such moments of calmness, because they brought back the image of my father's drooping shoulders as he stared at the letter on the kitchen counter and wiped the corner of his eye with a finger. He slipped the letter in the drawer, stalked outside and loaded his truck with a one-man canoe, glanced at the ocean's horizon, and drove off.

I waited for the rumble of the truck to crest the hill and fade down into the valley, then drifted toward the kitchen drawer. I couldn't help myself.

Niele! my mother always said. *So nosey!*

After fifteen years of marriage and six years of separation, my mother, Emiko Hunter, made it final—divorce papers, citing "irreconcilable differences."

Lani reached into her fanny pack, pulled out a doobie, and lit up. She didn't offer the joint to me; I hated the high of marijuana, which converted my brain and body into a run-of-the-mill garden slug. The worst part was having a bag of potato chips as the center of my universe.

With inaction and the silence of the forest, the thought in the back of my mind blurted forward. "I need money, Lan."

Lani inhaled and blew smoke into the light breeze. "For school?"

"Part of it."

"Easy solution," she said, staring at the city below. "Do what I did."

I shook my head. "You know I can't do that."

"Why not?" She took another hit, this time holding it in.

"Why?" I made a face. "Because it's illegal."

Lani tilted her head toward the blue sky and blew another stream of smoke. The sweet aroma of marijuana blended nicely with the wetness of the forest. "Money's damn good. Hey, I bought a new car for my *tutu* and an SUV for me."

"Yeah, see, I don't love school or my grandmother that much."

"It's not like I robbed a bank."

"But it's a massage parlor, man."

"So?"

"So? It's a massage parlor and they don't even offer massages."

"So I jerk guys off." Lani pinched the joint between her fingers and watched its slow burn. "But there's no sex. I show them some titties, and if the dude tries to touch 'em, I'd fuckin' bite his fingers off. Once they get the message, I'll fake a massage by throwing on a pair of latex gloves, add a little bit of lotion, and in a few minutes it's over, *pau*, done."

"No way, dude. I'm not like you." I cringed; I didn't care whether it was called whacking the doodle, polishing the dolphin, or shaking hands with Mr. Happy. I forced the sickening images from my head. "Besides, I hate it when men use women for—"

"Are you kidding me?" Lani quickly cut me off. "Men have been exploiting the female gender since the beginning of time. Wake up, girl!"

Lani would do what she needed to do in order to achieve what she wanted in life, yet there was a red line she would never cross. In most cases, her red line was much further out than mine. Lani didn't care what people thought or said about her, something I totally admired, and perhaps that was what cemented our close friendship.

Of all the times that Lani shoplifted, she got busted lifting a pair of Gucci earrings from Ala Moana. I didn't know why I did it, but I told the police that I stole the earrings, said that I stuffed them in her pocket when she wasn't looking. The cops didn't buy it, but they had no choice. My parents grounded me for three weeks. Lani would call every day asking, "How's it going?" We'd chat for hours into the night, and from that moment on we became inseparable.

"Two cars, eh?" I asked out of curiosity, but I knew someone would have to put a blowtorch to my brain to get me to cross that line.

"Damn right." Lani held up two fingers, took another hit, and said in a nasal voice, "If you need bucks for school, why not ask your dad again?"

"Can't, unless I promise not to drop out . . . again. I'm on my own." I stood and worked my legs to keep them from tightening in the cold air. I paced in front of Lani to warm up, then said in frustration, "Hell, I can't even buy an airline ticket."

"Again, ask your dad."

"If I told him the reason, he'd say no."

"You know the difference between us. You're just too fuckin' nice." A phrase that Lani had repeated often enough. "You force me to rush across a damn crosswalk because you don't want to keep drivers waiting. Then you cut short talking-story 'cause you worry about taking up people's time. Holy moly, Gen."

"Okay, okay." I started jogging in place. "I get your point."

"You know I love you, but you'll probably give the guy a blowjob to be employee of the month."

I winced disgust. "You done?"

"Yeah, I'm done," she said, but held up a finger. "And one more thing, then I'll shut up . . . You're too damn sensitive."

"Yeah, yeah." I cut her off and faced the trail. "I heard that before. Now you're done?"

Lani nodded.

"Then break's over, let's go."

I strolled along the narrow trail for another hundred feet before I turned back and asked, "Why'd you stop if the money was that good?"

"Two reasons." Lani rotated her right arm in a winding circle, like a baseball pitcher, and made a face of intense pain. "One—tennis elbow."

I spun to face the trail, continued walking, and burst out laughing. Lani chuckled from behind.

"Well,"—I pivoted back again— "what's the second reason?"

Lani carefully tiptoed around a mud hole in the trail and shrugged. "Sorry, but can't tell you that."

"Uhh . . . big secret, eh?"

She forced a smile and shooed me forward with a wave. "Better if you didn't know."

"Whatevas." I huffed, pretending to be upset. "Then how 'bout we pick up the pace?"

"Hold your horses, Sista." Lani sneered, snorted phlegm from deep within her sinus cavity, and expertly spat a glob on the side of the trail. "Okay . . . get the hell out of here and leave me to the wolves. And say hi to Zeus for me when you get to the top of Mount Olympus."

Once we reached the peak, it took us half the time to get back down to where Lani's SUV was parked. She'd left it on a side road, at the bottom of a sloped property belonging to a two-story log cabin house that blended naturally with the surrounding trees.

Then it registered, and I cracked up laughing.

Lani was spread out on the hood of her SUV as though she'd just returned to Earth after three months in outer space. She twisted her head sideward. "What's up with you?"

"I get it now. Why you named your SUV White Whale."

"Boy you're slow, Gen." She brought her hand to her mouth like a megaphone and shouted, "There she blows!"

A little after five, we drove up the steep winding incline to my home on Mariners Ridge in Hawaii Kai, an exclusive hilltop neighborhood perched along the southeastern ridge of the Koolaus.

We had purchased our three-bedroom, two-bath house in this quiet cul-de-sac eleven years ago. Although the divorce papers had stated that the ownership of the house would be transferred to my dad, I definitely preferred my mother greeting me whenever I came home.

Our house was two stories, split-level with a high ceiling and stemmed overhead fans. A large plate-glass window in the living room provided glimpses of the shoreline and the shopping area of Koko Marina below, with its eight-screen Cineplex theaters, Costco, and an assortment of restaurants and other businesses.

More of a muscle car than utilitarian hauler, a 1992 Chevy C1500 pickup truck was parked in our neighbor's driveway, painted burgundy with white flames on the hood. The once-polished, custom-chromed mag wheels were now tarnished with neglected grime. A joyful routine for Mr. Kapena was to dress in a black gas monkey sweatshirt, blue jeans, and backward baseball cap, and cruise down Waikiki on Sundays with a convoy of other muscle cars.

Lani pulled in front of my neighbor's mailbox. Mr. Kapena sprung from his wooden bench on the porch, waving a fist in the air.

"Oh shit," I mumbled under my breath. "Now you did it."

"What'd I do?"

"Mr. Kapena gets pissed if anybody parks in front of his mailbox. Getting the mail is his ritual. I picked up his mail a few times. It's mostly junk mail. You know, everybody's asking for donations or trying to scam old people out of their savings."

I climbed out of the White Whale and met the sixty-seven-year-old man at the front bumper. He was short and stocky, with hair too thin to hide his reddening scalp. His face was hardened, etched from time and experiences. Liko, his large pet Akita, barked non-stop inside of the house, with deep heavy woofs.

Mr. Kapena snarled. "Get that damn truck away from my mailbox."

I touched his dry, liver-spotted forearm. "Sorry Mr. Kapena. My friend is moving her truck right now."

I hand-signaled Lani to park farther down the street.

We had lived next to the Kapenas since I was ten years old. After Mrs. Kapena's death from cancer three years ago, her husband started showing early signs of dementia. At times he would forget that his wife had passed, and still talked about her in present tense.

"Eh *haole* girl, when you going bring me *kumu* again?" This time he was grinning, the mailbox incident quickly forgotten.

"I'll stop by Chinatown on Wednesday."

The old man chuckled. "Not like the old days. We had plenty

fish back den . . ." His eyes then shifted from side to side as though searching his memory. "You saw the drug bust on TV last night? We cornered the Big Island drug lord and . . ." His voice seemed to dissipate as the wind blew stronger from the ocean.

I guided my neighbor by his forearm, back to the porch. Mr. Kapena stared down at the cracked concrete walkway and started singing the lyrics from "Somewhere Over The Rainbow." His tone grew softer as I steered him onto the wooden bench.

"See you, Mr. Kapena." I squeezed his hand. "I'll drop fish off on Wednesday, okay?"

He didn't respond, instead pointed toward the ocean and the fast-approaching gray storm clouds.

I joined Lani, who was nervously waiting at the base of the driveway. She asked, "Is he okay?"

"I think so. Hard to believe he was once HPD's top detective." I still remembered the once vibrant man and said, "The drug bust he talked about happened eight years ago. Unfortunately, he was forced to retire in disgrace."

"Disgrace?"

"Yeah. A cop I know said he got framed. Because of his wife's chemo treatments at the time, he didn't fight the accusation. But let me tell you, when he's on, his mind is as sharp as a razor. He goes in and out, and doctors still can't figure out why."

As we headed for the house, Lani asked, "So what's up with the singing?"

"This doctor from Finland believes that singing is cognitively and emotionally beneficial in the early stages of dementia. He says that music helps dementia patients recall memories, emotions, and—"

Thunder suddenly cracked overhead. I cringed at the shock wave. My skin and bones felt welded together for a split second. At the horizon, the sky had darkened, and black thunderheads swirled and bulldozed toward land. Lightning flashed within the dark storm clouds, triggering that awful memory from fifteen years ago.

Lani reached up and placed a hand on my shoulder. "Hanalei?"

I nodded. "I thought I got over it totally, but . . . I guess not."

We walked to the side of the house and rinsed our feet and legs with the garden hose. The residual water drained into a small patch of mondo grass that Mom had planted at the edge of the walkway, another reminder of her absence.

The cloudbank burst overhead like a canon, vibrating the air. Heavy raindrops battered the roof. My hands trembled; I squeezed them into fists to stop them from shaking. Though I'd gotten better, a lot depended on my mood, and the letter sitting in the kitchen drawer wasn't helping.

My mother, Emiko Hunter, had made sure that her kitchen had all the modern appliances, and kept the place showroom spotless. Although my father and I tried to hold that same standard, an occasional cockroach would breakdance on the tiled floor, happy that we didn't.

While Lani washed off in the guest bathroom on the second level, I made tuna sandwiches and emptied a bag of chips onto paper plates before heading for the shower.

The house was built on an incline above the covered garage, and vibrated as the garage door rolled up. As I blow-dried my hair, I pictured my dad parking his Tundra. The door shuddered closed again. I donned a pair of track shorts and an extra-large T-shirt with the UCLA logo on the front, and headed for the kitchen.

Lani's voice rose above the sound of the rain on the tiled roof. "Hey Mr. H, how was the water?"

My father's deep, commanding voice funneled through the hallway. "It was choppy, but get this—a school of dolphins kept me company."

"For real . . . dolphins. That's super cool."

"Yeah, but they got bored with the land creature and eventually left me in the dusk."

Lani had changed into blue gym shorts and a T-shirt with *Poi Dog* stenciled on the front. She didn't hide the fact that she had a slight crush on my dad and every so often would tell me how handsome and cool he was for an old guy.

She was into macho guys with granite jaws, long, lean muscles, and killer smiles. My dad's full head of black hair was cut short, flecked with gray at the temples, and always well combed and trimmed.

Twice decorated for bravery, he was a dive officer based at Pearl Harbor, and part of Mobile Diving and Salvage Unit One, a group of Navy divers with salvage capabilities for the entire Pacific Fleet.

Lani often teased, "Wouldn't it be cool if I ended up being your mother?" After a beat, she'd add, "I bet your pop is a stud in bed."

"Don't even go there, girl." I would lightly shove her off balance, and we'd both crack up laughing.

Although I adored my dad, he was domineering and an excessive disciplinarian, and had tried many times to sculpt me in his own image. An excellent swimmer and an avid ocean man, he'd annually enter the 10K run, Honolulu Marathon, and any other outdoor sporting event held on Oahu.

John Hunter was my hero, but in many ways, I could never be like him. A gregarious extrovert, he could pounce on stage in front of a large crowd and sing like Engelbert Humperdinck and Blue Spanish Eyes at the drop of a hat.

Whenever he called for his little girl to join him on stage, I would slouch my shoulders and slump lower under the table. Many times, it was my mom who came to the rescue by laughing as though it were a family joke, lifting me up from under the table and giving me a big hug.

"Hey Sport," my father said when I walked into the kitchen. I gave him a peck on the cheek and joined Lani, who was sitting at the kitchen island with its faux marble top.

The three of us chatted for half an hour. My dad described his day on the ocean. We talked about the awesome morning swell at sunrise, then the challenging hike to the top of the mountain.

Lani wolfed down two sandwiches, yawned with her closed fist covering her mouth, and stood from the stool. "Sorry, but time for me to rock-and-roll home, soak my little tootsies in hot water, and sleep for days."

"Why don't you stay for dinner, Lani?" My father had his head halfway in the refrigerator. "We got some steaks and slices of teriyaki meat, and we can bake a few potatoes."

"Mahalo, Mr. H. But if I'm not crashing out in an hour, they'll be peeling me from my truck with the jaws of life."

Lani had grabbed a tuna sandwich. At the front door, she held her fingers to her ear mimicking a phone, and mouthed, "Call me."

Although the storm had eased to a drizzle, I handed her an umbrella.

Lani dashed to Mr. Kapena sitting on the porch and gave him the sandwich. She dragged herself to the White Whale, started up, and pulled away from the curb.

From the driveway, I waved at Mr. Kapena and walked into the house, chuckling to myself. "There she blows, eh."

My father cried out from the kitchen, "I got some leftover chicken that I can micro. You good with that?"

"What happened to the steak and teri meat?"

"That's for guest."

"Oh . . . okay." I proceeded with our Sunday evening routine. Fatigue hit me like a brick as I ambled into the living room, where we'd watch the early evening news together, and switched on the TV.

The landline rang. From the kitchen, my father shouted, "I'll get it."

After a few minutes, the sound of a TV commercial on Hawaii's close cultural ties to Japan rose over the silence of the kitchen.

Thinking that my father had gone outside for some reason, I strolled into the kitchen and found him standing over the sink, his head down, face ashen white.

"Dad?" I shifted closer. "Are you okay?"

Still, he didn't move.

"Dad. What's wrong?"

A tear dribbled from the corner of his eye and down his cheek. He wiped it away with the back of his hand. "Your mother is dead."

2

My father sat stunned on a bar stool at the kitchen counter, staring at a space in front of him. I needed to move, so I walked into the living room and glanced out the picture window overlooking the bustling community of Koko Marina after a downpour.

As the shadowed ocean merged with the gray sky, vehicles weaved through the gridded streets below. A pleasure boat made its way through the rippling water in the marina on its way back from the open ocean. A flock of wild ducks flew across the valley —life went on.

But our world had collapsed onto itself under this bottomless pain. The deep emptiness of hearing that my mother had died thousands of miles away felt like a stun gun to my chest. All of my energy drained in a fraction of a second—an immediate fatigue, heavy with indescribable loss. No amount of physical pain could compare to the sharpness, this wretched hollowness that frightened me.

Pain built on numbness, built on emptiness. Tears ran down my cheeks. I said, in a voice that didn't sound like my own, "Dad, tell me what happened."

His hands, steel-hardened from his daily workouts, were now lifeless. He dug his palms into his swollen eyes and shook his head back and forth. Not looking at me, he murmured in flat monotone, slightly above a whisper, "That was your mother's business partner, Kiyomi. She got the news from the police just a few minutes ago. It happened early this morning, and . . ."

I clutched my father's hands.

The strings in his neck tightened. He swallowed. "Kiyomi said that she was stabbed in a robbery while closing the bar. The police are investigating. As of yet, there's no suspect."

"Robbery." The word left my mouth in a whisper. People on the six o'clock news get killed in robberies, their names read off a teleprompter. This was not happening.

She can't be dead.

I struggled to ask, "Did she suffer?"

He shook his head, dazed, and said, "I don't know. She didn't get into the details. I don't think she knows herself. The police had called her just a few minutes ago . . ." His voice trailed off.

My father slid from the bar stool as though life's energy had drained from his entire body. His once powerful shoulders were now slumped like branches from a dying giant banyan tree.

Feeling abandoned and alone on the stool, salty tears ran down my cheek. I went to him and rested my head on his chest like when I was little. The comfort—his strong arms, the scent of Old Spice aftershave, the warmth of his body—caused my lips and throat to contract. I wept without restraint.

The woman newscaster's voice filled the silence with the day's news. "Honolulu police raided a Chinatown gambling den and confiscated illegal drugs and video poker machines. This continuous series of busts includes a crackdown on prostitution operating out of massage parlors . . ."

His face tightened; his Adam's apple pulsed. He fingered the corner of his eye.

My dad never ever displayed his frustration or emotion in public, or in front of me for that matter. Though he pretended that his wife leaving had no effect on him, I knew it was eating him up inside.

John Hunter had been the rock of our family. He made both my mother and me feel safe and secure. He was always there for us, especially for me. He'd picked me up within an hour's time from school whenever I felt sick. He helped me with homework and sold stacks of chili for my track team fundraiser. When I got a flat tire on the H1 freeway, he was just a phone call away.

I waited with him in silence for an hour, with a heavy heart. I had never seen my father looking as though he didn't know what to do next. I let out a breath, stood, and headed for the door to the garage.

He lifted his head. "Where're you going?"

I stopped at the door. "We need to start packing. Gonna get the suitcases. You need to call the airline and get whatever flight there is to Tokyo."

I turned back to the door, but his following words froze my next step.

"I'm not going."

I faced him, breath caught in my throat. "What do you mean you're not going? You have to go. She's your wife. My mother."

"Like I said, I'm not going." Dad stood up without looking at me and dragged himself into the living room.

The voice of the newscaster vanished with a flick of the remote. Footsteps trailed out the front door, followed by the sound of water flowing through the pipes. My mother's stern instruction before she left us was to water the plants. A man of his word, seemingly on autopilot, my father performed his ritual even though it had been pouring rain just a few minutes ago.

I booked two tickets to Narita on Delta Airlines for mid-morning the next day and headed to the garage for our luggage.

Two hours later, my father's suitcase was still open and empty on the living room floor.

I glanced at the clock on the wall—twelve midnight, which meant early evening in Japan. Like my mother, Kiyomi-chan normally hated to be disturbed while busy with customers, but things were *not* normal. Her business partner was dead.

I dialed the bar. The phone rang ten times before a young woman's voice answered with an accent, "Club Blue Diamond."

I was born in Japan when Dad was stationed at Yokosuka Naval Base, and found out while attending Japanese school and learning the language that my classmates and I were of that unique group of kids referred to as military brats. Although I still understood the language, I regrettably couldn't speak Japanese fluently. Now I wished I'd studied harder.

Speaking slowly in Japanese, I asked for Kiyomi-chan. Whoever answered the phone dropped it on a hard surface. I listened to a mixture of bar sounds—loud chattering, drunken laughter, glasses clinking, an occasional cough, and a man singing karaoke off-tune to Morris Albert's "Feelings."

As I waited, I cringed at the man's awful singing. I thought of how my dad would have mocked him by now. "Where's my Glock? I gotta put that damn cat out of its misery." While most families went on picnics for the holidays, my father and I spent time at the Koko Head shooting range.

In five minutes, the voice on the phone came back, more mature this time. "Hai." Kiyomi was forty-five, two years older than my mother.

"Konbanwa . . . this is Gena . . . Emiko's daughter from Hawaii."

She let out a loud huff, her voice thickly accented. "I very busy. No can talk to you."

Before she could end the call, I shouted into the phone, "Just one minute, please. One minute."

With the din of bar noise in the background, Kiyomi hesitated, then replied, "Hai, one minute."

I said in Japanese, "I need to know what happened to my mother."

The karaoke singing faded as she shuffled to another location. "Your mama was stabbed when closing."

I shivered at hearing the word "stabbed." The idea of having a knife or sharp metal object penetrate any part of my body did not register as reality. My eyes started to well, but I held back and bit my lower lip. I had to stay strong, or I would not get to the truth.

"Weren't you there at closing?" I may have come across as blaming her, because the phone went silent. "I'm sorry. I'm very upset at the moment. And I really appreciate you taking the time to tell me what happened."

Kiyomi's voice erupted through the tiny speaker. "We open at two in the afternoon. I open the bar and work to ten. Emiko-chan, your mother, starts at six and she works to two in the morning. So she closes the place. Because we open every day of the week, we decided that eight hours per day is better than both of us putting twelve. After three months, we would change shift. She would open the place and I would close it. That was our agreement."

Although Kiyomi couldn't see me, I nodded, understanding.

"Her money and Rolex were stolen. The police think that it was a random robbery." Kiyomi sounded as though my mother had cut her finger while preparing a meal, not been stabbed to death.

Random was like saying unlucky.

I was starting to hate this woman, but I needed information.

"The police said she was in the wrong place at the wrong time." Kiyomi sounded colder now, disinterested.

I needed to keep her talking. "Do you know—where's her body?"

The phone went silent a few seconds before she replied, "You need to ask the Shinjuku police. They will not release her for burial until a family member identifies the body. They are also performing the investigation to the robbery."

She didn't say the word murdered or killed, and I was thankful for that.

Kiyomi stopped talking and yelled to someone in the bar, "Where are you going?"

A man roared with disgust. "I wait for you, but you take too long."

"You promised to buy me a drink before you go back to the sagging bosom of your wife." Kiyomi faked a giggle.

The man laughed and yelled at the bartender to bring mama-Kiyomi a glass of shochu. The noise got louder as she walked back to the crowd.

Kiyomi shouted over the noise, "I very busy. I must go."

Just as well. I didn't know what else to say, or what else to ask.

I was about to hang up when Kiyomi's tone of voice turned standoffish. "Your mother and I had an agreement."

I waited a few seconds to let her coldness soak in. "What agreement?"

"That on the death of either one of us, the other would automatically inherit the business."

Through clenched teeth, I held back what I really wanted to say, knowing that I might regret it. I took a deep breath. "Arigato Kiyomi-chan. My father and I will be coming to Japan to bury my mother. We will talk more."

"I will take care of all the funeral arrangements and expenses." This time I felt her sincerity. "Your mother and I were not only partners; she was also my friend."

My mother and Kiyomi started working the water trade, *mizu shobai*, in their late teens. Although they'd had their disagreements about how to run the business, they were still friends. That was what my mother had told me.

I thanked Kiyomi again and ended the call.

I glanced at my father's empty suitcase. He hadn't moved from the living room sofa, where he was staring at the blank TV screen.

I sat cross-legged on the floor in front of him. "Dad, you have to go. If you don't, I know you'll regret it for the rest of your life."

If he had said something, anything, to explain why he didn't want to go, I could have debated with him and hopefully convinced him otherwise. He too knew that, so he said nothing, just gave me his patented stone-cold expression. At that moment, I hated the military and how they had molded this man with pure pride and ego, two powerful and dominant character traits with strengths as well as weaknesses.

"You are always so stubborn." I blew out a breath. "Can't you for once listen to another point of view?"

"Like father, like daughter." He mumbled softly.

Through gritted teeth, I tried a comeback, but with my head about to explode I couldn't form simple sentences, so I just grunted.

I stood up from the floor and paced in front of him to help vent my anger when I stubbed my toe on the open suitcase. I squinted from the intense pain, growled at the inanimate object, and gave it a heel kick. The suitcase slid a couple feet on the carpet.

My father looked on, but didn't react to my battle with the suitcase.

A streak of lightning flashed across the window. I closed the living room drapes and left my dad sitting on the sofa with his own thoughts.

Knowing that tomorrow would be a long day, I headed for my

bedroom to get some sleep. After thirty minutes, I was still awake. Rain came down hard again, pounding the roof in a continuous roar. My hands shook more than ever. The back door hinged open, then closed. Through the rain, I heard the high-pitched squeaks of the double swing in the backyard. This swing, which my father and mother had built together, where they'd relax, soaking in the setting sun and savoring a nice Bordeaux.

I peeked through the bedroom curtain. My father's hair was plastered to his scalp. His clothes sagged from the weight of water. He rode the swing back and forth, staring out into the darkness and the glimmering lights of Koko Marina through flashes of lightning.

Fear struck me with each crack of thunder. But this time it wasn't so much the past that terrified me, but the unknown, the uncertainty of traveling to Japan by myself, and having to deal with what would be the worst time of my life—alone.

3

Eight o'clock the following morning, my father's luggage was where I'd left it, empty on the living room floor.

I refused to talk or look at him at the breakfast table. He had prepared eggs and sausages with hot coffee.

With an invisible barrier between us, he stared at his plate and muttered in his deep baritone, "You gonna be a sourpuss all day?"

A smiled cracked across my sourpuss face. "Sorry."

After breakfast, my dad waited in his truck, parked in the driveway, staring out through the windshield, fingers drumming on the steering wheel.

I had on a plain, black, sleeveless jumpsuit, worn a little baggy. Instead of pumps, I'd chosen comfortable black wedge sandals. All of my clothes tended to be on the modest and conservative side. Lani accused me of dressing like an accountant, an engineer, or someone in a TV series from the sixties.

When I hopped into the passenger seat, my father handed me $3,000 in cash, started the engine, and pulled out from the cul-de-sac, toward the airport.

We stopped at Lani's apartment in Kapahulu, a subdivision located at the base of Diamond Head Crater. Failing to convince my dad to attend his wife's funeral, I'd called Lani at two in the morning. Lani burst into tears on the phone when she heard the bad news.

Between sobs, when I asked her to tag along, Lani's voice rose. "You got it. I can take emergency vacation. Becky Melchor owes me a favor. She can cover for me."

"You're the best, Lan."

"I just need to be back by next Monday." Her voice had a tinge of regret, as though she'd be deserting me.

"No problem, Lan. That gives you seven days."

After working for the city for three years, Lani was suing her employer for sexual harassment in the workplace. Her immediate supervisor had denied her promotion because she wouldn't go out with him. She'd taped conversations of the jerk making sexist remarks, and her lawyer said that the case was strong.

Dressed in comfortable blue jeans, sneakers, a long-sleeved green sweater, and a thick jacket with the UH football logo in back, Lani had a carry-on strapped over her shoulder and was pulling a large suitcase. My father loaded her luggage onto the truck bed.

Lani loved my mother. We traveled to Japan on a graduation trip and bunked at Mom's apartment in Shibuya. Staying up late on her nights off, we drank sake and talked about everything, like comparing the differences between Japanese and American men.

That night Mom slurred, "Japanese guys fight for the bill. They would swoop in like a ninja and attack the dinner check before you could reach for your wallet. White guys . . . hmm, they keep talking for another thirty minutes. They avoid looking at the check on the table as if it were a dead toad."

Lani cried out, "And some guys go, 'How 'bout we go Dutch?'"

We cracked up laughing.

"Here's one." Lani drank the tiny ceramic cup of sake,

croaked like a frog, and giggled. "Sorry. And—and Japanese guys got better manners."

"Not necessarily." My mother burped too, adding to the symphony of dispersing human gas. "They do not open doors, or help you put on your coat . . . And—and some pick their nose in public."

"I got another." Lani raised her hand like in school. "What about penis size?"

Mom's brow crinkled and she leaned closer. "Let me tell you Lani-chan. From my personal experience, I'd say not true, but . . . but—I've never took an official survey, so I'll leave that one alone."

Again, we cracked up laughing.

The way they bonded sent a pang of jealousy through me, but in the end I shrugged it off, because they were two people I loved and adored.

On the ride to the airport, my father didn't say a word. Lani and I also said nothing, so the twenty-minute ride was tense.

"Crap," I said and pulled my cell out.

Lani gave me her usual side-eyed look—*what the hell now?*

I placed the call on speaker. "Hey Angel, I need a favor."

"Gena?"

"Yeah, it's me. I need you to stop by Chinatown and buy a kumu this Wednesday and drop it off to my neighbor, Mr. Kapena."

"Shoowa." Angel exhaled.

"Mahalo . . . I owe you one."

Angel was a high school classmate. He was three hundred pounds and of Hawaiian-Portuguese ethnicity; a quiet guy. If he hadn't been built like a Detroit Lions defensive tackle, you wouldn't know he was in the room. He and Lani dated a couple times, then figured out they were better as friends.

Before hanging up, Lani tapped my shoulder from the back seat. "Tell that panty-ass Hawaiian *braddah*—don't mess this up."

Angel roared with laughter. "Yeah . . . I heard my future wife."

Lani cupped her hands and shouted at the phone, "What about your present wife and two kids?"

"My wife is only in it for my debonair personality and sexy body." His voice lowered as if he were sharing a secret. "I'll sell the kids." Angel made kissy sounds before ending the call.

Five minutes later, the truck pulled up to the curb under the overhead sign for Delta Airlines. As though on autopilot, my dad jumped from the cab, strolled in back, and unloaded our luggage from the truck bed onto the sidewalk.

He walked up to me standing on the curb and gave me a hug. "You be careful, okay?"

I nodded, with tears in my eyes. "I love you, Dad."

"I love you too, Sport." He wiped my tears with a finger, turned to Lani, and gave her a hug. "You be careful too."

"I will, Mr. H," she said, grinning. "And don't worry about Sport, I got her back."

My dad climbed back into his truck and drove away.

NINE HOURS to Tokyo with an estimated time of arrival at 3:20 p.m. I tried catching some Zs on the plane, but my head was spinning and my thoughts drifted.

After the beverage cart made its second pass, I fell asleep, and awoke twenty minutes later with my left leg tingling and my neck stiff. My stomach stirred with the anxiety of knowing that I was getting closer to the reality of my mother's death.

Lani jolted awake when I gripped her hand. "You scared the shit out of me, man . . . thought we were crashing."

"Sorry, but we'll be landing in thirty minutes."

Though we were bruised and dazed, our day was just starting.

Our luggage came up on the first conveyor-belt load. We took the west exit at Narita Airport and caught a taxi to Shinjuku Police Station.

My mind was stuck on the shocking thought that I would not be seeing my mother alive on this trip, or ever again.

A couple hours later, the cabbie pulled in front of a box-shaped building consisting of a dozen floors of glass and faded, cedar-colored concrete. A sign labeled *Shinjuku Police Station* was attached to the side of the building. Black-and-white police cars with red light bars bolted across the top were parked in front.

The golden arches of a McDonald's protruded from the top of an adjacent building. A dozen men and women dressed in warm clothes strolled in both directions across the sidewalk in front of the fast-food restaurant, holding election posters for someone named Kazuo Hayashida. Pictured in a dark suit and red tie, the man was handsome enough to be a film actor.

Lani stumbled out on her side of the taxi, stretched her arms, and lazily performed a few jumping jacks.

The entry door greeted us with hostility as our stuffed suit-cases got sandwiched between the revolving glass panes. Tokyo's finest came to our rescue. Two young men dressed in navy blue pants with broad suspenders hurried to protect the distressed women from the aggressive door. Lani thanked them with her Scarlett O'Hara smile. One of the guys stumbled on his partner's foot while backing away, staring as though he wanted to ask me on a date.

I had earned my share of adolescent scars, like when I stood above the tallest boy for our elementary school class picture, and someone shouted, "Fee-fi-fo-fum." The worst was being called Cry Baby in the playground. Lanky and uncoordinated, I never considered myself attractive, and still don't. My forehead was too wide, my ears stood out like motorcycle handles, my legs were too muscular. Lani would tease me, saying I could break walnuts with my big toes. It freaked me out when men made a fuss trying to get my attention.

The elevator opened on a floor sectioned by low partitions and a cacophony of loud chatter. A woman sat at a computer monitor behind the front desk. She was in her mid-forties and wore a dark blue two-piece suit. Her fingers flew across the keyboard non-stop. A Japanese man, also in his forties and with slick black hair, sat sidesaddle on her desk, jokingly asking her out to dinner and telling her what a great lover he was.

We lugged our suitcases in front of them.

"Sumimasen," I said with politeness—real Japanese.

But the woman kept typing and the man kept flirting. Lani shrugged, yawned, and inched her hand toward an inbox on the desk.

"Sorry, pardon me." I raised my voice—less Japanese.

"Yes," the woman with shoulder-length black hair replied without looking up from her typing. The man frowned at being interrupted, slid off the desk, and strutted past us to the elevator.

"I'm looking for anyone who can help me." I bowed courteously and spoke over the din of office chatter. "My mother was killed—" I stopped to keep my voice from cracking. Lani placed a comforting hand on my arm. "She was robbed and killed Sunday night."

The woman didn't break her stride, her fingers still a blur.

Lani huffed out a breath. Using her index finger, she discretely pushed the woman's inbox, filled with brown inter-department envelopes, over the edge of the desk. Like a gunshot in a crowded room, the metal box crashed to the tiled floor with a loud bang.

The chattering stopped. Eyes fell upon us.

The woman glared. "What do you want?"

"My mother. I, ahh . . . who can I speak to about a woman

killed at the Blue Diamond?" I bent to pick up the inbox and straightened the stack of envelopes.

"Inspector Akio Honma is assigned to the case." She pointed down the hallway. "Take a right at the water cooler and walk down the aisle. His office will be on the left."

As though she were the conductor of an orchestra, the moment she started typing again, the chatter in the office also resumed.

I turned and looked into Lani's bloodshot eyes. "Why don't you wait here?" I pointed to twin sofas and a glass table scattered with Japanese magazines.

"Good idea." She attacked the sofa as though it were a cure for jetlag.

I walked to where the woman had indicated. Low partitions were arranged in symmetrical blocks, metal filing cabinets aligned against the wall. Two men were in a strained argument by a desk stacked with folders. They hushed when I got within arm's length.

"I'm looking for Inspector Honma."

One guy glared at me with shifty eyes, turned, and walked to a nearby office.

The other guy, in a wrinkled dark suit, light-blue shirt, and dark tie, frowned. "Hai, I'm Honma." His clothes smelled like an ashtray.

With broad shoulders and a leathery smoker's complexion, he stood around five-six, about an inch shorter than me. He looked to be in his early- to mid-fifties but could have been much younger —his doughy, pale body screamed of a diet of cheap booze, four packs a day, and stress.

I extended my hand. "Pleased to meet you. I'm Gena Hunter. You're the head inspector on the Emiko Hunter case?"

Inspector Honma glanced at my left hand as he shook with his right; his gaze felt shrewd and calculating. He squinted and said, in English, "You are referring to the robbery and death of Emiko Yamashita."

It stung when he referred to my mother by her maiden name.

His voice was low and flat, cold and unemotional. "How do you know the victim?"

"I'm her daughter. Her married name is Hunter."

As if scripted, he glanced down at his hands and said, "I'm sorry for your loss, Miss Hunter."

Honma led me to his office in the corner and pointed at a chair across from his desk. With nicotine-stained fingers, he pushed his black-rimmed glasses higher on his flat nose. His thick black hair was well-groomed, not a strand out of place. He squinted as if he were in glaring sunlight and slid into a high-backed chair.

"You are American?"

"Yes, I am. I just flew in from Hawaii and I'm exhausted. But I can't stay put, or sleep, until I find out what happened to my mother. She died in a robbery. Please tell me what you have so far."

He didn't reply, instead stared out the window at the Tokyo skyline.

I hated being ignored and brushed off. My voice rose. "I traveled many hours. I'm moody and cranky, and I can't continue without knowing. I'm pleading with you to share what you know on the case. Please—" I caught myself leaning forward in the chair, so I took a breath and inched back. "I'm sorry, sir. I didn't mean to . . ."

Honma studied me for a few seconds. "The crime lab is still examining clues. There was a lot of blood, but we suspect that all of it was from your mother, not the person who killed her. He was wearing gloves. There was a footprint in the blood, so we'll be matching the print with size and type of shoe. She was stabbed repeatedly with a knife. From first inspection, it is believed that the knife might have been about a foot long. He probably hid in the shadowed darkness and surprised her when she locked up her bar."

He rattled off the information as if he wanted to purge what was in his mind, and was not about to repeat it.

"You said *he*. How do you know it was a man?"

Honma's sigh sounded like the burner of a hot air balloon. "Because, the perpetrator was strong like a man. After he stabbed the victim, we suspect he was strong enough to lift the body off the ground, because the knife went in below the belly button and cut up to the sternum. It would take a man's strength to do that." He paused before adding, "But it doesn't rule out a woman, however the likelihood is slim."

He must have seen the sheen in my eyes, because he tilted his head as though exasperated with me for demanding that he state the facts but being unable to handle the blunt truth.

"So sorry, Miss Hunter." Although Honma expressed empathy, I wasn't buying it. "I was notified ten minutes ago that there was another murder and . . ." He waved his hand in front like he had already said too much.

The word "murder" finally hit home. Until now, my mother's death had been referred to as a robbery that went sideways.

Truth be told, she was murdered.

Honma retrieved a file and flipped through pages. "Says here that your mother's business partner, Kiyomi Nakagawa, had identified the body, but she's not family."

I nodded.

Honma glanced at the desk clock, five thirty. He was stone-faced, no laugh marks, and his eyes shifted as if gauging his surroundings. "You, being family, should identify the body. We have a few minutes before the morgue closes for the day. If we don't do it today, you'll have to return tomorrow."

"Let's do it now, please." I wiped my face with a tissue I'd pulled from my handbag.

We walked back through the partitioned aisle, then the hall-way. The woman continued rattling on the keyboard. Lani was stretched out on the sofa, her jacket rolled into a bundle and used as a pillow. She was snoring lightly.

Honma ushered me to the elevator. We stood silent and uncomfortable until the door opened. People stepped back and made room for two more. All of the riders got off on the ground floor except us. The door shut and we continued to the basement.

We exited the elevator and walked down a hall. Turning right, we faced a balding man dressed in a white coat, sitting behind a tiny desk in an office no bigger than a closet. Inspector Honma and the man exchanged words in Japanese.

Our footsteps echoed in the hallway as we walked toward a door made of metal and frosted glass. The bald man opened the door with a key.

Honma waved me ahead. "We keep bodies here, as a tempo-rary morgue for recent cases under investigation."

I hesitated about entering but walked through. The air smelled stale and old and had an awful scent of formaldehyde. Honma followed behind me. The room contained two gurneys standing alongside a blue-tiled wall. Fluorescent lights hummed overhead. We approached a wall of refrigerated stainless-steel cubes, like those I had seen so many times on TV.

The bald man glanced at the slip of paper and moved to the cube farthest to the right. I steeled my nerves, my heart. He pulled the handle; it sounded like a walk-in refrigerator door opening. The body inside was covered with a white sheet from head to toe.

I took a half-step back, hoping and praying that it was a big mistake and that this was not my mother. I pleaded to myself—*please don't let it be her, please don't let it be her, please . . .*

The bald man slid the body out on rollers. He peeled the sheet down to the neck, hiding any bodily injuries. My breath caught in my throat. Mom's face, her body, lay motionless on the stainless-steel slab.

I hoped, or perhaps expected, to smell her scented perfume, but all I smelled was death. Her eyes were closed as though she were asleep, but her face was pasty white. Her lip was pulled up unnaturally to one side, exposing her teeth in a grotesque sneer. The tiny birthmark on her left forearm confirmed my nightmare.

My legs buckled. I held on to the edge of the drawer. Tears welled. I felt Honma over my left shoulder.

Sniffling, I nodded.

Despite how much I wanted not to break down, tears trickled from my eyes. I placed my hand on Mom's cheek, leaned over, kissed her forehead, and whispered, "I'm sorry about David."

Honma stepped back. The bald man had drifted to the corner of the room.

I didn't know how long I stood over my mother. I finally pulled away and convinced myself that it was not her lying there, just her body. Mom's spirit had left, the spirit that made her who she was when she was alive.

Anger rose from my gut. Who could have done such an awful thing?

I wiped my nose and eyes with a tissue. The bald man pulled the white sheet over her face and rolled the body back into the cube.

Again, Honma repeated as if scripted, "I am very sorry."

I nodded thank you.

Back in Honma's office, I reeled in my emotions, pulling myself together. "You must find who did this."

Honma's voice came out cold. "Miss Hunter, random robberies that end badly are extremely difficult to solve."

The reluctance on Honma's chiseled face cast doubt on whether I should continue probing or simply accept everything I was being told.

With his elbows on his desk, Honma stared at his hands, then looked up at me. "We have photographs, but I don't think you should see them."

Before I chickened out, I nodded. "Hai, I want to see them, please."

Honma reached for a folder, held it for a few seconds in hesitation, then reluctantly slid it across the desk.

I knew that once I viewed the photos, I wouldn't be able to purge them from my memory for the rest of my life. But it was something I needed to do. I took a deep breath, peeled off the top flap, reached inside, and pulled out a handful of eight-by-ten glossies.

I took one quick glance and turned away, my chest on fire. I cringed, took another breath, this time forcing myself to look, while attempting to avoid focusing on Mom's bloodied face.

Her body was positioned in a fetal position on the wet pavement, lying in a puddle of black. Her hair was matted and clumped together with blood. I flipped to the second photograph, a frontal view of the large incision from belly to sternum. My mother's insides leaked from the deep cut.

Honma reached over his desk and stopped me from flipping to the next photo. My hands were trembling. With true sincerity and concern on his hardened face, Honma gripped my hand. "Enough. You don't need to see the rest."

He was right. I slid the deck of pictures back into the folder and handed it to him.

"In the photos," I started, bile caught in my throat, "it looks like the crime was done in rage—violent rage. Am I wrong?"

Honma shrugged. "Could be . . . it all depends on the mental state of the robber. He might have already been worked up about something. Or he could have been high on drugs."

"Is it possible that the crime was an act of revenge, someone settling a score?"

Honma's eyes rolled upward. "Your mother ran a bar. Bars can at times attract men without scruples. Some minds are unstable. How do you Americans call it . . . mentally unstable?"

I didn't answer him.

"May I?" I motioned to the folder again. Honma hesitated, but passed it back.

In the first photo, a bloodied airline ticket jacket was spread on the ground next to the body.

I pointed to the photograph. "There are smeared finger marks on the ticket jacket. Were there any fingerprints?"

"The man used gloves." Honma leaned forward as though just now remembering the ticket jacket. "Ahh . . . maybe I'm getting ahead of myself, but—"

"But what?"

"Well, the airline ticket jacket was empty. We couldn't find the ticket anywhere."

"It was a ticket voucher. I gave it to her as a gift to use whenever she wanted to visit us in Hawaii."

Honma squinted. "Her credit cards and money were gone. When we asked her business partner if she wore any jewelry, Kiyomi-chan said she usually wore a locket and a Rolex wristwatch. Both were missing."

"What's the chance of finding the person who did this?"

He made a *tsk* sound. "Perhaps it was a druggie looking for cash and his next fix. Japan has a growing drug problem that is driving crime upward."

Honma had avoided my question.

He must have read the frustration on my face. "I know you don't want to hear this, but the odds of finding the killer are slim to none."

I refused to accept that and blurted out, "Did you find out if anybody used the voucher?"

"Not yet." He shook his head. "Unless the person who stole

the ticket—the voucher—had your mother's ID, passport, that person won't be able to use it."

I shot out, with a touch of sarcasm, "What about pawn shops? The person may have sold her watch."

The locket had contained a family photograph of my father, mother, kid brother, and me taken at the Cherry Blossom Festival when I was four years old.

"Why would he take the locket?" With my grief pushed down for the time being, my anger rose. "It had no value except sentimental."

Honma blankly stared back at me and said nothing.

I pushed harder. "Was there a diamond wedding ring?"

He flipped through his notebook. "The co-owner didn't mention a diamond ring, so for now we will assume that she wasn't wearing one."

Questions spilled out of me in rapid fire: "Do you have any suspects? Did she have any enemies? What's your next move?"

"We plan to talk to more people." His mouth curled upward into a frustrated snarl, punctuating that our meeting was over. "I will do all I can to solve the crime, Miss Hunter."

Honma escorted me to the door.

I bowed politely from the office entrance. "I don't have a phone number now, but when I do, please keep me abreast of the investigation."

He nodded.

I strolled to the front and woke Lani. She was blurry-eyed as I led her to the elevator, our luggage rolling behind us.

When we entered the elevator, one of three men in a group by the receptionist's desk said loudly in Japanese, "What does she expect when her mother owns a bar? Serves her right."

My hand shot out. The doors bounced open. I glared at the men. Two of them turned and faced the opposite direction. The other, probably the guy who made the comment, stood defiant, male dominance written across a smug face.

I spat out, "*Osu butas*." Male pigs.

As the elevator door closed, Honma shouted, "Takashi!" An inch before the elevator door shut completely, I could see Honma motion the man to his office.

Lani let me steam and said nothing on the way down to ground level.

I tried to push my anger aside, but the guy's words kept reverberating in my head like a hammer against an anvil. "Something doesn't feel right, Lan. Things are not adding up."

Lani stared at me with eyes more alive after her quick nap. "What's not adding up?"

"It felt like he was holding back on things." I recalled Honma's defiant body language and narrative of deflection. "I think in his mind the case is closed."

"What'd you say when we left? From the way they reacted, I doubt you wished for them to have a nice day."

I told her about the comment from the cop.

Lani's voice sounded like someone jacking a twelve-gauge shotgun. "Let's go back up and give him a taste of Hawaiian punch."

"Forget it. They could put us in one of the holding cells, and no one is going to care that you need to be home in seven days."

We walked to the street, flagged down a taxi, and headed to my mother's apartment in Shibuya.

Images of Mom's body lying in the refrigerated cube, of the photographs of her bloodied face, of her mutilated body, flashed in a continuous loop in my head as the sun set in Tokyo and neon lights flickered on.

4

Although nineteen years old, she passed herself off as sixteen, because he wanted his girls that way—between the ages of fourteen and sixteen, maybe younger, but never older.

Aom's petite size had convinced the Soapland Sayonara mama-san to set up the meeting with the yakuza *oyabun*. Rumors of the old man's obsession circulated, but the promise of earning ten times her usual fee for satisfying his sexual fantasy was one Aom couldn't refuse.

The catch was giving the greedy bitch five percent of her money.

Mama-san-Fukumi was in her late forties, round-faced, with sculpted hair and heavy makeup. She was on edge—deceiving one of the most powerful men in Japan would make anyone nervous.

Aom asked Fukumi for the third time, "What if he finds out?"

"He won't." She spun Aom around to face the mirror. "You look like twelve, see."

Aom wore a plain schoolgirl outfit—long-sleeved white dress-shirt, plaid skirt, thigh-high white stockings, and a pair of ordinary black leather shoes. She accentuated the look with a set of plastic-framed glasses and a child's Hello Kitty wristwatch. To add to the innocent-yet-naughty little schoolgirl image, she wore a pair of hoop earrings, another one of Tamura's turn-ons. Though petite in size, Aom was well proportioned, so to tease and conceal, she had wound compression-wrap, the kind used for sprained ankles, around her large breasts.

Although Isaan women were usually dark-skinned, Aom's complexion was light and smooth. A surgically altered flat nose gave her the look of a child of mixed race. Her hair was raven black and flowed like silk whenever she moved. Large dark eyes and exotically full lips captivated her johns.

"But he will know I am not a virgin," she said with a slight British accent.

"He not want virgin. He want innocent. To control the *helpless* is what drive his manhood. This is about desires of the mind. He will not hurt you."

Aom tried to re-live her innocence as a sixteen-year-old, but that part of her life had never existed. Her parents, in Thailand's northeastern Isaan region, had sold her to the Englishman at the age of eleven. This brought food and more farming property for the family, plus schooling for her three younger sisters, so they too wouldn't be sold.

Forty years her senior, the Englishman sculpted her, inducting her into womanhood. He educated her using words like *sophistication, elegance,* and *dignity.*

That all changed after living with him for six years in a Bangkok high-rise apartment. There she learned the true meaning of *betrayal* when the Englishman sold her to a Triad drug lord in Pattaya, then left Thailand for Europe.

Although money was the motivation, Aom accepted the invitation from Tamura because the Englishman had introduced bondage into their sex play a number of times. The Englishman explained why it excited him, *that ropes can inflict pain as well as pleasure.* The act itself was one of beauty. He cited the Japanese practice of *shibari* as he snapped photograph after photograph of her bound, naked and blindfolded, in erotic poses.

As he slid the rope between her legs, Aom told the Englishman that her father would tie up their ox to keep it from running away, but the animal didn't like it and would thrash and kick trying to escape. For some reason the Englishman thought that was funny.

A GIANT of a human escorted Aom up a private elevator to the penthouse suite. The man was barrel-chested, his forearms thicker than her thighs. He was dressed in a dark suit, tight across the chest, wore dark glasses, and stunk of four-day-old sweat.

Standing outside the suite's door, he spoke Japanese into a cellphone. A mechanical latch unbolted. The giant pushed the door open and waved Aom inside with a meaty hand. He remained outside as the door clicked shut.

Aom cautiously wandered into the suite, which was covered in plush white carpeting, the walls splashed with psychedelic reds, blacks, and yellows. Although Fukumi never entered the yakuza boss's home, she'd described it accurately.

The glass shelves displayed priceless artifacts from the Toku-gawa Edo era. At the transition between the living room and the expansive kitchen was the battered armor of a samurai warrior who had died at the battle of Shiroyama. Aom had shrugged with disinterest until Fukumi mentioned that the battle was what inspired Tom Cruise's *The Last Samurai*. Aom brightened, telling Fukumi she had watched the movie with Thai subtitles.

She stared at the amazing view through the floor-to-ceiling glass, the lights of Tokyo spread out below, with the large dark patch of Yoyogi Park in the foreground.

"Stay focused." The Englishman's voice rang in her ear. "Do not lose sight of the objective."

Tamura-san entered from an adjoining bedroom wearing a bleached, white *fundoshi,* a man's loincloth underwear. His sagging, aged butt cheeks grotesquely reminded her of two rotten durian fruits hanging from a stem.

He might have been attractive and robust in his youth. Now his thinning hair, cut to the scalp and filled with flecks of white and gray, matched his penciled mustache, painted on a face marked by a life full of battles for power. She had seen his type of eyes many times before on customers, men who took more than they gave. Although he was in his late sixties, she still felt the power and strength emitting from his body when he led her into the living room.

A tinge of fear pierced her to the bone as she stared up at the ceiling and the makeshift pulley system built in the middle of the large room. The leather sofa and sharp, dark, decorative metal chairs inlaid with chrome formed a circle. She froze at seeing the thick construction-plastic spread underneath.

"He will not hurt you," Fukumi's voice rang.

The old man stared at her, studying her, not saying a word. Her fear escalated with the transformation of his cold lifeless eyes, now filled with lust. He emitted a nauseating scent of tobacco smoke, which she could smell from ten feet away. His old body was etched with tattoos—fading colors on flaccid gray skin —accentuating his protruding ribs, like those of a carcass left on the side of the road in the heat of summer. The once-prominent tattoo of a fierce dragon now looked more like a shriveled gecko on his wrinkled skin.

She choked at what lay on the glass tabletop. Folded within a roll of canvas were knives. One knife was as large as a butcher's, another as thin as a surgeon's scalpel.

The Englishman, Aom knew, wouldn't hurt her.

She didn't feel sure here.

Tamura slithered to a cabinet in the corner of the living room, retrieved lengths of hemp rope, and shifted toward her like a hungry panther. When he made the first knot around her wrist, she was convinced that Fukumi had lied.

Although she had experienced men's parted lips, heavy breathing, and the trickle of saliva beaded at the corner of their mouths before, it was the old man's wolf eyes that convinced her. He had the sinister squint of a customer whose penis got harder whenever he struck her face.

As he knelt down to tie the second knot around her ankle, Aom grabbed for whatever item was within reach. Terror mixed with anger at Fukumi's lies, she slammed a large vase on the graying crewcut. A deep gash turned the old man's scalp into a stream of red.

She dashed for the door, avoided the private elevator, and ran for the fire exit. Everything happened in fast-forward. Six stories, five stories. How many stairs had she fumbled and stumbled down? Her shoes were not made for running down twenty-six flights of stairs; she yanked them off in her descent to the bottom.

Pumping fear, she heard menacing footsteps pounding behind her, echoing like thunder, reverberating between the stairwell walls. The large man moved fast, closing the distance. His heavy breathing echoed hollow. The footsteps were frantic—getting closer, closer, closer. Three floors behind. Two floors. If she got caught, she would *not* be deported, but killed, her body left in a dark, empty alley as rat food.

Breathing hard and heavy, she reached the ground level and slammed into the horizontal bar of the fire exit door like a sumo wrestler. The shocking chill smacked her sweaty skin. A large hand grabbed her left shoulder like a metal claw. Out of reflex, she twisted her torso clockwise against the grip, tearing fabric. She tripped and stumbled. Her body crashed to the concrete sidewalk, skinning her left elbow in bracing her fall. When she fell, the big man's legs slammed against her ribs, a mass of humanity the size of a small planet shot over her.

If she hadn't tripped and taken the man's legs out from under him, she would be in a headlock, and with the same miniscule muscle effort it takes to scratch an itch, he'd snap her neck.

Suffocating and gasping for air, her ribs were on fire. The giant must have tripped and judo-rolled, because he stood ten meters in front of her. At six feet tall, this monster had short, slick black hair parted down the middle and a large scar across his left cheek. He dusted off his suit as though checking himself in front of a mirror before a night on the town.

She froze in the giant's riveted stare. To break the spell, she rolled onto her side like a gymnast, scraping her knee on the pavement, got up, and took off running toward Shinjuku Station, hoping to blend in with the crowd in the busiest train station in the world.

She knew a shortcut, dashed left on a narrow street, and headed for a weathered wooden fence. The rusted nails that held the boards to the base of two-by-fours were loose. Her hands shook as she pried a board to the side and frantically squeezed through. A meaty palm grabbed her left ankle. Aom twisted and mule-kicked the loose board with her right heel. The big man screamed. She glanced back. Rage burned in the giant's eyes as he tore the board off, tossed it to the side, and glared at her through the missing fence board. She kept running.

A light breeze swooped between the towering skyscrapers, carrying the sweet aroma of marinated broiled squid and hot ramen from nearby street vendors feeding the drunken hunger of night zombies.

Surrounded by modern glass and steel, bright colorful lights strained to disguise the gloom of night. Giant TVs flashed advertisements for trendy women's fashions, with anorexic models strutting on catwalks ten stories above the sidewalk.

She glanced at her reflection in a storefront window. The once-pressed schoolgirl outfit was now tattered and torn. Excruciating pain shot up her right leg as she grimaced at the blood dotting her thigh-high white stocking. She was shoeless, and the cold, wet pavement numbed her toes and blackened her feet with street grime.

The free-flowing money still couldn't erase the hatred Aom had for this city. Two months in Tokyo was two months too long. Determined to get somewhere, the people here were always in a hurry. They were eternally well dressed, walking in quiet solitude with their heads down, plowing ahead as if against a gust of wind. She hated their subtle prejudices toward darker-skinned Asians. She hated the Japanese language and the choppy tone it had, sounding like a meat cleaver on a wooden chopping block in contrast to the elegant tonal sounds of Thai.

She reached for the pouch strapped around her neck. Her hands fumbled in desperation, frantically patting her upper torso, but the pouch holding two hundred thousand yen and her cell-phone was gone. Aom's stomach twisted into knots. How could she have been so careless? If only she'd gripped the pouch in her hand. If only she'd used a cord instead of the thin chain. If only she'd refused Tamura's offer.

Reality smacked her harder than the cold. What now? She could turn tricks to make money for airfare to Bangkok, but that would take time—time she didn't have.

The old man's influences and vengeful tentacles were far-reaching. How much time did she have before they started looking for her through his network of loyal informants and spies?

"Stay focused." The Englishman's words hammered in her head.

As an escape from the feeling of hopelessness, Aom reflected on the elephant village in Thailand, a place that always brought her pure joy. She remembered showing mama-Emiko the photograph of a spider monkey dressed in a black-and-white tuxedo with a miniature derby atop its small head, and balancing on a giant elephant. Mama-Em couldn't stop laughing, sounding like a jungle hyena.

Aom now knew what to do. From Shinjuku Station she headed northeast toward Kabukicho, Tokyo's red-light district.

Soapland Sayonara was a brothel masquerading as an exclusive massage spa. The competition for customers was fierce. If Aom was lucky, in one night she would have, at most, three customers. Men rarely asked for her services because she was new to the city, so the mama-san placed her in a queue with twenty other girls.

Time kept ticking and she wasn't making money.

To supplement her income, Aom moonlighted as a hostess in a *nomiya,* a small bar, four blocks away, situated in a maze of alleys and narrow lanes.

Mama-Emiko was a kind lady who ran the hostess bar where Aom moonlighted. Even though she couldn't speak Japanese, mama-Em still hired her as a hostess.

Aom would ask mama-Em for a loan. She would promise to pay her back. She herself didn't know when, but she would. If mama-Em decided *not* to help her, she'd be back where she was now. She had nothing to lose.

Although Kabukicho was shutting down, it was still ablaze with flickering neon lights in a kaleidoscope of rich colors. Hundreds of signs and bright billboards advertised sex clubs, host and hostess bars, and adult bookshops. Touts and hawkers walked the corners and out on the sidewalks and streets. Dressed in leather jackets, fur-lined boots, lambskin gloves, and dark trench coats, they shouted at straggling men as if selling used cars. But instead, they offered blowjobs from teenage girls.

Mama-Em's bar closed at 2 a.m. By 2:30, she would be in a taxi to Shibuya where her apartment was. The dots of Hello Kitty's eyes stared up from Aom's wrist. The digital numbers flipped from 2:31 to 2:32.

Aom jogged through the maze of alleys, her breath a cold mist. The stink of detritus from the night's businesses, discarded for the morning pickup, permeated the air. A rat the size of her forearm scurried out from some torn black trash bags left in the alleyway.

She followed the edge of a storm canal that dipped to the right of a narrow lane, her feet numb against the chilled stone slabs. The sound of trickling water floated up from the darkness of the stream bottom. Made of poured cement and giant stone boulders, the large canal was built to control and contain the raging river during the typhoon season.

Aom's hope came crashing down when she peeked through the bamboo. The blue-and-white neon glow of the club's sign was turned off. Deflated, she plopped down on the gravel road and wrapped her arms around herself, shivering from the cold.

What now?

She turned to leave, but heard scuffling in front of the club.

Mama-Em? Ahh . . . Buddha provides.

Aom squinted through the bamboo again. This time she froze when she saw the shadow lurking in darkness. Dressed in a strapless, black sheath mini-dress and thigh-high leather boots, a woman stood over a motionless body on the ground. Thick, shoulder-length black hair and tinted glasses hid the woman's age. She moved like an athlete, smooth and agile. The faint lighting couldn't hide her ghost-white complexion and painted rosy cheeks.

Aom covered her scream with both hands. Mama-Em's body lay in a pool of black.

She quickly retreated to the edge of the inclined embankment and crawled along the boulders like she'd seen Spiderman do many times on TV, her stockings grabbing the coarse surface like cloth gloves.

She peeked over the edge.

The woman in high boots squatted in front of the lifeless body. She poured the contents of mama-Em's handbag onto the ground, removing money and credit cards. She ripped the locket from mama-Em's neck, glanced at its contents, then tossed it against the building wall. Momentary light revealed a tattoo on the assailant's forearm—part light, part dark, circular. The dark part looked like four tadpoles swimming counterclockwise, forming the light portion, which looked like a ninja throwing star.

Was mama-Em still alive? Maybe she was unconscious. Aom could try to yell for help, but the surrounding shops were all closed. Her cellphone was in the lost pouch. Should she attack the woman? Aom glanced around for a rock, something solid, but it was a stupid idea—she was not a hero. The woman's movements were forceful and manly, maybe those of a weightlifter. She had just hurt or killed mama-Em. If they fought, Aom might break an arm or be left bedridden for days with medical bills to pay. She could injure and scar her face. Her appearance was her livelihood.

Or worst of all . . . she could be killed.

Aom rolled into a ball on the inclined slab of stone. She clutched her knees to her chest, trying to ignore the scuffling and heavy breathing happening in front of the club.

Unable to resist, she again peeked over the embankment and wished she hadn't. The woman viciously kicked mama-Em's head as if it were a soccer ball. Thigh-high boots forced her legs apart. She stared down at the white of mama's underwear and violently kicked her once, twice, three times in the crotch.

The woman's next move sent chills down Aom's forearm.

Deliberate steps crunched on loose gravel, heading directly toward her. Could the killer smell her fear? Aom calmed her breathing, pressing her face flush against the icy stone. She shrunk herself to a point, practicing the Buddhist single-point mediation to calm and stabilize her mind.

Waiting, waiting . . . waiting for a knife slash across her throat.

The scent of Coco Chanel was close. A rat scurried up from the stream, jarring a pebble that rattled down the incline. The crunching footsteps stopped. Aom slowed her heartbeat as though she wasn't a part of this three-dimensional plane. The rat stood on its hind legs, stared at her, then dashed for the rubbish bin.

With the air dead silent, she waited for the footsteps. Would they get closer or farther away from her? Aom held her breath. A distant siren wailed. She heard the heavy crunch of gravel, like the woman had shifted her weight. The footsteps then hurried away.

Aom puffed out a breath and sucked air into her lungs.

The passing siren kept going and faded away—*Buddha provides*.

Aom pried her hands loose from the concrete, crept to mama-Em's mutilated body, and held her breath at the awful smell. The kind lady's eyes stared lifeless into the night sky, a large pool of black puddled on the pavement beneath her neck. Her once immaculate hair was now tangled and smeared with blood.

Aom dashed to the base of the bamboo and vomited. She wiped her mouth with the back of her hand and turned to leave, but she had nowhere to go.

She crept back to the body. Breathing through her mouth, she glanced at the contents of mama-Em's bag, spread on the ground. Together with a hairbrush, compact mirror, and assorted makeup, she saw what looked like a bloodstained Japan Airlines ticket jacket. Using the edge of her skirt, she opened the blood-soaked jacket. In it was a voucher for a flight to Hawaii. She could use the ticket if she only had more time to buy a fake passport.

She carefully removed mama-Em's bloodstained Rolex from her wrist. The Englishman had taught her how to identify a real from a fake. She wiped the blood off with her skirt, felt its weight, studied the dial and serial number engraving. With the Rolex to her ear, she listened—no ticking. The second hand was not jerky, so not a quartz. She smiled. This could bring four to five hundred thousand yen, maybe more.

Why didn't the killer take the Rolex? Maybe she thought it could be traced or that a pre-owned timepiece needed provenance.

Aom again remembered mama-Em laughing like a jungle hyena at the photo of the elephant and monkey. She walked to the locket on the ground and opened it. Inside was a picture of mama-Em, a man, and a young girl and boy. She shoved the locket and ticket voucher in her skirt pocket.

She'd never visited Hawaii before, but had heard there were many military men there. The money could be good, and most importantly, there were miles of Pacific between Hawaii and this wet and stinking hell pit.

Her hand suddenly shot to her left ear. One of her hoop earrings was missing. It could be anywhere between Tamura's apartment and here.

Aom re-focused, considering what to do next. A powerful man was looking for her and would not stop until he found and killed her.

Like the phantom assailant, Aom scurried into the Kabukicho night, heading to a pawnshop in Shinagawa. From Platform two at Keikyu Shinagawa Station, she would catch the Keikyu Airport Kaitoku train bound for Narita International Airport, then Honolulu, Hawaii, and return mama-Em's locket to her family.

Karma.

5

Most of what happened following my mother's death was a blur. Although my body moved from one location to another, my mind was everywhere else, draped in numbness and detached.

Just ten minutes walking distance from the Shibuya train station, my mother's gray studio apartment building ran along a narrow street. Surrounded by a bakery, numerous small restaurants, and other low-rise apartments, the five-story building had a wide walkway that led up to a glass door with security cameras all around.

Situated on the third floor, the compact studio could have fit within the space of our living room in Hawaii. The queen-size bed occupied a large chunk of living area. The tiny kitchen had an angled countertop with two electric burners, a microwave, and a mini refrigerator pushed in the corner. Every piece of furniture and appliance seemed an exact fit, like pieces in a jigsaw puzzle.

I lifted my suitcase onto the bed and heard a distant, "Gena."

My mom's voice floated through the sliding window, which I had opened earlier to clear the studio's stale and stagnant air.

I stopped and adjusted my ears. Thinking it must be my imagination after an exhaustingly long day, I brushed it off.

A few seconds later, my mother's voice came through clearer. "Gena."

My forearms shivered, now covered in goosebumps. I rubbed my arms with both hands to stop the chill. I twisted toward the bathroom. From behind the closed sliding door came the sound of Lani showering.

A large part of me wished that Mom was standing on the sidewalk calling up to me, but reality kept tugging my brain in a different direction. I pulled myself to the open window, hoping that I was wrong, that her death didn't happen. Down below on the street, bundled up and layered in warm clothes, a mother and child walked hand in hand toward the bakery.

I mumbled. "Too tired . . . hearing things." I returned to the suitcase, pulled my funeral clothes from the bottom, and placed them on hangers.

The shower stopped five minutes later and the bathroom door slid open. One towel covered Lani's upper body as she fluffed her wet hair with another one.

Lani took a quick glance at me. "What's up, Sista? You look like you seen a ghost."

I hesitated to tell her, thinking she might think I was cracking up, but said anyway, "I swear, Lan. I heard my mom calling me from the outside. It was the same tone of voice she used when calling me to dinner. Man . . . I must be losing my mind."

"You're not losing your mind." She stared into the mirror and ran a finger under her puffy eyes. "You think Japan's got some kind of miracle anti-aging cream?"

I laughed. "Girl, you're twenty-one. What do you want to look like, seventeen?"

"Hey, you're not hallucinating," she said. She cupped her breasts and lifted them, posing left, then right. "Yep, still got it."

"Focus, Lani," I said, acknowledging how crazy I must have sounded. "What about my hallucination?"

"Let's face it, Gen. I think you're still in shock."

She was probably right.

Early that evening, I called Kiyomi at the bar, needing details about the funeral arrangements. Kiyomi answered with the din of karaoke music, glasses clinking, and mumbling voices in the background.

In Japanese, she half-shouted over the bar noise. "The eldest son is responsible for organizing the funeral."

Sorry, but I'm the default daughter.

"Certain days are better than other days for funerals. I have picked a good day."

Kiyomi sounded like she wanted praise, but how bizarre it was to have a good day for a funeral.

"Your mother's name will be placed in the obituary in the newspapers. The wake is set for Friday, the funeral to follow. Are you Buddhist?"

"No, I'm not."

"Oh." She sounded disappointed. "Either way, it will be held at a Buddhist temple in the Kanagawa Prefecture. Your mother will be traditionally cremated. A nice plot has already been selected and—"

"I don't want to sound like I don't appreciate what you're doing," I quickly interrupted her. "And I don't want to cause any trouble, but is it possible to do the same thing we do in Hawaii?"

"What is that?"

"We hold the wake, funeral, and burial on the same day," I replied, thinking of the Buddhist funeral I attended at the Wahiawa Hongwanji Mission a few years ago.

Expecting an angry voice at the change in plans, Kiyomi surprised me with her accommodatingly polite tone. "I will get back to you."

Perhaps Kiyomi hated having to take time away from her business on multiple occasions.

Kiyomi called back in an hour. "Because of situation, the *obousan* agree to combine the three events on same day." Obousan was the Buddhist priest.

Before Kiyomi hung up, I probed. "Did my mother say or do anything that was unusual or different, like maybe her behavior, or her—"

"I have to go." Kiyomi cut me off, quick as a slap. "I am very busy and have customers waiting." She ended the call.

Why was Kiyomi so unwilling to get to the truth? Even after being brushed off, I was still grateful to her for organizing everything, because I wouldn't know where to start if I had to do it myself.

FRIDAY CAME FAST. My mother's funeral service was scheduled for ten in the morning at the Aoyama Cemetery, located in the Minato District of Tokyo, just a few minutes away from Shibuya with the Metro Ginza Line.

I woke at five and let Lani continue to snore like a buzz saw. I crept silently out of bed hoping not to disturb her, although a nuclear explosion probably wouldn't have woken her.

Looking out from the apartment window, I scanned the grayness of the city, maybe hoping for a miracle, my mother standing on the sidewalk. But that wasn't the case. The bakery across the street was closed, and a light grayish frost hazed the air.

I searched for an umbrella in the closet adjacent to the bed. Something caught my attention. Under several pairs of pumps and sandals, part of the brown laminated flooring was black. I moved an assortment of shoes and uncovered a floor safe.

Although Mom would never have written down the combination, I took a chance and searched her drawers for a slip of paper with the four numbers. Finding nothing, I tried birthdates and anniversaries, but that didn't work.

What I did find was a phone book, which I used to call the first locksmith listed. The man from Shibuya Locks and Keys said he could stop by at eleven tomorrow.

I had purchased a temporary SIM card that gave me full access to my phone, plus Internet. I called Honma six times over the next three days, but his secretary said he was either in a meeting or in the field on a case and didn't want to be disturbed. I left a callback message with my number, but he still hadn't used it.

It took an hour to prepare for the funeral. I had on a black midi dress with matching classic black pumps. Lani looked hot, maybe too hot for a funeral, wearing a scalloped V-neck dress in black velvet with a ruffled hem that came to her knees. Knowing that we'd be outdoors for some time, we wore buttoned black cardigans and black leggings. We both spritzed ourselves with a gender-neutral fragrance smelling of jasmine and musk.

At 7 a.m., we took the elevator down to the ground floor. Lani had her eyes closed and leaned against the elevator wall. She yawned, her mouth stretched wide, like a lioness shaking out sleep.

I said to her, "I'm thinking . . . like in the movies, whoever murdered my mom could show up at her funeral."

Lani stared at me with one open eye. "Like a sicko would do to admire his work."

"The killing seemed done in rage, Lan."

With now both eyes open, she palmed her phone. "I can take pictures of the crowd and we can check out the faces later on."

"I don't think people will like it if you go around snapping photos of them."

"I'll make it like I'm trying to capture the moment—you

know, like tourist." Her brow creased. "Besides, I'd sure like to help catch this creep and see him rot in jail."

I nodded in agreement.

We took the train to Aoyama, the biggest cemetery in the twenty-three wards of Tokyo. Rolling hills ran throughout it. The sky held a dreary gray; a chilling breeze blew up the hillside and dropped the ambient temperature by a couple degrees. The calm and tranquility of the area pressed down on us as we strolled among cherry and pine trees. Stone paths were dotted with shrubs and small gardens, and led to graves ranging from ancient to modern. The view from this high elevation looked down upon the smog-capped city below.

The Buddhist temple towered as high as the tallest tree. The roof sloped down and then curved into upturned, flaring corners. Thick wooden columns painted a brownish red blended in naturally with the surroundings trees, as if they too had sprouted from the earth. The smell of incense flowed thick from brass burners.

I thanked the obousan, Higashi-san, for accommodating my request to hold the wake, funeral, and burial on the same day.

Higashi's body was slim and pale-skinned, which didn't match the deep baritone with which he said, "There is usually a long waiting time. Your mother has very *close* friends." His tone was submissive, like he didn't have a choice.

The service started exactly on time in a building adjacent to the main temple. I gauged about two hundred people in attendance. Men dressed in black suits, white shirts, and black ties, women in either black dresses or black kimonos. Younger women, from their early twenties to early thirties, were dressed in more stylish black.

A few women around my mother's age wore high, colored wigs that appeared more like helmets than hair. They had thick-powdered faces, cashmere coats, expensive furs, and surgically altered body parts.

Most of the guests must have been connected to my mother's business, probably club owners, bar girls, maybe vendors and loyal customers.

Lani and I sat in the front row. Guests on benches and folding chairs sat behind us, extending to the back wall. Blue drapes formed the background of a shrine framed by decorative scalloped curtains. With the room packed, mourners overflowed along the side walls.

Dressed in a black robe with prayer beads around his wrist, Higashi-san sat facing an ornate shrine of gold and polished redwood. Fresh flowers decorated the shrine, with a portrait of Mom in the center. A bronze urn rested beneath the picture of my mother in her twenties, a youthful, optimistic smile on her pretty face.

With the formal service over, we strolled outside, into the cold. In a group procession, we marched a hundred yards to Mom's gravesite, which was surrounded by well-manicured greenery, groomed shrubberies, and spaced between other densely packed graves.

It saddened me to see "Yamashita" and not "Hunter" written in white lettering on the coal-colored marble headstone.

After the burial, the crowd gathered in an adjoining high-ceiling hall. Tables were set up with mostly finger foods like sushi and *takoyaki*, with full bars in two of the corners. The hall opened onto a small tea garden. Rounded rock steps led through a pair of wooden gates into an enclosed courtyard. Camellia and Japanese roses lined the gravel-strewn walkway that led to the edge of the small koi pond. Benches were scattered under bright-red parasols where kimono-clad women gracefully served tea and sake.

In a matter of minutes, the service had turned into more of a reunion or sorority gathering. My heart sank at the thought that maybe these people had been more her family than my father and I, and perhaps the ones who really knew my mother's true self.

One girl kept looking at me like she wanted to talk. She had eyebrows like slashes across her face, wide-set eyes fringed with long, thick lashes, and shoulder-length wavy hair. Slim and in her early twenties, she wore a black turtleneck, faux cashmere trench coat, and ankle-high sheep-skin boots.

Whenever I turned to meet the girl's stare, she quickly pivoted away.

I approached Kiyomi and interrupted her conversation with Higashi-san. "Excuse me, Kiyomi-chan. Can I talk to you a minute?"

Kiyomi ignored me and continued chatting with the obousan. Higashi-san nodded and smiled at me then walked away.

The scowl at being interrupted hardened like stone on Kiyomi's face. I said to her, "My father agreed to pay whatever needed to be paid."

She pointed to the old man in the dark suit and said, "He pay everything."

I started toward him, but Kiyomi grabbed me. I glared at the hand gripping my arm and said, "I want to thank him personally."

Kiyomi shook her unnaturally black wig. "Not needed. I thank him many times." She marched away as I continued to stare at the old man.

My father's suits were usually bought from a mail order catalog, so I'd never seen a $2,000 suit in my life, until now. The four muscular men in the man's entourage wore dark glasses. Even though Japan outlawed handguns, the bulges of holstered weapons under their coats were obvious.

Behind the old man, a super-sized Japanese hunk built like a Humvee towered. He had short, slick black hair parted down the middle and a large scar across his left cheek, which gave me the heebie-jeebies.

Most people had already given their condolences when I felt a light tap on my back. I turned, looking into an oval-shaped face with high, curving cheekbones. The girl. Her eyes wandered from side to side, hands trembling as she pulled me under the wide eaves of the building, away from the crowd.

The girl whispered in Japanese, "I could get into trouble talking to you. The rumor is that the killing was done by yakuza."

A chill ran up my spine. The fear that the yakuza instilled in people had been ingrained in me since I was a child living in Japan. She was taking a chance by making such an allegation. To deceive any wandering stares floating in our direction, I nodded as though gratefully receiving her condolences.

I faked a smile and asked, "Why yakuza?"

The girl struggled to disguise her fear. She shifted her head back and forth, but didn't answer me.

With her non-answer, I asked another question. "Why are you telling me this?"

"If it wasn't for your mother, I would probably be dead." Her gaze roamed from face to face. "She helped me off drugs and gave me a job." Her cute facial features suddenly froze as though she'd been caught shoplifting.

I followed her fearful gaze. Kiyomi was staring at us from the hall stairs. I ignored her and turned back to the girl, but she had vanished into the crowd.

Throughout, Lani kept snapping photos of the guests. The majority of people posed and smiled.

She positioned herself on the other side of the koi pond and snapped a photo of the old man in the expensive suit. The giant standing behind him moved with surprising agility and speed for his humungous size, dashing around the edges of the pond like a middle linebacker on an all-out blitz. He yanked the phone away from Lani.

Caught off guard, she shouted, "What da fuck!"

The big man scrolled through the phone with his salami-sized fingers. He grunted and tossed her smart phone into the pond.

"Hey!" she screamed at him, reaching to claw his eyes with her sharp fingernails.

I yanked her back by the arm.

The place went dead silent. People anxiously watched, some leaning forward, as the old man slowly strolled toward us. He stopped in front of Lani and eyed her with interest. He grinned, flashing a gold tooth, and nudged his chin at her.

The giant reached into his trench coat pocket, pulled out a roll of cash, and peeled off enough yen to purchase two phones. He tossed the money on the ground. The old man turned and made his way to a black stretch-limo parked in front of the temple. His scary-looking entourage followed behind. I thought about what Honma had said, that the killer had to be a man to have driven the one-foot knife from my mother's belly to her sternum. Any one of these brutes could easily have generated that kind of strength.

The old man leaving signaled to everyone that the funeral was over. Within ten minutes, the area was empty, and the cleaning crew moved in.

Higashi-san walked up to me, bowed, and said with deep sincerity, "I wish you well." He then shuffled around the corner of the temple.

On our walk to the train station, I tapped Lani on the shoulder as we climbed the stairs to the platform. "Sorry for suggesting you take pictures of the crowd. It was a bad idea."

She brushed me off. "Don't get nuts. I did this on my own. If it wasn't for Godzilla, we could have had the killer on pixels."

We caught the three o'clock to Shibuya. Passengers were crammed together like toy soldiers in a matchbox. No one spoke. People were either locked onto their phones or in their own worlds with their eyes closed.

Having downed a few shots of warm sake, Lani was now lightly snoring next to me, her water-soaked phone cradled in her lap like a dead pet bird.

I glanced out the train window as the city of Tokyo flashed by in a passing blur. I couldn't get the nagging question out of my head. *Mom, what the heck were you involved in?*

6

M y father never objected to his wife being cremated in a Buddhist ceremony and buried in an urn in her beloved country. Yet I sensed the emptiness he felt in having the woman he still loved remain in Japan.

His voice came across distant and hollow on the phone. "How was the service?"

"It turned out good. Many of her friends and co-workers were there." Though I now despised her, I relayed the truth: "Kiyomi did an excellent job in arranging everything."

"How much do we owe her?" The touch of satisfaction I heard in his voice at his offer to contribute to his ex-wife's funeral warmed me.

I avoided telling him that one man paid for everything, instead saying, "The money received for the funeral covered the cost of everything."

"Oh . . . so how was it?"

I paused at his repeated question and said in an upbeat tone— as though I were describing a four-star hotel— "I'm sure Mom likes where she is. It's called Aoyama Cemetery and has lots of greenery. She got a nice view of the city. Mostly, she'll love the cherry blossoms when in bloom and—"

A puff came from the tiny speaker, so I stopped.

"When will you be coming home?"

"I'll stay here for a while longer to wrap up whatever loose ends."

"What kind of loose ends?" He spoke with the same desperation as he had when Mom left us for Japan.

I wanted to hug my dad more than ever. "Like figuring out what bills to pay, closing credit card accounts, and finding out what other legalities I need to take care of. Then there's packing up her stuff. And I need to clean her apartment, and—"

He grunted, signaling that he wanted to change the subject.

I waited, not knowing what else to talk about.

"Okay," he sighed, as though he too didn't know what else to say. "Call me if you need anything."

My throat tightened; a tear welled at the corner of my eye. "I will. Bye Dad."

"Bye."

I stared at the phone after hanging up.

"He's taking it hard, huh?" Lani turned away from the floor safe. For the past hour, she'd kept trying to crack the safe's combination and swore every time she failed.

THE NEXT DAY was just as difficult as talking to my dad had been. Lani and I never held hands before because Lani always joked that she didn't want us to look like lesbos, but on the bus to the airport, we kept our palms clasped together.

We hugged at the end of a passenger line that snaked back and forth a few times, the final destination being the Delta Airlines ticket counter.

With tears in our eyes, it was not our style to be overly

emotional, but something between us felt desperate. I handed Lani a tissue. We wiped more tears and chuckled at how silly we were being. Reality seemed to have struck us at the same time; she was just going back home to Hawaii, not to death row.

Lani wiped her nose with a tissue. "I wish that I could stay with you, but I have my day in court and—"

I waved her off. Although the meeting with her attorney was early Monday morning, I'd convinced Lani to travel on Saturday and take all Sunday to get over her jetlag.

My lips formed a tight smile. "I'm just super happy you were here with me through all this. I'll tell you what, Lan. I don't think I would have come out of this in one piece if you weren't here with me. And I'm not just saying that."

"You know I'm here for you, Sista."

"Yeah, I know." I didn't want our farewell to continue in glumness. "Besides, I know you gotta get back and face that suave man of the world, Taguchi the Toad."

"Very funny." She snickered at my sarcasm toward her supervisor. "Hey, he'll get his due. His twenty plus years with the city will be down in the toilet, just la-dat." She snapped her fingers.

After getting her boarding pass and checking in her luggage, we hugged again and I whispered in her ear, "I'll miss you."

"Same here, Gen." She scrunched her lips together, willing herself not to cry. Her brow furrowed; smudged makeup accentuated the seriousness on her face. "Please be careful, Sista. I don't know why I feel the way I do, but something is going on here that's kinda screwy."

I nodded and said, "Hey, one more thing—"

"You know I will." She cut me off, headed for the security line, then spun to face me. "I'll check on your dad and see if he's all right." She held her fingers up like a phone and mouthed, "Call me."

Though not on any type of schedule, I rushed to the subway

station before the well in my throat rose into my eyes again. Alone and filled with emptiness, the ride to Shibuya by train provided time to think. Lani was right; something was kinda screwy. For some reason, no one wanted to talk about what really happened. Maybe it was because I was *gaijin,* a foreigner, or maybe because I was half Japanese.

The studio apartment felt hollow and void without Lani. I hated being alone. The air smelled musty and cold. I glanced at the vanity mirror. My hair was a tangled mess, my eyes tired, droopy, and bloodshot.

After a hot shower, I found a bottle of merlot in the cabinet. Loud pounding at the front door stopped me from opening the wine. I pressed my eye to the peephole. The resident manager, Mr. Cucumber Nipples, frowned into the fisheye.

From the start, I refused to refer to my mom's apartment as her home because *home* was where we were all together.

When we first arrived at Mom's apartment, this middle-aged Japanese man with silvery hair and a bald pate greeted us. He was bone thin, with a liver-spotted face, and wore a paper-thin, see-through bleached white undershirt.

Lani had quickly turned away. She'd made a face and whispered, "I cannot look at old men's nipples. They look like sea cucumbers about to squirt water."

The resident manager had introduced himself as Tomo Shigemitsu. No handshake, just a polite nod. When I said I was Emiko Yamashita's daughter, he stared, but not in the lecherous or sexual way men usually did.

Today he wore a blue *happi* coat and looked like a chef from Benihana. Place a *ginsu* knife and an onion in his hand and he could build a small volcano in the lobby.

Tomo hesitated before speaking in Japanese. "You have a locksmith downstairs."

"Okay, please send him up."

He didn't budge and asked, "The other person move out?"

"Hai, she had to get back to Hawaii."

Even with that explanation, Tomo still stood motionless. He licked his lips. "You owe money for one day since she stayed half day over what you paid."

"You gotta be kidding me." I retaliated in English, but he wasn't smiling. "How much?"

"Five thousand yen."

"That's too much. I have only one thousand."

Tomo shook his head and made a noise in his throat, but he took the money and shoved it into his coat pocket.

I shouted as he walked to the elevator, "Can I have a receipt?"

He puffed out a breath. "I will send up locksmith."

The locksmith was a middle-aged man in gray coveralls who carried a green canvas tool bag. I led him to the floor safe, and within thirty minutes he had it open and kept grinning as though waiting for a standing ovation. It cost me six thousand yen for half an hour of work. I sensed I was getting ripped off, but what could I have done? I hadn't had TNT to blow up the safe, plus Tomo would probably have charged me for the noise and missing floor.

After showing the locksmith to the door, I popped the bottle of wine and filled a glass to the top. I sipped it while pulling the contents of the safe onto my mother's bed. It saddened and pained me to search through her personal items, but there might be clues as to why she was killed.

The safe contained an insurance policy for 219,000 yen, my mother's American and Japanese passports, her *koseki*, similar to a US birth certificate, twenty thousand yen in cash, and a bank-book from a bank in Hawaii. The balance in the book showed twelve thousand US dollars. I lifted an envelope, and out rolled an unmarked key with four numbers etched onto it. Was this a key to a safety deposit box? A bankbook from the Bank of Japan contained ten thousand plus yen.

In a folded envelope I found her will. I was the sole beneficiary. I then found what I was looking for in a brown paper bag. In a small jewelry box was Mom's one-carat diamond wedding ring.

Finally, I pulled a faded newspaper clipping from the bottom of the safe. My Japanese reading skills had dwindled from lack of practice, but I managed to make out that a fourteen-year-old girl, the daughter of the Chief Justice of Japan, had gone missing, her body discovered in a storm drain four days later.

Like I always did with hotel room safes when checking out, I ran my hand over the lining to make sure I hadn't left anything behind. Along the bottom edge, I felt a bump. I lifted the black felt lining and pulled out an old photograph.

When I glanced at the photo, my cellphone chirped.

"Is this Miss Hunter?"

"Inspector Honma?"

"Hai."

"Thank you for returning my call. I was wondering if there are any updates on your investigation."

A heavy sigh floated from the speaker. "As I told you in my office, finding the culprit in a random robbery is extremely difficult."

"Did you find out if anybody used the airline voucher?"

"Umm—" He hesitated, as if only now remembering. "We notified Japan Airlines, but haven't received anything yet."

"What about the footprint?"

He paused again, seeming to choose his words carefully. "The footprint was smeared to the point where we couldn't use it."

"What about the pawn shops and my mother's Rolex or locket . . . anything?"

Honma didn't reply. I realized that my voice had risen in anger again. "I apologize, Inspector Honma."

He paused, longer this time. "I will inform you if we find anything significant. So please do not keep calling because I do have many other cases to work on."

"Arigato, Inspector." I hung up.

I returned to the photograph from the safe. The picture was taken maybe twenty to twenty-five years ago. My younger-looking mother sat on the left side of a black leather sofa. She had a restrained smile, the type that screamed for the photographer to hurry up and take the damn picture. I recognized a younger Kiyomi, fifteen pounds lighter, sitting on the right side of the sofa. I didn't know the woman in the center, who was cradling a baby in her arms and grinning from ear to ear. What stood out from the photograph was the way Kiyomi was side-eyeing her. Kiyomi's mouth was down-turned, bottom lip pouty, and arms folded across her chest.

They looked like three contestants in a beauty contest, placed side by side, but my mother's beauty stood out from the rest. She looked sultry and sensual, even with that restrained smile. Her eyes hadn't changed much with time. They must have been what captivated John Hunter at first glance. The photograph captured her once-flawless milky complexion, which with time, and the strong Hawaiian sun, had aged and darkened.

Between sips of wine, I sighed, hugged myself, and let the tears flow.

Since I'd heard about my mother's death, I'd tried to convince myself it didn't happen. I would experience a rush of relief, as though I'd woken from a nightmare and Mom was still alive. Then my mind would twist and turn with clarity, my mother once again was dead.

Like with my own diary, I thought maybe she too had a journal, or something where she had captured her thoughts, moments that would bring her back to life, but I found nothing.

Sitting on the floor, I pushed boxes aside and found one labeled "Wedding Photos." I opened the box. Inside was a wedding album, synthetic gemstones decorating a youthful photograph of Dad in a tuxedo and Mom posing in a strapless, white lace wedding gown. I shut the album, placed it back into the box, and slid the cover back on.

The nagging question that now might never be answered kept creeping into my mind: why did she choose this life over our family?

My father never forgave his wife for choosing a bar over him, but ironically, the two of them had met in a bar in Tokyo. He was a second lieutenant on leave and stationed in Yokosuka Naval Base, the homeport for the United States Seventh Fleet.

Emiko Yamashita had started as a hostess when she was seventeen in the *mizu shobai,* the water trade. Some say the name was derived from the large number of natural hot springs in Japan and the ancient practice of men and women bathing together without sexual discrimination. So came the association of water and pleasure.

My father hated that she continued to work as a hostess. He urged her to quit, saying that he could take care of her financially. Mom did try to stop, but it lasted for just five months. It drove her crazy because entertaining was in her blood. She enjoyed singing karaoke and being out at night.

We lived together in Japan until I was four years old, and my brother two, then we moved to Hawaii because my father got reassigned to Pearl Harbor Naval Base.

After their separation, Dad never said a bad word against her. His remarks were always positive, commenting, "Gena, always remember that your mother is one of the most kind and generous people . . ." He'd turn silent for a few seconds before saying, "We were just different."

Yet he would jump up to answer the phone whenever it rang, hoping Mom was on the other end. Or he would listen intently to the TV news whenever anyone mentioned Japan for any reason.

All this kept running through my mind before I downed the last glass of wine. I wanted to stay in bed, to cry and wallow in grief, but the morbid photographs of my mother kept popping into my head. Tears dribbled down my cheeks and onto the pillow.

I tried to sleep, but couldn't. Sitting up, I stared at the light from the outside streetlight making patterns on the ceiling.

I needed to find the truth, or I would be stuck at home in Hawaii, never knowing. I envisioned the many sleepless nights, continually thinking about things I could or should have done while here in Japan.

My father had lectured me many times about never living in regret. "You make a decision and stick to it no matter how good or bad it turns out to be." Though I respected his advice, it was still tough, because he and I were so different.

I nibbled on my lower lip, rubbed my hands over my face, and took a deep breath. Perhaps if I scraped away the hardened Japanese barnacles of shame and fear, it would reveal the courage I needed to go all in instead of constantly measuring my decisions, frozen with all the possible consequences.

If the police were not taking my mother's death seriously, no one would. I tipped the bottle upside down, lapped up the remaining drops, and burped.

Already convinced it was more than a robbery, I said out loud, "Yakuza or no yakuza, I need to find out the truth."

7

Ever since the defeat of World War II, Japanese men had gotten weaker and Japanese women stronger. The pull of tradition, once ingrained with male domination and supremacy, had dwindled in Japan. Now, Japanese men seemed to have absorbed some of the American male's wimpiness, which, to the Kami's luck, made them perfect targets.

Kami is defined as either the divine wind or the spirit worshipped in the Shinto religion. She didn't care which, because she lived by the duality of oneness.

The Kami hated Americans because of their arrogance, which was perpetuated by the breeding of little prima donna brats who were taught how special they were, drilling into their tiny developing brains the lifelong sense of entitlement.

But she loved American movies, so in a sense they themselves became tolerable. Crime films taught her about microscopic evidence: DNA left behind in hair, saliva, or semen. When a murder was committed, cops first tried to figure out the motive, so the chances of getting caught diminished greatly when there was no reason behind a killing. She learned many gruesome ways of ending people's lives from watching horror movies. That ski-masked monster, Jason, was her favorite. The fucker just wouldn't die—someone to admire.

She dwelled on the injustice of her ancestors' deaths on the intense nights when a hundred thousand bombs rained from the sky. The fires burned for days, followed by more firebombing of Nagasaki, and still more of Hiroshima.

Six months later, for insurance, the Americans had dropped *Little Boy* over Hiroshima with a force equal to thirteen thousand tons of TNT. Three days later, for insurance-on-insurance, a B-29 dropped *Fat Boy*—a more powerful plutonium bomb equal to twenty kilotons of TNT—on Nagasaki.

Insurance my ass, the Kami thought. Civilians—her ancestors —had died by the thousands. The spineless Americans claimed they had been targeting military installations, the industrial war capabilities of Japan. When that didn't add up, they said that the destruction was intended to have a psychological effect and crush the kamikaze mindset of the county.

Domo . . . bullshit!

The truth was that, like scientists experimenting on guinea pigs, the Americans had wanted to test their new weapon of war on living, breathing human beings.

Mutherfuckers.

There should have been a tribunal for war crimes committed by the American leaders who'd decided to massacre millions of women and children. Instead, they received praise for a job well done.

The Kami had received a scholarship to study at Stanford University in California, and spent two years there before dropping out, learning more about American arrogance that they were better at reforming than at repenting.

She believed that life was about the survival of the strongest and the extinction of the weak. Weakness was not samurai. Her mother's genealogical bloodline, *bushido,* represented honor, loyalty, and bravery.

Shitting bombs from the sky reflected none of those things.

The Kami extended herself into the night like a hawk on the hunt. Tonight, another night of justice, her mother's suffering and the pull of vengeance weighed heavy on her heart. The Kami, a creature of the night, was in her element. She was sensitive to sounds, odors, and vibrations, and tonight's revenge took on a life of its own.

Roppongi appeared as a concrete confusion by day, but transformed into a heady, colorful playground for the evening nighthawks and trolls.

Justice would come in the form of another hostess bar. The same old story: young girls in their early twenties, wearing sexy clothes, pretending to enjoy themselves with drunken men twice their age. Degrading themselves, making sure there was a steady flow of drinks, lighting cigarettes, discussing boring subjects, nodding, smiling, and laughing at the customers' dumb jokes.

The Kami despised the men who patronized these bars, her hatred burning inside her belly like a welding torch. She squeezed the razor-sharp, icy-cool steel of her *tanto*, a knife a little less than a foot long. The single-edged blade was slightly curved, designed for soft targets, for slicing vital veins and throats—a hidden samurai weapon for close-up fighting.

The juice of the gods flowed through her veins, cocaine gripping her soul.

Shadowed behind a pillar, the Kami held her breath, arms tensed, right fist gripping the tanto, squeezing it in rhythm with her own heartbeat.

A few more minutes and the bars would be closing for the night. She knew that dressing in a form-fitting, strapless, gold sequin dress would do the trick. This outfit accentuated her curves and complemented her shoulder-length blonde hair. Japanese men craved blondes with big tits, so she was prepared.

She waited in silence; at times her heartbeat accelerated, but she calmed herself with a deep breath followed by an exhale of cool, white mist.

The Kami sniffed another line of cocaine. In the darkness, she relived the killing in Kabukicho a few nights ago. The bar was six kilometers away from Roppongi, far enough away to confuse the police when they tried to connect the motive.

THE SMELL of blood had invigorated her. She relived the woman's heels clicking against the pavement as the lock on the door snapped close. She despised this woman to the core, because *she* was the root cause of the Kami's mother's suffering.

The Kami had watched the woman on the street—three months of surveillance. Violating her free space had felt comforting and vindicating. The woman's aging legs and sagging breasts would soon be lumps of dead meat. She lived alone, didn't have a lover, and did not pursue companionship through one-night stands. Maybe she was dried up like a prune, the Kami thought with a snicker.

That night, the cocaine had flowed through her genitals like the devil's semen—pure euphoria, heightening her sense of awareness, increasing sensory stimulation. She couldn't decide which she preferred after snorting a line: sexual pleasure or sadistic killing.

In one fluid, continuous motion, she had slipped from darkness. The woman's eyes snapped open, startled. In a flash, the Kami slammed her against the wall, hands against her aging neck, and pinned her upward at an angle. The woman's eyes bulged with fear.

Through gritted teeth, the Kami demanded, "Where's the video?"

The terror on the woman's face changed to recognition. She choked back a scream and struggled to form the words. "There's no video."

"You lie!" The Kami increased pressure to her throat. "Where!"

"No vi . . . de . . . o," she croaked.

The tanto had penetrated, swift and smooth, into her lower abdomen. The woman's eyes sprung open, staring lifeless into the black sky. She dropped to the ground; a large pool of blood puddled underneath her. The police would find a disemboweled whore, her intestines boiling out onto the cold pavement.

After the initial stab, the Kami's rage had taken over. She'd blacked out, now unable to recall the pleasure of the kill. Blood had dripped from spider fingers, splattered on her face and dress, coating the ground like an oil spill.

She'd made it look like a robbery. She discovered a letter along with an airline voucher in the woman's handbag signed, *Love Always, Gena.* She slipped the letter into her garter. A locket. She snapped the chain from the woman's neck, opened it, glanced at the photograph inside, and flung it against the building wall.

The Kami knew she'd made a mistake when rage dominated logic.

"What video?" she repeated, and her hate escalated. *Lies!*

Standing above the whore and admiring the result of her work, she'd heard a noise coming from the stream area. The tanto snapped out. A rat, a damn rat stood on its hind legs at the edge of the embankment. When she walked toward it, the rodent scurried away. There, on the ground, was a hoop earring. She picked it up and fingered the cheap metal. It looked recently purchased and not tarnished by the elements. The Kami scanned the darkness.

Was someone hiding?

TWO A.M. She was giddy from remembering, but the chatter brought her back to the task at hand. Six middle-aged men staggered down the street with four young girls, who wore long coats that opened to expose short miniskirts, gyrating hips, and young, fleshy thighs. The girls giggled and weaved, arm in arm with the drunken men.

Must be careful, she must be quick. Jack jumped over the candlestick.

The Kami recalled watching National Geographic on TV. A lion would select and isolate a buffalo calf from the herd of bigger adults. Lions were natural hunters, and she liked to mimic them.

She stood at the edge of the streetlight and pulled her shoulders back, breasts protruding outward like bait to a fish. Her left leg was seductively extended forward, exposing a firm thigh in a white stocking. Hands on hips, she stared at the group of drunks as if in an alluring advertisement.

The men stopped to stare at her, eyes thirsty, hungry. The four girls sulked at the men's diverted attention, but like most hostesses, sex was not part of their work, so they snubbed the prostitute and moved on.

The men roared louder, slapping each other on the backs and giving high-fives. One man in a dark, wrinkled suit broke away from the group. The Kami grinned victoriously at the young buffalo calf. He staggered toward her. The others continued with the four girls down the alleyway to the main street, their voices and drunken laughter fading.

The Kami flashed a smile, took the man's hand, and led him into the darkness of the nearest alley. The stink of the night's trash permeated the area like a disease.

She ran a slender finger along the man's crotch and spoke in Japanese. "Ten thousand yen."

He fumbled for his wallet and paid.

The man slobbered on her neck and groped at her breasts. She shoved him off her. A look of shock sprung from his face when he felt the woman's physical strength. She smiled sexily at him to ease his concern, slithered to her knees, and slowly unbuckled his pants.

His eyes rolled upward, then closed.

Men were so easy to control. With her left hand busy, her right hand clutched the tanto. In one continuous, rotating motion, she stabbed him in the perineum, the area between the anus and scrotum. Known as the *Gate of Life and Death*, it paralyzed him, stifling his scream.

The Kami stood up and stared into the man's eyes, which were full of terror, knowing that death was imminent. She used the strength of her legs to rip the tanto upward, from the lower abdomen to the sternum.

Like the six others had, his eyes bulged, frozen in shock. Blood splattered onto the sidewalk and the Kami's dress. She pinned the man's body against the concrete wall and pulled the knife blade out with a sucking sound. The once shiny steel, as well as her gloved hand, were now covered with blood. She slashed the knife between his legs, and with one merciless thrust upward, twisted the blade clockwise as it dislodged human tissue.

The man's body dropped to the wet pavement with a loud thud. She glanced around—no one. The Kami stood over her motionless prey for a second before shoving his lifeless body toward the stairs with the heel of her shoe.

As the final encore, she dropped her trophy into a sealed plastic bag.

8

I spent the next day cleaning Mom's apartment, mostly killing time and waiting for the night to arrive.

At nine, I rode the train from Shibuya to Shinjuku and walked ten minutes north to Kabukicho, Tokyo's red-light district, with its porn cinemas, pink salons, no-panties cafes, peep shows, soap land brothels, and hundreds of hostess bars scattered in dark alleyways.

The skyscrapers of Shinjuku loomed overhead like giant sentinels, seemingly whispering to me under the hazy moonlight, urging me to keep going. Yet my push to move forward wasn't as determined as when I'd made up my mind to seek out the girl from the funeral. Time and sobering up tended to do that—cool the steam once the fire from the booze was removed.

I strolled along the cramped alleys and bright neon of Kabukicho, and halfway to the bar I got hit with the urge to turn back, as second thoughts hit me about how insane it was.

I asked myself aloud, "What am I doing? Who am I to investigate a murder? I know nothing about how to go about it except what I see on cop movies and TV shows."

A light-headed dizziness clobbered me. I had only gotten two hours of sleep that night, and not much more on any other night since the news of my mother's death. I was operating on pure, high-octane adrenaline.

I relived seeing the images of my mother's dead body lying prone on wet concrete, followed by the police mocking her death.

My anger, my hate, built at the injustice.

Reaching deep within, I gathered the strength to break away from the gravitational pull of the safety of Hawaii. I focused on the bizarre task ahead and continued walking.

Hostess clubs were as prevalent in Tokyo as sushi and sake. Being a pocket-sized hole-in-the-wall, my mom's small bar was hard to find. I felt shamefully sad that Mom had owned and run such an establishment in this seedy area, but who was I to judge. My only regret was never getting another chance to ask her why.

She once tried to explain it to me. Drunk at the time, she said, "When I was a child, my great grandmother showed me a chest filled with the most exquisite silk kimonos I'd ever seen in my life. The silk was incredibly soft. If the fabric were any softer it would have vanished into thin air at my touch. Next to the kimonos was a *shamisen*, the three-stringed musical instrument of the geisha."

And that was the extent of her explanation. Perhaps it was her way of reinforcing that it was her calling, her geisha destiny.

Although I'd been led to believe that hostesses were not prostitutes—that there was no sex involved, that a hostess used her sexuality to make money by flirting and providing female companionship—I still found it hard to believe that sex didn't happen. All of the key ingredients were included in one place— pretty young girls hungry for money, rich men, and booze.

The route to Club Blue Diamond was not straight-forward and did not always follow the right angles of a well-planned city grid. New buildings were built around old buildings, or wherever there was available real estate. Part of the street I was on curved into a half moon before straightening. I felt like a lab rat searching for the cheese at the end of a maze.

I finally came to a dead-end alleyway, a ten-by-twelve-foot enclosure. Thick bamboo trees decorated the entrance of the bar. In the back, a cinder-block wall bordered a side street, providing glimpses of neon lights and patches of the night sky above it. The enclosure muffled the sounds of the city; distant car horns drifted in to fill the silence.

The front of the bar was a façade, the old, gabled wooden roof of a rural house with overhanging eaves. The weathered roof gave the entrance an ancient seventeenth-century look. The alleyway and worn concrete looked as if it was swept twice daily by a whiskbroom.

The pavement. I recognized the spot from the photograph where my mother's body lay in her own blood. In time, no one would know what happened here. Avoiding the spot as if it were a bear trap, I took a wide detour and walked down three shallow stairs to the entrance.

I slid the door open and stepped into a tiny, dimly lit sepia-toned room, the yellow mixing with the purple haze of cigarette smoke and black lights.

When the door opened, women shouted in unison as if on cue, "Irasshai-mase."

Also in unison, they moaned at seeing a woman and not a male customer enter. In a cramped booth, four girls in their early twenties were laughing with a group of four men dressed in pressed slacks and expensive suits, taking long drags off their cigarettes as smoke snaked up toward the low ceiling.

The tiny bar could fit twelve to fifteen people comfortably. It was decorated in a traditional Japanese style—blacks and whites in harmony with polished frames, a few pottery pieces scattered throughout, and colorful paper lanterns suspended from the ceiling. Silk mosaics of birds and flowers hung on the walls in a losing effort to hide a wallpaper that was shabby and sagging in places. The place screamed for needed maintenance.

I wondered if it turned a profit.

An L-shaped, thatched bamboo bar sat in front of a shelf lined with bottles of liquor. It was backlit, shining through the liquids— many different shades of amber, some clear, and a few green. Clean drinking glasses were stacked upside down on a lower shelf.

Two men sandwiched the girl from the funeral in a high-back booth. One guy was slurring and had an arm wrapped around her. His hand cupped her breast as he jabbered on and on.

I flinched, wondering how any woman could demean herself like that, letting herself be violated in that way. I hated being here.

I didn't see Kiyomi, so I sidled up to the bar and sat down on a high stool. Everyone ignored me; the girls were too busy with paying customers. A thirty-two-inch flat-screen TV mounted on the wall at the end of the bar was showing a sumo wrestling match, the images reflecting on the polished bar counter. Photographs covered the entire wall closest to the karaoke electronics. The details of the pictures were too far away to make out, but they overlapped one another to form a large disorganized collage.

Kiyomi walked through the entrance holding two bags of groceries in each arm. She stared at me. Her eyes narrowed into a harsh squint, which transformed into a frightful sneer.

She stood at arm's length from me and said in Japanese, "What are you doing here? You shouldn't be here."

I couldn't tell her the truth, so said, "I'm looking for a job."

Kiyomi-chan stared at me for a couple seconds, then grimaced.

Before she could ask, I injected, "I need money to stay in Japan for a few days to clean my mother's apartment, sell what I can, and ship whatever else to Hawaii."

The change in the woman's face struck an agreeable note. "You ever worked as a hostess?"

I shook my head. "I'm willing to try."

Kiyomi placed a finger under her chin, slow-paced toward the wall of photos, then turned back. She smirked. "No. I have too many girls already." She pointed to the six women, spun around, and walked away carrying the grocery bags in her arms.

I followed her. "Please, Kiyomi-chan. I need a job for just a few days."

She ignored me, sliding cans and boxes into cabinet shelves.

One of the four men, maybe a businessman, shot up from his seat with a goofy smile on his drunken red face. His hair was mostly black, with a few white streaks, and was slicked down and side-combed. He staggered toward me, stumbled once, and received a chorus of *ooohs* from everyone, followed by laughter when he regained his balance, holding on for dear life to the edge of the bamboo bar.

Kiyomi rushed at me like a charging bull in pumps. Her hands fluttered in front of her, and she blurted out in rapid English, "Come, come. You sit here with customer."

She had transformed from the cold bitch of a few seconds ago to a gracious hostess wanting to drum up business.

I didn't move and thought: *What would Lani do?*

Kiyomi took hold of the drunken man's hand and pulled him toward an empty booth, flagging me to follow. "Hayaku, hayaku."

Lani would play her.

I didn't follow her like some obedient dog. I remained on the barstool. If Kiyomi'd had a rolled-up newspaper, she would have smacked me across the nose.

Kiyomi's anxiety seemed to increase, and she turned to me with pleading eyes. I brushed aside the ounce of guilt I felt and didn't budge.

The man grinned and shouted, "Hai!" He dug into the pocket

of his pleated pants, pulled out a roll of money, fanned it out, and started waving it above his head.

He cried out, "Come here, beautiful girl."

I wanted to throw up on the jerk. I stood up and headed for the door. The slow-moving Kiyomi seemed to kick into overdrive and chased after me.

She huffed out a breath, which smelled of garlic. "Okay, you start work tonight."

"Tomorrow night." I stood my ground, refusing to be pushed into an occupation I had despised all my life.

The drunkard gave up on me and stumbled back to join the others, immune to the ridicule he was getting for failing to entice the pretty girl. A young hostess took his arm, held up his wrist, and waved the hand holding the bundle of money like a tree branch with leaves. Before the night was over, the money would be hers.

Kiyomi faced me, and this time came across as a drill sergeant. "Okay, you work tomorrow. You dress in proper clothes. Sexy clothes. No jeans and T-shirts."

I had on blue jeans and a red, long-sleeved blouse, jogging shoes, and a little face makeup. I hadn't showered yet and smelled of dust and sweat.

Kiyomi drew her finger along her cleavage. "You wear sexy dresses, low-cut."

I nodded, knowing that I needed to go shopping tomorrow.

"Out of respect for your mother, I will give you work for one night." Although Kiyomi tried to make it clear why she was hiring me, I didn't believe her. "If you meet the requirements, you can work another night."

I knew what "meeting the requirements" meant—making money for her.

"Emiko-chan and I agreed that if either one of us should die, the other would inherit the business." She repeated what she'd said on the phone.

My hands shook and my face warmed. I ignored her lie.

I glanced around the bar. Run-down and appearing to be barely surviving, Kiyomi had more things to worry about than right to proprietorship. I had no intention of claiming any part of this dump, none at all, but I decided to keep Kiyomi guessing.

"Arigato for the job." I projected coolness. "What time tomorrow?"

Kiyomi's chubby face contorted at my non-response about ownership. Her voice rose in anger. "You start at eight and work till closing at two. Don't be late. If you are late, there will be no job."

I walked out without saying a word.

9

"Who da hell are you?" The next day, Lani couldn't believe my crazy plan to find my mother's killer. "You're kidding me, right?"

"Look. Nobody's doing anything to find who killed her." I continued to reassure myself that I was doing the right thing.

"So you need help in picking a hot number for tonight?"

"Yeah, I'm calling from the mall." I had already scanned through the dress racks and taken pictures of six outfits. "I'll send you what I have."

After each picture, I received: *Boring*. Six times.

Lani texted: *Where's the cleavage?*

I texted back: *You know I don't have your assets.*

After an hour, we settled on a dress.

I stood vogueing in my new dress in my mother's apartment, wearing a pair of killer new shoes. I sent Lani the final picture, me standing in front of the full-length mirror.

Lani sent an emoji—a mouth with large lips and a red tongue hanging out. Her text read: *Sexy, but not slutty.*

I sent back a smiley face.

You're really gonna do this, huh? Lani expressed concern that the most sensible person she knew was doing something so bizarre. She texted: *Be careful, Sista! You'll be entering a whole different world.*

The black dress fit my shape nicely. The sequin bodice, held up by spaghetti straps, had a plunging V neckline, and the velvet skirt ended above the knees, a slit down the side accentuating my athletic legs. The shoes topped it off: smooth black leather, open-toed with thin ankle straps and leg-lengthening stiletto heels.

I wore a coat on the train ride from Shibuya to Shinjuku and changed into low sandals to walk the remaining distance. Before I entered Club Blue Diamond, I removed the coat and sandals, placed them in my backpack, and slipped on my new shoes.

I checked the time: 7:50 p.m. I entered the club paralyzed with fear, not knowing what to expect. All the while, I kept thinking about what to ask the girl from the funeral.

I took a quick glance around the club. She wasn't here. The two girls from last night were with two customers in a booth. A third was hanging out at the bamboo bar sipping a drink, a fourth busy singing karaoke with a customer.

The wonderful aroma of marinated teriyaki beef triggered my hunger. I had eaten only a small sandwich for dinner, because I wanted to fit comfortably into my new dress. The sizzling sound of beef grilling from the tiny kitchen in back floated throughout the small bar, creating a light haze of cooking smoke.

Kiyomi screamed, "You're late!" She pointed to the digital clock on the wall, which showed five after eight.

I re-checked my wristwatch and knew I wasn't. "No, I'm not. Your time is wrong."

Just when Kiyomi was about to cuss, shout, and refuse to give me a job, two Japanese men, both about my father's age, strolled through the entrance.

The first man stared and smiled at me. He was breathing hard for a man in his forties and had an ample belly protruding over a strained belt. His dark blue suit fit snuggly, stretched to its limit at the seams.

To get in Kiyomi's good graces, I bowed to the man and said, "Irasshai-mase."

Kiyomi's rounded cheeks went slack. She'd lost her opportunity to reject my employment and was still angry that I had not acknowledged her as the true owner of the bar.

I wondered if I made a mistake in playing Kiyomi by stringing her along.

A pretty girl, early twenties with an oval face and high curving cheekbones, rushed toward us. Furious, she shoved me away from the man. My new shoes weren't made for balancing in, so I grabbed the bar countertop to avoid falling to the floor. The girl clutched the man's arm and led him to a booth.

I felt like a passenger standing alone as the train pulled out from the station.

The irate girl had long, silky, flowing black hair and was dressed like a racecar driver. Her two-piece outfit consisted of a stylish red leather top and matching hot pants. With long legs and six-inch heels, she towered over the other girls.

Sitting with the customer, the girl's wide-set eyes, fringed with thick, long lashes, continued to send evil-eye darts at me from across the room.

What the heck did I get myself into?

Another girl had heavy-lidded bedroom eyes that looked sleepy yet seductive. She had shoulder-length espresso-colored hair. Her name was Yui.

Yui chuckled and said in Japanese, "That is her regular customer. You do not steal anyone's regular customer."

"But I didn't—"

She walked away, not bothering to let me finish.

I wandered to the bar where the lone girl sipped her drink. She barely looked eighteen. She had a small but straight nose and her lips were naturally pouty, so her look matched the adolescent schoolgirl outfit she wore.

I asked her, "Do you speak English?"

"Sukoshi . . . little bit."

"I'm Gena."

"Junko."

"How can I tell who the regular customers are? I don't want to cause any trouble."

She stared back at me like I was an idiot.

"When girl busy with customer, you can have that customer." Junko talked as though it were one of the Ten Commandments of hostessing. "Some girls work more than one customer, same time. If customer see another girl he like with other hostess, he can choose her. But price go up. This called *shimei*."

"So how would I know all this?"

She shrugged like that wasn't her problem.

In the first hour, I at least learned where my locker was in back. To make the money issue clear, Kiyomi huffed, saying all bars paid differently. "I pay commission on the customer's bill. If customer drinks beer that costs two thousand yen, you get four hundred yen. I will not pay—" she stopped, then glanced at the door as though expecting someone, but no one entered. She didn't finish her explanation, instead turned and walked away.

For the next hour, I sat at the bar while five girls catered to six customers. I noticed that four of the customers wore wedding bands. Mei was the girl in the red racecar-driver outfit. She worked two customers and shifted from one to the other every ten to fifteen minutes.

I got thirsty and hungry waiting and doing nothing. When I asked for a beer and teriyaki beef, Kiyomi placed the charge on a running tab. Two hours went by and I owed the club money. This wasn't working out as planned.

With nothing else to do, I wandered over to the wall of photos.

There were hundreds, maybe a thousand candid photographs of drunken customers with hostesses. Like a large collage, each photo was pinned on a corkboard. Young girls posed frozen on customers' laps, sitting side by side, or laughing in playful embraces. My mother appeared five years younger in some pictures, while others looked as though taken a few weeks ago, maybe even days before she died.

In the hodgepodge of pictures, I recognized someone familiar. The photograph had been taken at the entrance of the bar. She was the woman from the image I had found in the floor safe. Here, the woman who'd been holding a child in the center of the sofa looked about ten years older.

Boredom gave me time to reflect. During my short stint attending university, I'd wanted to know more about my half-culture and the Asian blood that ran through my veins. I read a book by an author named Ruth Benedict called *The Chrysanthemum and the Sword*, which explored how Japan's ideology developed and how it was reflected in the manners and customs of everyday life.

One thing Benedict studied was why the Japanese had been willing to keep fighting during WWII even when they were losing, why they had been ready to die rather than be taken prisoners, why young men crashed their airplanes into American ships in suicide kamikaze attacks.

Additionally, with regard to sex, I found it interesting that the Japanese did not condemn self-gratification, that they considered physical pleasures good and worthy of cultivation, as long as they did not intrude on the serious affairs of life. They cultivated the pleasures of the flesh like fine arts, and once they had been savored, they sacrificed them to duty. Sex was like any human feeling and regarded as good, as a minor aspect of life. In Japanese philosophy, the flesh was not evil and therefore they were not moralistic about sexual pleasure—enjoying it was not a sin. The spirit and body were not opposing forces.

At 11:30 p.m., a customer walked in alone. Kiyomi glanced at me and nudged her chin toward the door. At this point I didn't feel desirable, more like a wallflower at a high school dance.

The guy was in his late twenties and dressed in jeans and a pullover sweater with a hoodie. Just my luck. My first customer turned out to be the Unabomber. I took his hand, which was cold and clammy, and led him to a booth. I slid in first. He sat on the outside.

We communicated in Japanese. For the first thirty minutes we small-talked and took shots of *shochu*. Tipsy, I giggled more than I should have, trying to convince Kiyomi that I could do this.

Kiyomi watched from a barstool. Her wide smile said everything—at least for now, I was "meeting the requirements."

At midnight, the girl from the funeral walked into the club. She wore a black leather corset with a matching skirt. Her hair was wild and uncombed, which accentuated her elfin look and firm pointy jaw. She flashed a cute little girly smile at men who looked at her for more than two seconds. A customer sitting at the bar poured her sake from a porcelain flask into a small ceramic cup.

The girl saw me sitting with my customer and quickly turned away.

The Unabomber slid his hand over my knee. I gently pushed it away like it was a tickling feather, yet I kept smiling at him. His face pouted at the rejection. He'd had twice as much shochu as me and was slurring his words. Like teenage boys do in high school at movie theaters, the guy pretended to yawn with outstretched arms, then dropped his arm around my shoulder and leaned in to kiss me.

I wanted to smack him across the face, but didn't. I giggled like a silly fool, politely removed his arm and said, "Benjo . . . toilet."

He sulked, stood up, wobbled, and let me out of the booth.

I headed for the toilet, stepped inside, and sobbed quietly. I placed my face in my hands and said out loud, "What the hell am I doing here?"

I dried my tears and decided to call for help.

Lani answered groggily, "Hello, Sista."

I forgot that 12:10 a.m. was 5:10 a.m. in Hawaii. "Sorry, Lan, I forgot about the time difference."

A long, drawn-out yawn was followed by, "What's up?"

I gave her a summary of my horrible night. "I don't know how you did it."

"You mean jerking guys off?"

"Yeah."

"Let me tell you the key." Lani yawned again. "You know that small shop along Maunakea Street in Chinatown where they sell roast duck on metal hooks?"

I sniffled and wiped my nose. "Sure, I buy duck there every New Year."

"So there's this skinny Chinese guy with this gigantic butcher knife, right? I mean this guy was bone thin with noodles for arms, and I don't know how da fuck he lifts that huge blade all day long. Chopping roast duck on this humongous wood chopping block, you know. And everybody's waiting to order roast duck, at the same time watching this guy like a sideshow." I heard Lani strike a lighter, inhale a breath, then say in a nasal voice, "Yep, fuckin' boring job. All he does all day is cut-duck, cut-duck, cut-duck, cut-duck. Next customer: cut-duck, cut-duck, cut-duck, cut . . ."

"Okay, okay, I get it. And so?" Talking to Lani had cheered me up a little.

"And so." Lani snickered. "All I did all day was, hand-job, hand-job, hand-job. Next customer: hand-job, hand-job."

I burst out laughing; snot flew from my nose.

Lani seemed to ponder her next few words. In a calming, sisterly voice she said, "Think of hostessing the same way. Do the same thing over and over. Just don't overthink these guys, Gen. Men are pretty simple to figure out. They have only one thing on their minds."

"Maybe I'm taking this hostessing way too serious."

"Yep, just think of the of the Duck Man in Chinatown."

"Cha—wait." I jumped off the toilet, faced the bowl, and heaved up vomit.

After I gathered myself, Lani chuckled. "Good one, Gen . . . from da gut, eh."

"Yeah, I better slow down with the booze." I wiped my mouth with another tissue pulled from my handbag. "Thanks, Lan."

"Easy Sista." She hung up.

I dragged myself to the mirror, turned on the faucet, and washed my mouth. I didn't swallow water, afraid of cholera or something else nasty. Other than my bloodshot eyes, everything was in place.

I walked out of the restroom. The Unabomber stared at me like I'd tried to sneak out the backdoor.

As I sat down next to him, the girl from the funeral staggered toward our booth and swiped my drink off the table. She made a fist and smacked the Unabomber in the eye.

She shouted in Japanese, "Get out of here before I call the police."

The Unabomber shoved me to the ground and dashed for the door. Everyone in the club stared, but nothing else.

Shaken, I grabbed the edge of the table and pulled myself up. I asked the girl, "What happened? You just clobbered my only customer."

"That fucker put pill in drink."

"Date rape drug?"

"Could be anything," she said, and turned and headed back to the bamboo bar and her waiting customer. But she stopped and faced me. "And one more thing—do not sit on inside. A drunk customer can trap you inside the booth."

I nodded and said, "Arigato."

I found out from Junko that the girl from the funeral was named Reiko. Whenever Reiko wasn't with a customer, I tried to get closer to her, but she always drifted farther away. I didn't get it, until I scanned the club and caught Kiyomi staring with her vulture eyes.

All six girls were busy with customers for most of the evening, so there was never an opportunity to talk to anyone about my mother.

My plan was failing miserably, and at the end of the night I'd learned nothing except that my shochu tolerance was low, never to leave my drink unattended, and that the safest place to sit in a booth was on the outside.

At closing, Kiyomi handed me 3200 yen for the night, which was about thirty bucks. I didn't care about money, but obviously Kiyomi did, given that sour scowl she gave when paying me.

"You cannot be a hostess." Kiyomi frowned, but was holding back a grin. "A good hostess must pretend that her customer is her best. Not only that, but she must pretend that he is the best at the club. She must make her customers spend more."

"This is my first night," I said defensively. "I can do better."

Kiyomi placed a finger to her lips. "The customer can feel your disgust. You have tomorrow night to do better or you do not have a job here."

Given that ultimatum, I decided to take a chance with Kiyomi. "Did Detective Honma talk to you about my mother's death?"

Her chubby cheeks quivered as she glanced at the floor, her reaction delayed. "Hai."

"What did he ask you?"

"It's not important."

"Why don't you want to talk about my mother's murder? You might know something that's not apparent to you, but it might be significant to the investigation."

Kiyomi pivoted and walked away, stopped and faced me again, and pointed a stern finger at me.

I got the message.

Exhausted from the evening, and the mental and physical strain, I lumbered to my locker to gather my things. At the beginning of the night, Kiyomi had sold me a combination lock that I could have bought on the street for half the price. The lockers were in a separate room. Seven feet high, triple-tiered, and made of flimsy sheet metal, the freestanding structure also acted as a partition that separated two stalls from the restroom door.

I screamed at what was crawling in my locker. Giant, brown, squiggly cockroaches scurried over my backpack. I brushed off the roaches and slammed the door.

People at the bar outside stared as I exited. Mei snickered and whispered to a young woman in a long white sequined evening dress. Through the silence of the bar at closing, their laughter carried into the night as I left through the front door.

On my taxi ride to Shibuya, I stared out the side window as Tokyo slept, and wondered: *What was Kiyomi hiding?*

10

Aom arrived on the island of Oahu late in the afternoon and needed to find work before she ran out of the money from mama-Em's pawned Rolex. While at the pawnshop, she had purchased secondhand clothes: a thick, yellow winter sweater, a dress from another generation, and running shoes that were one size too big. To complete the illusion of normalcy, she bought a battered carryon and filled it with an assortment of clothes.

After purchasing a one-way ticket from Narita to Honolulu, she had a little over $200 left.

Through a Chinese Triad crime syndicate, she was issued a Japanese passport for servicing important Chinese clients visiting Japan for diplomatic reasons. The passport gave Aom ninety days access to the United States without needing a visa. So, the count-down to make money before returning to Thailand was on.

Believing that she was in control of her ultimate fate, she clutched the locket, determined not to leave Hawaii until she found mama-Em's family. The hard part was telling them what she'd witnessed that night. To describe the killer as best she could, especially the tattoo on her forearm.

Aom was sure mama-Em's family would try to convince her to talk to the police, but she hated and distrusted law enforcement. In her experience, the police in Thailand were as corrupt as the thieves, some even more corrupt. She didn't know much about the police in Hawaii, but at this point she trusted no one, especially with the yakuza wanting her dead.

When she asked for possible lodging, the security guard at the airport first suggested he lived alone in an apartment and would consider a roommate. He was flatfooted, two hundred plus pounds of lard; she didn't think about it for long. Although he implied sex as payment, it came across as jest, so when Aom didn't respond, he suggested, "Got a woman's homeless shelter in Iwilei."

Aom caught a taxi to Iwilei, a business district on the south side of the island. She pictured herself standing out like a yellow highlighter against the darkness of winos and bums lined up for their free meals.

The lady behind the counter looked Aom up and down. She was in her mid-forties, plump with a double chin. She instructed, "We don't turn anyone away who needs lodging, but we have very strict rules here. If you steal anything, even a cup, you're gone. You are required to bathe every day. You will be served breakfast, lunch, and dinner in that room." She pointed in the direction of a line of women holding empty trays.

Aom wrapped her sweater tighter around herself and looked down at her oversized running shoes. Reaching out for help brought back memories of her childhood. She'd hated begging for handouts after the monsoons wiped out her family's crops, but it was her destiny.

The double-chinned woman continued, "We secure the doors at 7 p.m., so if you're not here you'll be locked out."

The offer sounded like heaven to her after having escaped death in Japan.

She sat alone and ate her serving of hot chili, two hotdogs, and two scoops of white rice on a folding table and chair. When done, they assigned her a sleeping cot in a room packed with thirty other homeless women. The men were housed in another part of the building. The humidity in the air added to the stench. The overhead and ground fans weren't enough to air out the human sorrow.

A brown-skinned woman brushed the hair of a little girl clutching a teddy bear. A white woman in her twenties breastfed a child while humming a nursery tune. No one spoke out loud. The air was thick with gloom.

Aom leaned over to the lady on the cot next to her. She lay prone, with her eyes closed. Her hand trembled non-stop.

"Hi, I am new to Honolulu. Where I can find work?"

The lady twisted her head sideward and smiled, exposing a large gap where two front teeth once were. Her turkey neck wobbled. "What can you do?"

"You might say I am an entertainer."

"Hmm." She gave Aom the once over. "If you put on some nice clothes and a little makeup, I think men will find work for you."

Aom wondered if her profession was that obvious.

The woman had small beads of sweat on her brow. "I used to be a dancer, but as you can see, I ran into some hard times."

"It happens." Aom's tone of voice signaled, *that's life*. She had met, and knew, enough druggies to see that this lady had a bad case of chasing the dragon.

Her jaw quivered. "You wanna strip?"

"I was thinking more of a hostess."

"Hmm." The lady turned on her side, bracing her tangled blonde head with her palm. "Looks like you got a killer bod under that sweater. You might make more money stripping than hostessing. They got some pretty good strip clubs here in

Honolulu. When the ships get into Pearl Harbor, the clubs are packed. You might also get some side action with some cute young studs too." She giggled. Spit flew from between the gap in her teeth.

Aom admitted, "I have never stripped before."

The lady again giggled and went into a coughing fit. Phlegm caught in her throat before she added, "Fuck, man . . . what's so hard about taking your clothes off?"

"But I cannot dance."

"You don't have to dance. Just stand on stage and strut, move your hips a little, move your hands a little, cup your titties a little, then pull your garter open for guys to feed you money. A dollar at a time—after a while it adds up. It's not rocket science."

"Do you know of any good hostess clubs? It is more my style."

"They got a few here in this area, but I worked at only one personally. A few blocks from here there's a club for both hostesses and strippers. But I wouldn't call it a gentlemen's club either."

The lights flicked a couple times, signaling bedtime.

Aom turned face up and thanked the lady.

"No problema." The lady coughed phlegm. "For me . . . I like it here. Fuckin' rat race out there, bust my butt to make a living, but this city had beaten the shit out of me."

The following day, before curfew, Aom checked out the hostess club that the lady had talked about. She got directions and walked a few blocks. The area was an industrial district with a car repair shop, a store selling refurbished rattan furniture, and another selling wholesale ceramic tiles.

Building shadows stretched with the setting sun, and a small neon sign glowed dimly across the building's front: Club Star. Aom split the olive-green drapes that separated the street from the inside. Unsurprisingly, the place was a dump, dreary, and smelled like mildew and Pine-Sol. There was a small bar counter by the entrance and neon beer signs illuminating the darkness.

Raised about a foot off the floor, the scarred stage held a stripper pole that reached from the stage to the ceiling, looking as if it were the only thing holding up the roof. On stage, there was a chubby white woman in a black G-string who appeared to be north of forty. Her hips were large, her thighs pocked with cellulite, and her full breasts sagged. An elderly man wearing a tank top and a light-blue construction hardhat chewed on a tooth-pick and mechanically stuck dollar bills into her garter.

She'd seen enough.

Even the worst club she worked in Bangkok was better than the one she'd just left. She was in big trouble if this was the best that Hawaii had to offer.

Aom made it back to the shelter in time for curfew. She lay down and turned to face the lady on the neighboring cot again. "You were right. That sure was no gentleman's club."

The lady didn't move. Aom reached over. Her skin was cold to the touch. She sat up straight; the thin shelter blanket fell to the side. Aom scanned for someone, anyone nearby who could help. All the cots were full of sleeping bodies, or dead ones.

A shelter worker passed the side door.

"Help!" she shouted and waved.

Men in white suits soon came and took the woman's body away on a gurney; a white sheet covered her from head to toe.

A Black woman two cots down—prison butch cut, wearing a T-shirt big enough to be a tent—snickered and said, "Happens all the time. You wind up here usually 'cause you're at your bottom. Some don't leave till they got a sheet over their head."

The next day Aom, knowing nothing about computers, convinced a cute shelter volunteer named Henry to use the office computer and search the Internet for the name written on the airline voucher: Emiko Yamashita. His search showed an

Emiko Yamashita in California, but none in Hawaii. Henry also searched through the phone directory, but that too turned up empty. He mentioned that the phone number might be unlisted.

Late afternoon, before curfew, Aom took the dead woman's advice and checked out the strip club. The club had three stages that could each fit four dancers at once, and three smaller stages for singles. Every stage had its own stainless-steel stripper pole. Mirror balls rotated above, blending and mixing with colorful spotlights and flashing strobes. The place was half-full of men, old and young.

The club opened at two in the afternoon and closed at two in the morning. Aom was hired on the spot. The mama-san said that the day crowd was smaller compared to the one at night.

Time to make money—Aom walked up to a man at the bar sitting next to a stripper sipping a drink on the rocks. The short Filipino girl was dark-skinned with deep smoky eyes, had large breasts, and wore a red teddy.

As she did in Bangkok, Aom ran her hand along the man's thigh, inching closer to his crotch. She leaned in and whispered, "Come . . . let's have some fun." She cradled his hand to her breasts and led him to an empty booth.

The Filipino stripper shot off the barstool and screamed, "Hey bitch! You can't just steal customers like that."

After thirty minutes, the customer left. Mama-san, a statuesque Korean woman in her early fifties with a face stretched like a drum and breasts that could land an airplane, flagged Aom over. "Cut it out. This is not a cutthroat place."

"Cutthroat?" Aom feigned ignorance. "I do not know what that means."

"You cannot take a customer away from another girl like that."

"I am just trying to make money." She thought about what the

Englishman had taught her about win-win. "The more I make, the more you make."

The mama-san nodded, but glanced at the Filipino stripper glaring at her. "One look at you and I know you can make more money than anybody here, but I gotta keep the peace. So stop it, or you have to leave."

Aom needed the job, so she'd play by whatever stupid rules the place had. At the end of the week, she left the shelter because she could make more money at night, and in order to do that she had to break curfew.

She found a termite-eaten two-story walkup on Piikoi Street. Though she treasured having her own place, a huge chunk of her earnings went to rent and food, because the cost of living on Oahu was crazy.

Although working nights was better, she still wasn't making the kind of money she needed to return to Thailand. Time was ticking.

The next night at the club, she asked a waiter, "How can I find out who owns this? The woman's name is Emiko Yamashita."

Randy was a local Japanese guy in his mid-twenties with monolid eyes, a wide forehead, and high cheekbones. He studied the photograph inside the locket. "You tried the phone book or Internet?"

"Did that, but got nothing."

"Have you tried facial recognition?"

"What is that?"

"If you have a photograph of a person, you use the photograph and set up an algorithm to scan social media sites like Facebook, Instagram, or whatever."

"Can you do this kind of thing?"

"Not me, but I can find out who can. I work here only part time. I'm really a student at the university. They got some major computer brains there that can do this kinda stuff."

"It is important I find these people."

He shrugged. "I'll ask around, but it might cost you."

Aom knew she should be making money, not spending it, but asked, "How much?"

"Don't know, but I'll make a call." He reached into his jeans pocket and pulled out a cell. "Be right back."

He exited the club.

In ten minutes, he was back. "Two hundred."

"Whoosh . . . why so much?"

Randy shrugged his broad shoulders.

"When can he get this done?

"The guy said in a day or two."

"Do it. I need it fast."

After two weeks of living in Honolulu, Club Om kept popping up as the place to make big money consistently, because the clientele consisted mainly of wealthy men from Japan—businessmen, CEOs, and diplomats. An icy chill ran up Aom's spine when she learned that the clientele also included yakuza.

Even though she was hiding on a speck of rock in the middle of the Pacific, Tamura's scorn was far-reaching. It would be only a matter of time before he found her. She had to keep moving and not stay in one place for too long.

She hated the club's name, Om, because it disrespected the Buddhist chant, but she needed to make money faster than a dollar at a time.

11

I arrived at Club Blue Diamond twenty minutes before eight. When I entered the bar, the digital clock on the wall matched that on my wristwatch. As I suspected, Kiyomi or one of her henchwomen had moved the time forward last night.

"Okay," I told myself. "If that's the way she wants to play."

Kiyomi squinted at my dress, the same one I'd worn last night, but she said nothing. I sure as heck wasn't going to purchase another outfit when I might not be here after tonight.

I thought of what Junko had said about shimei. "If a customer sits down and sees another girl he likes sitting at another table, he can select her, but the price goes up." This included commission on drinks and food, and if a customer stayed beyond ninety minutes, each hour would cost more.

Tonight, I planned to do something I'd never done before in my life, which was to *flirt*.

Throughout the day I practiced with Lani on Skype. On my first attempt, Lani laughed so hard I felt insulted. I said, "What the hell, this isn't easy for me."

Lani gathered herself and snickered. "Gen, you really looked constipated."

"Come on, Lan. Help me out here. If I don't make some serious money tonight, it's over, and the old bat will fire me."

Her laughter tapered off. "Okay, Sista. You got the most gorgeous *hapa* eyes on the planet." Lani had always made a big deal of my *perfect* mixed-race eyes. "You gotta use it, man."

Lani described how she flirted, but with her physical assets, pushing a cart with a broken wheel filled with plumbing supplies in Home Depot could be considered flirting, drawing attention from men and even some women.

Three girls were sitting with four customers and singing karaoke, badly. All four Japanese men wore dark suits and had been there a while, judging by the red glow on their faces.

Mei sat with a skinny, geeky-looking young man.

"Well, here goes." I mumbled, still not sure if I could do this.

I didn't just walk up to the bamboo bar—instead I pretended I was strolling down a catwalk like a fashion model. When Mei's customer saw me, I held his gaze for about five seconds, then looked away. I turned back to him with a fleeting smile. I slid onto the barstool, making certain that the slit in my skirt exposed my firm runner's thigh. Trying hard, but not too hard, I relaxed my eyebrows and focused my eyes on his, moving my gaze down his lips, then back. I straightened my shoulders to emphasize my breasts. Slowly and sensually, I ran a finger along my throat.

Mei saw what I was doing and pulled her customer's chin toward her, but her customer had already flagged mama-Kiyomi and said a few words to her. If Mei got any angrier, steam would be coming out of her ears.

The man stood and tried to act cool when he walked toward me. He stumbled but regained his balance. When he was within reach, I touched his arm, brushed against his shoulder, and led him to an empty booth.

In my peripheral vision, I glimpsed Mei screaming at mama-Kiyomi. The loud karaoke music drowned her tantrum.

When the customer left, I copied what the other girls did. I hated it, but the guy spent generously. I escorted him to the door. With my heels on, he was shorter than me, so I had to bend down to give him a hug. He stared at my chest when I pulled away. Though it made my flesh crawl, I forced a seductive smile.

And that was how it went throughout the rest of the night. Through shimei, I stole two of Mei's customers and one of Kimi's, the girl who'd laughed along with Mei at the roaches in my locker.

Kiyomi grinned like she'd won the lottery. At the end of the night, she handed me 97,500 yen, or about $900.

I opened my locker expecting another nest of roaches, but found a piece of paper, a note from Reiko. It wrote to meet her at 3 a.m. at a soba stand. She drew a rough sketch of how to get there.

A night of drinking made Reiko look like a tightrope walker in a strong wind when she weaved toward me. She wore a Goth snakeskin-print sleeveless dress, and ankle boots with three-inch heels.

The soba noodle stand was a few blocks from the bar, far enough from the main path most travelers took that hopefully no one we knew would see us together. Nestled between towering buildings, the noodle stand consisted of a single table made of unfinished three-quarter-inch plywood covered with a food-stained tablecloth. Knee-high stools with duct-taped seat covers surrounded the table on three sides. A dim, yellow paper lantern hung above the table from a short bamboo pole tied with twine.

A woman in her seventies with silvery hair worked the food stand wearing a rust-colored sweater and a dirt-brown knitted cap. A blue tarp, the kind you'd find in a typical hardware store, was securely tied above the table at a forty-five-degree slant to serve as a shelter from rain. The old woman hunched over a gas burner with a pot of hot water boiling right next to her, oblivious to the denseness of the city buildings that surrounded her like steep canyon walls.

We sat on different sides at the same corner of the table. Reiko ordered hot noodles in a bowl, called *toshikoshi* soba. I had the same.

Reiko often swiveled her head toward the narrow alleyway that led to Club Blue Diamond, cocked and ready to bolt if anyone she recognized came down the path.

The old woman set two steaming bowls of soba noodles in front of us within a couple of minutes.

"I want to thank you, Reiko, for meeting with me."

Reiko glanced into the bowl of soba, then at me. "Mama-Kiyomi warned me to stay away from you."

"What she's got to hide?" I asked, not interested in eating my meal. "I'm just trying to find out why my mother was killed. The police aren't doing anything about it. They already made up their mind this was a random robbery, and said to my face that the odds of finding the person who did this are slim to none."

Reiko's head spun as if on a spindle. I didn't think she'd heard a word I said. Her attention kept shifting, attuned to even the slightest movements in her sphere of awareness.

The old woman accidentally tipped over a wooden cutting board with a loud bang.

Reiko jumped from the stool. I held her arm and stopped her from running. I reassured her. "It's okay."

Her nerves were as tight as bowstrings. If I had plucked her bicep, it might have vibrated out a musical note. I needed her to calm down, or else she wouldn't open up.

In the club, Reiko was a little chatterbox. It didn't take much to get her talking once she started. She needed familiarity. I had to start the fire under her, and asked, "Do you think mama-san will force me to get *dohans*?"

A dohan was like an insurance policy for a hostess. It ensured that she had a customer to service for the evening by arranging a dinner date, later bringing him to the club to spend more of his money.

I might finally have Reiko's full attention, because she stopped looking around as if a SWAT team was about to rappel down from the surrounding buildings.

Reiko slurped her soba, poured green tea into a cup, and took a sip. With her elbows on the tabletop, she folded her fingers together. "In one week, average, I bring minimum six men to club. This make mama very happy. She push us to get many dohans, so there is . . ." Her eyes rolled up as though searching her mind for the right word. "Pressure. There is many pressure."

"You can speak Japanese if you feel more comfortable." I wondered if my mother also forced the girls to do things against their will.

Reiko's jittery eyes relaxed. She said in Japanese, "Your mother never did that—force us to get dohans." I felt relieved in hearing it. She continued, "I hate it because almost all of my dohans are married men. I attract only *oyajimachi*. Dirty old men."

I pushed on. "You said my mother saved you. That she got you off drugs and gave you a job."

"Hai, your mother was a good person. I think many of the hostesses will leave with Kiyomi running the bar."

The corner of her mouth twitched. Reiko had stopped talking and stared at me as if I had two noses.

"What?" I felt self-conscious with her looking at me.

"The club is thick with jealousy." Reiko's demeanor was now calmer. "Every night is the same. Who's making the most money? And if it's someone else, spikes of jealousy will come from every direction, and they will spread nasty rumors about you. That you have a child. That you have a boyfriend, a husband. You got hepatitis B. You're a lesbian. You name it and they'll make it up.

When you're making money and they're not, watch out. And what you did to Mei in shimei, her revenge will come. You just don't know when and where."

I told her about the roaches.

Reiko snickered nasally. "That's nothing. It was her message to you that she's the top hostess here."

To keep her talking, I decided to play along. "What can I do about it?"

Reiko pointed a finger at me, but not in a condescending way. "If you complain to mama-Kiyomi, she won't do anything. She encourages competition, and will pit one girl against another because it means more money for her."

I shook my head, disgusted. Another lesson learned in the water trade.

The old woman glanced up at us while her hand continued to cut carrots and onions into thin strips. I was convinced that this woman could de-bone a whole chicken blindfolded.

Reiko exhaled as if she'd just run a hundred-yard sprint, her voice filled with sadness. "I hate all my customers. Sometimes they touch me. The conversations are such that I feel like I'm like a kindergarten teacher. But they give me money and gifts, so I try very hard to ignore the negatives."

Reiko sniffled.

I sensed that she was high on more than booze.

"We have many different kinds of customers—" Reiko stopped and slurped her soba noodles. She looked up at me. "There is this one guy that comes every day."

"Is he the one with the dark glasses and elevator shoes?"

"You noticed him." Reiko chuckled. "He wants to look like Jason Momoa. The problem is he's two feet too short, twenty pounds too heavy, and bald."

We laughed at the little guy.

Reiko continued snickering. "And he has no money. But

mama allows him to run a tab because he pays it right on his payday."

"Mama really has to trust the guy's not running away, huh?"

"Hai," Reiko replied. "Mama has to be a pretty good judge of character to allow him to do that, but most regular customers know that the bar is connected."

"You mean with the police?"

Reiko shook her head. "Yakuza."

Her comment slammed my head like a wooden mallet. "Does the bar pay protection money?"

"I don't know, but I would say yes." Reiko hesitated then added, "Your mother was very close to a yakuza boss, so the regular customers who run up tabs know that they have to pay."

I now wondered if my mother leaving us had anything to do with the yakuza.

"Although being a hostess is tough work"—Reiko shivered, and not from the chilly air— "the yakuza scares me."

Reiko's nervousness returned. She glanced around quickly, then reached into her handbag and palmed a photograph across the stained tabletop.

I recognized it from the wall of photographs. The picture was of a white middle-aged male posing with my mother.

"This was one of your mother's best customers. He liked her and spent a lot of nights at the bar. It may mean nothing at all, but he died a few weeks before your mother's death."

I took the photograph. The man had a military crewcut and thick body. His right arm was around my mother's shoulders, caught in frozen laughter by the snap of a shutter.

I handed the photograph back, now hurting for my dad, starting to understand why he hadn't been able to attend her funeral. The urge came to call Dad and tell him that I loved him.

Reiko added, "On his last night at the bar, your mother got a phone call. Her face turned white, but she said nothing. She handed the customer the phone. The man stormed out of the bar. The next day, the news headlines stated that the man's wife had killed him with a knife while he slept, then taken her own life through the samurai ritual of *seppuku*."

Reiko paused as a gust of wind spiraled a sheet of newspaper into the air.

The old woman was cleaning cooking utensils in a plastic container filled with soapy water. I wondered, if she'd had the opportunity to become a hostess when in her twenties, would she have done it? With thousands of bars in Japan, beginning after World War II, young girls had to make money any way possible. Maybe she had been a hostess once upon a time. In the way she could de-bone a whole chicken blindfolded, maybe back then she could de-bone a man blindfolded.

Cut-Duck.

Reiko leaned closer and whispered, "Hideo Tamura. He's the yakuza boss, the oyabun. He would visit the bar every so often."

"Was he the old man at the funeral?"

She nodded. "He's one of the most powerful men in Japan."

Reiko's jitteriness had now turned to outright fear. "Whenever Tamura-san came into the bar, every girl was terrified because he was the *only* customer that mama-Kiyomi would demand that the girls have sex with."

"What about the no touching policy?"

Reiko laughed at my naiveté. "That applies only to regular customers. He's not into the usual kind of sex, but rough sex. Whenever he showed up, every girl would be scared that she would be the unlucky one."

My stomach twisted into a knot.

"The older hostesses aren't afraid because the yakuza boss is only into new and young girls and—"

Reiko stopped when I turned away, blankly staring into the night. Who was this person Reiko was describing? Mom as a solicitor of sex, basically a pimp, was not the woman I knew all my life. Had I really known who she truly was?

Something, someone, had to have driven her to do the unspeakable.

"Sorry, I didn't mean to . . ." Reiko touched my hand resting on the tabletop.

If I couldn't keep myself detached, and avoid connecting Reiko's words to my mother, I wouldn't get to the truth.

I steadied myself and said, "Go on. I need to know."

"There was a new girl. She was beautiful, a very beautiful Thai girl. She worked at the club for just a week. I think her name was Arm. Or Aom, or something like that. She wouldn't admit it, but I think she was making money somewhere else. My guess, she was a prostitute. But unlucky for her, Tamura-san was captivated with her striking beauty. I think she was older than she looked, but who knows. Even if she knew about Tamura's obsession, she still wouldn't refuse. The look in this girl's eyes said it all—she could smell money. Anyway, she disappeared."

"Killed?"

"To this day, no one knows what happened to her."

To me, the scenario where the yakuza killed my mother didn't make any sense, because why would such a powerful crime figure want to kill a small-time bar owner?

The deep, drawn-out silence signaled that our discussion had come to an end.

To break the silence, I asked, "Will you continue as a hostess much longer?"

Reiko cheered up a little. "One day, if I have the courage to tell my parents. They think I'm working at an English pub at night. Right now, I need money. I also need to improve my English so that I can speak more fluently. I want to go to America and live. Maybe even Hawaii."

"You speak English pretty good already." I sensed that Reiko was hinting that she would like to hook up when I returned home, but I didn't leave an open invitation.

"Hostessing is like a Christmas cake." Reiko's tone of voice turned defiant, perhaps subtly telling me that she could live in America without anyone's help.

Much like how Christmas cakes were no good after December 25, women over the age of twenty-five were often seen as used goods in the business, with men no longer interested in them.

"Men spend money on me because of my youth." Reiko's eyes were downturned. "I am not beautiful and will be less desirable as I age. You, me, the other girls go through hell with advances from drunks, but that's the nature of the business. As long as there are young girls, the water business will continue."

I now understood why my mother had helped Reiko. She was a survivor. There have been, and will always be, downfalls. It happens to everyone. But survivors keep moving forward.

My mother admired survivors because she too was one. I always wondered if I had that same survival gene as her.

Reiko's voice softened. "With your mother gone, I hate working there more and more. Kiyomi's a bitch. She runs the place as if she's Genghis Khan. I am thinking of quitting because I want to spend my time with people I like."

"Thank you for meeting with me, Reiko."

"I must purposely ignore you at work. I don't want to, but that is something I must do."

I nodded in agreement, paid the old woman for the noodles, and left a generous tip because I didn't want her to think I hated her food by leaving the soba untouched.

We stood an arm's length apart and stared at each other for a few seconds. Reiko then spun around and hurried down the dark alley.

Maybe before I left Japan, I would give Reiko my phone number.

———————

12

My mom had paid for Internet service for the month, so I searched online for the murder-suicide that Reiko had mentioned. It seemed like a stretch, a coincidence that this could be tied to my mother's murder, but that was all I had to work with.

The two-inch newspaper article on my screen stated that William Novak, the man murdered, was a second lieutenant stationed at Yokota Air Base near the city of Fussa. Based on the position of the man's body in bed, he had been stabbed repeatedly in the neck, stomach, and chest while he slept. His blood had soaked through the mattress onto the tiled floor beneath and flowed to a low spot in the corner of the room.

The wife was the obvious suspect. With her flannel nightgown covered in blood, she'd tracked it from the bedroom to the living room. She knelt down in front of the home shrine and stabbed herself in the abdomen with the same knife that killed her husband. Her name was Misaki Novak. Married for ten years, the couple had lived together in the apartment for five. The article noted that the incident was under investigation. However, everything pointed to a domestic crime.

I kept searching for other newspaper clippings online. Clicking the mouse, I froze at what I discovered next. Another newspaper had headshots of the man and woman. I recognized her. It was the woman with the child from the photo in my mother's safe. The man in the picture with my mother from the wall of photographs was William Novak, the murdered victim.

I needed to look further into Mom's customers. Located in the western portion of Tokyo, Yokota Air Base housed fourteen thousand military personnel. I wasn't quite looking for a needle in a haystack, because I had a name, but the nine calls I made all resulted in dead-ends. I received the major military run-around for about an hour until the tenth call. A sergeant told me that Lieutenant William Novak had died.

Having finally found someone who knew him, I asked, "Is there anybody I can talk to who can vouch for Lieutenant Novak?"

"What for?"

"I'm with Global Insurance. Lieutenant Novak has moved from one base to another, so we were not sure of his latest address. We just need confirmation that he served at Yokota Air Base, so if I could speak with his commanding officer, I would appreciate the help."

Tap, tap, tap on the computer keyboard, followed by more shuffling. The guy came back. "Ma'am, there's a Lieutenant Baxter down at Maintenance. I gave him a call, but he's not in."

"Could you please relay a message for me?"

"Just a second." I heard the sound of someone looking for a piece of paper and pen on a cluttered desk. "Okay, go ahead."

"Please have him call Gena Hunter." I gave my phone number, thanked him, and hung up.

An hour later, my cell chirped.

"Hello, is this Gena Hunter of Global Insurance?" It was a voice with authority, low and confident.

"Yes," I replied, holding my breath, hopeful. "Is this Lieutenant Baxter?"

"Yours truly."

I couldn't continue with the charade. "I'll be frank with you, sir. I'm not with Global Insurance, or any insurance company for that matter. I'm sorry, but I had to say what I said to get someone to talk to me."

Suspicious silence fell on the other end.

I spoke quickly. "Please don't hang up on me. I needed to get in touch with someone, anyone, who knew Second Lieutenant William Novak. My name really is Gena Hunter. Have you heard about the murder of a woman a few days ago, a bar owner?"

More silence.

I couldn't have faked the sadness in my voice. "Well, that woman was my mother."

"And you think that Novak killed her?"

"No, no, no." I had to start from the beginning. "I went to the police and they told me it was a random robbery that went bad. They have no suspects. But I heard from someone who worked in the bar that night that when Lieutenant Novak received a phone call, his entire demeanor changed. He went from having a good time to being angry. After the call, he stormed out of the bar in wild rage."

"You're wondering if there is some kind of connection between Bill's behavior and your mother's death."

"It might sound farfetched, but—" My voice cracked. "The police won't do anything to find my mother's killer, and somehow I sense a connection of some kind, but at the moment I don't know what it is. I need your help, Lieutenant Baxter. To find out more about Novak and maybe—"

"Do you know how Bill, ah, Lieutenant Novak died?"

"Only that it was a murder-suicide," I answered. "According to the news, his wife killed him, then herself."

I decided not to mention the photograph I'd found in the safe.

"Yeah, in summary, that's about it." Baxter sighed. "So, I don't see what that has to do with your mother being robbed and —I'm sorry—killed in the process."

Process. He made it sound like a formula for murder. "Like I said, it sounds implausible and highly unlikely, but I have nothing to go on right now and I can't go home until I find out the truth."

Baxter blew out another sigh. "Listen, Ms. Hunter. I'm really sorry about what happened to your mother, but I don't think the two cases are related. You should go home to wherever it is and let the police—"

"Can we meet?" I stopped him from continuing. "I'd like to ask you a few questions. That's all. It won't take long. I can come to Fussa. Please, Lieutenant Baxter. I hope that you understand. Just a few minutes."

He let out a softer sigh, a busy man with a busy schedule. "Okay, just a few minutes. You said you'll come here to Fussa?"

"Yes."

"There's a Starbucks near the train station. You can't miss it. I'll meet you there at fourteen thirty tomorrow."

I glanced at the clock on my phone. Already eleven twenty. "Can we meet today?"

Silence, before he said, "I'll meet you there at three. And don't be late because I have a meeting an hour after that."

"Thank you, Lieutenant." I ended the call.

I read online that Yokota served as the headquarters for United States Forces Japan, and was currently being used for airlift missions throughout East Asia. The eastern portion of the city's economy focused on the military base. To make the troops and families feel at home, there were American-style bars, shops, and restaurants within walking distance from the main gate.

I speed-walked to the train station and caught the Yamanote

Line from Shibuya to Shinjuku, and from there took another forty-six-minute train ride to Fussa.

The busy commercial area surrounding Fussa Station had several department stores, restaurants, and fast-food joints. The most prominent building was the large six-story Seiyu Department Store. A sky bridge connected the two buildings like a vital artery, the train station was the heart pumping life into the adjoining stores with its constant flow of people.

Starbucks was easy to find. The ceiling was high with round, recessed lighting. The service counter was built exactly like those at home in Hawaii, and probably everywhere else in the world. Floor-to-ceiling glass windows on the right stretched the length of the coffee shop. A barista shouted orders, and there were a few people scattered throughout.

I glanced at my watch. I was ten minutes early, so I bought a latte and took a seat at a round table with two chairs facing each other.

I sat next to the glass, overlooking the street and taxicabs lining up below. After two sips of my latte, an African American man entered wearing blue jeans and a tan long-sleeved shirt. In his forties, he had flecks of white in his close-cropped hair. He stood over six feet tall, muscular with broad shoulders. His deep-set eyes scanned the room from left to right, and stopped when I waved. He nodded and stepped toward me with long stork-like strides.

I stood when he reached the table. "Lieutenant Baxter, thank you for meeting with me." I extended my hand for him to shake.

"Sure." His grip was firm, and he held my hand longer than a usual greeting. Baxter glanced at the service counter. "I'll grab a cup of coffee and will be right back." He grinned; his mouth full of white teeth.

I forced a smile, but didn't like the way he kept looking at me. Maybe I was just imagining it—perhaps working as a hostess had made me suspicious toward men I didn't know and their hidden intentions.

Imagined or not, I'd purposely dressed in what I thought were the most unappealing clothes in my suitcase: a baggy short-sleeved tunic, plain cotton sweater, and a dark-brown, high-waisted wide-leg pant.

Five minutes later, he sat across from me holding a steaming cup of black coffee.

I thanked him again for meeting with me. I folded my arms across my chest and got to the point. "Did you know my mother?"

Baxter stared down into his steaming coffee, then up at me. "I met your mother, but I didn't know her well. Novak was the bar guy. My wife went back to the States because her mother was ill, so I hated staying home and watching the paint dry. When Bill asked if I wanted to tag along with him, I thought, why not."

He grinned as if we were on a date. I hated it, but I had to endure. Perhaps the reaction of disgust and mistrust had somehow crept into my psyche as an automatic defense mechanism from hostessing.

"Yokota Air Base is home to C-130 Hercules," Baxter boasted with pride. "We work to keep those planes flying. And—"

"Like I said," I interrupted him. "I can't go home until I find out the truth."

He frowned and forced a smile. "And where's home?"

"I'm from Hawaii."

His eyes sprung open. "No kidding, Hawaii. I was stationed at Hickam when I first enlisted."

"My dad works at Pearl Harbor."

His lecherous behavior seemed to have retreated back into his body. Now a postured gentleman, he smiled at reminiscing. "They still got that small shop in Kapahulu where they sell the best *laulau*?"

He was referring to Keoki's, but I wasn't here to talk about food. "Yep, it's still there. I don't want to be rude, but . . ."

"I got it—get down to business." He frowned, hesitating. Maybe it was against his manly code of conduct to share information exchanged between drinking buddies.

After a few seconds of silence, he let out an unconscious sigh, the kind of sound one made when trapped in traffic. Baxter glanced out the window and said, as if not of his own volition, "Novak liked to gamble. There were rumors that Bill was deep in debt and owed a lot of money, but like I said—just rumors."

If Novak was in debt to the yakuza, he would be in deep, deep trouble.

"Bill was a pretty good guy." He paused and took a sip of coffee. "Whenever he wasn't drinking that is. He just couldn't handle booze well and would turn violent. But he kept going to the bars. Since I know how much he makes in wages, frankly, I don't know where he got the money from."

"Maybe gambling winnings."

He rubbed the bristle on his chin. "Maybe . . . but I never saw the cash because he seemed to get comp a lot."

"Comp?"

"You know, free booze and food."

No one gets comp, except maybe politicians, a way to brown-nose and get something back in return.

"The time we went out together was going to be my last." Baxter didn't wait for me to ask why. "Because he would easily lose his temper and wanted to fight with everyone. I'd go out expecting a good time and we'd end up fighting. And this was with each other."

"Where does he live?"

"I went to his apartment once. It's in Tachikawa City." Baxter pulled out his phone and scrolled Google Maps. With shifting and expanding fingers, he then passed the phone to me. "Here it is."

I took a snapshot of the screen with my phone and handed his back.

"One more thing—and this might be the reason for the murder." He squinted and hesitated, his face hardened. "There were rumors that he would beat his wife. But it was never confirmed because nothing was reported. The military likes to keep this kind of stuff quiet."

I didn't realize that I was smiling until Baxter gave me that lecherous grin again. Perhaps I was outwardly projecting feeling good about myself for what I had accomplished in trying to gather information.

To get him to stop gawking at me, I asked, "Did you know his wife?"

"Well, I met her once, but wouldn't recognize her again even if I sat next to her on the train. You might want to talk to people at the bar."

"I actually got a job there now—" I stopped mid-sentence, sensing I'd said more than necessary.

"So you work as a hostess?" Baxter glanced at my chest as though it were an ingrained habit before settling his gaze on my face.

My cheeks warmed. The quick lesson I learned as a hostess was to keep smiling, even when I wanted to smash the customer's face in. I smiled at Baxter, mechanically thanked him, and made a rush for the train station.

The train ride from Ushihama Station to Tachikawa Station took twenty minutes on the southeast Ome Line.

Baxter called them *gaijin*, or foreigner-friendly, apartments. The map led to a three-story walkup with sparse parking stalls below.

A *Beware of Dog* sign was posted on the building's ground floor, next to a sign that read, *Manager, Natsuo Abe*. I knocked, expecting a bark from the other side of the door, but nothing came.

A middle-aged Japanese man answered with a sad frown. He stared as though not registering that he had a visitor standing in front of him. His forehead and eyebrows contracted upward; the corners of his mouth pulled down.

I spoke in Japanese. "I am a friend of the Novaks."

The building manager remained emotionless and said nothing.

"I'm here to pay my respects, and—"

"The apartment will be vacant for a while." Abe's jaw clenched, wavering between anger and hurt. He swatted the air. "People do not want to live in an apartment with two deaths, fearing *obake*."

My brother's voice rang in my head: *Sugi-sugi-obake*.

With my brother having been four years old, I didn't take his warning of sugi-sugi-obake seriously. Sugi was his best friend in our old neighborhood in Kalihi, a couple blocks away from Honolulu's Chinatown.

The problem was that Sugi wasn't real. He was David's imaginary friend. Sugi was supposed to be a Japanese boy who arrived with the first immigrants from Japan to work in the sugar cane fields. At the age of ten, Sugi died from the black plague of Honolulu.

At the time, there was an epidemic in Asia. A ship had sailed into Honolulu harbor with a dead crewmember on board who was diagnosed with the plague. Though the ship was quarantined, the rats carried the disease across the mooring lines, over the water to the docks, and into Chinatown.

Sugi-sugi-obake was my brother's warning that the area had ghosts and not to go there because bad things would happen. I didn't believe in such nonsense. I wished I could turn back time, but instead I had to live in this haunting loop, wishing I'd done things differently.

I refocused and motioned to get Abe's full attention. "They were associates of mine. Can I see the apartment?"

"I am still making repairs." He gave me a bitter scowl. "Their deposit doesn't cover the cost of materials and labor. There was much blood."

The manager led me up two flights of stairs. His keychain caught my attention when he opened the door. On it was a picture of a cute toy poodle. Abe followed my gaze. With downturned eyes, he covered the dog's photograph with his palm.

The one-bedroom apartment was empty except for a mini shrine on a knee-high table, with burnt incense and melted candles.

I pointed to the shrine. "Is this theirs?"

"Hai. Even though their ashes are not here, I will still honor the thirty-five days Buddhist ritual before burial."

I strolled closer. A photograph of a handsome boy, about twelve years old, stood in a golden picture frame.

"Who's that?" I pointed to the boy.

Abe faced the empty room, seemingly in a world of his own.

"Sir." I flagged to get his attention again. He slowly faced me, his eyes blank and empty. I asked, "Who's the boy?"

His voice came out distant and unsure. "I think it was the woman's son."

"Was?"

"I think he died." Abe's jaw trembled as he gripped the photograph on the keychain.

When we were done, he led me back to the ground level. I turned to thank him, but he was already heading to his apartment.

On the ride back to Shibuya by train, the view revealed the majestic Mount Fuji in the distance, with its snow-capped peak. Orange-colored clouds caused by the reflection of the setting sun surrounded the iconic mountain. I gasped at the postcard image and realized why the Japanese considered this mountain a god. The view did take my breath away.

My mind drifted. I thought of Abe's dog, because we had a dog once when I was a child. Our cocker spaniel was a *dog* and not a companion. But the man's grief for his friend felt palpable.

I thought of my mother's business. It sold more than drinks and food—it sold illusions. A hostess's short skirt and skimpy top might fuel a customer's desires, but that was her job. To the customer, it was a world free of rejection and filled with possibilities, but mostly it was one that provided companionship.

I was certain that, after these short entanglements, neither hostess nor customer would grieve like Natsuo Abe grieved the loss of his companion.

13

Once on stage, she always captured the oneness of the tempo, sending her rainbow-colored kimono fluttering as though it had a life of its own. The audience, leaning forward, was captivated by her moves—her spinning quickly with an arched back, seductively shielding her face with a folding fan, tilting her head just enough to gaze deeply into the darkness of the theater, tantalizing each and every person in their seat.

Heavily made up, her face painted bleach-white with pouty, blood-red lips, the dancer spun and twirled to the heart-thumping rhythm of *taikos,* bamboo flutes, and the amplified sounds of falling rain. Colorful lights and flashing lasers modernized the show and raised the energy level in the theater with its packed house of two hundred in the audience.

She expertly captured the old-fashioned Japanese femininity, her movements exuding gracefulness with a strong-willed undercurrent below the surface, mesmerizing the audience with the beauty and sex appeal of her performance.

As she exited the stage, a young man ran up, trembling at being only two feet away from her, his voice high-pitched with excitement. "You are so beautiful, I cried at the end." She gave him an autographed picture and kissed the bottom, which left a dark-red imprint of her lips. The young man clutched the photograph to his chest and bowed respectfully, unable to hide his jubilation.

In the solitude of her dressing room, with its bright lights and large assortment of kimonos and costumes on wooden racks, she glanced at the delicate blue porcelain jars of powders and paints and the array of fine brushes atop a makeup vanity table with lighted mirrors.

The Kami hated whenever the performance came to an end because she would have to return to a life of plainness. She shimmied in front of the full-length mirror and performed her usual final pose to the left, then to the right. Tonight, she'd played a young girl, so her gestures were less confident. Last week she'd played an older noblewoman during the Kamakura period, which made her gestures more deliberate. She favored the performance of the young girl because of her ability to flirt with men and the means of control that afforded her.

Finally, with the elaborate waxed wig of human hair and ornaments lifted from her head, she stared at the image in the mirror, and frowned. "Now, I am *he*."

Sebastian, the man, tall and handsome and masculine, stood erect with distinctly soft, feminine facial features.

Since debuting at the age of four, he'd dedicated his life to the kabuki stage. Having a high voice and slender body, as a teenager it had been logical for him to become an *onna-gata,* a man who played female roles.

Onna-gata had been a part of Japanese mainstream entertainment and culture for centuries, tracing its roots to the seventeenth century traditional kabuki theatre.

He recalled an interview on a network television talk show, explaining the secret to playing female roles.

"It's all in the movement." Sebastian was ecstatic at his building fame. "My shoulders were getting broad and high, so I made up for it by using my body and moving my shoulders more."

At the time, fifteen-year-old Sebastian had been praised by the media for his feminine elegance and understated seductiveness. Now, at the age of twenty-two, the only surgical procedure he'd had was to his Adam's apple. His androgynous facial features were so subtle that when he grew older, he didn't need plastic surgery.

Disappointed that the evening had come to an end, he relived images of his last kill to excite him. The drunkard in the alleyway had gotten his comeuppance. Such thoughts about the eradication of scums from the earth always brought fulfillment and joy.

According to the *Hi No Maki,* or *Fire Book,* if you practice day and night polishing your skills of bushido, you will be able to attain freedom and the ultimate power to perform miracles, thus gaining supernatural powers. The ancients of bushido mastered the art and skills of killing, reaching unprecedented supernatural levels. This was the secret of *Heiho,* a swordsman's concept of strategy and tactics in combat.

The theater had developed Sebastian's necessary skills of appearing non-threatening, projecting innocence and seduction, and becoming the perfect hunter at night.

The whore did not deserve a proper burial. The Kami's hands had dug deep into the soft dirt, reliving squeezing the softness of her neck. Bar whores, all of them. Customers were just as bad or even worse. Just like with drugs, if there weren't customers to buy, the dealer would be out of business. It was the stupidity of the men who patronized the bars that kept *all* of them up and running.

Disguised as a gardener for the cemetery, Sebastian immediately recognized the girl, Gena, from the photograph he'd found in the woman's purse. She was older than her picture, maybe now in her early twenties.

After the funeral service, he'd followed the girl and her friend to the woman's apartment in Shibuya. His plan came crashing down when they rode a bus to the airport the next day. Was she leaving Japan? Days of preparation now down the drain, he had to develop a new plan. But things weren't as they appeared, and the girl returned to the apartment alone. He couldn't have planned it better when she started working at the bar as a conniving, money-hungry hostess. At first, he couldn't understand her reason for doing it, but then found out that she was trying to find her mother's killer.

Interesting.

He didn't know whether to laugh at her stupidity or admire her courage.

With her dying breath, the whore had said she didn't know of any video. Liar! His rage at being lied to made him lose control, and he'd killed her before knowing if she was telling the truth. Whether she was stupid or courageous, he needed the girl as part of his plan.

Staking out her apartment, this time disguised as a college student wearing a T-shirt, faded jeans, and headphones, he followed her to Yokota Air Base. There she met a Black man in Starbucks, then rode a train to the apartment in Tachikawa.

Maybe he underestimated her. Had that twerp Abe talked?

He didn't think so, because acid would work just as well on human skin as it did on dog fur. That awful smell had clung to the follicles of his hair throughout the day even after multiple scrubbings.

He'd smiled wryly at the landlord and said with terrifying calmness, "Say nothing . . . or you're next."

To Gena's credit, the Kami hadn't thought she'd get this far.

She had persistence and determination, key traits he admired and which were honored by his ancestors and the code of Bushido.

Could the woman have placed the video in a bank safety deposit box in Japan or Hawaii? If that were the case, he would need the beneficiary to have access to her bank accounts. He'd gotten the address in Hawaii from a letter. His planned trip had disappointing results with the father, but he didn't dwell on it. Did Gena have the video? He didn't think so, but she would be the one to help him get it.

He picked up the hoop earring he'd found that night he killed the whore. His stomach twisted into knots at the thought that someone might have witnessed the killing. He hated the flaws in his plan. He hated loose ends.

Glancing in the mirror, he placed the wig back on, chuckled at looking like a half-dressed clown, and air-kissed the reflection looking back at him.

His pulse accelerated—she was tracking him.

Once again, he recalled the last kill.

Dry-mouthed and with lightness in his chest, he knew that strong desires could easily be manipulate and control. He thirsted for the tingle of the game, the tingle before a kill.

Sebastian knew of the rumor spreading around Kabukicho, that the bar owner's killing was yakuza. He had an idea.

14

W hen I arrived at 8 p.m. at Club Blue Diamond, I found an envelope taped to the front of my locker with "Gena" written on it.

Instead of tearing it open, I glanced around and wondered who could have put it there. It had to be someone who worked here, or else somebody might have asked or paid any one of the girls to do it.

Two girls were already at work, each with a customer. None of them looked in my direction when I entered the bar, but that didn't prove anything.

My next thought was that this might be Mei's revenge. Taking precautions, I scanned the envelope for any sign of white powder, a bit embarrassed at being so paranoid. Seeing no anthrax, I pulled the envelope from the locker and slowly fingered the adhesive that sealed it close.

Inside was a four-by-four note: *I HAVE INFORMATION.*

Below was written the location and a sketch of the meeting place: *Shin Okubo Korean Town at 11 p.m.* Two words stood out: *COME ALONE!!!*

Then it struck me. If it wasn't someone here who'd left the

note, then whoever wrote it knew who I was and my objective. A penetrating chill ran through me when I thought of the yakuza having anything to do with this.

My gaze went to the bottom of the note. It was signed, *A FRIEND.*

Friend?

Questions kept popping into my head: Should I meet whoever left the note and find out what was going on or should I call the police? My first thought was asking Reiko to tag along, but I wouldn't want to put her in harm's way if something did go wrong. Plus, Reiko was the only one in the bar who knew why I was here. Maybe I'd trusted someone I shouldn't have, but Reiko was the only person who'd offered help.

I had three hours to make a decision. Though my mind jittered with uncertainty, I tried to focus on my customers. A part of me wanted to meet the letter writer and discover more, but another part wanted to ignore the note and continue with what I had discovered thus far.

More to kill time than to make money, I sat at the bar watching a baseball game on TV. A customer about my age tapped my shoulder. With slurred speech, he said in Japanese, "I knew your mother. We used to talk."

An adrenaline rush hit my brain. I grabbed his hand and led him to a booth farther away from the loud noise of the bamboo bar.

I leaned in closer than usual. "Tell me what you know."

He chuckled; spittle flew from his lips. "What do you Americans say? You scratch my back and I scratch yours."

I had a bad feeling about this, but I needed to know what he knew.

The dude undid the top two buttons of his shirt. "Pinch my nipple and I will tell you all you want to know about your mother."

"Fuck dat." I stood to leave.

He touched my arm. "Your mother told me stories about your family vacations in Hanalei."

The dude was a funny little guy, really white-skinned, and his chest was totally flat, with no shape to it. His little nipples hung from his scrawny body. He welcomed my fingers as he rubbed his crotch outside his pants.

I sat back down. "If you're lying to me, I'm going to smack you."

He grinned, handed me twelve thousand yen, and said, "Plus I'll give you this."

"Ah shit . . . what the hell." I reluctantly slid my hand inside his shirt and pinched his nipple. As soon as I did, his eyes rolled up, and he came in his pants. I yanked my hand from his shirt as though I'd been bitten by a centipede. It took him a minute to regain consciousness.

My voice rose in disgust. "Now talk."

He scanned left then right, squinted, and whispered. I couldn't hear him, so I leaned closer. The moment I did, the little sneak kissed me on the lips.

I hammered his face with an open palm strike. His head snapped back, blood gushing from his nose. Within a minute, Kiyomi handed him a wet towel. The guy placed it on his nose. Kiyomi glared at me then walked away.

I had enough of his bullshit. "You fucker. Tell me now."

He recoiled and shook his head. "I never knew your mother. Mei told me what to say."

Mei was sitting with a customer, clutching her stomach in laughter.

I rushed to the restroom and washed the blood from my hands and arms. My dress was ruined from the blood splatter. When I got back, the guy was gone.

My stomach twisted with anger at being set up. I should have known better. Word of my desperation must have circulated within the bar. I wanted to kick myself in the butt for being so naïve. My mother could have spoken to her co-workers about our vacations before she died.

For the rest of the evening, I sat at the bar and nursed a beer. At 10 p.m., I headed for my locker. I changed into street clothes— blue jeans, a comfortable halter-top, and a gray sweatshirt. As I reached for my street shoes, a live scorpion crawled out from the right one. I pulled back but stifled a scream. Mei and the others outside were probably waiting to hear it. I squashed the scorpion with my left shoe.

How was she getting into my locker? I walked behind it and saw the issue. No other locker had four screws holding the back plate to the frame.

Kiyomi stood in front of me when I existed the locker area. "Where you going?"

"I have something I need to do."

"If you leave, you not have a job."

I brushed pass her and spat out, "Whatevas."

Mei and Kimi whispered to each other and frowned with disappointment as I calmly walked past them.

I had visited Shin Okubo Korean Town once before. The twelve-minute walk would take less time than catching a train.

Once an affordable neighborhood, the area became popular with Korean students and laborers in the '80s, and slowly evolved into a replica of South Korea. I wandered the main street, a gauntlet of four- to five-story buildings, some even taller. Illumi- nated neon advertised karaoke entertainment and stores selling K- Pop CDs and DVDs by the latest Korean boy bands. Cosmetic shops selling K-Beauty products seemed to be on every corner, because Shin Okubo was the latest hotspot for teenage girls who had taken to the Korean pop culture craze.

I needed a weapon. I found a small shop selling kitchen utensils on a road connected to the main street. A thin Japanese lady in her fifties approached me when I entered the shop. To the side was a glass case displaying prime cutlery as though it were precious jewelry.

I smiled at her and said in Japanese, "I'm having guests over for dinner and looking for a good chef's knife."

She motioned to the glass case. "Japan has the finest knives in the world because the ancient technique of samurai sword-making has been applied in the making of kitchen knives."

"How's about that one?" I pointed to an eight-inch knife.

"Ah, good choice." The lady retrieved the knife from the display and handed it to me. "There are actually thirty-two layers of steel in this single blade. The steel's surface is slightly textured so as to slice through literally anything, and it's also completely rust-resistant. Plus, it's dishwasher safe for easy cleanup."

How bizarre the woman sounded when I thought about the real reason, I was purchasing the knife.

"Okay, I'll take it."

The woman gave me a 10 percent discount on a black leather case for it.

As I exited her shop, the woman cried out, "One other thing, your knife comes with a lifetime replacement and sharpening warranty."

"Arigato." I smiled at her, but mumbled to myself, "I don't think I'll be using it."

I followed the sketch on the note and walked east from the main street. The surrounding buildings drowned out the noise from the street, teeming with life just two blocks away. They would have the same effect on a scream, and no one would hear me.

I cautiously walked down a narrow street with cars parked along one side of the sidewalk. Electrical wires crisscrossed and hung from power poles and buildings. The street was deserted at this time of night; a black cat scurried across the alleyway.

The sketch led to the entrance of an abandoned two-story building. There were two flags crossing each other engraved on the side of the structure. One flag was the national flag of South Korea and the other was that of Japan. The map's arrow directed me to go under the crossed flags and around the right side of the building.

A large "No Trespassing" sign hung to the side of the entrance.

I removed the knife from its leather case, and I slipped into my back pocket. I stopped at the corner of the building. My surroundings were pitch-black because of the arched canopy overhead.

This is crazy. What am I doing here?

I took a deep breath and flicked on my cell phone light, which dimly illuminated a cracked and chipped and water-puddled narrow walkway. I pointed the light upward. Spider webs covered the building's joists and corners.

The arrow on the map pointed to a side door on the left, about fifty feet in.

I gave the metal door a slight shove. The door squeaked on its hinges and opened into more darkness. My phone's flashlight couldn't cover much distance, but I could see that many of the windows were cracked and coated with dirt and grime.

Being scared shitless should have made me turn back, but I would never know what was waiting for me unless I continued onward. I clutched the handle of the knife tighter and took a step inside; stale air smacked me in the face.

The building's walls and foundation appeared as if they had been slammed by an earthquake, then condemned. Although many of the building codes in Japan now required houses to be earthquake resistant, the older buildings were still susceptible to the shifting earth. The islands of Japan were located along the Pacific Ring of Fire, the most active earthquake belt in the world.

I cried out, "Hello."

The air smelled thick, dusty, and stale. Broken glass was scattered throughout a floor of bare concrete. The tiny cone of cell phone light showed footprints in the thick dust. I followed the prints deeper into the building. My echoing footsteps mixed with the sound of dripping water. I stepped between pieces of glass, at the same time avoiding the footprints. The tracks led to a flight of stairs and continued up. I slowly scaled the stairs, twisting the light upward, and back, in case someone came up from behind.

I stopped at the top of the stairs. The second floor had a high ceiling and was as barren as the bottom floor. Rusty light fixtures lay on the floor among shards of glass and thick coats of dust. The footsteps continued deeper into the room and led to a closed door in the corner. Light leaked from around its edges. I turned around to check for footprints in the opposite direction, but they only headed one way, toward the door.

I shouldn't be here. I don't know what I'm doing.

A noise came from the opposite corner of the room. My head snapped in that direction, the knife up and ready.

I cried out, "If you don't show yourself, I'm leaving."

Another sound behind me—I spun, knife in hand. Someone smothered my nose and mouth with a cloth smelling of paralyzing fumes. Panic shot through me like an icicle. I held my breath and swung the knife blindly, hoping to cut whoever was attacking me.

The person was strong and bear-hugged my arms together from behind. I dropped my body into a horse stance, which instantly lowered my height six inches, in order to break the grasp. The sudden move threw my assailant off balance for a split second. I delivered two rapid elbow strikes, right-left, behind me. The first elbow made contact with a body of pure muscle. The attacker rebounded quickly, absorbing and deflecting my second elbow strike.

My attacker was a skilled fighter.

I took a breath. The toxic vapor instantly invaded my respiratory system. My legs buckled. The strength and power confirmed that my assailant was a man. I continued to slash the knife blindly, but he was strong, and I getting weaker. He struck my limp wrist; the weapon flew from my hand. Out of desperation, I thrashed and head-butted back at him. But the more I struggled, the more fumes I inhaled.

The world spun around and around, then went black.

I woke up with a splitting headache. My hands were bound in back. I was stripped to my panties and bra in the freezing cold, blindfolded, and tied in a chair with rope.

I knew immediately I hadn't been raped.

The man's voice was heavy and guttural. "Why are you nosing around?"

I tried to speak, but my throat was dry, my teeth chattering from the cold. I swallowed a few times. "The woman that died, murdered outside of Club Blue Diamond at closing, was my mother. I don't believe it was a random robbery like the police indicated. I need to know. Why was she killed?"

He shifted around me. His feet shuffled on the concrete floor, at times crunching glass. Though blindfolded, I could sense him studying me.

I asked, straight to the point. "Are you the one who killed my mother?"

"No," he quickly replied. "It was yakuza."

I twisted my hands to test the rope. He reached over my shoulder and pinched my left nipple. I tensed from the pain. My body shook with rage.

I composed myself, biting back my anger, and asked, "Why kill her?"

He didn't respond. Instead, the chilling blade of a knife traced along my chest. My lips trembled, sweat dribbled from my forehead and into the blindfold.

I cannot . . . die . . . this way.

I needed to talk my way out of it. At best, I could pick up clues in order to identify him later—if there was a later.

I became a sponge, listening to the tone of his voice, which was low and at times edgy. Although he spoke fluent English, I detected a slight accent. I sensed that he was Asian. The rhythm of his speech sounded forceful, but with moments of calmness, as though he were contemplating what to say next. I smelled a scent I could place. It wasn't completely masculine. It had a touch of sweetness, sort of like a woman's fragrance. I studied his mannerisms. He had sniffled five times since I woke up.

Cocaine?

"There are powerful people who you should not cross," he said, then paused long enough to bring to mind images of a gun firing into the back of my head or a knife stabbing my chest. He cleared his throat with disgust. "Where's the video?"

"Video? What video? I don't know what you're talking about."

"The video that your mother used to blackmail the oyabun."

"Blackmail?" My thoughts flashed to the man with the expensive suit. "I still don't know what you're talking about."

He huffed out a breath. "Get me the video and I will tell you who killed your mother."

"But—" I started, then wondered if I should pretend that I had the video so that he'd let me go. I could then go to the police for protection. Instead, I said, "I will try to get whatever you want, but you must keep your word."

His laughter echoed in the empty room.

"I don't know where to start."

"That's your problem."

He ran the knife along the top of my shoulder. With a flick, the strap of my bra was severed, exposing my left breast. He pinched my nipple again, harder. Tears of pain welled in my eyes.

I screamed, "Stop! It hurts."

A cork popped from a bottle. I froze at the thought of what would happen next. The toxic fumes floated in my direction as he walked closer across crunching glass. From behind, he shoved the rag over my nose and mouth.

I held my breath as long as I could, but within seconds, I blacked out.

15

I was standing on the highest spot on the riverbank, a cliff, watching a twenty-foot wall of violent brown water thundering down the narrow river passage that just a few minutes ago had been a quiet mountain stream.

David was standing frozen in its path.

I screamed and screamed.

I sprung awake from my recurring nightmare. My skin was on fire from the freezing cold. I glanced around. Now I remembered being held captive, tied to a chair. I pulled the cut strap of my bra up to cover myself and made a square knot to hold it in place. The rope that once bound me was now coiled on the ground like a dead snake.

Sunlight filtered through the heavy grime on the cracked glass above. It was early morning, that much I could tell. I hugged myself. Cold. I searched the floor for my clothes and phone and purse, but they were all gone.

I rose from the chair and got slammed with vertigo. I grabbed its wooden back for balance. I took a step toward the stairs, but stumbled and fell to the cold concrete. I brushed crushed glass from my hands, regained my balance, and made it to the top of the staircase. I searched for something to pull over me, to cover my nakedness and shield me from the freezing cold, but found nothing.

I staggered downstairs. From the outside, the abandoned building looked ominously dangerous in daylight, with large sections appearing to be about to collapse. I tiptoed across the street, the uneven asphalt biting into my bare feet.

A middle-aged, gray-haired woman carrying a bag of groceries squinted in disbelief, as if I had reappeared from a magic trick.

The woman shuffled over to me and asked in Japanese, "Are you alright?"

"Please. Help me call a taxi."

She placed her bag of groceries on the sidewalk and scrambled to the intersection two blocks away. By the time she shuffled back, a taxi had rounded the corner and stopped in front of me.

A young Japanese cabbie scurried from the driver's seat and hurried to the trunk of the car. He pulled out a towel and wrapped it around me, but it covered only the upper half of my body. My teeth continued to chatter non-stop. I'd already lost feeling in my fingers and toes.

I smiled at the woman. "Domo arigato."

The woman nodded, picked up her bag of groceries, and continued strolling down the sidewalk.

The young cabbie ushered me into the back seat and jumped in front.

"Please take me to Shinjuku Police Station," I said, then remembered I didn't have any money. "I cannot pay you now, but I will when I'm back at my apartment."

The young cabbie glanced in the rearview mirror. "The trip is short and you are in trouble. You do not have to pay."

His kindness filled me with a warmth that I hadn't felt in a while. The grocery lady and this cabbie had helped out a stranger when they didn't have to. Was hostessing corrupting my belief in basic human goodness? People at the bar seemed to only be out for themselves, perhaps tossing aside *pono*, a Hawaiian expression meaning "to live with righteousness and care for those around you."

The young cabbie dashed into the police station. Two officers trailed him out to where I was standing in my black bikini panties and towel. One young man had a long raincoat draped over his forearm and handed it to me. I pulled the raincoat on, slid the towel off, and gave it back to the cabbie. Although the raincoat smelled bad and stuck to my skin, it filled me with warmth because it reached down to my ankles.

I clutched the young man's hand. "Arigato."

He responded with two short bows, smiled, got in his cab, and drove away.

A young officer led me to the same floor Honma's office was on. He wasn't in. The same receptionist who'd ignored us a few days ago hurried away, came back with a long, black wool coat, and handed it to me. I thanked her, headed for the restroom, and came back wearing her coat.

The moment I stepped back into the office, my face dropped. The officer who made the despicable comment about my mother deserving to be killed because she was a bar owner was grinning at me.

I'd describe this cop as a human weasel, skinny with shifty eyes and a sallow face that appeared malnourished. He sniggered and grinned smugly, likely remembering me calling him a pig, and later being chewed out by Honma for his heartless comment.

"Please." He waved me into his office with a spiny hand.

I sat across from the human weasel.

"I'm Inspector Takashi. Second to Chief Inspector Honma."

I explained what had happened, from the moment I received

the note taped to my locker, to entering the abandoned building, to when I woke this morning.

Although Takashi appeared to be listening, I sensed that he wasn't interested in hearing my story.

After a couple minutes of fingering his bony jaw, he interrupted by asking, "Were you sexually assaulted?"

I paused at the question because it stunned me. It was as if his words had come from a dark part of his brain.

"No. I—" I stopped, and didn't see the point on continuing.

Takashi's exhale was loud and exaggerated. "Are you saying that a beautiful young woman like yourself—a naked woman— was not raped?"

I spun away from him. "No Inspector, I was not raped." Yeah, I made a stupid decision, but I sure as hell wasn't going to admit it to him.

"A beautiful young girl, naked in an abandoned building, walking out untouched seems highly unlikely." Takashi snickered. "What do you do now, Miss . . ." and he flipped through a notepad and continued, "Hunter?"

"What do you mean?"

"I mean, how do you make a living?" His tone of voice was snotty. "Money. You must make money to live here in Japan."

I sensed that he already knew the answer, yet I replied, "I work at my mother's club as a hostess."

His gaze shifted from his desk to me. "Hostess?"

I nodded, not wanting to look into his weaselly eyes.

"Yes, I remember you now." He pretended to only now be recognizing me. "You made a scene here. Accusing us of not doing enough to solve your mother's murder. Your mother who was a bar owner."

"Look, Inspector Takashi. I have a note that's proof that there was foul play with the death of my mother, because I was threatened to stop meddling or else."

I held back on telling him about the video.

Takashi frowned as though he thought I was an insignificant bar girl wasting his precious time, but asked, "What note?"

I showed it to him. He placed a white glove on his right hand and picked up the note. "Were you the only one who touched this?"

I never thought of fingerprints because of the closing "A FRIEND" written on the bottom. "Yes, me and probably the person who wrote it and maybe the person who taped it to my locker."

"I will hold on to this and send it to the lab for examination." He let out a bored sigh. "We will do all we can to look into this. I suggest that you change your line of work, because hostessing will attract people who will do this kind of thing."

Though speechless, I was seething inside.

"We will be sending officers to the abandoned building to validate your story." He smirked with enjoyment. "That building has been condemned for eight years. The owner does not have the funding to bring it up to the standard earthquake building codes. You were lucky that the building didn't collapse on you while you were inside."

I stared blankly out the window at the adjacent building.

Takashi cleared his throat. "I decided to not charge you for trespassing."

"What?" I couldn't believe where this was going.

"You illegally trespassed on private property." He paused to let it sink in. "Property that had been condemned and categorized as unsafe. If you had been hurt or injured, and unable to exit the building, our brave police officers and men of the fire department would have had to risk their lives in order to save you."

I glared at a space in front of me, my voice a cold monotone. "Are we done?"

Takashi didn't give a verbal reply, but jerked his chin toward the door.

I rose from the chair, started for the exit, then turned to face him. "My money was taken. Can you please help me with a police car and take me to my apartment in Shibuya?"

The weasel of a man shook his head, and gave no further explanation.

On the way to the elevator, I thanked the receptionist for the coat and reassured her that I would get it dry-cleaned. She smiled and nodded.

When I stepped from the entrance of Shinjuku Police Station, I craved a bath—not because I had been drugged, stripped naked, threatened, and spent the evening in an abandoned building, but because I needed to wash the stink of Takashi's toxic presence off me.

Shibuya was about two miles away. When I started walking, I heard footsteps shuffling behind me. I spun around and into an out-of-breath policewoman. She wore white gloves and a crisply pressed blue-black uniform with a matching short-brimmed cap atop a bob haircut. Her skirt was down to her knees. She had a round face and pretended to be searching the streets.

Not looking at me, the policewoman spoke from the corner of her mouth. "There's a ramen shop two blocks from McDonald's. Meet me there." She turned and scurried back to the entrance of the police station.

The front of the ramen shop had a white canvas awning with round Japanese paper lanterns above and to the sides. I pushed the sliding wooden door open and entered the tiny restaurant. The place had a narrow counter that angled around propane burners, with short wooden stools in front. Still too early for lunch, there were no customers.

A man in his fifties wearing a white paper skullcap and a dirty white apron stood behind the counter, boiling water in a large pot. Cooking utensils hung from hooks.

He kept cutting vegetables on a cutting board with a large knife, then looked up at me and cried out, "Irasshaimase."

His knife reminded me of the knife I bought the night before. After waking, I'd searched the floor, but it too had been gone. Maybe I'd cut my attacker when I was blindly slashing at him. If so, the blade would have his DNA on it.

I told the owner that someone would be joining me shortly. The tiny restaurant had three small tables crammed against the wall about four feet from the counter. I sat on a stool at one of them.

Ten minutes later, the policewoman entered the restaurant. Short and bone thin, her black leather duty belt looked oversized and heavy.

I said to her, "I would have ordered something for both of us to eat, but my money was stolen."

"You must be hungry." The policewoman took a few steps to the counter and ordered two bowls of ramen. She sat on the stool opposite me. "My name is Hanako Sakamoto."

We shook. "I'm Gena." I waited for Hanako to tell me why I was in a ramen shop instead of a shower.

Hanako cleared her throat, started, then stopped abruptly. The man walked up to our table with two bowls of steaming noodle soup.

When the guy returned back behind the counter, Hanako said, "I know it was your mother who was murdered. I am very sorry."

"Thank you."

"I saw you the other day with Chief Inspector Honma." She side-eyed the chef, who was still cutting vegetables.

"Honma is rarely in and he doesn't return my calls." I paused, unsure of her relationship with Honma. "Does he ever work?"

Hanako chuckled. "Inspector Honma is under a lot of stress

because there's a serial killer roaming the streets of Tokyo, leaving a trail of dead men who patronize hostess clubs and bars."

"I guess that would keep anyone very busy."

Hanako snickered at my sarcasm.

"By the way, why is Inspector Takashi so hostile to me? I did nothing to him. In fact, we just met."

"Takashi's a snake." Hanako's cute face sneered. "He fell in love with a hostess and worked hard to make her happy, and happy meant providing for her financially. They had two kids, but she abandoned her family. He raised them alone. Takashi hates anything and anyone in the hostess business."

His story sounded familiar.

Hanako leaned closer and whispered, "I feel very uncomfortable about what I have to say to you, because I can get into trouble."

I broke the pair of chopsticks in half and attacked the ramen noodles. "Sorry, the food looks so *oishi*."

She nodded and smiled.

Hanako slurped the ramen with chopsticks. She wiped her mouth with a paper napkin and paused. Her voice came out low and barely audible. "A few months ago, the chief justice's daughter was kidnapped and later found dead."

I stopped eating and recalled the newspaper clipping in my mother's safe.

"Her name was Yumiko Matsumoto. She was a troubled fourteen-year-old who craved attention, so she regularly hung out on the streets of Harajuku. The word around the station was that she was tied up and raped in some kind of deranged sexual encounter."

I wondered where this was going.

Hanako cleared her throat. "The suspect is Tamura-san, the powerful yakuza oyabun. There are rumors that your mother may have evidence that he did it—a video."

I thought of the man in the warehouse and asked, "Do you know what's on it?"

"It's mere rumors and nothing substantiated. It might be the act itself or maybe documents of witnesses." She shook her head with determination. "Whoever has this video will have power over the oyabun."

"Why are you telling me this?"

"Because the murdered girl had a friend." She chomped down on a piece of roasted pork glistening with fat. "No one, including Chief Inspector Honma, interviewed the girl's best friend who was there on the day of the kidnapping."

"Sounds like you want me to question this girl?" I frowned, because it seemed odd that the police would send a civilian to do their job.

"She might be able to tell you more," Hanako replied. "I am not an investigator, I am only a traffic officer."

"Why don't you go to your superiors and have someone push from the top to investigate further?"

"Because I have two children and a lazy husband who hasn't worked a permanent job in two years." She stared into her hands. "I need this job. I have studied and passed the inspector's exam but was denied the position because I am not willing to follow Honma's orders in covering up his own corruption."

"Corruption?"

"Hai." She glanced at the entrance, then back at me. "Honma is yakuza. Or he has deep connections with the yakuza."

"Oh shit." A chill ran through me.

Hanako huffed. "I hate the yakuza. They pretend to run legitimate businesses by rubbing elbows with politicians and giving donations to the needy, but that is just a front for corruption. The chief justice is heavily against the yakuza because they broke the once honored code after the financial bubble, that is, to leave the public alone. But they didn't, because they had become too inter-twined with the public."

"Where can I find the girl?"

"She usually hangs out on Takeshita Dori in Harajuku."

"Do you have a photograph of her?"

Hanako slid a picture across the table. "I was able to acquire this from her yearbook. The school says she rarely attends her classes."

I stared at the photograph. The girl had rosy cheeks and fright-ened eyes. Her legs were short, her arms stubby and puffy, as if she hadn't yet lost her baby fat.

"What's her name?"

"Suzume Hayakawa." Hanako nervously stared at the door. "She goes by the nickname Sparrow."

After I borrowed taxi money from Hanako, we stood outside the restaurant and stared at each other. Perhaps we both sensed that if I unearthed things that some people didn't want found out, we could both be crossing a very dangerous line.

I thanked Hanako. The policewoman then scurried in the direction of the station.

16

Earlier the next day, I purchased a new phone and downloaded my contacts from the Cloud. I also picked up the receptionist's wool coat from a dry cleaner and dropped it off at the police station's information desk with a thank you note. I would have delivered it personally, but hated the thought of running into Takashi again.

I spotted Suzume from a distance at the Yoyogi Train Station. Hanako had said that it was her daily starting point. She would then take the two-minute train ride to Harajuku.

Suzume was tinier than she'd looked in the photograph—less than five feet tall. She did have the smoky eyes and narrow face of a sparrow, but that was where the similarities ended.

She was dressed entirely in pink: a pink top with a darker pink miniskirt, pink shoes, and pink stockings. Her light pink, frizzy hair, looked as if she'd been placed in front of a giant fan.

Suzume's tiny body leaned forward to counterbalance the weight of her humungous backpack. She struggled to hoist it onto the train. I ran toward the train and slid between the closing doors. Suzume bumped against frowning passengers as if they didn't exist. Although the cabin was not fully packed, no one offered us seats, so we both stood holding the stainless-steel pole in the center, facing each other.

When the train jolted forward, her bag yanked her backward and slammed her to the floor. Suzume fought to stand, but the large backpack pinned her down, her thin arms and legs sprawling in midair. She looked like a turtle on its back struggling to flip over. The passengers around her pointed and laughed; nobody helped.

I shoved and pushed my way through, separating bodies, and struggled to pull her upright. The backpack was heavier than I thought. I grabbed the pole and lifted Suzume off the floor. Items clicked inside her bag, sounding like shifting rocks. Once standing, Suzume continued as though it was business as usual, like this kind of stuff happened all the time.

We ended up facing each other again, holding on to the pole.

I felt sorry for her because of the way people had mocked her. I asked in Japanese, "Can I offer you a cup of coffee at the next stop?"

Not looking at me, Suzume answered, "I do not drink coffee." Her gaze drifted to the overhead screen, a line showing the train's route with colored dots highlighting the station stops.

While I thought of my next approach, Suzume said, "I would prefer a meal at McDonald's."

I pretended not knowing where Suzume's next stop would be, suggesting, "There's a McDonald's in Harajuku. We can stop there."

Referred to as the birthplace of many of Japan's fashion trends, pop culture and cosplay, I'd visited Harajuku numerous times. The main street, Takeshita Dori, was narrow and usually packed curb to curb with people. Four hundred meters of street were lined with shops, boutiques, cafes and fast-food outlets, all targeting Tokyo's teenagers.

We stepped off the train into the station. Suzume walked

down the wrong way to the exit, against the arrows printed on the steps. Immune to people pushing and shoving her like a pinball, she made it to the exit turnstile, which turned into a wrestling match with Suzume battling her backpack through the narrow opening. I helped her through.

As we walked toward Takeshita Dori, I had to glance back every so often to make certain she hadn't gone in another direction. At times, Suzume would lose her balance and stagger like a drunkard, her backpack seemingly having a life of its own, perhaps shifting with the earth's rotation. A ten-minute walk turned into twenty.

McDonald's was crowded. Luckily a teenage couple vacated a round standing table as we walked down the crammed aisle.

I spoke slowly. "Stay here. I will get us some food." Suzume's eyes roamed from one side of the restaurant to the other.

I thought she hadn't heard me until she said, "I'll have a double filet of fish, fries, and a large coke."

The counter order took longer than anticipated, and I wondered if Suzume would still be where I'd left her. I let out a breath when I saw her shuffling through items in her backpack. She opened one plastic container after another, placing them on the already crowded table. The contents in the containers looked like dirt.

I slid the food across the tiny table. "I'll be honest with you, Suzume." I remained calm, sensing she might freak out at any type of edginess. "I wanted to talk to you about a friend of yours."

Her gaze drifted to the ceiling.

I touched her hand. "What's the matter?"

Suzume stared as though seeing me for the first time. Her voice was high-pitched and scratchy. "My name is Sparrow."

"Okay, Sparrow." I started, but wondered about the containers. "What's the dirt for?"

She squinted at me like it was a stupid question. "These are lands I visited." She lifted plastic containers labeled as being from Singapore, Korea, and other places.

I stopped her hand at one labeled Hawaii. The container held crushed lava rock.

Superstition abounded in Hawaii about ancient legends of war gods and other deities; Madame Pele was the goddess of volcanoes and fire, and the creator of the Hawaiian Islands. I didn't want to burst Sparrow's bubble by telling her that Pele's curse says that any visitor who removes lava or black sand from the islands will suffer bad luck until the items are returned.

"*Hashi*." Sparrow made a face as if I'd pissed on her leg.

"What?" I blew out a breath, feeling exhausted just being around her. "I don't understand."

Sparrow stood and walked away like she was about to leave, but she wouldn't, not without her backpack.

When she returned, Sparrow slid chopsticks from its sleeve, broke them in two, then picked up a single French fry. She evenly spread ketchup across the length of it. Her upper lip was chapped and split, and she nibbled the food like a mouse from one end to the other.

Maybe she was looking at me. Maybe she wasn't. She had sort of a cockeyed grin that made me wonder if she was high. But I didn't think so. In some strange way, I admired Sparrow for being herself, without any inhibitions whatsoever.

After ritualistically eating a few fries, Sparrow unwrapped her fish burger as though she were disassembling a bomb.

"I want to talk to you about your best friend, Yumiko Matsumoto."

She stopped working on her fish burger. Her voice softened. "Yumiko doesn't come here anymore."

"Do you know where she is?"

She shook her head. "Yumiko and I planned our escapes."

"Escapes?"

"We would send key phrases by text and we would skip school and meet here in Harajuku for the day, or days, depending on when people came to force us back home to our parents."

"It sounds like you miss her a lot. What happened to her?"

Without making eye contact, Sparrow started talking. "Yumiko and I were in Harajuku hanging out. I needed to go to the toilet. I ran into Kazue on the way back. He was dressed in a Little Orphan Annie dress with red and white horizontal stripes. His wig was a coordinated yellow and red and—"

I held up both hands in a "stop" gesture, but Sparrow didn't, she continued to ramble about meeting her friend. "His lips were painted like clown lips, deep red with a permanent smile to show happiness even when the world around us is crumbling. It was a very nice outfit and brought out Kazue's true self."

"Sparrow, please—this is very important."

She frowned. "When I got back to Yumiko, I saw her being led into a car."

"Was she being forced?"

"No."

"What type of car? Did you see the driver?"

"I do not know the types of cars, but it was a big black car. And that was the last I saw of my best friend." Tears dribbled down her cheek.

She wiped tears away, but stopped, something caught her attention. She twisted her hand around and licked a smear of ketchup off a finger.

"Can you tell me anything else that happened that night?"

"Yumiko would never have gotten into any strange car without a fight. She either knew the person or was told a story to lure her away."

"Did the police interview you?"

"No."

"Did you ever think of going to the police?"

Sparrow started to rock back and forth. She began humming. Not a song that I recognized, but it had a dreary rhythm.

As she hummed and swayed like a pendulum, she'd say a word every time she swung right.

"I"—a swing to the left then to the right—"have"—swing back and forth—"the"—swing—"car"—swing to the left then to the right—"license"—swing—"number."

My elbows slipped off the table. "You have the car license plate number?"

Sparrow's eyes rolled upward like she was scanning files in her head. She closed her eyes and began blurting out numbers.

I didn't interrupt her. When Sparrow was done, she asked, "Did you write it down?"

"Sorry, but I didn't." I pulled a pen and an old store receipt from my handbag and said, "Please repeat what you said."

I expected Sparrow to put up a fuss and complain, but she didn't. Once again, her eyes rolled up, and she repeated, "Eight-two-nine-eight-two-four."

Sparrow closed her eyes, and then they sprung open. She snatched the receipt off the tabletop, stared at it, and put her palm out as though wanting to give me five.

Without looking at me, she said, "Pen."

I placed one in her hand. Sparrow sketched a Japanese character, then another, and handed back the receipt. I pointed to the two characters. "What's this?"

She shrugged. "That's what I saw."

I exhaled. Although being with her was like trying to hit a moving target, in a nice way she also made me laugh with her innocent antics and odd behavior.

Sparrow dug into her backpack, unfolded an envelope, and handed me a picture of Yumiko. She was maybe fourteen, and her close-cropped brown hair framed her face, making it appear rounder and child-like. No makeup and no nail polish. She wasn't pretty.

Sparrow did not nod, blink, or eat another fry with chopsticks. She seemed to be studying my reactions, perhaps watching everything the way a goldfish watches the world from its bowl.

She mimicked Yumiko's way of speaking. "She said to her father, 'I put on this dress especially for the dinner banquet. Isn't it pretty?' He tells her, 'Can't you do something about your hair?' She cried."

Sparrow's left eye fluttered. She rubbed her fingers across her lashes, opened then closed her mouth, and crossed her arms. She chewed her upper lip. The fingers on her right hand began pinching her left side—hard, nervous pinches.

She continued, "Yumiko's eyes were red and watery. She began to rock and finally told him, 'I hope they change their minds and don't give you that fucking award.' She didn't say it to me, but just sort of whispered it."

"What award?"

"Something to do with the yakuza."

The fingers on Sparrow's right hand moved faster, digging and squeezing into the soft flesh of her side. She probably didn't even know she was doing it. I wanted to reach out and stop her.

Tears rolled down her cheeks and landed in her mouth. Sparrow giggled, then made a wet sound. Her tiny body shook and heaved. She put her face in her hands and cried. I shifted closer and held her. I wasn't going to leave her side until she stopped crying.

A few minutes later, a girl walked in and strolled like a zombie toward Sparrow, and hugged her from behind. She wore a black corset, black coat—black everything, except her hair was red and filled with red paper roses. Sparrow stopped crying.

I smiled, thinking she had someone around who cared for her, even if they were different from most people. My first thought was *not normal*, but who was I to say that Sparrow wasn't the normal one compared to everybody else.

Before I left McDonald's, I ordered a to-go bag of cheeseburgers and a milkshake and took it back to the apartment. Milkshake in hand, I thumbed through my new phone for Hanako's number.

"Hello, Hanako." I sipped on the drink, savoring the little pleasures of life during these times of confusion. "I talked to Suzume, and she witnessed her friend get into a car. She couldn't see the driver, but she was able to get the license plate number. I'm taking a photo and sending it right now."

The familiar ping came from the phone speaker. I visualized Hanako opening the photo, expanding and studying it.

Hanako explained: "The left symbol represents the location of the office where this car was registered. In this case, the area is Shinagawa."

"What's the other symbol?"

"Next is the Japanese letter assigned from the *hiragana* alphabet. Some letters are reserved for rental cars, some for businesses such as taxis and so forth."

"So the key is still the numbers."

"Hai." Her voice had an edge of nervousness. "It will take some time to get this information, because I do not have the authorization and need someone to help me. I'll get back to you when that happens." She hung up.

I fished Mom's diamond wedding ring from the safe and walked to the window with the melting milkshake in my hand.

Bundled in warm coats, the same mother and child from the other day strolled hand in hand along the sidewalk. I wondered if Mom had stood at this same spot, perhaps imagining her and David going for a walk.

I took a sip of milkshake and thought: *Mom, how did any of this lead to you winding up on a morgue table?*

17

N ot sure if I still had a job at Club Blue Diamond or not, I decided to find out, because I needed to reach Reiko. My gut feeling was that Kiyomi's greed exceeded her hatred for me.

I'd made a bad decision going to the abandoned building alone, but if I hadn't, I wouldn't have known that part of this, or maybe all of it, was happening because of a video. Had I made a bad decision in meeting with Sparrow and doing police work? But I'd gotten the license plate number for a suspect in the murder of the chief justice's fourteen-year-old daughter. Why didn't the police interview her? I had pieces of the puzzle, but a huge chunk of it was still missing. Did my mother blackmail Tamura with a video? It sure didn't sound like her, but if she did, she may have had a very good reason.

I entered the club as usual before eight. A half dozen people anxiously turned to face me, twisting heads searching for Kiyomi, anticipating a showdown.

What if Kiyomi fired me on the spot? Then I would wait for Reiko outside the club, and if needed, drag the information out of her in some way.

At this point, my patience was wearing fuckin' thin.

Heading for the lockers, I passed Kiyomi. The old bat ignored me as though I was floor dust. I had assumed correctly in thinking that making money was the most important thing to her.

I added a strip of transparent tape over one of the screws on the back panel of my locker. I slipped a note into Reiko's, wanting to meet at the same soba stand after work. An hour later, looking up from flirting with a customer at the bamboo bar, Reiko nodded that our meeting was on.

That evening, I had four customers. Time dragged in anticipation of the meeting with Reiko.

They say that the witching hour, or the devil's hour, is the time when the powers of darkness are believed to be the strongest. While most refer to this as the hours between 2 and 4 a.m., Hamlet designated the *witching time of night* as midnight.

Time seemed to stop at midnight when the super-sized Japanese man from the funeral entered the tiny bar. His body blocked the entrance like a giant boulder blocking a cave, sealing everyone inside with no way out. The chatter in the bar stopped.

His prominent short-slicked black hair, parted down the middle, and the deep scar across his cheek had left indelible imprints on my psyche. He had come to me in a nightmare one night. I woke in a cold sweat from being hunted down by this scarred devil.

Kiyomi shuffled toward the entrance. Though her face trembled with fear, she forced a smile. Even with dark glasses on, the man's eyes seemed to scan from one hostess to another. His gaze locked on Mei. She was sitting with one of her regular customers in a booth.

"Irasshaimase." Kiyomi's voice quivered. She kowtowed as though the giant was the emperor of Japan.

He was dressed in the same style dark suit he'd worn at the funeral. He pointed a meaty finger at Mei. Kiyomi shuffled to the booth, gripped her by the hand, and yanked her toward the giant. Mei resisted by pulling away. Kiyomi grabbed her arm. Up close in Kiyomi's face, Mei yelled in rapid Japanese. I couldn't make out what she said. Kiyomi slapped Mei across her face then spoke firmly into her ear. Mei pouted, her head down, she folded her arms together.

Kiyomi ushered Mei toward the private karaoke room. The purplish glow of fluorescent black lights filled the mirrored room. The giant followed both women to the sliding door. He entered. With one hand, he shoved the table in front of the raised, cushioned booth as though it were made of cardboard. He plopped onto the sofa, faced the door, and removed his dark glasses.

Mei stood to the side like a statue.

Godzilla stared at me and grinned. Did he remember me from the funeral?

Kiyomi shuffled backward to the door, bowing repeatedly as she went. She was about to slide the door shut when the giant grunted. She bowed and left the sliding door open.

A number of hostesses and their customers occupied three booths facing the karaoke room. Unless they purposely turned away, there was no avoiding what was about to happen. If there had been an empty booth, I would have moved there with my customer and not be any part of this.

Mei wore a black-and-white-striped backless evening dress with spaghetti straps. The white on her dress glowed in the black light. With her back to the door, she slipped the straps of the dress off her shoulders. The dress dropped and bundled on the floor. No underwear. The whiteness of her body accentuated her feminine curves.

The giant licked his lips, but his focus wasn't on Mei. I could tell from the whites of the man's eyes; his attention was on me. My legs turned to Jell-O, and I was a breath away from peeing in my underwear.

Kiyomi signaled for Junko to start the karaoke music. She played an older, upbeat tune, "Yellow River," to raise the energy in the place. Its lyrics floated on the bottom of the screen.

No one sang.

Light from the LCD TV screen leaked into the dark room. Mei stepped out of her dress and knelt in front of the giant. The ceiling mirror reflected her undoing his belt, then unzipping his pants. Although Godzilla's head leaned back, his gaze never left me as Mei's head pumped between his legs. Her hands worked along with her mouth. His cheeks soon tensed, then drooped. Mei swallowed. She wiped her mouth with the back of her hand.

Kiyomi waited beside the door with a tray of sake and four small logs of hot towels. She shuffled into the room and handed Mei a towel. Mei wiped between Godzilla's legs, redid his zipper, then belt. She stood naked in front of him for a couple seconds, shifted over to her dress on the floor, pulled it up, then slipped the straps over her shoulders. She bowed respectfully, turned, and scurried from the room.

The giant downed five cups of sake. Kiyomi handed him two hot towels. He wiped his face and hands, reached into his wallet, and dropped a roll of yen on the floor.

Godzilla rose from the sofa, headed for the entrance, then stopped. He turned to face me, pointed a finger, and grinned. The deep scar on his cheek twitched. This time I lost control of my bladder and dashed for the restroom.

After I changed my underwear, I stood at the sink and splashed water on my face. Sobs came from behind the door of a stall. Though I despised Mei, no one—no one—should have had to go through that.

My knees wobbled when I walked back into the bar. The bar had erupted with loud chatter. I hated this place more than ever. I hated everyone here.

At closing, Mei sat in the corner booth, her head on the table, an empty bottle of whisky next to her.

The screw on the back of the locker still had the strip of transparent tape over it. I changed into my street clothes and strolled back into the club. Kiyomi sat on a stool, her face caught in its permanent scowl. She counted off 80,000 yen and shoved it at me like she was giving up a late tax payment to the government. I pocketed about $750—filthy money.

I needed to stay focused.

Who'd taped the note on my locker to meet in Korea Town? Reiko was first on the list. Although she'd helped identify the Novaks, I didn't trust her.

At three in the morning, we sat at the same food-stained table, hunkered under the same blue tarp. Under the dim yellow paper lantern that hung above the table, we again ordered two bowls of hot soba from the old lady.

"I hate yakuza," Reiko slurred after a night of drinking more than usual. "What are you going to do?"

"Do? What do you mean?"

"You cannot say no to Yoshi." She stared at me like a chess player, waiting for my next move. "If you do, he'll kill you. You don't know when it would happen. Could be anywhere, anytime."

Cold sweat beaded on my neck. I didn't answer her.

With my silence, Reiko changed the subject. "Kiyomi knows about your incident in the abandoned building."

I'd thought the night couldn't get any worse, but it just had. The information had to have leaked from the police station, because I told no one at the club.

The moment the old woman placed the bowls in front of us, Reiko attacked the hot meal like a starving animal.

"Kiyomi was furious, and shouted that she will fire you . . . again." Reiko slurped soba noodles as though that were her top priority. "But she won't because you're making money for her."

Knowing that police investigative information was reaching Kiyomi frightened me. I needed to move faster. One dead end led to another dead end. I needed to push harder.

I remembered a quote that my father would repeat often: "There's a time for positive thinking and there's a time for righteous anger."

Not being able to purge the images of my mother's mutilated body from my mind, I felt beyond righteous anger—more like righteously pissed off.

I decided to gamble with Reiko. "I know you put the note on my locker to meet that guy in the warehouse."

Unable to look me in the eyes, Reiko turned away, and said in a garbled voice, "I don't know what you're talking about."

"I checked with other girls and they confirmed that my mother helped you get off drugs and the street, but not one person said that they trusted you. Why are you lying to me?"

Reiko stared into her bowl of noodles, then lifted her head, deciding. "I-I got back on drugs."

"You placed the note."

She looked down at her hands, nodded, then squeaked out, "I was paid."

"By who?"

She fumbled with the chopsticks. "The person made contact through text. I don't know who it is."

"What else did you do for this person?"

"I lied at your mother's funeral service." She didn't look at me. "I was instructed to meet you and tell you that there was yakuza involved. I'm very sorry, Gena. But I needed money."

My voice came out stern and unforgiving. "I want to talk to Tamura. Where can I meet him?"

Reiko choked, but it wasn't from slurping her soup. She stared at me with blank eyes. "That's like committing suicide."

"I just want to talk to him. Ask him some questions. From

what I've heard around the club, it sounds like he liked and admired my mother. I won't accuse him of anything, that would be stupid and unsubstantiated."

"Even to insinuate that he ordered the killing is more than suicidal." Color was returning to Reiko's face after getting some food in her stomach. "You'll feel the wrath of a very vindictive man because he never forgets." She emphasized *never* like it was a curse.

"Vindictive?"

Her eyes blinked as though she were trying to swat flies with glued-on eyelashes, then nodded.

My phone buzzed. Lani. I answered, happy to hear a friendly voice. "What's up?"

"Gena, I got bad news," Lani blurted out, her voice frantic. "Your father went canoe paddling and he hasn't returned."

"What?"

"Your dad—"

An icy chill ran through me, my eyes blinking back shock. "My dad's missing?"

"Yes." Lani's voice cracked with worry. "Your father took a couple days off from work, so he had a four-day weekend. When he didn't show up for work on the fifth day, his co-worker, Josh Venezuela, found his truck where he usually parked at Moanalua Bay. His canoe was gone, and his truck was broken into."

My dad always carried his cell phone, even when practicing. "Did they try calling him?"

"Yes, but no answer."

"Are the coast guard or fire department looking for him?"

"Yes." She calmed down a little, then added, "The Navy is also involved."

"I'm coming home, Lan, on the first flight I can book."

"I'll pick you up at the airport. Text me when your flight is."

A long pause followed before she said, "And Gen, it's going to be all right. Your father is a pro on the ocean."

"Thanks, Lan."

I pivoted to Reiko. With high heels in hand, I watched her scramble like a jackrabbit down the dark alleyway.

My mind became a blender of possibilities thinking about what could have happened to him.

I called the airlines.

My heart jumped when the buzzer mounted by the door of the apartment went off. I pressed the receive button and answered, "Yes?"

"It's me, Hanako," came the tinny voice through the speaker box.

I pressed the enter button, heard the downstairs door unlatch, and waited with the apartment door open.

Hanako entered and did a quick scan of the apartment. "You left a message that you were leaving."

"How'd you find me?"

"I'm a police officer." Her tone was flat. "I wanted to talk to you face-to-face. If you leave, I cannot do this myself."

"Sorry, but my father is missing. I hate going back, but I must."

She squinted. "What about finding your mother's killer?"

I felt lightheaded; anxiety eating away at me. "I'm torn between not being able to stay and see this through, and leaving."

I thought about being used by Kiyomi to make money, Mei and the silly games she played to be the number one hostess at the club, pinching some creep's nipples to get him off, and about Mei being forced to blow the yakuza guy. The images made me sick to my stomach. I needed to get away from here.

Hanako squinted again. "Do the police suspect foul play?"

"I don't know what they know," I answered, and looked away. Maybe if I hadn't acted as an amateur detective, my father would be home right now watering my mother's plants. I pressed my palms to my eyes. "He went canoeing and never came back."

"I'm sorry," Hanako said with downturned eyes. "When will you be returning?"

"I don't know." Then it dawned on me. "Do you think you'll be able to track my missing phone? We might get lucky, and the guy who abducted me in the abandoned building hasn't destroyed it."

"Every modern cellphone has its own unique identifier called the IMEI number. And your SIM card also has a unique number called an IMSI. We can use either to track your phone."

"Since I bought the SIM card here in Tokyo, you need to go to the vendor who sold it to me." I gave her the mobile phone vendor's name. "I don't know my IMEI number, but I can get it to you."

A bright smile finally broke across her previously serious face. "I'll see what I can do."

Before walking out the door, I gave Hanako a hug. "I'll be in touch."

Prior to boarding the flight at Narita Airport in Tokyo, I had called Josh Venezuela, a co-worker of my father's. We agreed to meet at Moanalua Bay in one to two hours after I landed on Oahu. I gave him my flight number and estimated time of arrival of 8:30 a.m.

Josh said over the phone what I already knew—that my father was always prompt, and if he didn't show, he would call. When Dad hadn't shown up for work and didn't call, Josh drove to where he usually began his canoe paddling and found his truck broken into. He called 911.

Lani was waiting at the curb for arrivals at the Daniel K. Inouye International Airport at little before 9 a.m.

Moanalua Bay was a horseshoe-shaped bay. The southeastern edge extended out into the ocean, with multimillion-dollar homes perched on a peninsula of land called Portlock, which also formed a natural breakwater from the strong ocean currents.

As Lani and I waited in her White Whale, a shirtless elderly man wearing shorts and dark-green *tabis* waded in ankle-deep water. The morning's low tide exposed the reef. With the angle of the rising sun reflecting off the water surface like a mirror, the man appeared to be violating the laws of physics and able to walk on water. He held a three-pronged spear. His eyes were focused down at the reef, searching for fish or octopus engaged in their own morning hunt for food.

Although my father often talked about Josh, who was also part of the team of Navy divers, I'd never met him until now.

Josh was born and raised on the Big Island, and one of the best blue ocean spearfishing divers in Hawaii. Using a boat and without scuba gear, he'd free-dive for big game like marlin, *ahi* tuna, mahi-mahi, *ono*, and *ulua*.

Lani gasped when Josh got out of his truck and sort of strutted toward us. He stood about five-ten and had a rock-solid body in a thin T-shirt with a picture of a *tako* stenciled in front. With his chiseled face, he was knockout gorgeous. He was of mixed race: Filipino with double eyelids, dark hypnotic irises, maybe a little Hawaiian with his thick, wavy black hair, and likely part Caucasian, with big round eyes and a sharp nose.

I hopped off the truck and extended my hand. "Thank you for meeting me, Josh."

We shook hands. He smiled, the whiteness of his teeth standing out against his mocha-tanned face.

"This is my friend, Lani."

If I hadn't pulled her away, Lani would still be holding on to his hand. I led them to a green-painted picnic table/bench combination by the grassy portion at the edge of the parking lot.

"I'm sorry to hear about your mother," Josh said sincerely.

I nodded thank you.

Josh sat opposite us, facing the ocean. Lani and I faced *mauka*, toward the mountain, as well as the busy stoplight and intersection of Kalanianaole Highway.

He placed his elbows on the tabletop, and his voice held a sadness that touched my heart. "There's nothin' yet on your dad. The Coast Guard is searchin' from here to Diamond Head where he usually practices. We also have a couple Navy choppers searchin' the western side of the island, because that's how the ocean currents run. Let me tell you, after a day or two, the ocean currents are fast and strong and can easily take anythin' that floats from here to Kauai." Kauai was about a hundred miles from Oahu.

"My father is more at home on the ocean than anybody. He's always prepared for whatever could happen at sea. He can't be missing . . . he just can't."

The sound of my voice amplified the guilt I felt for putting pressure on Dad to attend his wife's funeral service.

Josh glanced at his hands then up at us. "I don't know how to say this, but I feel that I better."

I nodded to go ahead.

"Although your dad pretended like your mother's death didn't bother him, he was takin' it pretty hard, Gena. He wasn't right. You know, emotionally. I think he was grievin' in his own way."

"How's that?" Lani asked before I did.

"He felt guilty for not attendin' your mother's funeral, so he poured into trainin' to cope with the loss." Not that anyone was comfortable giving bad news, but Josh's body seemed to be crumbling in front of us. "You probably already know how obsessed your father is with workin' out, but in this case, I never saw him this intense, maybe to the point of keepin' a step or two ahead of being depressed. He pushed himself from sunrise to sunset, paddlin' like he was competin' in a race of life and death."

My face soured. The word *death* brought the reality that something terrible may have happened to him.

Josh glanced at the tabletop then up at me. "Sorry, that came out wrong."

"That's okay, I know what you meant."

"Did your dad have an emergency beacon on his canoe, like EPIRB?" Josh squinted in the morning sun. "The Coast Guard asked but I didn't know."

"No, because whenever he trained he was always within sight of land, so he could use his cell phone if needed."

The mention of EPIRB made me think of his phone GPS. Josh seemed to have read my mind. "The police tried your dad's phone GPS, but got nothin'. So right now, they just don't know until they find the canoe."

Josh stood and pulled a slip of paper from his jeans pocket. He passed it across the table. "Here's the police officer that I've been talkin' to."

I read the note: Detective Frank Lau, Honolulu Police Department.

Josh said, "Lau has been very helpful and is doin' all he can to help find your dad."

Even with the Coast Guard and Navy on the search, realistically I knew that finding a one-man canoe in the vastness of the ocean would be extremely difficult, if not impossible, without GPS or an emergency beacon.

"Your dad is the best on the ocean," he reassured me. "If anybody can survive out there it will be him."

Lani cleared her throat. "Could he have . . . you know . . . being that he was so depressed?"

"Could he have what?" Though I did think of it for a second, I refused to acknowledge it consciously.

"Never mind." Lani paused a second then added, "I was just thinking of what could have happened—ah, never mind."

"No, don't cop out now, Lan." My voice rose at the thought. "You're saying that my father could have taken his own life?"

Josh fidgeted and ran a hand across his mouth.

"It was just a thought, because he was depressed and all that." She fumbled with the collar of her shirt. "Forget that I brought it up."

I glared at her. "Let's get one thing straight. My dad would never, ever, commit suicide. Never."

"I think Gena's right," Josh injected, hoping to calm the tension between us. "Her dad is not like that. He always faced up to whatever came up. He's not someone who would feel sorry for himself and give up."

Lani blinked rapidly a few times. "Well . . . I never really thought he would do anything like that. I just thought—ah, never mind."

Perhaps my resistance in acknowledging a possible suicide was because at seventeen, I wanted to just sleep and never wake up from the reality of deceit and betrayal of someone I thought I was in love with. Back then, was I feeling sorry for myself and gave up on life? I don't know. All I know was that I hurt really, really bad.

I turned to Josh. "Please call me if you hear anything."

He stared at the horizon over the ocean and said nothing. Lani and I looked out at the mountain ridge and also said nothing. Breaking the silence, a twirling wind circled around us, sending a paper cup skidding across the pavement. The three of us gazed up at the sky.

I cringed at the possibility of a storm happening at the worst possible time. In any search and rescue operation, success depended on the weather. It was difficult enough trying to locate a tiny canoe in a massive ocean, but it became ten to a hundred times more difficult with increased white caps and large waves.

I asked Josh, "By the way, where's my dad's truck?"

"Probably impounded by the police. You might wanna call Lau."

"Those are my only wheels."

He nodded. "We'll find him, Gena."

I thanked him again.

Josh stood from the bench and walked to his truck. Lani pretended not to be checking out his butt, but I knew her well enough to know her patterns.

I was still hurting from Lani insinuating that my dad could have committed suicide, and the ride to my house was driven in deafening silence.

When Lani pulled to the curb, I said, "Sorry Lan. I didn't mean to bite your head off."

We hugged. Lani said, "I know, Sista. I'm sorry for thinking that way."

To lighten the situation, I poked Lani in the ribs. "Josh is hot, huh?"

Lani snorted. "I didn't notice."

"Okay, if you say so."

Lani clutched my hand. "Hey, do you want me to hang with you tonight?"

"Nah." I forced a smile. "I'll be okay. I got things to do."

Lani held up a finger phone. "Call me." Within seconds, her White Whale rumbled down the street.

With closed windows, the house felt stuffy and muggy, and smelled of stale air. I opened all the nearby windows and headed for the kitchen. The refrigerator offered nothing edible. My father must have gone out to eat.

I found a pack of dried saimin noodles, boiled water with *dashi*, and had that for lunch. I opened a bottle of red wine, went outside, sat on the outdoor swing, and thought about the things I needed to do.

I held up the safety deposit box key that I'd found in my mother's safe. I unfolded the photograph of the three women in their younger days: my mother, Kiyomi, and the woman with the baby.

On Tokyo time, jetlagged, I couldn't sleep with all these thoughts exploding in my head, but eventually dozed off on the swing from exhaustion and wine.

Loud pounding jolted me awake. The knocking came from the front door.

I glanced at my wristwatch: 7:25 p.m.

At the kitchen sink, I scooped water into my hands and splashed some on my face a few times. The knocking got louder, impatient.

I opened the front door. Two police officers in HPD blue stood in front. The short, chubby local cop held up a piece of paper and shoved it in my face. He had the air of someone who has been on the job too long. One step behind him was a second police officer, younger. She was also local, probably part Portuguese, with wavy brown hair bundled under an HPD cap, a pear-shaped body, and a strong jawline. Standing on the lower porch were three male officers with navy blue jackets with HPD written in white lettering on back. They all looked as if they'd recently graduated from the police academy.

"Are you the owner of this house?" The short, chubby lead cop had his chest out as though compensating for his shortness. He was an Asian guy, maybe local Korean or local Japanese, with small brown eyes and tanned skin.

"My father—" I started, then said, "Yes, I live here."

"I have a search warrant," the lead cop said with attitude.

"Are you kidding me?" Now fully awake, I asked, "What for?"

"We found cocaine in the truck that was impounded at Moanalua Bay." The cop spoke loudly, as though he wanted the neighbors to hear. "Please step aside."

The lead cop signaled the three guys standing in the back to start the search inside. I paced the driveway as strangers invaded our house. I couldn't take it anymore, so I wandered down the street. When I got back thirty minutes later, I went back to pacing the driveway.

After an hour, the lead cop came outside and held up a Ziploc bag. He pointed to the woman officer and asked, "Where'd you find the cocaine?"

"It was it in the freezer. In a Tupperware container under a box of frozen shrimp."

My voice rose at how crazy this was. "No way, my father don't do drugs!"

"It could be yours."

I came a millimeter away from telling him to fuck off, but bit my lower lip. "Think about it. Whoever broke into my father's truck had the garage remote, so whoever it was put the cocaine there."

The short, chubby lead ordered, "We're taking you in to get your blood tested for drugs. We'll match fingerprints as well."

I then did something I would never have done before. I shouted at the police, "Are you fuckin' kidding me? I'd like to talk to my lawyer."

I tried to walk away, but the woman cop came up from behind and held me in place. "Stop, don't resist. If you're innocent, the facts will show that you are."

The lead cop removed his cap and ran a hand over his receding hairline. "Were you drinking?"

"Just a little wine. I just got in from Japan after hearing that my father was missing at sea."

He grunted like he didn't care. "We're doing this for your own good, because you're intoxicated and impaired enough that you may hurt yourself or others."

I knew it was a bunch of crap. Besides searching online or through the Yellow Pages, I didn't know where to look for a lawyer, so I reasonably conceded.

The woman cop followed me around as I locked up the house.

Mr. Kapena stepped from his porch dressed in shorts and T-shirt and scowled at the short, chubby cop. "What's going on here?"

"This does not concern you, Kapena. You got your own problems."

"This is my business." He stepped closer. "She's my neighbor and a good girl. What's the damn charges?"

The woman cop stepped forward. "No charges."

I rubbed both hands over my face. "My father is being set up for using cocaine."

Kapena's jaw dropped. "Your father? Not ever in this lifetime or the next would he do that."

By the time a taxi brought me back home, the wind had picked up.

Mr. Kapena was waiting on his porch. He stood and cried out, "Sorry, I couldn't pick you up at the station. My driver's license was taken away from me. They said I pressed the gas when parking at Walmart when I should have pressed the brakes. The DMV noted that I could be a danger to society. Thirty years on the police force and now I'm a danger to society."

"No problem, Mr. Kapena." Anticipating his next question, I said, "They tested me for drugs, and of course I was clean. They also took fingerprints from the drug packets. They didn't find my father's or my prints on it."

His expression went sharp. I could see him for what he was— a respected law enforcement officer.

"What a day," I said, and couldn't believe this was happening.

Mr. Kapena called out, "Goodnight, Gena. Everything will be okay. If I can do anything to help don't hesitate asking, okay?"

"I will." I smiled at his offer. "Goodnight, Mr. Kapena."

I showered and drank two beers. Once again, I couldn't sleep, and stared up at the ceiling, listening to the patter of raindrops on the roof. I cringed at the potential consequences of bad weather and spoke to the sky. "Please stop raining, please . . ."

Between patters of rain, a squeak came from outside. The same sound as when my dad swung back and forth on the swing.

"Dad?" I slipped out the backdoor. Bigger drops started falling, darkening the concrete by the swing. The nearby streetlight dimly illuminated the area.

The empty swing moved back and forth. Then I saw it. I cautiously surveyed the bushes in the darkness and twisted back toward the house, wondering if I should get my father's gun. I changed my mind and walked over to the swing.

I had last seen it around my mother's neck when she was alive. The locket I gave her dangled from the swing; a piece of paper was folded and stuck into the chain-link.

I held the paper up in the dim light. On it was a phone number.

19

The girl and boy in the locket had been too young when the photograph was taken, so Aom focused on the man.

Using the facial recognition program that Randy, the waiter, had supplied, and which had cost her $200, she found three people on social media that sort of looked like the man in the picture after using a computer aging process.

Of the three possible men, two were from Hawaii. One lived in an area called Kaneohe and another in Hawaii Kai.

Aom caught a taxi to the address in Kaneohe and waited under a plumeria tree around the side of the man's house. Within half an hour, a blue-and-white police car arrived on the scene. One police officer asked her what she was doing hanging around this subdivision. Because she didn't know what a subdivision was, she didn't respond.

The policeman spoke with authority. "We got a call from someone. Said you've been hanging around back here, and that's not your house."

She feigned ignorance. "I am from Thailand and shopping for potential real estate properties in this area."

A man and his wife drove up to the house in a black Chevy

van, and four kids piled out. If this was the same man from the facial recognition program, he had let himself go, and was now overweight. He looked to be in his thirties, maybe remarried, because the kids looked different from the ones in the locket. This was not the guy.

The other policeman said, "My wife is a real estate agent." And he handed Aom a business card.

Once back at her apartment, Aom chuckled, thinking that she had turned into a pretty good actor. She threw the business card into the trash.

The second man from the facial recognition program was in the military and stationed at Pearl Harbor. She met many military guys as a stripper and had asked around the club if they recognized this guy, showing them the man's aged photograph. They'd laughed at her and told her that there are a few thousand men at Pearl Harbor.

She caught another taxi to Hawaii Kai and waited across the street from the house. A neighbor must have called the police again, because another blue-and-white drove up to her and asked, "What are you doing here?"

Aom repeated the same reason, but this time neither officer gave her a real estate business card. She promised the police that she would be leaving soon and mentioned that she'd called a taxi because she wanted to check out another property closer to town.

When the police left, Aom decided to talk to the man sitting on the wooden porch staring at the horizon.

She strolled up the concrete walkway. "Excuse me."

The man was maybe in his late sixties and gave her a blank stare. "What do you want?"

"Will the man who lives in that house be home soon?" Aom pointed next door.

"Who's asking?"

"I am a real estate agent and shopping for property for my

client. That house is perfect for what my client is looking for. They are a young couple with two lovely children."

The man was grouchy. "If you're a real estate agent then where's your damn real estate car?"

She looked down at the cracked walkway leading up to his house and then up at him, "You are right. The reason why is that I am lost."

"You're also a liar," he scoffed, his brow furrowed. "Now get the hell out of here before I call the boys back and have them cuff you and take you downtown."

As she was about to leave, a white SUV pulled into the driveway next door. A woman in her early twenties hugged the driver. Aom thought they were lesbians saying goodbye.

Aom studied the young woman. She had a long nose, thin face, sharp jaw, and the skin tone of a mixed *farang*, a white person in Thailand. She noted that the girl in the locket was also of mixed race, but in this case her father was farang and mother *yeepoon,* Japanese.

The woman's lesbian partner drove away.

Knowing she needed to flee the area or the grouchy old man would likely call the police, she pretended to walk down the road, then doubled back. She jumped over a low rock wall and maneuvered through thick bushes with branches that scratched her skin. At about a hundred meters away, she hunkered behind a cluster of short guava trees.

It was early evening and she was hungry, so she munched on three candy bars while waiting. The girl exited the house, sat on the swing, stared at the horizon, and drank an entire bottle of wine.

Aom cursed her bad luck in having to rely on the actions of an alcoholic. She had lived through countless nights when her father was blind drunk on Thai whisky. Aom dozed off watching the girl sleep. Luckily Hawaii didn't have the same mosquito problem as

Thailand or she'd have been covered in red welts and scratching her skin raw.

She awoke when two police cars drove up to the house. Two hours passed before the police loaded the girl into one of the blue-and-white cars and drove away. Aom again cursed her bad luck. The girl was not only an alcoholic, but also a criminal.

"What now?" Because this was her only lead, she chose to stick it out. Her luck got even worse as it began to rain.

Her patience paid off when a taxi brought the girl back. The grouchy neighbor talked with her for a while then left. Without seeing the man, she would never know for sure if this was the house, but she decided to take a chance.

When the house lights went out, Aom wrote her cell phone number on a piece of paper, snuck to the back of the house, hung the locket on the swing, and slid the piece of paper between the links in the chain that held the swing. She pushed the swing back and forth a few times and headed for the cover of trees.

Dressed in shorts and a sweater, the girl exited the house, stared at the locket, and twisted her head around. She lifted the locket from the swing and read the note. Like a magician making things appear from nowhere, she pulled a phone from her sweater pocket and punched in the number.

Aom didn't want to talk to the girl yet, so she didn't answer; instead, she walked to the bottom of the hill by streetlight. She phoned the same taxi company that dropped her off earlier and headed for Club Om.

With the club catering to yakuza, she had to tread carefully. Like the Englishman would have warned her, "You're going into the belly of the beast."

There were two reasons why Aom had decided to work at Club Om. For one, she needed money fast, and the men there were richer and tipped better. Additionally, fuckin' Randy and his friend had ripped her off by selling her facial recognition software that she could have found for free on the Internet. He seemed like the type of guy who would sell her out if he knew she was on the run.

Halfway through the night and between customers, Aom glanced at her phone—five messages.

She listened to her voicemail: "I'm calling about the locket. Please call as soon as you can." The other three messages said the same thing, with slight variations. In the last message, the girl sounded like she was on the edge of a meltdown. "You had my mother's locket. You must have seen what happened to her in Japan. Please, please, call me."

Aom walked to the water's edge, where fishing boats moored for the night and prepared to cast off before sunrise to catch the prized yellow fin tuna. She took a deep breath, smelled the salty air, and punched redial.

"Hello," a voice answered urgently.

"Is the locket yours?"

"It was my mother's," the girl said with sadness. "How did you get it? Did you witness what happened to her?"

"Yes," Aom replied. "I saw everything. Till this day I wish I had not, but Buddha gives us a path and we do not have a choice."

"Will you come with me to the police and report what you witnessed?"

Aom had prepared for the question. "I fear the police. They are not honest. I will disappear like many others who tell the truth."

"What's your name?"

"I cannot tell you that." There was a long pause before she asked, "Was mama-Em your mother?"

"Yes." Her voice was full of hurt. "I went to Japan but no one will help me. Even the police."

"Eh . . . like I said, I trust no one."

"Why not come forward?" the girl persisted desperately. "You were in Japan and now you're here in Hawaii. It seems like you are seeking justice, like I seek justice."

"Your mother was good to me." The sounds of lapping waves under the wooden docks in the background could give away her location. "This is the only way I know how to repay her."

"Where are you from?"

She didn't answer.

"Okay, sorry, I'm asking too much."

Aom decided to come clean about being a witness. "I did not see who the killer was but I will never forget the tattoo on the forearm."

"Tattoo." She expressed disappointment, but bounced back. "What kind of tattoo?"

"It was sort of circular—black on light skin. The dark part looked like four tadpoles swimming in a counterclockwise circle, and maybe formed the outline of one of those ninja throwing stars."

"*Shuriken.*"

"If you say so."

"Can you draw it out and send it to me?"

"Let me think about it." She paused then added, "And it is a *she.*"

"What?" A voice in shock. "The killer was a woman?"

"That is what I saw." Aom glanced at her watch, needing to hurry back into the club to make money. "I am risking a lot to give you the locket."

"Risking how?" The voice grew increasingly desperate, seemingly not wanting Aom to hang up. "I can get you help."

Aom knew that with Tamura hunting her, being seen openly in public or engaging with police would make her an immediate target.

"I must go." Aom felt herself bending with empathy toward

mama-Em's daughter. If she talked longer, she would give in to her wishes.

"No wait." The girl's voice rose. "Why don't—"

Aom ended the call before she could finish. A few seconds later, her phone chirped, but she turned it off.

She stood on the dock listening to the lapping waves and soaking in the quiet of the night as she nodded to herself—karma fulfilled.

20

The TV news kept flashing a photograph of my father. The Coast Guard continued the search, but they were delayed due to bad weather, rough seas, and strong winds.

I cringed when I overheard a member of the search team say, "Searching for a one-man canoe in the ocean is like looking for a green contact lens on an eighteen-hole golf course."

An occasional missing boat or person at sea was nothing new in Hawaii because of its close attachment to commercial and sports fishing, kayaking, canoeing, surfing, scuba or skin diving, and anything else involving the ocean. The longer it took to find my dad, the more the chances of doing so diminished.

I had failed to convince the woman with the locket to come forward as a witness to my mother's murder. Her trembling voice had indicated that she was terrified. But scared of what, of whom?

I focused on the guy from the abandoned building talking about a video, saying that my mother had been blackmailing someone very powerful. I refused to believe that Mom would have done that; that was not the person I had known all my life. But I needed the video as a bargaining chip.

Was the guy from the warehouse one of Tamura's henchmen? Or maybe from another yakuza organization in competition with Tamura?

All this kept going through my head when my phone buzzed.

"Ms. Hunter." Lau's voice was steady and calm. "The Coast Guard received a radio call from a long-line fishing vessel that a one-man canoe was found about two hundred miles northeast of Kauai."

I catapulted off the sofa. "Was my dad with the canoe?"

"Sorry, but no," he replied. "The canoe is badly battered from the elements. The crew of the fishing boat hauled it on board, but they're unable to return until they meet their quota of fish. The Coast Guard will be sending a vessel to meet them and haul the canoe to shore."

"When do you expect it to arrive on land?"

"I'd say in a day or two?"

"Why so long?"

Lau sighed as though it were out of his hands. "It's a big ocean and their resources are limited."

"What if I can get help?" I thought of Josh Venezuela.

"What kind of help?"

"I may be able to get the Navy to help."

Silence. "Well, if you can do that then sure, do it."

I hung up, then called Josh. I explained to him what Lau had told me. Josh said he would see what he could do.

Forty-five minutes later my phone buzzed. "Gena?"

I held my breath. "Yes, Josh."

"My commandin' officer was able to schedule a chopper to retrieve the canoe." He cleared his throat. "Anyway, I'll work with the Coast Guard and get the coordinates. We should be able to get the canoe back on land by the end of today."

"Thank you, Josh."

I hung up. The numbers on my phone read 10:43.

At 1:06 p.m., Josh called back. "Hi Gena. A Sea Hawk heli-copter is airborne with the canoe latched to its belly. They're takin' it to the Coast Guard station on Sand Island. I already phoned Lau and he's headin' there now."

With Lau's help, I got my father's impounded truck back. The only damage was to the busted driver's side window. I found an empty box in the garage from an Amazon delivery and, using a utility knife, cut a large piece of cardboard to cover the widow, securing it with duct tape.

I jumped in the Tundra and arrived at the Coast Guard Station on Sand Island an hour after hanging up with Josh.

I parked outside the fenced-off area across the street from the station and walked to the security gate. The young, skinny guard stepped forward. He wore a vest over a light-blue short-sleeved shirt with epaulets, blue wool pants, and a matching blue baseball cap. The young guard had a sidearm and appeared prepared to use it if he had to.

To the right was a grassy area next to the building. Four men gathered around a canoe; frowns etched on their serious faces. Three wore the standard blue of the Coast Guard.

One guy knelt next to the battered canoe. I assumed he was Detective Lau. He wore a printed, dark green aloha shirt, black pants, and black shoes. I expected a man in his forties, instead he was mid-thirties with a military-style haircut. The rhythm of his voice had been distinct and careful on the phone. Obviously raised in Hawaii, Lau occasionally slipped into pidgin English when he spoke. He was a nice-looking man and had a runner's physique, with well-toned, stringy muscles.

Security stopped me at the gate.

I shouted to Detective Lau. He looked up. I waved to him. Lau stood up and talked to a man in uniform standing behind him. He walked toward me and the guard shack.

Lau said to the guard, "Your station commander said to let this woman through."

He nodded. I followed Lau to the canoe.

"Is this your father's?" Lau asked, hope rising in his voice.

I knelt down and touched the slim, molded carbon-fiber hull. "It is his canoe. I've never seen it this beaten up before."

Lau spoke, loud enough so everyone could hear. "I don't think we'll get any type of forensics data. The ocean washed everything clean."

Everyone nodded in unison.

Lau pointed to the front of the canoe and asked me, "Did your father always attach a leash from the canoe to himself?" He pinched the cut leash between his fingers.

"Always." I sighed, aware of the reality of the trouble my father was in. Dazed at the discovery, I said, "He'd strap the leash to his ankle and the other end he'd clamp to the front. So, if he should *huli*—" I mimed tipping over. "My dad always tried to anticipate the unpredictable."

Dad had often lectured me about the ocean currents being extremely fast and powerful. Even if a paddler were an Olympic swimmer, the chance of catching up with the canoe after detaching from it was slim.

Lau pointed at the right corner of the canoe, where a deep gash marked with blue paint had penetrated the canoe's shell.

"Was this on the canoe before he went out?"

I knelt and examined the damage. It looked like it had been made by the claw of a raptor from one of the Jurassic Park movies. "My father was very meticulous about maintaining his equipment. If this had been here before he went out to sea, he would have repaired it. This must have happened on the ocean."

Lau squinted, and the lines in his forehead loosened, brushy brows arching upward. He turned to the commander, who looked to be in his late forties with sun-bleached short hair. I couldn't hear their discussion, but the man nodded and strolled into the building.

Lau faced me. "The commander will dispatch the fishing boat and ask if their vessel may have caused the gash."

Two minutes later Lau's phone rang. He listened, then said to everyone, "The fishing boat's captain said that the gash was already there when they pulled it from the ocean."

The man who was kneeling next to the canoe twisted upward. "It could be from floating debris? There's a lot of junk out there."

"That's a possibility," Lau replied, but with reluctance.

"Something bad happened to him that doesn't involve nature," I mumbled to no one in particular.

"Foul play?" Lau shifted closer. "What makes you think . . . Did he receive any threats? What about enemies, did he have any that you know of?"

"I don't know, Detective. Most people will go through life and eventually die of natural causes. The cut ankle leash on my father's canoe tells me that there was foul play involved. I just got back from Japan where my mother was murdered. The police claim it was a random robbery, but I don't buy it. Now my father, who's an expert ocean guy, is missing at sea."

I still refused to give up hope. Dad had to be alive. Perhaps he'd been able to latch on to floating sea debris. Or maybe by chance he'd drifted onto one of the weather buoys that surrounded the islands. These buoys were strategically located five to ten miles from shore. They measured a range of weather variables such as wave height and direction, and wind speed and gust. My dad could then damage the communication system so someone would have to eventually investigate.

But with his battered canoe in front of me, reality struck me like a freight train: no one could survive in the ocean without a floatation device.

No one. Not even John Hunter.

I tried convincing Lau that they needed to find the boat that caused the gash in my father's canoe. He didn't know how to respond, so said, "Do you know what you're requesting is—"

"Nuts." I finished his sentence. "If my father was involved in foul play, the vessel or boat that caused the gash might be the answer."

Lau rolled his head as though working a kink out of his neck. "I'll be frank with you, Gena. HPD do not have the manpower to search every boat on this island and compare paint fragments with your father's canoe. Plus, we still haven't ruled out that ocean debris may have caused the gash."

"So that's it"—my voice hardened in desperation— "my father is missing at sea and you'll do nothing but say . . ."

Lau pulled out his phone and scrolled his directory. "Here's the number for a private investigator that may be able to help."

I punched the number into my phone.

Lau took his phone back. "His name is Jack Gilman. He's not cheap, but he's good at finding things that don't want to be found."

While driving home from Sand Island, I called the private investigator to get a cost estimate and time frame. The man had the raspy voice of an ex-smoker. "I need ten thousand in advance plus expenses."

"To look for a boat on the island?"

"My price is non-negotiable."

"Let me think about it," I said, but was already shaking my head. I wasn't hiring him to find lost treasure from World War II.

I pulled into the driveway and waved to Mr. Kapena sitting on his porch. He flagged me over. From the clarity in his eyes, I sensed he was himself. His large Akita jumped on me, tail wagging, tongue lopping out the side of his mouth.

Mr. Kapena shouted, "Liko, down!" The dog listened and crouched to the side.

I sat on the wooden bench and patted Liko's large head.

"I forgot to thank you for the fish." Mr. Kapena chuckled. "Your giant friend scared the shit out of me when he knocked on my door. I was about to shoot him, until he showed me the kumu he brought from Chinatown."

"You're welcome, Mr. Kapena." I leaned back on the wooden bench. "When things settle down, I'll get to Chinatown again and pick you up some fresh *uku* or *onaga*."

Kapena stared out at the horizon. "You're a good person, Gena. When I was a cop, I started to lose hope in the goodness of human beings after investigating endless beatings, rapes, murders . . ."

"You're a good person too, Mr. Kapena."

He frowned as though only now remembering something important. "I'm sorry for what happened to your mother in Japan. I wrote it down somewhere to remind me to tell you that, but I seemed to have misplaced the note."

I smiled at him. "Thank you, Mr. Kapena. When my mother

was living with us, she always said to me, 'Mr. and Mrs. Kapena are the nicest people.'"

The neighbors had been curious about what happened to my mother, and the rumors were many: She left because she'd had an affair with a younger man. She left because she hit the lottery and bought a hot spring *onsen*. No one really knew the truth, because neither my dad nor I talked about it openly with anybody.

Mr. Kapena kept studying me. He had known me nearly my entire life, dropped candy in my bucket every Halloween, bought something for whatever school fundraiser I was involved in, and twice a week I trained with him and his two sons in Wing Chun kung fu in his garage.

He stared as though wanting to ask me a question.

"Are things okay, Mr. Kapena?"

He looked down into his hands and cleared his throat. "I know that I go in and out with this dementia thing, but I'd like to help you if I can."

I would have instantly accepted the offer from the *old* Mr. Kapena, but wondered if now he would be more of a liability than an asset. I promised myself one thing though: that I would never hurt his feelings no matter what.

Sitting next to him on the wooden bench, I talked about my experience in Japan and my father missing at sea. I talked about working in the mizu shobai business trying to find information about my mother's death. We chatted about the abandoned building, the guy wanting a video, and the suspicion of yakuza involvement—specifically Hideo Tamura. I got into as much detail as I could, and that went on for about forty minutes. Mr. Kapena didn't say a word, just listened and took everything in like absorbing clues to a case.

"Yakuza, yakuza, yakuza." He spoke the word as though it were a profanity. "At the end of the twentieth century, the yakuza owned properties in most of the world's major trade and resort centers. Because millions of Japanese tourists visited here and spent billions, Hawaii became a target. By the early seventies, yakuza thugs were seen sunning themselves, showing their full-body tattoos on the beaches of Waikiki. They then got into gunrunning, gambling, and drugs here. But the big money was in shopping malls and golf courses."

"Golf courses?"

"Yep. Billions poured into buying and developing golf courses for two reasons. One, because it was a big moneymaker, and two, it was a great way to launder money."

"I didn't know that. I just thought Japanese people liked to golf."

Mr. Kapena laughed. "Yeah, that too. At the time, the Japanese had money to burn. Housewives in Nara would sip a $500 cup of coffee sprinkled with gold dust, and businessmen spent tens of thousands of dollars on Tokyo's flashy nightlife."

"Here's a story I heard from my mom," I interjected. "Back in the day, customers would purchase a small cut diamond and place it into the bottom of a champagne glass. The hostess would then chug the champagne and diamond together. To retrieve the diamond, the hostess had to wait until it passed through her, standing by the toilet with a screen filter. I know it sounds gross, until she shared the secret. It was a trick. With practice, the hostess would skillfully slip the diamond under her tongue before swallowing the champagne."

Mr. Kapena's face soured. "Yep, it was pure extravagance back then. What gets me is the way the yakuza tried to legitima-tize what they did by fashioning themselves in line with the ancient samurai's ideal of *giri,* or duty, and *ninjo,* or social obliga-tion. What a bunch of crap. It came down to pure extortion, because it's the yakuza's biggest moneymaker, and a favorite target was the mizu shobai."

I thought of Mom's tiny bar and her possibly being extorted, but at this point I wanted to change the topic. "Can I ask you a personal question?"

He squinted and nodded.

"What happened between you and the yakuza?"

"Kenji Kusaka," he moaned with disgust. "I was hot on the trail of this porn slime-ball. Not only does he make sicko movies, but he also owns a high-end hostess club called Om, a few brothels disguised as massage parlors, as well as adult video stores."

I thought of Lani and how she spoke negatively about Club Om.

"I pursued the arrest of Kusaka because the shit-face was involved in human trafficking."

Kapena rubbed his eyes with both hands. There seemed to be a battle going on inside of him, as though—if at all possible—he was holding his dementia at bay.

With his eyes still clear, he continued, "Through deception and false promises, he would lure young women into porn. He'd advertise modeling jobs with a $5,000 cash payment, but they were duped into performing sexual acts captured on video for eternity. Some women were pressured into signing documents without reviewing them and then they were threatened with legal action if they failed to comply. These were mainly local and mainland girls. He then went further and trafficked girls from Thailand, Myanmar, Cambodia, and Laos, and confiscated their passports until they paid off what they owed, which took three to four times longer to repay than expected."

Stunned to hear anything like this had ever happened in Hawaii, I couldn't stomach the cruelty with which one human being could treat another.

"The crime was conspiracy to commit sex trafficking by force, fraud and coercion." His hand formed a fist. "On several occasions, women were raped, and several more were sexually assaulted and abused."

I decided to tiptoe around the subject. "They say you were framed."

"My wife was in the fourth stage of breast cancer, and I received a search warrant at the door from HPD." Kapena patted the top of Liko's head. "It was the same snob that came to your house with the warrant. Anyway, to make a long story short, the police found $50,000 in a place where I would never hide $50,000."

Where? The question must have been written on my face.

"In the toilet tank," he said. "That would be the first place I would look if I did a search."

"You were set up."

"I was accused of being on the take for the yakuza porn industry." His faced filled with loathing. "The prosecuting attorney had documents, bank accounts and whatnot as evidence. I'd never seen these documents before in my life, so I decided to fight the false accusations, but I . . ." He huffed out a breath.

I placed a hand on his.

"But then I get a readout of my wife's cardiac data in the mail. Someone drew a red horizontal line where the usual heartbeat should be. My wife was in the hospital fighting for her life, and the yakuza had someone in the hospital."

I couldn't believe what I was hearing.

"In the mail, someone sent pictures of my grandchildren playing in the front yard at their home in Washington State. And another picture of my second boy's children in California . . ." He paused, swallowed, and added, "They knew where my two boys and their families lived."

"So you retired."

"I retired," he spat out, then said, "Everything on the investigation of Kusaka came to a halt."

I trusted Mr. Kapena, and he would be the perfect person to help me, but his dementia was too unpredictable.

"I observed Tamura rise in power in the yakuza as the authorities stood by helplessly." Mr. Kapena's nostrils flared with anger. "I heard he's a sick fuck. He likes girls, young girls, and does perverted things to them."

I cringed to think that my mother had associated with such a person.

"Like many rich and powerful people, they fear their mortality." He shook his head as though unable to comprehend human stupidity. "And get this—he visited this place called Huangshan, or the Yellow Mountain in the southern Anhui province in eastern China for three months to seek guidance from a Taoist priest about the secrets of immortality. Rumors say he paid the priest a million dollars."

"To battle time?" I asked with skepticism.

"Yep, the guy's out there."

If Tamura had instigated all this mayhem in my life, then maybe Mr. Kapena would have an idea on how I could defeat him if I needed to, so I asked, "Does he have a weakness that can be exploited?"

He thought for a few seconds. "There's an election for a new Attorney General happening in a few days. Tamara has pulled out all the stops in trying to rig the election, but the new guy has a very good chance of winning."

I recalled the people in front of McDonald's holding election posters for Kazuo Hayashida. "What does this got to—"

"If this man wins the election, Tamura could go to jail and lose all of his power as an oyabun."

"I would think that people would be positioning themselves to take his place."

"You got that right," he answered. "Unless the reign is handed over to someone by Tamura himself. But he's so self-centered that he would never do that."

A silence fell over us, he then glanced at my house. "A woman—she looked Indonesian, or Thai, or something like that—she was watching your house. She said she was looking for real estate, then she lied further and said she was lost."

I thought about the locket I found on the swing. "I think I know who it was. What'd she look like?"

"She was very beautiful—very." Mr. Kapena paused a few beats and fingered his chin. "On the day your father was reported missing, the garage door accordioned up and his truck drove in. It was about two or three in the afternoon."

"That can't be, because his friend said he trained from sunrise to sunset." Things weren't adding up. "Maybe that's when the drugs were planted."

"Can I take a look inside your house?" Mr. Kapena stood from the wooden bench.

I scanned his eyes. They were still clear. "Sure, but why do—"

He lifted a hand and I shut up.

We walked over to my house and I opened the front door. He shuffled past and motioned for me to sit on the sofa. He clicked the remote, turning on the TV.

There was a rerun of the A-Team movie playing, and the sounds that Mr. Kapena made as he moved from one room to the next were drowned by bombs going off and Hannibal Smith and the rest of the characters playing their parts.

After an hour, Mr. Kapena lifted the notepad and pen by the landline and shifted to where I was sitting on the sofa. He wrote: "Your house is bugged."

My eyes sprung open. He shushed me with a finger to his lips.

22

M y paranoia-meter was pegging to the stratosphere. I thought back on things I'd done, things I'd said. Who would do such a thing? Was I being watched too? Electronics stores sold those miniature cameras online, which anyone could buy.

I had to know. I led Mr. Kapena outside to the curb and whispered, "Are we far enough away that we can't be heard?"

He nodded. His gaze wandered the neighborhood as if someone might be watching us.

"Was there video too?" I was trying to remember the many times I'd walked around naked, at times having had too much to drink and talking to myself.

"No video," he replied. "I found one bug in the kitchen, hidden behind the faceplate of the landline outlet. Another was in the living room behind the TV. You may not like this, but the last was in your bedroom."

I thought about the cops with the search warrant. "Why didn't the police find the bugs?"

"Probably because the devices blended in with the furnishing and tough to spot if you're not looking for them. I think the searchers were also rookies and instructed to look for drugs."

My hands shook with rage knowing I had been violated. I spun to the front door, about to rush into the house and tear all the bugs out, when Mr. Kapena grabbed my wrist. "Where you going?"

"Where else?" My face was burning mad. "I'm going to—"

"And what?"

"Soak them in gasoline and watch them burn."

He shook his head and grimaced. "The person who planted them don't know we know. We can use it to our advantage."

"How?"

"Don't know right now. But I'll know when the opportunity arises. The important thing is you act like everything is normal. Just be aware you're being listened to."

"Do you think whoever did this is also watching my house?"

"Quite possibly, but I don't think all the time, or else your neighborhood watch would have reported it to the police, but then again, you got all those bushes on the sloping land next to your property. You see the road down there?" He pointed to a part of the subdivision in the valley. "The person who installed the bugs could park a van or car on that road. Maybe put the hood up or fake a flat tire and eavesdrop on you. Or, there might be a recording instrument that automatically downloads whatever's on the devices."

"So the range isn't too far?"

"I'd max it at three hundred meters because you're high up and in a clear line of sight."

"I like to see them."

I followed Mr. Kapena into the kitchen. He pointed to the landline outlet. He wrote on a pad of paper: *Power supply is the telephone line current, no battery needed.*

He led me into the living room and pointed behind the television and the mess of wires that cluttered the floor and wrote on the pad: *Power supplied by the AC power.*

We headed for my bedroom. He walked to my desk and pointed at a decorated pen-and-pencil holder made from a Campbell soup can when I was in preschool. He fingered one pen. Now paying attention, I knew that pen wasn't mine. Mr. Kapena wrote on the pad: *Long alkaline battery life, maybe forty to fifty hours.*

We went back outside. I paced in front of him. "I don't feel comfortable with someone listening . . ."

"You cannot change your daily pattern, or the person will know."

I realized that I'd talked to the girl who'd witnessed my mother's murder in my bedroom. What did I say out loud? Did I place her in danger? She hadn't given her name or said where I could find her. The girl identified the killer as a *she* and emphasized a tattoo.

If not for Mr. Kapena, I wouldn't have known that my privacy was being violated. I trusted him. I needed his help.

"If your offer is still open, Mr. Kapena, I'd like your help finding a boat that could have gashed my father's canoe."

He rubbed his chin. "You know about my dementia, and you still want my help?"

"I trust you more than anybody."

"Actually, that sounds easy enough." He was already moving. "Let's go."

"Now?"

"I think there are more boats parked in garages than at harbor docks."

I threw out what was on my mind. "If there's a killer—and if he's yakuza—then the boat more than likely was a rental."

Mr. Kapena grinned. "Maybe you should take up police work."

I was not about to tell him that I'd dropped out of school twice.

"I suggest we check out the obvious places first," he said, energized and back on the hunt. "Ala Wai Boat Harbor and Kewalo Basin."

I drove us into Waikiki by way of Diamond Head Road, then along Ala Wai Boulevard, with the wide canal flat and glassy on the right. The largest small boat and yacht harbor in Hawaii, it accommodated about seven hundred berths. Situated at the mouth of the Ala Wai Canal, between Waikiki and downtown Honolulu, sailing masts filled the skyline.

Lucky for us, most of the vessels were white. I parked close to the shoreline in a metered stall. We decided to split up and cover more ground.

Mr. Kapena pointed. "You go that way and cover from there to there." He twisted his finger in the other direction. "I'll go that way."

I weaved from one dock to another to another, the sun beating down on my neck. I wished I'd brought a hat. My phone buzzed thirty minutes later.

"Hey Gena, I found a seventeen-foot Boston Whaler." His excitement burst from the tiny speakers. "The hull is blue and it looks like it's a little damaged."

"How do I find you?"

"Use the Prince Hotel as a guide. Stay Ewa of the building. It's about . . . one, two, three . . . four. Fourth row Ewa of the Prince."

I was sweating when I reached him. Mr. Kapena pointed to a boat low in the water, sandwiched between two large yachts.

"Come look at this." He led me to the front of the boat.

I dropped to my stomach on the hot concrete walkway and examined the damage closer. I studied the color of the boat, comparing it in my mind to that of the gash.

My voice echoed between the boat's hull and the stanchioned concrete docks. "This might be it, Mr. Kapena."

He didn't answer. He started to wander, walking to the front entrance of the Prince Hotel.

"Mr. Kapena." I shifted toward him, not sure how he'd react. "Where are you going?"

"Huh?" His eyes looked less clear than before and stared blankly at me. He started to hum a tune that I didn't recognize, a local contemporary Hawaiian song.

"Are you okay?"

He straightened his posture and shimmied his shoulders. "I'm good, Gena. I'm good."

I called the main office of the Department of Land and Natural Resources because I knew that this was their *kuleana,* their area of responsibility. A woman gave me the owner's name. Ralph Martinez owned a fishing supply store and boat rental business located in Kakaako, about ten-minute drive away.

Late afternoon, I parked in front of the small fishing supply store. The sign on the door was flipped to CLOSED. I strolled into the shop next door, a dry cleaner full of racks of freshly pressed shirts and blouses.

Behind a waist-high counter, a young, gum-chewing girl smiled at me. "Can I help you?" I glanced at the nametag: Erin.

As she continued clacking on the computer keyboard in front of her, I said, "Hi Erin. Who's the owner of the shop next door?"

She stopped and gave me her full attention. "You mean the bald middle-aged guy who smells of booze in the morning?"

"I guess."

"That guy thinks he's Mr. Romeo." Erin placed a finger in her mouth and pretended to vomit. "Jerk keeps hitting on me. I love this part-time job, but he makes me want to barf and quit this job just to get away from him."

"What time does his shop open?"

"It should be open by now. He's usually open six days a week, but it's been closed for the past few days."

I thanked Erin and went outside to join Mr. Kapena.

He had slipped behind the closed shop and said, as I approached, "Something's definitely wrong. The back door is closed and I don't want to mess up the crime scene if it comes to that."

"Crime scene?"

"There's a smell I've never gotten used to." Before I could ask, he answered, "Death. The smell is very faint, probably because the AC is set to the max to keep the place cold as a refrigerator."

Mr. Kapena dialed 911. Within five minutes, a squad car pulled up in front of the building. Mr. Kapena identified himself as a retired police officer and explained to the two cops what he suspected. "The front and back doors are locked. I used a towel so as not to leave my fingerprints."

The moment the police got the back door open, the scent went beyond a stench. It smacked my brain like nothing I'd ever smelled before in my life. The closest thing I could think of was when I'd run into a cow carcass while hiking in the mountains. The carcass had been covered with a black sheet. When I got closer, I realized it was a layer of flies. Underneath, thousands of white maggots wriggled.

More cops arrived and soon began questioning us. Many of the older cops remembered Mr. Kapena respectfully. One told him that he'd gotten a raw deal.

Detective Lau arrived and winked. "I shouldn't have doubted you."

I shrugged, no big deal.

After I described the location of the blue boat, Lau said he would compare the paint with that from my father's canoe.

Lau now looked as though he'd lost his best friend. "I got bad news, Gena. The authorities have called off the search. It was a tough decision and the debate went back and forth, but without a floatation device . . ."

"You can't—" But then I looked down at the pavement and submitted. "I do want to thank you for all you did."

Lau turned and headed for his car.

Hearing that they'd stopped the search for my dad filled me with the same hollowed-out emptiness that I'd felt when my brother died just tens of feet away from me as I helplessly looked on.

I REMEMBERED how the hiking trail had branched left, right, and straight ahead. My kid brother's warning continuously echoed in my head. *Sugi-sugi-obake.* David had pointed to the left of the trail.

Immersed in learning to work my new damn phone, I half-heartedly shook my head and told him to take the left trail. My brother cried out, but I wasn't listening. Half of me kept concentrating on my phone and other half was trying not to step in ankle-deep mud. I'd taken the right leg of the trail. We ended up in different locations. I'd stood on the edge of a cliff and watched him below, kneeling on the side of a trickling stream, stirring the pond surface trying to corner tiny fish.

I yelled at him, "What are you doing down there?"

He looked up and shouted back, "You told me to go this way."

We heard the heavy rumble at the same time. David quickly stood up. I read the fright in his eyes. I jumped up and down, screaming at him to run, but David stood frozen. He pivoted and stared at a mountainous wave crashing directly toward him. His little body disappeared, swooped away with the wall of raging water. The river rose twenty feet and continued to rumble downstream like a freight train out of control.

Everyone on the North Shore came out to search for his body. Some people suggested that he had been carried out to sea. Others said he might be buried under eight feet of mud. The dogs had sniffed along the river, but found nothing.

I cried for days. My father and mother stopped talking to each other for three weeks, until the fourth week when, without preamble, they rushed into each other's arms and cried together. On the third day of that fourth week, David would have turned five years old.

I didn't deserve their hugs. With my head down, I'd started for the front door, but Mom waved for me to join them. Our grieving family cried together until long shadows slid across the terrazzo floor.

My mother eventually told me that her moving back to Japan was not because of David's death. But no matter how much I'd wanted to believe her, I couldn't after seeing the pain in her eyes, the pain in her movements. The hollowness, the emptiness, felt like my soul had been ripped out of me.

Had I made the wrong decision in remaining in Japan to hunt for a killer? I could have simply accepted everything I was told as fact, even though deep down I'd known it wasn't true. Perhaps it had been a gut feeling, or maybe pure logic, that convinced me that the desperation to acquire the video would go beyond continental borders.

Night had fallen by the time we were finished with the police. Horrified that the investigation into the gash on my father's canoe had led to a dead body, I felt terror in my bones that people were dying around me.

Mr. Kapena sat silently in the passenger seat. He had that dementia-distant stare. I tapped him on the arm. "We're home."

He turned to me; his eyes were cloudy. I ushered him to his house.

Liko barked from the porch. Leashed to the railing, his tail whipped back and forth as we strolled up the walkway. The dog quickly calmed and whimpered after sniffing Mr. Kapena's hand, sensing his owner's condition.

"Thank you, Mr. Kapena." I guided him into the house. I patted the large dog on the head. "Take care of your friend, Liko."

Mr. Kapena shut the door behind him without saying a word.

23

I woke up knowing that no one was searching for my dad.

Detective Lau had called last night. He confirmed that the paint on the Boston Whaler matched that found on my father's canoe. The death of the shop owner solidified suspicions of foul play as the reason my dad was missing at sea.

Breakfast. I thought about skipping it again like I had the past two mornings, but by midday I couldn't lift a five-pound dumbbell. I ate a bowl of oatmeal mixed with sliced banana and apple when I heard pounding drifting from Mr. Kapena's garage.

I recognized the sound, and so put on a pair of gray sweatpants, pulled a large T-shirt over a sports bra, and slipped on a pair of Nike running shoes.

I hurried over to my neighbor's house and peeked in from the side door of the garage. Mr. Kapena's tank top was soaked with sweat, his face intense and focused. The heavy punching bag dangled from the large beam that stretched across the two-car garage. Sixty-seven years old, Mr. Kapena still hammered the heavy bag with loud, powerful punches and kicks.

I cleared my throat to get his attention. He turned and said,

"Morning Gena, I thought I'd get some sweat going and sharpen some of my aging skills."

"Man, Mr. Kapena, I could hear your blows from the kitchen. I thought your house was about to collapse."

He chuckled. "When I first installed this heavy bag on that beam, the house shook like crazy. One day my wife rushed downstairs screaming, signaling for me to stop. When I asked her why, she said that the kitchen cabinet upstairs had shifted downward from the pounding and vibration to the house structure."

I remembered. "You hired a structural engineer to survey for damages. Then you had him re-enforce the cross beam to support the punching bag."

"That's why I loved my wife so much. Well, that and many other reasons." He stared down at the thin leather gloves on his hands. "She never stopped me from doing what I had a passion for, which was the martial arts."

"Can I?" I pointed to the heavy bag. I needed to purge all of my restrained frustrations.

Mr. Kapena offered me a set of leather gloves, but I declined. My first punch felt awkward and uncoordinated. The heavy bag swung a little, as though laughing at me. I hit it with a one-two combination. The left felt soft, but the right landed square in the center of the bag. For the next ten minutes, I poured out everything I had—punches, elbows, front thrusts and roundhouse kicks—mixing it up from one move to the next. The solid thud of the bag signaled that I'd hit the sweet spot, with power.

Every ounce of frustration, anger, retribution, pain, hurt, disappointment—every emotion tossing around in my body—exploded from me into this inanimate object.

I hadn't noticed the blood on my knuckles until Mr. Kapena wet a paper towel with rubbing alcohol and held it to the minor wound. Though it stung, it invigorated me. Sweat dripped from my forehead, down my neck, and drenched my large T-shirt.

I said, more to myself, "Who needs to pay hundreds of dollars for a shrink?"

Mr. Kapena laughed and motioned for me to assume a half lotus position on the concrete garage floor, my legs crossed and back straight.

Eyes closed, I listened to his soothing voice. "Slowly inhale. Hold for a second. Now slowly exhale. Visualize your breathing. Erase any thoughts in your mind. Relax your shoulders. Relax your facial muscles. Relax your body. Keep your back, your spine, vertical to the heavens." He pushed my lower back inward and made a minor adjustment to my posture.

"Open your eyes." Mr. Kapena instructed, then asked, "When was the last time you sparred?"

"It's been too long. I'm guessing six, seven years, maybe longer."

"Do you remember *chi sao*, eyes closed, sticky hands, sensitivity training?"

"Yes, but I'm probably rusty."

We faced each other in the closed *bi jong*, or ready position. Mr. Kapena extended both his arms toward me. I matched him by extending mine, our wrists loosely locked and resting upon each other. This exercise improved touch sensitivity, rapid-fire reflexes, trapping, and footwork. The key was to feel your opponent's energy and either respond or re-direct the attack.

With our eyes closed, we went by feel and our senses, flowing and matching each other's energies. When I flowed, about to strike his head, Mr. Kapena would instantly *pak sao*, blocking my strike. Following the concepts of Wing Chun kung fu, I was regaining the rhythm that I'd lost because of time and non-practice.

His movements were soft and loose, when necessary, yet powerful whenever he sensed an opening to strike. I thought I was doing a pretty good job until he warned me, "I'm going to pick up the pace. Okay?"

I might have made a mistake in agreeing. "Go ahead."

His attack came from the side, so I flowed naturally with the techniques taught by my now opponent. Then—*wham!*—his open hand stung my cheek and felt like it might have loosened a tooth. My body tensed. But Mr. Kapena didn't let up; he delivered a combination of lightning strikes that I wouldn't have been able to stop even if I knew they were coming.

Although every punch he delivered would have caused devastating damage to my body, he eased off his full power, turning each strike into a slap, signaling where my weaknesses and openings were.

I wanted to scream at him to stop, but I didn't.

After a barrage of multiple blows to my cheek, stomach, neck, chin, and jaw, Mr. Kapena pulled away.

I opened my eyes. He had his two hands together in a kung fu salute and said calmly, "Bow."

With clenched teeth, feeling humiliated and battered, I respectfully returned his bow.

I didn't know why I felt the way I did, but I sensed that Mr. Kapena had just taught me something that I needed to know at this point in my life.

"When you get hit, the first thing you do is freeze up. Your entire body stiffens. The problem is when you freeze, you create more openings, so I'm able to delivery multiple strikes with ease. As in sparring, as in the martial arts, as in life, accept the fact that you will get hit. The idea is to take the hit, absorb the blows, and not freeze up."

He motioned for me to stand. Again with our eyes closed, we started in the closed bi jong and chi sao position. Mr. Kapena delivered a hard slap to my face. I reflexively tensed, body and mind stiffened. Then came a flurry of strikes, as if he had four hands. I got hit five, maybe six times, because I froze at the initial hit.

As Mr. Kapena's strikes increased in power and speed, I emptied my mind and felt oneness with his energy. Another powerful slap landed across my ear. It stung, and my ear rang, but this time I didn't freeze. I absorbed the blow and continued.

He stopped suddenly and said, "Better."

I didn't know whether to thank him for pulverizing my confidence.

"Open your eyes." He waved me into a half lotus position again and said, "The other day when I found the listening devices in your house, your first reaction was panic, then anger—you basically froze."

I understood his teachings.

"In sparring, like in life, you will get hurt. To put it in more context, if you're in a knife fight, protect your vitals where a strike could put you down quickly, like your chest or stomach. Although you should try to avoid the blade, you will get cut. If you freeze, you'll be dead against an experienced fighter. Accept that fact and fight back with everything you got."

I thanked Mr. Kapena and limped home like a beaten warrior.

The moment I opened the door, my phone buzzed. A photograph popped up on the screen. I was bound and gagged on a bed, blindfolded and naked.

Blood drained from my face. I grabbed hold of the kitchen counter and lowered myself onto a stool. I flashed back to the emergency room. Blinding bright lights shone in my eyes, and there were muffled but stern frantic voices in the background. People in white coats hovered over me, rushing to pump my stomach of sleeping pills.

To say that I made an error in judgment back then was an understatement. My then boyfriend Stanford Ueno thought it would be fun to try Japanese bondage. At first, he'd hint after we made love, but it became increasingly obvious that he wanted to try it, mostly as a life experience. I reluctantly agreed because I thought we were in love.

Stanford was my first. He was four years older and experienced with sex, and once he'd tied me up like a Japanese girl he'd seen in a bondage video, I was at his mercy. He gagged me, so I couldn't cry out. It got stranger when tears started running down my cheeks, because my helplessness excited him more.

When he took out a camera, I froze in terror. He grinned, almost sinister, knowing that I was watching him slowly mount the camera on a tripod. Most of what he did to me after that I couldn't recall in detail because I just wanted it to end.

After that horrible ordeal, Stanford tried to comfort me by holding me tight, but it didn't work. I hated him with every ounce of my being.

Before dropping me off at home, Stanford's guilt overflowed. Excessively apologetic, he politely asked if I was hungry. "We can go to your favorite lunch place then dessert at Liliha Bakery." But I'd said nothing and stared at my hands resting in my lap.

I hadn't quite understood my mother when she first told me, "If you trust someone, whoever it is, they will disappoint you if you wait long enough." Then, at seventeen, I did.

How could someone who said he loved me do something so atrocious, heartless, and evil? I told only Lani. If my father ever found out, he would have killed Stanford.

"Where's the video?" The voice on the phone brought me back to the reality of the moment.

I screamed into the phone, "You sick fuck!"

"Nice pictures. If I knew you got hot with kinky stuff, I would have done it to you in that abandoned building."

"Fuck you!"

His tone of voice went from playful to suddenly threatening.

"I want the video in my hand by this evening or the other pictures will be posted on the Internet."

"I don't have—"

He hung up. I hit redial, but he didn't pick up. I texted: *I DO NOT HAVE THE VIDEO!!!*

A text came back: *I loved your ultimate fantasy.*

I glared at the screen. What did he mean?

Another text: *To be the finisher of a Magic Johnson fast break would also be up there as a dream come true.*

I dashed into my bedroom. My journal was gone.

Everyone on my contact list, and maybe more, would see the bondage photos. How could I show my face anywhere? People would snicker under their breaths. I wanted to escape, to hide somewhere, anywhere. I rapidly paced from the living room to the kitchen and back to the living room.

How could I have been so stupid! I hated Stanford, but I hated myself more for being so easily manipulated. I clenched my teeth at the ugliness of life. My eyes squeezed tight; the tendons in my neck tensed like ropes. My head was about to explode, my body numb with shame and the humiliation to come. I pressed my face into a pillow and screamed until my throat hurt and I got dizzy from lack of oxygen.

I opened a bottle of wine and filled a glass to the brim.

Everything hinged on a video that I didn't have. Things ran through my mind as I tried to recall information, smells, sounds, and even nuances of the smallest details in the abandoned building.

Though the blood in my veins boiled, and I wanted to strike out at anything, everything, I closed my eyes, took a deep breath, and re-lived Mr. Kapena's open palm smacking me hard across the ear.

His voice carried, reverberating in my head. "Take the hit. Take the hit. Take the hit." I entered a meditative frame of mind and slowed my breathing. Inhaling, exhaling . . . slow and rhythmic.

I didn't realize that I'd fallen asleep on the sofa until my phone buzzed. I opened my eyes to morning sunlight. Last night didn't happen. It couldn't have happened. It was just a bad nightmare.

The glass of wine was where I'd left it, untouched.

I answered, "Hello."

Lani yelled, "The fucker Ueno posted your pictures on social media."

I opened the website, shocked but not surprised, and stared at five photographs of me naked, blindfolded, and tied up like an animal in different positions taken from different angles.

Lani remained silent, possibly waiting for me to go off like a skyrocket with rage.

Screw it. I took another deep breath, calmly pulled myself together, and said, "I like the third picture the best."

After five seconds of silence, Lani cracked up laughing, and screamed so loud it hurt my ears, "*Imua*, Sista!" Imuaa Hawaiian expression meaning "to go forward with strength, courage, and strong spirit."

"Thanks, Lan."

"For what?"

"For supporting me all the time."

"Easy, Sista."

We hung up.

This asshole was always one step ahead of me. I needed to change that.

24

Ever since that night in the abandoned building, the Kami hadn't been able to get Gena Hunter out of his head. He went back to his apartment and couldn't sleep for what little remained of the night. Every time he closed his eyes, all he could see was her, helpless, naked, and bound.

He'd listened to the phone call from a parked car a couple hundred meters away from the house. He didn't recognize the girl's voice, but it had a mixture of an Asian accent with an occasional British pronunciation thrown in. The witness who saw him kill the bar owner had left Japan to give Gena a locket. Unless this girl was from Hawaii, why would she travel thousands of miles to return a worthless locket?

The Kami held the girl's hoop earring in his palm and rolled his fingers over the cheap metal. She hadn't seen what he looked like except for the tattoo on his forearm. He smiled when he heard that. Was it worth taking the chance of eliminating her as a witness when she couldn't identify him but for the tattoo?

His body tensed, hating loose ends because they grated at his desire for perfection.

What to do? What to do?

The Kami thought the threat of exposing the naked photos on the Internet would have done the trick, and that Gena would kill to retrieve the video. But from the sound of her snoring, she'd probably drunk herself to sleep. If Gena didn't have the video, then she needed to try harder.

His mother had said Kami traditionally possessed two souls: one gentle, called *nigi-mitama*, and the other aggressive, *ara-mitama*. She referred to her son as Kami to steer him away from his temper tantrums, explaining that it was his choice to be nigi-mitama or ara-mitama.

The Kami found the garage remote in the glove compartment of the truck, snuck into the house at night, and found the truck's spare key in the kitchen drawer. Thinking he would be less conspicuous in the truck; he drove to the house and into the garage. He planted the cocaine and installed the three listening devices, hoping to find from her where the video might be.

He hit what he considered to be a treasure-trove hidden behind Gena's dresser drawer in a Ziploc bag. Her journal. Excited to be invading her thoughts, he sat on the floor and read her innermost feelings from what looked like middle school to her senior year in high school.

In a moment of rambled scribbling, she wrote: *I feel inept at sex, and the pressure of being a virgin at seventeen. I know it shouldn't matter, but girls who have experienced sex seem to hold themselves differently; perhaps they know something that virgin girls don't. Like maybe it's one of those "been-there-done-that" kind of thing.*

"Self-confidence," she'd written in quotes, then continued: *Most people don't fuck and tell, but Lani talks about it like scratching an itch.*

Gena had sketched a smiley face. *Lani—When I start thinking about my grocery list or what I plan to do after this guy gets off of me then it's time to get a new lover. Guys have only one thing on their damn minds, 24/7. Even during eating they're thinking about sex. Kings of the past went to wars for sex. Men kill for sex. All I'm doing is what comes naturally. I use sex to manipulate men because they want to be manipulated.*

The Kami scanned the next two pages since most were gibberish about her pain. Blah, blah, blah . . . the shame . . . blah, blah, blah . . .

The next page got his attention: *Why did I allow Stanford to do that to me? I feel sick to my stomach. He proudly showed the bondage photographs to me and said they were beautiful. I don't think so. I feel so ashamed. I hurt so so bad that I don't know what to do. Help!*

He closed the journal and planned to take it with him to read in more detail later. He couldn't find the photographs she'd written about.

Kami tracked down Stanford Ueno via the Internet. Gena also had a photo of him that she'd torn to shreds, and maybe spit on. He chuckled and thought that maybe if he'd searched her room harder, he would have found a voodoo doll of Ueno with pins sticking into his dick. Built like a house, handsome, and older than her by maybe four or five years, Stanford gave off the same vibe as Gena's father.

Hmm . . . interesting.

He followed Ueno from his workplace in Mililani, an auto repair shop, and held him at gunpoint. Ueno drove his truck to a two-story townhouse in Wahiawa, thirty minutes away, with the Kami next to him. The gun never wavered.

Gena should be proud of this guy for the way he held out on giving him the bondage pics even at gunpoint. The Kami stripped the dude naked and bound his ankles and wrists together. He gagged him but, making certain Ueno watched everything that was about to happen, he left off the blindfold.

Ueno fidgeted and squirmed, hogtied at the Kami's feet.

Should he take pictures of him and send it to Gena as his gift of revenge? She might feel the same redemption he did whenever he killed men who patronized hostess bars, the type of men who'd disrespected and hurt his mother.

The Kami teased Ueno. "How does it feel to be on the receiving end, Lover Boy?" He ran a kitchen knife along the shaft of Ueno's penis. "Where's the pictures?"

Ueno started to cry. He nudged his chin toward the headboard of the bed. The Kami found the memory stick taped behind it, opened it on Ueno's laptop—making sure not to leave any fingerprints or evidence for the police—and said to the hogtied man, "Arigato very much."

His attention shifted from the man to Gena. Seeing her in bondage made him hard, as well as sick. Frightened and helpless, she brought out the warrior in him, and his duty to rescue her like in those hero movies, but it also excited him to see her like that, because like her friend Lani, he too loved the control.

How could this piece of shit do such horrible things to her?

"You're one sick puppy" were the last words that Ueno heard before the Kami slit his throat and gutted him like he'd seen the boar hunters of Hawaii do on YouTube.

Was she laughing at him when she'd said to her friend that she preferred the third picture the best? He didn't like being laughed at; he had heard that same ridiculing laughter from his mother's drunken customers as he waited outside the club every night.

Nope, Gena was not leaving his head anytime soon. She was faking samurai toughness. He couldn't blame her. But once they were together, she would forget everything that had happened in the past. He'd make sure of it.

Gena Hunter had left her imprint on his mind, and nothing felt the same anymore. He wondered if she looked at things the same way he did. Maybe if she got to know him as a person, she'd realize what a perfect match they were. She might even forgive him for killing both her mother and father. Or maybe not.

He spit on nigi-mitama. His gentle side wasn't getting things done, and he was running out of time. The election was in three days and he still didn't have the video.

Ara-mitama must dominate his thinking, his actions.

25

On the run and pursued by yakuza, Aom's sense of awareness was sharp, like a neurotic cat on full alert, always cognizant of anyone who entered Club Om.

At 12:15 a.m., a hooded man walked into the club wearing dark glasses.

Was he yakuza? Yakuza occasionally walked into the club, but he didn't carry himself like yakuza. Yakuza didn't walk like normal people, they strutted like bulls about to charge a matador.

This guy moved more like a snake, slithering through the club, suspiciously looking behind him as if he were being followed. Aom hadn't seen the woman's face in Kabukicho, but this man seemed to move with a similar grace and boldness. A long-sleeved sweater hid his forearm.

Maybe she was being overly paranoid, but as the Englishman used to preach, "Better safe than sorry." And sorry meant her death. Her bags were packed. She had purchased an open ticket to Bangkok and was ready to jump on the first available flight at any sign of trouble.

Her creep of a landlord made her pay monthly, without a

contract, and without a deposit *if*—he'd licked his lips— "you give me a pair of your used panties once a week."

Aom had met many crazies before, and she realized that men were all the same, even in so-called paradise.

Even with his eyes hidden behind dark glasses, Aom knew that the man was studying her. He was solidly built, athletic, sort of masculine, yet there was a strangely feminine feel to him.

She thought about leaving. But if she left abruptly, it'd be obvious and suspicious, plus that a-hole Kenji would devise a plan for revenge, which usually meant withholding money. Aom took a deep breath. The man could just be looking for a good time. Maybe she could make up something to convince him to remove his sweater.

Aom sauntered toward the man. "Are you looking for some company?" She walked her fingers along his forearm.

He smiled wickedly at her. "I'm like the Prince looking for Cinderella, but instead of a shoe, I'm hoping to match this," he said, holding up a hoop earring.

Aom didn't react, did not panic. He kept staring at her eyes, her face, maybe searching for a facial tic, rapid eye blink, or a sideways glance. Her profession had trained her not to react to the craziness of drunken men.

But it had been a woman in Kabukicho, not a man. Maybe this was one of Tamura's hunters who had found her earring in the stairwell when she ran from the oyabun's apartment. Or maybe this was the killer, and *she* could have been a *he*. Taller than the average Japanese woman, Aom couldn't remember if the killer had worn stiletto heels or not. Had he been in disguise that night?

Aom went through her routine and said to the hooded patron, "Come with me and I will show you a good time."

The man quickly turned away, ignoring her advances. He moved on to another Asian girl, showed her the hoop earring, and like he had with Aom, studied her reaction. After thirty minutes and showing the earring to all the Asian girls, he headed for the door.

The moment she took a step toward the locker area, the man stopped at the entrance and twisted back into the club. Aom steeled her nerves, leaned over, and pretended to fix her shoe.

He exited the club.

With four more hours till closing, she had a bad feeling. Screw Kenji. It was time to get out of here. Although she hadn't seen the tattoo, it was better safe than sorry.

She shuffled to her locker, grabbed her bag, and headed for the door. But then she stopped. He might be waiting outside.

She had an idea.

Aom slithered close to a doughy, middle-aged Japanese businessman wearing a bright aloha shirt with a tropical fish print, rubbed his crotch, and whispered in his ear, "I want to go back to your hotel."

Caught off guard by her proposition, the man stumbled and fumbled as he paid his tab. Arm in arm, they left the club. She playfully ran her fingers through his hair, faked laughter, kissed his neck, and pulled his hand to her breasts.

Once the taxi dropped them off at the Hyatt Hotel in Waikiki, she ditched him.

Before leaving Hawaii, she had one more thing she needed to do.

Aom made a call.

26

"Thank you for meeting with me," I said, aware that I needed to choose my words carefully so as to not spook her.

We met at 2 a.m., in the corner of the dark parking lot of a two-story Kahala restaurant open 24 hours a day. The girl's head swiveled nervously from side to side, and she shifted as though her arms were bound together.

She motioned me toward the entrance of the restaurant. I entered first. The girl twisted around, looking back into the darkness, then cautiously followed behind.

The restaurant had no customers on the ground floor, and from the outside, the wide glass showed none upstairs. Three young workers with paper caps and green aprons, jumped to attention. Although the girl worker yawned and shook her head back and forth from what appeared boredom, the two young men stared at their female customer like she was a contestant in a beauty pageant.

At the counter, I ordered a cup of coffee for myself, and hot tea and a croissant for her.

"*Khob khun kha,*" she said in Thai. "Or as you Hawaiians

would say, 'Mahalo'"

The nervous girl led me upstairs. We sat at a table overlooking the entrance and the dimly illuminated parking lot below.

From the way she constantly scrutinized her surroundings, I sensed she had lived a life of acute awareness, like prey always watching out for a predator.

"Tamura wants to kill me," she said, glancing at the parking lot then the stairs. Her eyes told a story of living in constant fear. "Coming to Hawaii has increased his chances because there is nowhere to run or hide on an island. Everything is so far away."

I recalled Reiko talking about her accepting an offer for sex from Tamura.

She got straight to the point. "Although people refer to me as a prostitute, I do not think I am one. I had no other choice. I am a survivor, not a whore."

I didn't know how to respond, so said nothing.

The girl munched on the croissant and sipped tea. "You might wonder why I am being so honest with you."

"Since we just met, yes, that came to mind."

"I want you to know who I really am, and have no reason to lie to you." She paused and nervously looked out the window as a car pulled into the parking lot. Two young women exited. She let out a breath. "As a child in northern Thailand, I was sold to a man forty years older than me. He betrayed me and sold me to a Triad drug lord, who eventually sold me to the yakuza in Japan. It took time, but I finally made enough money to buy my freedom."

"Jeez. While I was worried about doing my homework correctly, or wearing the right dress to wherever, you feared—"

She quickly waved me off. "That is not why we are here."

My lips tightened with hope. "Have you changed your mind and will come with me to the police?"

"Kenji is smuggling underage girls from Thailand, Laos, Cambodia, and Myanmar to make his sex videos." She ignored my question. Her voice was defiant, her face hardened. "I cannot stand by and let these girls go through what I went through. Any of them could be my younger sisters."

"Why are you telling me this?"

She continued as if not hearing me. "There is a ship arriving from Southeast Asia. I do not know how many girls are on it."

"How do you know this?"

"I overheard Kenji talking."

"When is the ship arriving?"

"In a week, maybe longer." She made eye contact, seemingly studying me as though gauging my reactions. "I do not know the exact day, but the ship's name is Dhia Malaysia. Here is what is important. Kenji will be there because I heard him say he wants to inspect the merchandise."

I instantly thought of Detective Lau.

"Someone must stop this from happening. I cannot do anything but tell people what I overheard. I am an entertainer, not a hero."

Since she'd said she wanted to do good, I pressed her again. "Please Aom, will you come with me to the police?"

Her face turned ashen white. "How do you know my name?"

I paused, thinking I'd made a big mistake. "I checked with people."

"Japan?"

"Yes, from Japan and the airline. I needed to find you to get to the truth about my mother's death."

"I must go." She stood; the chair scraped against the floor. "If Japan knows I am in Hawaii it is only a matter of time before I am dead."

Though she seemed like she wanted to flee, I sensed that another part of her didn't. I needed to calm her down. "Please, tell me . . . what happened."

Aom studied me again, as if deciding how much she could

trust me. She stared blankly straight ahead, blinked several times, then slowly sat back down.

She glanced toward the stairs. "My plane will not leave until eight tomorrow morning."

I was hoping she could fill in the gaps that I felt were missing.

Aom talked about working in the massage spa, struggling to make money, about moonlighting at Club Blue Diamond, and about accepting a night with Tamura for ten times the amount she would make from a regular customer.

"Tamura-san is into rough sex." Aom sneered with disgust. "I thought I could do it, but I could not. So I ran. I escaped, and almost got caught."

"I'm sorry. I didn't know. If I knew about your past, I wouldn't have—"

She held up a hand. "Like the Englishman used to say, 'Damage already done.'"

In our short time together, and with our brief phone conversations, I realized that even after being sold and used by men for most of her life, Aom had somehow managed to maintain a level of moral dignity. Maybe it was her faith in Buddha that helped ground her.

I liked her. I decided to change the topic to help ease some of the tension. "Tell me, what do you love about your country?"

Aom stared at me as though no one had ever asked such a simple question before.

Her infectious smile brought out my own. Then it hit me. Perhaps I knew why men were so attracted to her. It was not just her beauty; it was also the little-girl innocence that tinged her sexuality.

"I love elephants." She grinned jubilantly. "When I have enough money, I will retire and care for them back in Thailand."

"Why do you love elephants so much?"

"Elephants are the largest land animals living on the planet and some of the strongest, too. When I am near them, I can feel their kindness and wisdom. They are so smart. Whenever I hug them, I can actually feel them giving me love back. No matter how many men . . . I have never felt that kind of love before."

I nodded, understanding.

"I liked and respected your mother very much." Her eyes now appeared calm and welcoming. "She was a good lady that ran into some very bad people."

"Yes, I miss her a lot"

"I have made enough money. The Englishman told me not to be greedy because greed tends to bite you in the arse."

I laughed at her British accent, which snuck through every so often.

Aom cheered up. "Maybe one day we will meet again under different circumstances."

I stood up, stepped closer to her, and gave her a hug. Her body stiffened at first, then accepted my sisterly embrace.

Though I suspected she'd taken a cab, I asked anyway. "How did you get here?"

"Taxi."

"Let's go." I reached for the truck keys in my handbag.

"Where?"

"Come to my house. We'll pick up your bags. You can sleep over, and I'll take you to the airport tomorrow morning."

"No, the less people know where I am the better it is for me. And you—if they find me at your home . . ."

"Well then, where can I take you?"

"Chinatown."

"Are you sure? Chinatown can be dangerous this time of night, with lots of druggies and homeless people."

She shrugged; no big deal.

On the drive to Chinatown, Aom shouted, "Stop!"

We were adjacent to Iolani Palace, with nothing around but

dark government buildings. I pulled the truck to the side of Bere-tania Street. When Aom faced me, the dashboard light revealed an indescribable loneliness in her large eyes.

"You are in many ways like your mother." She smiled, and *wai*, her palms pressed together in a prayer-like fashion then bowed. "I'm glad that I met you, Gena."

"Same here, Aom."

She jumped from the truck and wandered through the dark-ness toward the royal residence of the rulers of the Kingdom of Hawaii, built by King Kalakaua in 1882. I kept watching as she sprinted across the expansive lawn, her white blouse vanishing into the night like a ghost into shadows.

27

"It's about time to use the bugs." Mr. Kapena whispered as though we were indoors with the listening devices close by, but we were standing outside, next to my mother's row of white ginger plants. A sweet, natural scent stirred with the light breeze that blew up from the valley.

"What's your plan?"

"You said the Thai girl already left the island, so we—me and you—have a conversation in your house saying that the witness to your mother's murder is working at Club Om. Then we wait until he shows."

"Aom did say she was leaving, but who knows, she could have changed her mind. And he's a *she*. She witnessed a woman murder my mom."

"Either way, we need to get into the club."

"She can only ID her by a tattoo on her forearm." I repeated Aom's description of the image.

Mr. Kapena nodded. "In our conversation you say you got another call from her, and that she has new information that will help identify the killer."

"I heard it's a private club." I recalled what Lani had said.

"They won't let us in unless we're Japanese nationals here on business, or yakuza."

"Ask for a job, maybe as a hostess. Before accepting the position, ask to check out the place. He—she—might already be inside."

I didn't want Lani involved, but she knew the club's manager. I picked a white ginger flower by the stem, sniffed it, then reluctantly added, "I have a friend that may be able to help."

"Kenji is vermin, a parasite," Lani cussed on the phone after hearing me out. "I know the bouncer. His name is Dante. He can get you in. But I need to come along or Dante won't agree."

At seven that night, Mr. Kapena was in the back of the truck's extended cab. Lani sat in the front passenger seat and couldn't believe my house was bugged. "So you guys already planted the bait with the fake conversation?"

"Yeah," I answered. "I hope those high school acting lessons helped me sound believable."

"I think it went well." Mr. Kapena exuded confidence, seemingly back in his element. "I'll be outside watching who goes into the club. If you see anyone with the four tadpoles swimming tattoo or whatever, call me, don't approach her."

"Please be careful," I said, concerned. "We don't know what we're up against."

Mr. Kapena opened his blue windbreaker and revealed a holstered Beretta. "I brought this just in case."

I tried to read the look in Mr. Kapena's eyes, but couldn't in the dark.

"Maybe we should let HPD know what might happen if this person turns out to be my mother's murderer," I suggested reluctantly.

"It will be all right, Gena." Mr. Kapena looked directly at me. "I got this."

"Kenji is local Japanese," Lani injected, changing the subject.

"Thirty-two years old and graduated from a private school in Honolulu. He speaks the language fluently."

"His mother was originally from Japan," Mr. Kapena added. "And here's the thing. He's got a guardian angel in high places."

I took the Kapiolani Boulevard off-ramp.

"This guy has one of those small-man complexes," Lani added, laughing. "Barely stands at five-two, yet he drives a GMC, a heavy-duty, four-door Sierra with an extended cab and double alloy wheels. A few of his employees caught him secretly sitting on a pillow so he could see above the steering wheel. He also drives a red Ferrari because he wants to be like Magnum PI."

Mr. Kapena venomously spat out, "Kenji's golden goose is making porn for the yakuza. He will send sexy girls dressed in hula skirts to pick up wealthy Japanese guests at the airport. He'll set up *golfu* tee times and arrange for young girls to keep them company at night. Kenji greases a lot of palms to stay out of jail."

I parked two blocks from the club.

Lani stared out the windshield. Her voice held a throaty sadness. "You remember my brother, Jess?"

I knew that Lani had been bailing Jess out of trouble since he was in his teens, but she couldn't protect him from serving eight years in Halawa prison after getting busted for dealing.

"Jess owed Kenji a ton of money because of his drug habit." Lani's voice cracked. "If . . . if I didn't do what he asked, Kenji would have had him killed. Neither my brother, nor I, had forty-seven grand."

"So you cut a deal," I said, the picture clearer.

Lani faced me. "Yeah, I had to work in one of his massage places until the debt was paid. And to turn a losing situation into a win, I sponged what I could."

"Kusaka is slime." Mr. Kapena cringed. "You recall when I told you that I was set up?"

I nodded. Lani pivoted back to face him.

"I suspect it was him because I was on the verge of busting his local porn business. I had two girls willing to testify as to how he took advantage of them and used them in his videos. This would have screwed him up, because any court hearing would have drawn huge amounts of media attention—"

"Something the yakuza highly disapproves of," Lani interrupted.

"Yep, and if this went to trial, the yakuza would have killed him before it started."

At nine sharp, we stood in darkness away from the entrance to Club Om. The place didn't stand out like a glitzy neon showcase, but was positioned between a Japanese restaurant and a Korean hostess bar. The air was thick with the sea-like smell of dashi broth and the aroma of sweet soy sauce coming from the restaurant. Rock music spewed from the Korean bar's curtained entrance.

The neon lights blaring from the restaurant and Korean hostess bar had pulled attention away from the entrance to Club Om. If it weren't for the sidewalk lighting and an illuminated, four-inch-tall box-sign in front, the place would be hidden in darkness.

Parked in front, to the side of the club's entrance, was a cherry-red Ferrari 458 Italia. Mounted on the edge of the single-story building, overhead spotlights and security cameras faced the $350,000 car.

Mr. Kapena signaled Lani and me to the door and motioned that he would stay outside of the cone of security light created by the strobes on an adjacent building. He walked over to a large tree with overhanging leaves and leaned against the trunk, holding a pair of binoculars.

Lani opened the right side of the black-painted double glass doors. Someone we knew met us with a huge grin. Standing between the two sets of doors was our friend Angel.

Lani poked a finger at his chest. "What happened to Dante? And what da fuck you doing hea?"

Angel broke into a wide grin. "Hi honey, did you come special to see me?"

Her frown deepened. "This place is bad, dude."

"Dante split, so I'm his replacement," Angel said. "I need money, coz. For school, and money to pay for things my kids need. You know how it is."

I glanced at the inner doors. Bright colorful lights, mirrored balls, and strobes flashed into the faces of inebriated men and women. Music vibrated through the glass.

Although Lani ribbed Angel a lot, she cared for him like a brother, and said, "Hey *braddah*, I'm the worst person to judge what people should do with their lives because let me tell you, I made some major bozo mistakes that I wish that I could take back. But this place is not for you."

"It pays well. And not much trouble 'cause this it's branded a yakuza hangout."

"Angel, I'm looking for a job," I said, wanting to stay focused.

He scratched the top of his baldness; the tip of this tongue flicked out then rolled in his mouth. "You're kidding me, right?"

Lani hadn't lost her edge. "She wants to ask Kenji for a waitress job. Is he here?"

"So, you're saying this place isn't for me, but you're cool with your best friend asking Kenji for a job?"

Lani crossed her arms and glared at the big man.

Angel withered and nodded his large head. "Yep, he's in his office."

I asked, "By the way, Angel. You ever seen a girl with a tattoo on her forearm like four tadpoles swimming in a circle?"

He snickered. "This is a yakuza bar, Gena. I'll show you a dozen people with tattooed forearms. But I saw nothing like that."

Lani pivoted, now facing in toward the club. "There is some serious money to be made here, but these chicks gotta get past the bullshit. There are dancers strung out on drugs. I tried talking some of them into leaving, but have you ever tried to convince snickering crack whores? They're paranoid, edgy, and erratic. It's like trying to teach a dog to spell 'dog.'"

Angel made a call on a cell phone he pulled from his coat pocket.

Lani faced me. "Tell Kenji you're looking for a waitress job. He'll ask you if you have any experience. Tell him you worked as a hostess in Japan. He's always looking for beautiful *hapa* women, of mixed race."

Angel nodded to no one in particular and ended the call. "Mr. Kusaka said he'll meet with you."

"Mr. Kusaka?" Lani snarled. "What da fuck."

Angel shrugged his boulder-sized shoulders.

Lani shifted to open the door, but Angel stopped her. "Sorry Lan, but Mr. Kusaka only wants to see Gena."

Her face turned to solid ice. She stood frozen, as though zapped with a stun gun.

I placed a hand on Lani's shoulder. "I'll be okay."

Lani's glare could have melted the skin off Angel's bones. The big guy fidgeted and turned away.

I followed Angel through the club. We passed four stages spaced apart in a diamond, each surrounded by chairs on the perimeter. There were Japanese men sliding money into garter belts. Strippers, dressed in sexy lingerie, teddies, pushup bras, dark nylons, and smelling as though they were marinated in pools of perfume, sauntered throughout the club. All model-gorgeous, either completely naked, or half-naked and working toward full nakedness. The place stank of cigarette smoke, a thick haze diffusing the twirling lights from a mirrored ball. The music ranged from Aerosmith to K-Pop.

Along the walls and in the middle, between the stages, were high-back booths. A bar counter stretched in a semicircle, occupying a large part of the club.

Angel led me to a door in the back, a few yards from the bar. Most of the customers wore short-sleeved shirts. Some were trendy and stylish, while others seemed from another era. I scanned everyone's forearm, but saw no ninja star tattoo.

Angel knocked on the door. A young woman's scratchy voice shouted, "Come in."

I entered a dark room that smelled of cigar smoke, mildew, and sex. The walls appeared to be oozing slime. Kenji shouted into his cell phone, "You fuck around with lots of guys. I'm not taking no damn DNA shit. Bitch!"

Kenji stared at his hands for a few seconds, then calmed down. He looked up at me and my skin crawled.

In the dim lighting, the girl who called for me to enter barely looked of legal age, with her slender body and punkish blonde hair. She crossed her legs at the knees on the black leather sofa and smiled a stoner's blank grin. Her eyes were blue and clueless. Her mouth worked furiously, chewing gum. She put on headphones and thrummed a beat, fingers drumming on her thigh.

Kenji had a half-cocked Fu Manchu mustache, greasy black hair parted in the center, and eyes that slanted at a sinister angle. His mouth formed a permanent frown, corners turned up slightly. One look at him and you would think *sleazebag*.

He nudged his chin toward the girl, then said to me, "You wanna be a star like her? All I see is potential. You'll pull in a fortune."

I made a face.

Kenji had on a light-blue cycling outfit, which he wore day and night. Lani said he dressed that way because it meant he was able to whip out his penis like he does at toilet stops without having to remove layers of clothing.

"Angel says you're looking for a waitress job." For such a small man, Kusaka had a commanding baritone voice. "I got enough waitresses. I need strippers."

Sticking to the plan, I reluctantly answered, "Okay, I need the money."

"You and everyone else," he snickered. "There's an interview process, honey."

"When do I come back?"

"Take off your clothes. The interview starts now."

My feet froze to the sticky, dark floor.

"If you want me to give you a job then you best show me what you're giving me in return."

I wasn't going to back down. Without hesitation, I undid the top button of my blouse.

Kenji yanked the girl's right headphone out. "What do you think, you want to eat her?"

The girl shoved his hand aside and replaced the earbud. She continued to drum her fingers on her thigh, uninterested in my job interview.

"Keep going." He snickered. "Jeans too."

My hands and knees shook, my body petrified in the dark office. Kenji was raping me with his eyes. I removed my jeans and stood there in my bra and mama-goto white panties. The cold air gave me goose bumps across my arms and legs.

"Your tits," he said, mocking my vulnerability. "They're real?"

I nodded; arms folded across my chest.

"Babe, you're hot. You'd be a natural in my movies." Kenji kept licking his lips, pointing at the rest of my clothes. "Everything. Let's go."

I reached in the back to undo my bra clasp, but stopped when I heard hard knocks on the door.

"What do you want?" Kenji cried out.

Lani shouted, "I'm looking for my friend."

Before Kenji could answer, I yelled, "Come in, Lan."

Lani barged in. Even in the darkness, she blushed at seeing me half naked.

Kusaka snickered. "Well, well—look who popped in. I could sure use a massage 'bout now." He burst out laughing.

Lani's gaze bored into the little man. "Let's get out of this fuckin' shithole."

I gave her a hard, questioning look.

Lani waved me toward the door. "Tell you about it later."

I still didn't move, my face questioning. *Wasn't this the plan?*

"Trust me," Lani said, and stepped forward to shield me from Kenji's lizard eyes.

I grabbed my clothes and dressed behind Lani, who kept glaring at the sleazebag.

Kenji screamed, "Where the hell you going? You come here to waste my fuckin' time! Bitches—all of you are all fuckin' bitches."

We rushed out of that hellhole and blew past Angel. Lani's voice rose over the din of the club as we rushed to the entrance. She said as we exited, "Mr. Kapena has a guy with that tattoo pinned on the ground."

Outside in the cool night air, at the far corner of the building, Mr. Kapena's knee was on the back of a man lying on the blacktop road in front of the Japanese restaurant.

The man on the ground had on a short-sleeved aloha shirt and had a circular tattoo on his forearm. He was in his mid-thirties, with greasy black hair, and eyes that were blinking with fear. Subdued on the pavement, the man shrieked in Japanese, "What do you want? Please do not tell my wife. I heard about this club from a friend. My wife went to have a massage . . ."

Mr. Kapena bent closer to the man's forearm, licked his

thumb, and rubbed at the tattoo. His face sank when the black pattern smeared. "Shit . . .We've been tricked."

He pushed off the Japanese man, who pounced off the ground and dashed down the dark alley.

"I fucked up." Mr. Kapena kicked the side of a parked car. The alarm wailed. He cussed under his breath. "I acted too damn fast."

"He had the tattoo," I said, trying to calm him down. But I knew we'd had one shot, and there was no way back in now.

Mr. Kapena glanced around at the cars parked in the dark, along the side street, and in the nearby paid parking lot. "We're being watched." The car alarm stopped. "Let's get out of here."

Before we left, Lani pulled a bunch of keys from her jeans pocket, walked along the cherry-red Ferrari, and scraped them against its side as she walked. The loud bar music drowned out the screeching of raw metal.

Angel did an about-face and quickly walked away.

When I got home, I took a long hot shower, like I had after meeting that creep Takashi. But that still wasn't enough to get Kenji's stink off me. I filled the tub with bubbles and soaked in it until the tips of my fingers wrinkled.

After downing three glasses of wine and trying to drown the images of all the toxic people I had met over the past few days, I still couldn't get over the sickening feeling in my gut that the worst was yet to come.

28

S itting in a car at the base of the mountainside, he could see her house through thick dried brush, perched on the slope a couple hundred meters up. Using a laptop, the Kami listened and replayed the recorded conversation between Gena and the old man who lived next door. They were in the living room.

Gena said, "The girl witness called my cell. She said she had new information that could help identify the killer."

"More than the tattoo of the four tadpoles swimming in a circle?"

"Yes. She works at a place called Club Om."

"That's here in Honolulu, on the edge of Waikiki," the old man said.

"What do we do?"

"I think we should talk to her."

"When?"

"The club opens at eight p.m. and closes at two." He paused then added, "I say we get there at nine and ask her what else she has. And if she did witness everything, we convince her to talk to the police."

The Kami concentrated on every microscopic sound. Shuffling feet were followed by the opening then closing of a door.

He glanced at the digital clock on the dashboard. 7:14 p.m. The sun had set about an hour ago. He needed to get to the witness before they did. What new information? He gritted his teeth, hating loose ends.

At 7:45 p.m., the Kami sat in a car parked among many other vehicles along Kapiolani Boulevard and watched the entrance to Club Om. Beautiful girls sauntered in with faces made up like centerfold models. Some wore jeans, loose halters, and jogging shoes, while others were dressed in high heels and long overcoats.

The Kami focused on the five Asian girls. Two looked like they were from Japan, another had dark, tanned skin, so he assumed she might be local Japanese. One girl was a statuesque Filipino, and the last one could have been either Chinese or Korean. None of them had reacted when he showed them the hoop earring earlier. She must have been prepared. Anyone of them could be the witness who'd seen him kill the bar owner. But one of them was missing, the Thai girl. He pinched the hoop earring between his fingers and thought about his next steps.

Something kept clawing in his gut like a little crab with pinchers. Maybe it was the vibe the girls gave off as they strolled into the club. They hadn't given off any air of nervousness or caution. Anyone who'd witnessed a killing just days ago in Tokyo would likely have a careful edge to her movements, maybe glancing behind her, worried she was being followed. Things didn't fit. Maybe it was the conversation between Gena and the old man that felt wrong.

At five after nine, Gena and her friend entered the club. Where the hell was the old man?

Something didn't feel right.

The Kami saw a Japanese man in a bright Hawaiian shirt stumble on the sidewalk a few meters from his parked car. He got out and scurried after him, partially in darkness, along the side of a building.

From behind the man, he asked in Japanese, "Are you from Japan?"

The man wobbled and turned toward the voice. He rubbed his eyes.

In tour-guide disguise, the Kami wore a bright, short-sleeved aloha shirt with a hula dancer print, a wide-brimmed Hawaiian straw hat, and the kind of dark glasses that he'd seen men wear on the beach during the day. He'd stuffed cotton balls in his cheeks and hid his tattoo with an armband. He repeated, putting on a welcoming smile. "Aloha. Are you from Japan?"

The man was husky and smelling of booze, and smiled at hearing his native language spoken.

He answered in Japanese, "Hai, I'm from Osaka."

"Are you going to Club Om?"

"Hai," he answered. "I heard of the popularity of the club, so I left my wife at a massage place down the street and decided to do a little exploring on my own for an hour."

"There are many pretty young girls in there," the Kami said with a devilish, friendly guy-to-guy grin. "You'll enjoy the company while your wife gets her massage."

As a precaution, he had purchased a black inkpad and had the owner of a small novelty shop duplicate his tattoo. As a quick fix, the guy had made a mold using silicone rubber that would work once or twice before smearing.

The Kami told the Japanese man, "For ten dollars I can give you a stamp that will get you a ten percent discount on every drink."

With raised eyebrows, the tourist said, "Just ten dollars?"

"Hai, about a thousand yen," the Kami said and anticipated the man's next question. "My job is to approach customers; as you can see the club is difficult to find."

He nodded with a drunken grin. "Like those people who stand outside restaurants in Japan encouraging passing customers to come inside."

"Exactly like that."

The tourist fumbled and got his wallet from his back pocket, slipped out a ten-dollar bill, and handed it over. The Kami pocketed the money, opened the inkpad, pressed the stamp to it, and inked the symbol onto the man's right forearm.

The tourist glanced at his forearm and the circular stamp.

"Just show this to the person at the door," the Kami said, continuing to smile like a friendly tour guide. "I'll give you a full refund if you want."

The tourist hurried toward the entrance to the club a happy customer, but it didn't work out as planned. As he approached the bright light that illuminated the Ferrari, a shadowy figure slid out from the darkness behind a tree along the boulevard.

Within seconds, the old man skillfully had the tourist on the ground, pinned down with a knee to his back.

The Kami stumbled backward and hid deeper in the shadows. He gritted his teeth. A setup. Where did he screw up? Gena couldn't have found the listening devices herself. It had to be the old man.

A giant bouncer wearing a dark suit rushed to the old man's side. They chatted as though they knew each other. The big man dashed back inside the club. Gena and her friend now stood above the old man pinning the tourist with his knee.

The old man twisted the man's forearm awkwardly behind him in a wrestler's hammerlock. He wet his thumb with spit and rubbed the stamp.

The Kami chuckled and said to himself, "Amateurs. They will pay for this."

His thoughts flashed to one of his favorite shootout movies, to the apartment scene in *Die Hard 4*, where the antagonists had tried to kill the computer genius. Machine gun fire ripped through the windows, furniture, appliances, TV, and everything in the room.

The Kami made a phone call, said a few words, hung up, and drove to Chinatown. The smalltime drug dealer who'd sold him a .45 also offered an AR-15, a lightweight semi-automatic rifle.

Ara-mitama!

29

Half asleep, I kept reliving the events of the night. What had gone wrong? My phone buzzed and vibrated on the nightstand. The digital clock read 3:37 a.m.

Any phone call at this time wasn't going to be good. I steadied my nerves and answered, hesitantly. "Yeah?"

The voice on the other end snickered. "How stupid do you think I am? Your trap was a big joke."

I said nothing.

"You and the old man will pay."

An icy chill shot through my body. "Don't . . ."

The next terrifying words floated from the phone speaker. "I've planted a bomb under your neighbor's house."

His words grabbed me by the throat. Was he bluffing?

"You have five minutes to get him out before it explodes." His voice held a pinch of vengeance and a twist of joy. His laughter was confident and convincing before he hung up.

I blasted through our front door, dashed to my neighbor's house, scrambled up the wooden porch, and slammed on the door like a maniac. "Mr. Kapena, get out of there! Get out!"

Liko barked like an attack dog, going crazy inside. A light flicked on, and Mr. Kapena shouted, "Quiet! Knock it off!"

Before he swung the door open, I cried out, "There's a bomb under your house. You must get out, now!"

Liko barged through the screen door, excited to see me. The playful Akita jumped up and down then landed both paws on my chest. The big dog forced me back onto the porch.

Mr. Kapena forced sleep from his eyes. "What da hell, who are you . . ." The Beretta he had earlier hung limply in his hand.

I grabbed him by the arm and pulled him toward the rear of the truck. It should shield us when the bomb went off. We'd scrambled half the length of the car when bullets began pinging all around us. The back window exploded. The two rear tires blew. I pushed Mr. Kapena's head down and reversed our course, steering us toward the front of the truck, because the shooting was coming from the bushes. Bullets pulverized the mailbox, and more ricocheted off the nearby rock wall. We hunkered on the ground in front of the truck's license plate.

Liko snuggled close. I clutched his collar as bullets struck the front fender and pulverized the side mirror, causing damage everywhere. Mr. Kapena's eyes were dazed and unresponsive. I gripped his hand and said close to his face, "Mr. Kapena, it's me, Gena."

He started singing softly to himself.

I kept my voice low and calm. "It's going to be all right, Mr. Kapena. The police—your guys—are on their way."

I remembered the Beretta. I twisted back. The weapon was on the porch, a couple feet away from the front door.

I placed my fingers under his chin and gazed into his empty eyes. "Mr. Kapena, do not move. Please do not move. I need to get your gun. Do not move, okay?"

He blinked twice. I hoped that signaled that he understood.

Another burst of gunfire strafed the thin metal of the truck, shattering the front windshield. I waited for the reload. Rather than the gunshot triggering a hundred-meter sprint in a track competition, it was silence I held out for. When it came, I dashed for the gun.

Fifty feet felt like fifty thousand. The moment I picked up the Beretta, the shooter opened fire. The windows of the house shattered, wood splintered, and tiles fell from the porch's overhang. Crouching low, trying to keep the truck between the shooter and me, I shuffled back to where Mr. Kapena was curled on the ground in a tight ball. I dove the remaining five feet like I was stealing second base and hit my head on the truck's front bumper.

Mr. Kapena continued to softly sing.

From my experience at the shooting range, I could make out the distinct sound of an AR-15 semiautomatic rifle. Being outmatched in terms of firepower, I needed to send a message. The shooter would think twice about getting closer to someone who was armed.

I disengaged the Beretta's safety, chambered a round, military-crawled deeper under the truck toward the back, and waited for a muzzle flash. More shots came in explosive spurts. I took a prone shooting position. Elbows resting on the ground, I pointed the gun at the flash and pulled the trigger three times. I aimed low and made sure no stray bullets would penetrate anyone's home while they slept.

Then it came, the sound of distant sirens approaching. The shooting stopped. The shooter must have also heard the police on their way.

I grabbed Mr. Kapena's shoulder. "We'll be okay now. Help is on the way."

Mr. Kapena's limp body was hunched over, a puddle of red forming on the ground. A coppery scent, mixed with my fear, filled the air. I carefully rolled him over to expose the front of his body. His white T-shirt bloomed red with blood. I had never seen an open stomach wound before in my life, and hoped I'd never see another, but I needed to stop the bleeding. I rushed to the truck's cab and found a beach towel behind the driver's seat. I placed the towel on Mr. Kapena's wound and applied pressure to slow the bleeding. He winced with pain.

"Hurry," I mumbled, and said to Mr. Kapena, "Help is on the way. Hold on . . . hold on." Only then did I notice his leg was bleeding.

He coughed, his face hardening, determined to gather enough strength to say something to me.

"What is it, Mr. Kapena?"

As if with his last breath, he blurted out, "Liko?" His eyes closed, his head slackened, and he passed out.

I had forgotten about the dog. When I turned toward the house, my heart sank to the pit of my stomach.

Liko lay on the wooden porch, not moving.

Emergency vehicle lights reflected off rooftops and house walls. Neighbors stood outside in bathrobes watching, worry etched on their faces at the violence so close to home.

Mr. Kapena was hooked up to an IV bag and carefully carried away on a gurney by an emergency medical technician, a woman in her mid-thirties, who had short black hair and was built like a locomotive.

Mr. Kapena's eyes were closed. Before they lifted him into the back of the ambulance, I cradled his hand, leaned down to his ear and said, "You're a fighter Mr. Kapena. Don't give up."

The EMT climbed into the back of the ambulance and closed the door.

I quickly shuffled closer to the second EMT. "Is he going to be all right?"

The guy had a receding hairline above a ruggedly etched face. He shrugged. "He looks to be in pretty good shape for his age. When we lifted him onto the gurney, he was solid as a rock." The EMT climbed into the driver's seat.

The ambulance siren wailed. I walked to the edge of the house. Flashlights crisscrossed in the thick brush; police were scanning the hillside for the shooter.

When I was done describing what had happened to the police, it was 4:30 a.m. I jumped into my father's truck and drove to the hospital on Punchbowl Street.

In the waiting room, I was told that Mr. Kapena was in the ICU. He'd sustained two gunshot wounds: one to his abdomen, the critical wound, and a second to his left calf.

"Everything happened so fast," I said to Detective Lau when he walked into the waiting room and stood in front of me. I described what we'd done earlier that night—trying to shake out my mother's murderer by feeding him false information about the girl who witnessed everything in Japan. Lau's frown grew deeper as I explained the details of what happened at Club Om.

Lau rested his chin on his chest. "Did you know that Kapena has dementia?"

I exhaled, anticipating where this was going. "Yes, I did. But he goes in and out, at some points he's the man he was before, then that changes and—"

Lau's lips tightened into a straight, horizontal line. "Mr. Kapena was a mentor for many of us younger guys, so it's very hard seeing him in this condition."

A deep silence fell between us.

"Will you fill me in on what you find on the shooter?" Even though I'd asked the question, my thoughts were focused on Mr. Kapena getting well.

"This guy is getting bolder and much more brazen." Lau sat

next to me with his elbows on his knees. "Like he's pressed for time, or something in his brain isn't wired quite right. I'll double the patrols in the Hawaii Kai area and make sure a car drives by your house more often."

I thanked Detective Lau before he left. I fell asleep in the ICU waiting room, waiting for word about Mr. Kapena.

I woke up at the sound of a door opening. I rubbed my eyes. The sun had risen, casting symmetrical beams of light on the gray carpet. The male nurse, Cesar, who was keeping me abreast of Mr. Kapena's status, grinned and handed me a paper cup full of steaming coffee from the vending machine.

He yawned, then smiled. "How you doing?"

"Long night." I rubbed my face with both hands and took the coffee. "How's Mr. Kapena doing?"

"He's doing good and wants to see you."

I jumped up from the chair.

"Keep it short, okay? He's still not out of the woods, but he's doing much better." He handed me a paper face mask. "And one more thing, he's heavily sedated, so I'm not sure what he wants to talk to you about, but it must be important to him."

I nodded. I knew what he wanted. I slipped on the mask.

"Thanks Cesar." I followed him to Mr. Kapena's room. "And mahalo for the coffee."

Cesar winked and left us alone.

I stood next to Mr. Kapena's bed, tubes disappearing under his hospital garment. He pried his eyes open, forced a smile, and croaked, "Hey."

"How you doing?"

"I'd rather be in Vegas with a chilled beer playing the quarter slots." He squinted with pain, and his voice was heavy with sleep. "But I guess life had other plans for me."

I clutched his hand.

His eyes brightened with anticipation. "How's Liko?"

I choked back tears. "Sorry Mr. Kapena, but Liko didn't make it. He got shot in—" I stopped because he had turned away and faced the window. The sadness in his eyes made me sick to my stomach.

I filled him in, saying that the police hadn't found the shooter. Cesar motioned to me that Mr. Kapena needed rest. Knowing that he was getting better, I headed home.

While driving along Kalanianaole Highway in stop-and-go traffic, I realized this was the second time that I had witnessed the heartache of someone who'd lost their four-legged best pal.

My phone buzzed when I was halfway home. Without looking at the number, I sensed who it was and answered, "You mutherfucker!"

"Temper, temper," he teased with delight. "This is your final warning for the video, or you and your closest friends will all die."

He hung up.

I frantically called Lani. The phone rang and went to voice mail. Shit. I tried again. This time Lani answered, "What . . . kinda early, eh?"

With my heart in my throat, I exhaled with relief. "Got stuff going on and I'm worried for your safety."

"You're telling me all this and I haven't even had my cup of joe yet."

"Sorry, but things happened last night after I dropped you off at your apartment." I gave her a quick summary. "Mr. Kapena has gotten better, but he's still not out of trouble."

Lani let out a concerned moan.

"Do me a favor." I tried to stay calm and in control because I was expecting pushback from her. "Lan, this is serious. Can you live with your tutu for a few days?"

There came a long silence on the other end, then Lani answered, "Okay, Sista."

"Thanks, Lan." We hung up.

When I arrived home, my thoughts went back to Liko and the pain in Mr. Kapena's eyes. It was the same pain I'd seen in Abe's eyes. The Novaks' resident manager had carried a photograph of his dog on his keychain like a cherished charm.

I needed to get back to Japan.

30

The dull, gray color of my mother's apartment building, which ran along the narrow street, depressed me. Even at this time of year, Hawaii could fill a camera angle with a multitude of bright colors.

The bakery was open. The smell of freshly baked bread had drawn customers who were waiting in a short line. I bought a chocolate éclair.

I walked to the five-story building, my luggage rolling behind me. I glanced up at the security camera—I'd known that Tomo was watching the moment I got out of the taxi at the street curb.

The resident manager, Mr. Cucumber Nipples, frowned when he met me at the front entrance.

Stone-faced, he said in Japanese, "Where's your friend?"

"She won't be coming."

"Too bad." He held his cucumber nipples together trying to mimic Lani's breasts and said, "I like."

I headed for the elevator and mumbled, "Asshole."

The studio apartment felt smaller, lonelier, and emptier than I remembered it being just a few days ago.

I boarded the train from Shibuya to Tachikawa Station. It took thirty-five minutes on the JR Chuo Rapid Service.

Once in Tachikawa, I searched the Internet for shopping centers with pet stores. I remembered that the dog in the photo on the manager's keychain had been a toy poodle.

A bell over the door jingled when I entered the store.

"May I help you?" a young girl greeted me politely in Japanese. In her hand was a rubber duck squeeze toy. A white cockatoo squawked in a cage above the cash register. The place smelled like a mixture of birdseed, sawdust, and cat poop.

I smiled at her. "I'm looking for a toy poodle." I scanned the cages in the corner but didn't see what I was hoping for.

The girl could read the disappointment on my face. "I just received a couple puppies, but I haven't had time to bring them up front yet."

The girl took me to the back. I pointed. "There, that's it." The puppy jumped up and down in the cage.

"How much for that one?"

"You're in luck." Her smile grew bigger. "We have a special price for puppies. This cutie is exactly 110,000 yen."

"Whoosh," I blurted out. That was around a thousand bucks.

The puppy seemed to be in on the sale, because it whimpered and barked on cue. Having just arrived, I needed to be careful with my cash, but this could open things up.

Cradling the puppy, I walked to the ground floor of the three-story building with the *Beware of Dog* sign out front. Natsuo Abe had the same sunken cheeks and depressed aura as last time.

When Abe saw the puppy in my arms, his forehead and eyebrows drew upward, and the corners of his mouth pulled into a wide grin.

I handed the puppy to him and said in Japanese, "For you."

At that moment, I didn't exist. Abe sniffed behind the puppy's ears and cuddled it to his cheek.

"I need to talk to you about the Novaks."

The manager's smile never wavered; his attention focused on his new friend.

He motioned me into the building. We climbed the two flights of stairs to the Novaks' apartment. The place was as it had been before, empty except for the mini shrine with burnt incense and melted candles.

Abe snuggled the puppy. "People still do not want to live in an apartment that has seen two deaths. It will be difficult to rent."

I strolled closer to the shrine. There was the photograph of the handsome twelve-year-old boy in its golden picture frame.

"Tell me about Novak, and what happened that night of the murder-suicide."

He stopped petting the puppy. His eyes turned gray with fear.

I pointed to the picture of the boy by the shrine. "That boy looks Japanese, but Novak was white."

The man nodded with downturned eyes. "Misaki lived here for many years, even before she got married to Novak." His look when he mentioned the man's name was one of pure disgust.

The puppy started whimpering. Abe focused on his new pet and ignored me. I pulled out a dog treat from a plastic bag and handed it to him. The puppy gnawed on the biscuit.

"Tell me about before she got married."

"Misaki used to be a hostess. She would work into the early morning hours. The boy—" Abe nudged his chin toward the photograph. "He refused to stay with a babysitter and also refused to remain at home, so he would wait outside of the bar until it closed. They would then return to the apartment together; at times he was freezing and shaking from the cold weather. No matter what, he would wait for her each and every night until she finished work. He hated the men who patronized the bars because of the demeaning and disrespectful way they treated her."

"When did she meet Novak?"

"They met in a bar. Novak sent the boy to an international school with other military children. He drank and gambled many nights, and would beat her often. They were married for maybe ten years. I don't remember."

"What was Misaki's surname?"

"Novak," he replied.

"I mean her maiden name, before she got married."

"Suzuki."

Abe stared at the puppy, who was working on the treat. "I liked Misaki because she was a nice lady."

"What about the son?" I asked, but somehow already knew the answer. "How did you feel about him?"

He clutched the puppy tighter. The dog yelped.

Natsuo Abe faced the empty room, seemingly in a world of his own, perhaps reliving something he wished to forget.

"Sir." I interrupted his thoughts. He turned with a blank stare. "Where's the boy?"

His voice came out distant, terrified. "He stops by whenever he feels the need."

"So he's not dead."

He cradled the puppy to his chest and shook his head.

I reached over and held his keychain with the photograph on it between my fingers. "He killed your dog."

His face tightened, tears dripped from his eyes and down his cheek. "Hai."

"He threatened you if you told anyone?"

The man nodded. The wrinkles on his neck wobbled when he hiccupped out more sobs and said, "He tied me to a chair and taped my eyelids open so I had to watch."

If Abe hugged the puppy any harder, he would suffocate it to death, so I tapped his arms, signaling for him to loosen his grip.

His face soured. "He poured acid . . ." Abe broke into tears again.

"What's the boy's name?"

"His father gave him an English name—Sebastian."

"No Japanese name?"

"Not that I know of, because they always referred to their son as Sebastian Novak."

"What else can you tell me about him?"

"He's famous. You can look on the Internet and there are pictures of him in costume."

"Costume?"

"Hai, he's an onna-gata performer."

"What's that?"

"Men who play kabuki female roles."

Aom had said that my mother's killer was a woman. Honma said that the killer was strong like a man.

Abe's hands were shaking. "Sebastian must not know I told you this or he will be back." He stared down at the puppy playfully nibbling his fingers.

"He will not know from me."

We walked down to the ground level. When I turned to thank him, he was already heading to his apartment, cradling the puppy.

On the train ride back to Shibuya, I stared at the majestic Mount Fuji with its snow-capped peak in the distance and mouthed, "Sebastian."

31

I dialed Hanako's number. She answered cheerily, but when I spoke my first words her good mood vanished. She hushed, "Wait, I need to change location."

Background voices faded.

"Since I hadn't heard from you, I thought . . . I don't know what I thought." She paused as though remembering something. "Did you find your father?"

My breath caught in my throat. "They found the canoe, but my dad is still missing."

"I'm sorry, Gena."

"The weird thing is that this might be related to my mother's murder." I needed to stay focused on the here and now. "I'm back in Japan because I need to pursue some things that right now don't make any sense."

"Any way that I can help." She paused. "Before I forget, we tried tracing your phone, the one he took from the abandoned building. He must have destroyed it."

"Well, it was worth a try." I'd already known they wouldn't get anything, because this guy was careful, and smart. "Here's the thing. I need to know more about the Novaks' murder-suicide."

"The case was quickly closed. All evidence pointed to the woman stabbing her husband while he slept. She then walked to the home shrine and committed seppuku with a knife. But here's where it got strange."

"Strange?"

"The woman's family was said to be of samurai linage. They had a suit of warrior body armor in the apartment and a matching pair of traditional swords worn by the samurai class in feudal Japan. Referred to as a katana, or long sword, and a *wakizashi,* or short sword. They also had a tanto, a samurai's knife."

Keeping my focus on the investigation, I asked, "Why so strange?"

"Being of a traditional samurai family, you would think if seppuku was appropriate, she would have used the wakizashi or tanto, but she didn't."

I waited her out.

"She used a kitchen knife." I got the impression that a critical samurai code had been violated. "Being of samurai bloodline, Misaki using a kitchen knife to commit seppuku or hara-kiri would be like using *Lipton* tea in a traditional Japanese tea ceremony."

"Could this be a double murder?"

"There were many unanswered questions," Hanako said. "But they still closed the case."

"Like what kind of questions?"

"Someone called Novak while at your mother's bar. No one knows who it was, or why he stormed from the bar after the call, nor what was said to him."

I pondered this before asking, "Did you get the vehicle belonging to the license plate number that Sparrow gave me?"

A long silence followed before Hanako answered, "Once again, something strange is happening, because it shouldn't have taken this long. When I probed my associate, she said she'd lost her clearance, so she has to get it another way."

I sensed that Hanako might be in trouble. Based on the cautious tone of her voice, Hanako knew it too.

"Call me if you hear or find anything," I said, fearful that people around me were dying. "And please be careful, Hanako"

That afternoon I tried reaching Reiko, but she wasn't answering her phone. When I called Club Blue Diamond, the girl who answered said that she had quit.

The rumor that my mother had secretly filmed Tamura with a hidden camera didn't make sense—Mom couldn't reset the clock on our DVD player. Though one of the smartest people I knew, she was simply disinterested in technology.

The rumor floated around that my mother was Tamura's favorite. If true, he had no reason to kill her, unless she'd done something to him that triggered his wrath. Mr. Kapena described Tamura as a narcissist, so he could easily have turned against somebody who was once loyal to him.

Before Club Blue Diamond opened, I waited in a tiny restaurant about fifty yards away from the entrance. I held my breath and crouched down low when Kiyomi walked past me along the alleyway on her way to work. I shushed the restaurant owners, an elderly man and woman behind the counter. To pacify them, I ordered two servings of takoyaki.

As Mei approached, I strolled out into the alleyway and stood in front of her. Mei's eyes flashed—fight or flight. She turned and ran in the opposite direction. I huffed, grabbed both orders of takoyaki, and gave chase. As I ran, I cursed. "Why does everything have to be so fuckin' hard?"

Dressed in blue jeans, a pink sweater, and Asics running shoes, Mei ran like a greyhound down a side street, hurtled over a stool just as an old man stood to serve a customer, and dashed up a hill at a 30-degree incline. Vendors screamed and shouted at her, but she kept going, the distance between us increasing as she toppled items behind her and into my path to slow me down.

I decided to take a shortcut and scampered down the huge, rocky storm drain, scurried across the meandering stream, and vaulted up the other side of the embankment. I exited on a narrow road and heard Mei's hurried footsteps approaching. She kept glancing back and didn't see me standing in front of her.

Five feet away and out of breath, I grabbed her by the arm and held on like a rodeo cowboy on a bucking bull—this one wearing Asics.

I screamed in her ear, "Stop Mei! Stop! I won't hurt you."

I had Mei in a headlock. Her body relaxed from exhaustion. Breathing hard, she struggled to say into my armpit, "What do you want?"

"I want to talk—that's all."

Though she nodded, I held on to her wrist. I didn't have the energy to chase after her again.

We sat down across from each other in a coffee shop. "I want to know where the rumor came from about my mother black-mailing Tamura. She would never blackmail anybody."

Mei sipped a cup of green tea and said in Japanese, "You know how it is in the club, or any club. Rumors fuel us. We thrive on rumors. At times we make up our own rumors just to spice things up a little and get away from the boredom of hostessing. At times we use rumors to manipulate others, like telling a customer that the hostess he's sitting with is pregnant, or has three children and a husband at home, or that she has a sexually transmitted disease."

I gulped down a chilled bottle of water; Mei had given me a pretty good workout.

Mei stopped and looked down at her hands. "I didn't mean to spread the rumor that you had an STD." She chuckled in a playful way.

"I was wondering where that came from." I laughed along with her. "I heard that Tamura enjoys rough sex with underage girls, and that there's a video of him killing the chief justice's young daughter while she's in bondage. Where do you think that rumor started? Or is it true?"

I could sense by the expression on Mei's face that she was tossing her response around in her head, perhaps trying to scrape away true from false, or maybe trying to blend both into a credible story.

"I'm not sure if that rumor is true. But if it's just a rumor, then it probably started here, spreading like wildfire through Tokyo's hostess and sex industry."

"Why here?"

"I'm not one hundred percent sure, but when a forest fire starts and everything in, let's say, a kilometer radius around it isn't burning, you kind of know where it started. It's the same with rumors. They start in one place, and if no one hears them outside a certain area, then you basically know where the source is."

"How do you know that?"

"Because I have many contacts throughout the Tokyo area. If I ask them, 'Did you hear this?' and they say no, my guess would be that the rumor hasn't reached there yet. It is not scientific and I'm not sure if it's accurate, but it seems to work if done right."

Although I doubted her theory because people had cell phones, I still asked, "Who could have started it?"

Mei shrugged. "You have to look at who has the most to gain."

"Kiyomi?" sprouted from my mouth.

"Quite possible, because she's one mean bitch." Mei's frown deepened. "Plus, she wants Blue Diamond for herself."

I hesitated before asking, "You don't like her?"

"All the girls hate her. But they stayed because of your

mother. Since your mother died, four girls have already left and started at other clubs."

I thought about it more. "Maybe someone paid one of the girls to spread the rumor for their own benefit." I thought of Reiko and her drug habit.

"Maybe, but the girls liked your mother because she was fair."

Although I despised the business, I was still curious, and asked, "Why do you like being a hostess?"

A cross between and smile and a smirk formed on her lovely face. She contemplated my question for a few seconds then said, "Control. Japan has been a male dominated country for centuries. I make my own money as a hostess; there are many Japanese women who must depend on men to survive. Though they hate it, they have few other options. As a hostess, I use my youth and sexuality to control men, and they give me their full attention. Ask any wife if her husband gives her his full attention and she'll laugh in your face. Men give me gifts. Some even promise to divorce their wives to be with me."

"But what will happen as you age and become less—"

"Desirable?" she jumped in, then adding, "Then I will have my own club."

"Don't you get lonely for companionship?"

"I have my friends. But they are not hostesses. They are regular people that I grew up with in school. They are my true friends, because they knew me when I had no money, no nothing."

I handed Mei the beat-up bag of takoyaki.

She opened the bag and sniffed. Her eyes rolled upward. "My favorite."

I thanked her and she went to work munching on the snack.

Halfway to the train station, my phone buzzed. Hanako. The moment I answered, Hanako rapidly fired out, "You must leave Japan, now!"

"Calm down, Hanako," I said, trying to get her to slow down. "Tell me what's going on."

"I got word from a friend in Homicide that Suzume Hayakawa was found dead last night on a side street in Harajuku."

"Sparrow is dead?"

"Inspector Honma is accusing you of the murder."

"But I didn't—"

"I know you didn't, and his higher-ups are questioning his reasoning at this very moment. An associate of mine excused herself to go to the restroom and called me to report what is now transpiring in the meeting. If Honma convinces them, you will be arrested."

"But I'm innocent."

"This is Japan, Gena-chan, and you are a foreigner. There are innocent people who are now in our prison system."

There must have been something that triggered this setup. "Is there something you're not telling me, Hanako?"

I was met with silence, then Hanako's nervously shaking voice. "The license plate number that Sparrow gave you was traced to a vehicle used by Inspector Honma."

"Oh shit." I clenched my teeth together, stopping my jaw from trembling.

"I will do my best to stall from here, but I do not have authority in the department. Honma will brush me aside like a gnat."

"Arigato, Hanako," I said and hung up.

I didn't go back to my mother's apartment in Shibuya. Instead, I caught a taxi to Haneda International Airport and booked the first flight I could out of Japan.

When I was stopped by security because I didn't have any luggage, I gave them half-truth: that my father was missing at sea and I needed to get to Hawaii immediately.

The man wasn't buying it until I said he could check it with the Honolulu Police Department. "You can confirm my emergency with Detective Frank Lau."

They finally let me through.

The next available flight left in an hour for San Francisco. I didn't book any connecting flights or hotel reservations; I just needed to get back to America. Besides when waiting for updates about my missing father at sea, the wait for my flight to board and then sitting on the plane during taxiing and lift-off, felt like the slowest that time had ever passed.

I tried sleeping on the eleven-hour flight, but every five to ten minutes I would stare at the screen in front of me, wishing that the little airplane on the map of the flight route would move faster.

32

T hroughout the flight I kept scanning up and down the aisle, maybe expecting the sky marshal to suddenly slap a pair of handcuffs on me. Worse yet, maybe they would wait until we landed and make me sweat through the entire flight.

Standing in line with the other passengers, still not cuffed, Immigration and Customs at San Francisco International also questioned me about why I didn't have any luggage. I gave them the same story—my father was missing at sea, and I'd gone straight to the airport from a shopping mall. The fastest route to Hawaii had me stopping in San Francisco. They could check with Detective Lau of the Honolulu Police Department if they needed confirmation.

If the authorities did check with Lau, I wondered what he'd tell them.

After waiting six hours at SFO, I boarded the first available flight to Hawaii. When we landed in Honolulu, I stopped at the entrance to the jetway, closed my eyes, inhaled a whiff of jet fuel, and smiled at being home.

Despite the eighty-degree heat, my body shivered when I saw

someone I hadn't expected at the gate. Detective Lau had on a dark sport coat. His gaze moved back and forth, scanning the faces of passengers until he spotted me. He motioned me over. We walked in silence toward baggage claim.

Lau finally spoke. "Do you have any luggage?"

I held up my handbag.

We walked past the luggage belts. At ground level, the departure terminals above shaded the arrivals from the noon sun. A young cop stood beside a blue-and-white parked at the curb. He ushered me into the back then jumped into the driver's seat. Lau slid in the front. We pulled out into traffic.

Lau spun around to face me. His bushy eyebrows formed a concerned mini triangle. "We got notification from the Shinjuku Police Department from an Inspector . . ." He read off a notepad. "Honma."

"He's the investigator in my mother's murder."

His face tightened as though he didn't know what to do with me. "The treaty of extradition between the U.S. and Japan proclaims that each country undertakes to extradite, to the other, any person found in its territory and sought by the other party for prosecution, or to execute punishment for designated offenses."

"Am I under arrest?"

Stone-faced, he didn't respond.

"I can explain everything." I paused, then asked, "Should I get a lawyer?"

"Gena," Lau said in a tone that was somewhere between that of a father and of an attorney. "I will not tell you whether you should or shouldn't, but it is your legal right."

With everything that had happened with my father and the incredible effort Detective Lau had put into helping me, I needed to trust him.

"I went back to Japan because things weren't adding up with my mother's murder . . ." I stopped and thought how crazy a conspiracy theory like this would sound. "I remembered after Liko was killed—Liko was Mr. Kapena's dog—there was a picture of a dog. I had a hunch I needed to see through. Can't you understand that? My mother is dead and my father is missing. I can't live with any more question marks. I got some info. And a name."

He didn't react, instead focused on me like I was a witness in front of a jury.

"The chief justice's daughter was found missing from Harajuku, and there was a witness. The witness got the license plate of the car that took her. My connection in the Shinjuku Police Department told me that Suzume Hayakawa, the witness, had been found dead. I can't believe it . . . I'm a suspect for her murder."

"And who's this police connection you're talking about?"

I shook my head. "Sorry, but can't tell you that. If I do, the person may be in danger."

Lau fingered his chin. "Did you meet with her—this Suzume person?"

"I did, but not this time. I'd given my connection in the Shinjuku Police the license plate number of the vehicle. I don't know how he's involved, but it led to Honma."

Lau squinted with disbelief. "Are you telling me he's yakuza?"

"Don't know." I raked my fingers through my hair. "I did not kill Suzume. I'm being framed; this is a setup. It's all connected. Don't you see? First my mother, my father, now me."

Detective Lau stared out the windshield at the slowing traffic ahead. "My response to the Shinjuku Police will be that this is under investigation. I will need your passport until it's finalized."

I retrieved my passport from my handbag and handed it to him. "Thank you, Detective."

Lau shifted his jaw from side to side, seemingly trying to

decide what to do next. "What has happened to you and your family is unfortunate. I don't know what's going on, but it's become obvious that you are involved in something very serious with some powerful people. And some crazies too, for strafing you and Kapena the other night."

The young cop took the Nimitz Highway along the southern coast. I asked Lau, "Are you taking me to the police station?"

He turned to face me. "We're taking you home."

"Can you drop me off at Queen's Medical Center on Punchbowl?"

Within fifteen minutes we pulled into the hospital driveway, and I stepped out of the car. Being nosy, I had to know. "Did the airline or anybody call you about my situation?"

"Yeah."

"What'd you tell them?"

"That's not important."

Lau lifted his chin to the driver. They drove away.

Information directed me to the third floor. I bought a flower arrangement of red carnations and baby's breath from the shop on the first floor before heading up. I approached Mr. Kapena's room, smelling hospital disinfectant and hearing CNN playing on a television. He was peering out the window at the Koolau Mountain Range.

"Hi, Mr. Kapena." His skin was pale, eyes sunken with blue shadows underneath them.

"Hey, Gena." He winced.

"How you doing?"

Although I sensed he was in extreme pain, he replied, "I'm doing okay."

"I wanted to let you know that I took Liko to the vet. They'll keep him there until you get out and we can give him a proper send-off."

When I told him that I was being accused of murder in Japan, he assured me that if they have no proof then they got nothing. We chatted about everything except the incident that night, avoiding anything to do with why he was lying in the hospital with gunshot wounds to his stomach and leg.

He talked about his wife, and her surprise birthday gift. She had placed a large red ribbon around the puppy's neck. Liko's tiny paws were on the kitchen table, staring at the lighted birthday candles. Mr. Kapena wiped away a tear and again stared blankly out the large window.

"I'm glad you're getting better, Mr. Kapena." I stood up to leave.

"Thanks for coming." His mind was already elsewhere.

When I arrived home by taxi, I removed the three listening devices and placed them in a box as evidence. I continued to behave as if the devices were still hidden, invading my privacy. I hated it and later planned to hire someone with professional electronic equipment to scan the entire house.

I recalled the bank account information and the key I'd found in my mother's safe, which I guessed had to lead to a safety deposit box. I changed into a comfortable, blue short-sleeved shirt, off-white pants, and leather sandals. I needed the damn video for leverage and find the truth about my mother's murder. What if it wasn't there? I thought of a backup plan.

I wished that Mr. Kapena were here to confirm that I was doing the right thing.

I slipped a *Dirty Harry* movie into a blank DVD case, but changed my mind and instead went with *Finding Nemo*. Eastwood was one of my dad's favorite actors.

In case someone was watching, I'd pretend retrieving the video from the safety deposit box to draw them out. The trouble with my plan was that I didn't know what to do next. The video better be there.

The McCully branch was smaller than the main bank downtown, and so less crowded and more personal. I brought my mother's death certificate, last will and testament, photo ID, and bank book, because I couldn't gain access to the vault without the proper documents.

Completing the authorization process, I followed the female manager into a room where the walls were covered with safety deposit boxes. The manager was in her mid-forties, and wore a rich-blue business suit with black pumps. She found my mother's box. I used the key from my mother's safe, and the bank manager used hers to open the lock. She pulled out the box and placed it on a standing tabletop, smiled, and exited the room.

I flipped open the top and quickly scanned the contents. A feeling of dread and hopelessness crash-landed on my chest. No video. The box contained another copy of Mom's will, exactly like the one from the floor safe. I lifted a black silk pouch tied with a silver cord and shook out the contents into my palm.

"Whoa." The word burst from my mouth. I counted four diamonds. I held one up to the fluorescent light overhead, sensing the high quality of the gem.

I fumbled with another silk bag. This one was dark red in color. Another four diamonds rolled into my palm. The third silk bag was purple and contained another four diamonds. The final was indigo blue with the same contents.

Sixteen diamonds. I wasn't a gemologist, but knew I held a small fortune in my palm. The colors black, red, purple, and indigo blue were favored colors in Japan. But why four diamonds per bag? Four was considered an unlucky number because it sounded like *shi,* or death.

I remembered a rumor from back when we lived in Japan, about yakuza members who challenged death choosing license plate numbers containing 4444 to express their contempt for their own mortality. On the roads, the message it sent was not to cut off this car. Maybe I was making too much of this, but why four bags and not one?

On the bottom of the safety deposit box was another key, like that for a lockbox.

Mom, what are you trying to tell me?

I lifted a brown eight-by-twelve envelope from the box, pulled out the contents, and perused the documents. Everything was written in Japanese, and I recognized it as a *koseki*, a system of identification in Japanese society.

In Japan, upon birth, each individual is listed in a family register, which sets out the relationship between family members and records births, deaths, marriages, divorces and adoptions. The koseki was based on a particular view of the family that centered on a couple's children and placed importance on birth order.

My phone got reception in the vault, so I researched the Internet for koseki. I found that, in the birth registration, "one person takes the position of the indexical 'head' or *hittosha*. All family members in the same koseki will have the same surname. Even if the father provides recognition of paternity, the child would be registered as illegitimate or *hi-chakushutsu-shi* if the parents were not married."

Here's where it got interesting: if the father was unknown, the child of an unmarried Japanese woman would be registered in the mother's koseki and take her surname, but would still be registered as illegitimate.

The koseki from the safety deposit box documented a male baby with a surname of *Nakagawa*. Kiyomi's surname was Nakagawa. I recognized the kanji character in the space for the first name—*Kami*.

I double-checked the box. Definitely no video.

The woman holding the baby in my mother's photograph, the one who'd killed her husband while he slept and taken her own life in seppuku, was Misaki Suzuki Novak. Assuming that this koseki was that of the baby in the picture, why was the child's surname listed as Nakagawa and not Suzuki? Was the child Kiyomi's? Why was this document so important to my mother?

Before exiting the bank, I froze at the glass door. Was I doing the right thing? I took a deep breath, lifted the DVD case from my handbag, slid on dark glasses, and walked out into the sunlight. I paused outside the entrance, smiled at a lady who walked past, glanced skyward for few seconds as though letting the sun warm my face, and placed the case back in my bag.

At every stoplight, at every turn, I glanced into the rearview mirror to see if anyone was following me. My phone chirped on the passenger seat. I left it there, anticipating a call from someone who might be watching and stalking me. The number on the screen was not the same one from before.

I answered with apprehension and caution. "Hello."

"Is this Gena?" a shaky woman's voice asked.

"Yes."

"This is Aom," she said, partly with relief, partly with terror. "They want the video."

"Who . . ."

"Tamura." Aom screamed in pain after what sounded like a loud slap to her face. "If they do not get the video, they will kill me!"

The line went dead.

I pulled the truck to the side of the road; my body trembling. I'd gotten it wrong. It was the yakuza following me.

I dialed Lani. No answer. I tried again. The call went to voicemail. I called Lani's grandmother who lived in Waimanalo.

"Hello," an elderly woman's voice said.

"Hi Mrs. Fernandez, this is Gena. Lani's friend."

"Oh yes, hi," she said, upbeat and cheerful. "How you been? Did you get a boyfriend yet?"

"No, Mrs. Fernandez," I answered. "Is Lani there?"

"She's another one who should already be married and giving me great-grandchildren, but—"

"Mrs. Fernandez." I felt bad for interrupting Lani's tutu and tried to control my own voice from going off the rails. "I need to get in touch with her. She planned to stay at your house for a few days."

"She did?" Her voice sounded surprised. "She neva tell me."

"Okay, sorry to bother you, Mrs. Fernandez. Bye." I hung up before she started asking me questions that I couldn't answer.

Maybe Lani had gone to the store and forgotten her cell. But she'd confessed to me many times that if she had to make a choice between having her phone with her or having an orgasm, there was no doubt she'd pick her phone.

I lifted *Finding Nemo* from my handbag and tensed with fear. "What have I done?"

33

Sebastian removed his wet clothes from one of a dozen washers, walked across the aisle, and tossed them into a large dryer. He could feel the heat from the adjacent dryers, which were tumbling wet garments in a dizzying clockwise rotation.

Dried lint, heavy machinery, a scent of flowery soap, and a tingle of electrical burning permeated the ground floor of the two-story building. The second floor was occupied by other small businesses.

The laundromat's entrance opened onto a two-lane asphalt road. It was situated diagonally across from a small restaurant specializing in catering fresh Hawaiian food. Only a short distance away from Waikiki, and with many two to three-story walkups in the area, the laundromat was always busy despite the small-town atmosphere of Kapahulu.

From the corner of his eye, Sebastian took a quick glance at Gena's best friend folding clothes into little piles. Lani was her name. A little hottie and a big tease, he knew from observing her how she used her sexuality to control men.

Sebastian nonchalantly ambled over to her. "Hi, I was

wondering if you got change for a couple dollars." He pointed at the change machine. "It's broken."

Lani smiled sexily at him. "That damn machine is always busted, so I bring my own loose."

She counted off change for two dollars and they made the exchange. He thanked her with a gracious smile.

He extended a hand. "I'm Sebastian."

"Lani." She shook it. "I haven't seen you here before."

"I passed this place when returning from snorkeling at Hanauma Bay. When people started giving me that 'bad smell' look . . ." He shrugged.

Lani chuckled at his joke and continued folding clothes. "Where're you from?"

"California, but I also spend a lot of time in Southeast Asia."

He wasn't sure if she'd chosen them intentionally, but she placed a pair of red thong panties to her nose and inhaled. "I just love the smell of clean clothes in the morning . . . It smells like—"

"Victory." Sebastian finished the popular movie phrase and said, "*Apocalypse Now*, 1979."

They cracked up laughing.

Between giggles, Lani interjected, "I have a friend you might want to meet."

"To tell you the truth, I wouldn't be interested in your friend."

The tease actually blushed.

"How's about a cup of coffee while we wait for our clothes to finish?" Sebastian offered with a flirty smile of his own. "My treat."

She folded her red thong panty, which looked like an exclamation point when added it to the stack of clothes. "That's my last."

"Then how's about I give you a lift home?"

"How do you know I didn't drive here?" Lani answered with a suspicious squint.

"Because I saw you on the sidewalk. I passed by when I went to buy breakfast at the corner restaurant down the street. I came straight here afterwards."

Her smile returned. "Sure, why not . . . cup of coffee sounds super." She placed her folded clothes into a plastic basket.

They walked out to the parking lot. She placed her basket in the back seat of his Nissan. When she opened the passenger side door and slid in, Sebastian pointed a handgun at her.

His voice turned cruel and determined. "Don't shout or do anything stupid that will cause me to pull the trigger. At this close range, I won't miss."

"What do you want?" Lani couldn't take her eyes off the gun. "I have a little money. It's all yours. Just lemme go."

"On second thought"—he clucked his tongue— "I am interested in your friend."

She looked like she was running names and faces through her head and asked, "Gena?"

He nodded and motioned with the gun for her to close the car door.

Lani stared out through the windshield and said through clenched teeth, "Ah, fuck."

With the handgun rolled up in a beach towel and pointed at her back, she followed Sebastian's instructions to the letter.

Thirty minutes later, he had her hands and ankles bound in his high-rise apartment in downtown Honolulu.

Her complaining and swearing soon wore on him. Every other word that came out of her filthy mouth was *fuck*—what da fuck, who da fuck, why da fuck . . . And it went on after he admitted interest in her best friend.

"Did you fuckin' kill Gena's mother?"

He didn't answer her.

"What da fuck are you gonna do with me?"

He didn't answer.

"Don't you have something to fuckin' eat in this dump?"

He'd had enough. He stomped to the dresser and lifted a knife from a drawer. Lani froze and didn't say a word. Sebastian retrieved a roll of gray duct tape and tore off a piece. Lani twisted her head away from the tape, but he slipped it over her mouth.

"Now maybe you'll just shut up."

"Mmm." She struggled to talk under the gag, but her next few words didn't need a cryptographic translation. "Mmuuk myuu."

Sebastian used another burner phone and called Gena.

She answered but said nothing.

He said in a low, threatening voice, "I have your friend."

Silence. Then, "I don't believe you."

He motioned to the girl sitting on the floor. "Say hello." He tore off the duct tape.

"Ouch, you dumb fuck." Lani cried out, "Fuck this guy, Gen!"

He slapped the duct tape back over her mouth and said into the phone, "You got your proof."

"I'll kill you if you harm her!"

Gena's threat made him laugh louder. "No, you won't. You'll trade her life for the video."

"I told you—" She stopped, and seemed wrestling with her emotions. "I'll give you money."

Sebastian grinned at the panic he heard on the other end of the phone call. "Her life for only the video."

Gena's once shaky voice suddenly calmed. "Give me a few days."

Sebastian grinned at her samurai toughness, but said, "No more days."

"I know you want this video more than anything. I'm sure you can be a little flexible."

"When?"

"I'll call you back in thirty minutes."

Sebastian hated being put on hold.

After forty minutes, his burner chimed. She said, "Day after tomorrow. Meet me on the island of Kauai on the north shore, a place called Mountain Paradise Villas in Hanalei. Be there at noon. If you harm Lani, I'll kill you."

"Bring the video." He ended the call, euphoric to have such control over her.

Sebastian turned to Lani sitting on the floor. "We'll be catching the inter-island flight to Kauai. I will be untying you. If you cry out for help or in any way fail to cooperate, I've got someone with a target on your friend's back. Do you understand?"

She didn't reply.

Sebastian slid behind her, reached over her shoulder, and pinched her right nipple hard. He took pleasure in her muffled scream.

With ice in his voice, he calmly asked again, "Do you understand me?"

She nodded rapidly and glared at him like a vicious Tasmanian devil locked in a cage.

Sebastian scratched his chin. "I wonder what your friend's up to?"

ngel had arranged for me to pick up a handgun at the airport on Kauai from an uncle whose primary means of income was selling marijuana, and not for medicinal purposes.

We met in the airport parking lot. I saw the family resemblance. He was a big, burly Hawaiian man with sunburnt brown skin. He was leaning against a raised black truck with giant wheels that looked like it should be in a monster truck show. He wore dark glasses and a tank top that looked a size too small for his three hundred pounds of humanity.

In low baritone he said, "You Gena?"

I nodded and smiled.

He waved a hand as large as a catcher's mitt. "Come."

Angel's uncle led me to the passenger side of his truck. A skinny younger guy with matching facial features sat in the passenger seat, picking his teeth with a toothpick.

He retrieved a plastic grocery bag, looking at me like I might shoot myself. "It's not marked. Fully loaded. Hollow points. No extra shells."

I peeked in the bag at a Glock 17 pistol and a seventeen-round

9mm magazine. I pulled the gun out and, leaning into the truck cab to hide from view, checked that the gun was unloaded and noted the safety trigger. I engaged the magazine and pulled the slide back to load a round. I then released the magazine, again pulling the slide slowly back to unload it.

The skinny guy snickered, his lips tight, the toothpick bouncing in his mouth. "You seem kinda prepared for a girl."

I placed the gun back in the bag. "My dad was military and proud of it. He never let me forget it."

"My nephew said you all right," the big man said. "Angel one good boy. Not too smart, but he got one good heart. Good luck."

Kauai was the oldest of the eight islands, and so the greenest. The life-pace sort of gave off a laid-back vibe, with quaint country towns originating during the plantation era.

I checked out a rental car and headed for the north shore. Because of the rugged mountainous terrain and cliffs on the north side of the island, there were no roads that circled Kauai, so once out of the Lihue Airport, turning right would lead you east, then north. The road then dead-ended in the Hanalei area thirty-two miles away.

My head in a daze, I started the hourlong drive. The radio news broadcast disrupted my trance, warning of a northern storm moving toward the island. I hadn't noticed the dark clouds forming overhead. The wind also picked up, but I kept hoping that this would be over before the storm hit.

Every year before David died, our family would spend a week on the North Shore, staying at Mountain Paradise Villas, vacation rentals with twelve exclusive luxury mountain cabins. We loved it because of the seclusion of the mountainous rainforest and the short distance to the horseshoe-shaped Hanalei Bay, with its pristine white-sand beach and aqua-blue ocean water.

After an hour of driving, I climbed out of the rental car to stretch my legs. A cool breeze blew across the valley, refreshing my body after being cooped up. Along the white wooden railing, I looked out over the majestic greenery of Hanalei Valley, carpeted below with acres of taro patches. The Hanalei River meandered along the edge of Hanalei, which back in the sixties had been a hippie town full of drugs and nakedness and was now a hot tourist destination.

The steep, mountainous terrain appeared ominous, yet it had a surreal calmness, with its dozens of waterfalls creating vertical streaks of white lines against dark green backgrounds.

This place brought back joy, as well as sadness.

A young tourist couple next to me said words that didn't register at first. The blonde woman repeated, "This valley is absolutely gorgeous."

"It sure is." I climbed back into the car and followed the rickety two-lane road that weaved down into the valley. I crossed a steel truss bridge, took a left, and followed a one-lane road that cut through acres of taro patches on both sides.

After ten minutes, I parked in front of the office building. Built for luxury and privacy, the twelve cabins were about two hundred feet apart, spaced out like the spokes of a bicycle wheel with the office centered as the hub. The twelve cabins were connected by gravel roads. Each cabin had a spectacular view of Hanalei Bay in the distance.

Footsteps approached from behind me. I spun into a teenage boy wearing a white blazer uniform with a clipped-on nametag reading, *Steve*. He had his hands on his knees, trying to catch his breath, and looked part-Hawaiian with his cocoa-colored complexion, slim body, and narrow face.

He took a breath. "Hew . . . glad I caught up with ya, lady. My boss had to take off, but he gave me da key to give ya."

Stepping through the raw-wood front door brought back memories. A hardwood floor encircled a fire pit with a large flue directly above it. A side door led to the master bedroom, and another door to a modernized bathroom.

The designer had maintained that raw, outdoorsy feel using mahogany and pine and *koa* wood throughout the cabin's interior. The kitchen had the basics. Pots and pans hung from hooks above an expansive smoke-colored granite counter, and in the corner was a tall rack with a great assortment of fine wines. The outdoor furniture on the wooden porch was made of framed wrought iron.

Cook pine trees, a hundred to a hundred-sixty feet tall, surrounded the cabins. I appreciated these towering trees more since I'd learned that, in the days of sailing, they were used to repair ship masts after long journeys across the Pacific Ocean.

It was three in the afternoon, so I had another three to four hours before darkness settled over the cabin villas. I drove to the community hardware store in Princeville ten minutes away and bought handsaws, rope, canvas, steel clamps, and everything else I needed.

One of my favorite college basketball coaches, Bobby Knight, used to say, "I don't believe in luck, I believe in preparation." But I was up against professional killers. With no disrespect to Coach Knight, I needed more than preparation; I needed Lady Luck on my side.

When I got back, night had fallen. I began prepping the fireplace, making a small pyramid of stacked wood from a pile next to it. Staring straight up at the ceiling and its open rafters, lightning flashed, illuminating the surrounding trees for a split second, casting instant shadows across the walls. In the blink of an eye, it went back to darkness. Thunder cracked violently overhead; the sound vibrated the air, creating a terrifying shockwave.

I pulled myself together and forced my hands from shaking.

In darkness, I listened. The wind grew stronger. It moaned, phantom-like, as it pressed against the windows. It whistled and howled through the hidden cracks in the cabin walls.

From the corner of my eye, I picked up movement outside the window. A shadow crossed the glass; a face peeked into the cabin. Fear shot through me with a cold, terrifying chill. The lightning flashed again, but the figure standing at the window had vanished just as quickly as it had appeared.

I grabbed the Glock.

Whoever was outside jiggled the door handle. I pointed the gun at the door and screamed, "Who is it?"

A heavy voice said, "You Gena?"

"Yes. Who are you?"

"Angel called. He thought you might need some help."

I unlocked the door and swung it inward. Standing on the wooden porch were three men and two women. They all wore shiny, wet ponchos, with the men wearing dripping baseball caps and the women rain bonnets. I let them in, and they hung their coats on a clothes rack inside the door.

The lead guy, the oldest of them, had a white beard that dangled to the top of a sunken chest. He wore a tank top, board shorts, and rubber slippers. "I'm Kimo. Angel said there's some bad dudes trying to do bad things to you. We're here to help."

"Mahaho, Kimo. I can use the help."

Kimo pointed, going from left to right in the semicircle. "That there is Puna." The large middle-aged Polynesian man nodded his wiry afro, which looked like something from the sixties.

"Ipo." The heavy-set woman in her forties smiled, showing a set of white teeth.

"Den there's Tundah." The man made a noise with his lips and said, "Howzit." He was thin as a twig, his voice low and rhythmic. Sort of like thunder, I thought.

"And this here is Maile." The woman wore a floral muumuu. "She's one of the best welders in Hawaii. Worked at Pearl Harbor Naval Shipyard and kept those rust buckets in tiptop shape."

Maile looked to be Samoan with her overhanging eyebrows, thick lips, and flat nose.

The last guy was Eddie. Kimo said, "Best carpenter on the island. He builds ancient Hawaiian canoes on the side."

The six of them sat around the warmth of the fire in the center of the room. After I explained my plan, Kimo leaned forward. "I served in 'Nam. You're talking about guerrilla tactics."

I nodded. "I do appreciate the help, but this is *my* fight. People have already been killed getting involved and I don't want harm come to any of you."

Maile had shifted to the back and out of the firelight. She stepped forward. "Dis Kauai . . . What da fuck is yakuza doing hea?"

Although I needed help, I wasn't going to place anyone's life at risk. "Like I said, these people are professional killers."

The group huddled together for a minute in the shadow of the cabin.

Ipo took a step closer. "We all have kids to think about. But we're willing to help you set up your plan tomorrow."

Warmth filled me, like it had when the young cabbie and old woman in Japan helped me in my time of need. I said, with deep-felt sincerity, "Mahalo everybody."

Kimo stood up. The others followed his lead. They pulled their ponchos on at the door. The two women and two other men left first.

Kimo stopped in the doorway. "I've seen enough death in 'Nam, but I will fight again for justice. You say these people killed your mother and you also think they are involved in your father going missing at sea?"

"I think there were other deaths, but I can't prove it."

Kimo nodded and shut the door behind him.

By firelight, I disassembled the Glock and thought of Sun Tzu's *The Art of War*— know your enemy.

What did I know about Tamura-san? Mr. Kapena had described him as a narcissistic bully. Killing was ingrained in Tamura like breathing; he was a merciless yakuza oyabun who'd gained power and respect by instilling fear in people and through death threats. His entourage of killers more than stacked the odds in his favor.

What did I know about Sebastian? Did Sebastian murder my mother? Hanako had talked about a serial killer murdering men who patronized hostess clubs. Although circumstantial, all evidence pointed to Sebastian. He despised all those who were involved in the water trade. As an onna-gata performer, he could have disguised himself as a woman and lured men into having sex, then killed them.

Some people say the geometry of an animal's eyes indicates whether it was the hunter or the hunted. The eyes of predators slant upward, like those of wolves, tigers, hawks, and gators, while the eyes of prey slant downward, like rabbits, gazelles, deer, sheep, and horses.

I strolled to the mirror and checked out my eyes. Was mine the image of predator or prey? Both my opponents were predators. Predators could smell fear.

I steeled my nerves. My dad's voice echoed in my head, "If you gotta use a gun, make sure it fires."

I snapped the clip into the Glock and pulled the slide catch down. I opened the cabin door, pointed the gun into the dark sky and pulled the trigger twice.

The wind muffled the loud blasts.

I glanced at the rack of wine, but decided against it. I needed a clear head. My plan had to work. Because of me, two innocent lives were at stake.

35

W e were done with the all-day preparations. The sun inched below the surrounding mountain peaks; the storm had taken a break, an intermission. The ground was saturated and spongy as I walked to the office building. A screeching cry from a Hawaiian *pueo*, a short-eared owl, echoed through the trees.

Steve, the teenage boy, stood in front of the office door. "Sounds like ya guys were busy out there doing something. I recognized Uncle Kimo. He one pretty cool old man 'cause he treats everybody with respect, even young people. He was in war. But when I ask him what it was like, he says he no talk about it 'cause it brings bad memories." Steve shrugged like it was no big deal.

"Hey Steve, why don't you take the day off tomorrow?"

Surprised at my suggestion, he said, "But my boss not hea and I'm responsible. And my boss said we closing da office cause of da storm, but he still want me to hang around in case ya need anything."

Closing the office? I hadn't seen his boss since arriving.

"Is there anybody in those cabins?" I nudged my chin toward

the eleven other cabins. Although I hadn't seen anyone walking around and heard only the wind and the owls, I still needed confirmation.

Steve looked down at his big toe sticking out from the edge of his slipper and avoided eye contact. "This time of year kinda slow 'cause it rains a lot hea. So my boss was super happy when ya booked this place for two nights."

"I'm the only one here?"

"Yeah." He shrugged his bony shoulders. "Hey, da weather lady on TV said dat it might reach twenty-eight inches in da next twenty-four hours." Steve looked up at the sky. "Maybe I should haul out da boat."

I reached into my pocket and pulled out a hundred-dollar bill. "Here, don't show up tomorrow, okay?"

He glanced at the money. His fingers twitched, but he said, "I can't, lady."

"Then this is for allowing us to modify the cabin." I didn't draw back my hand.

"You said ya'll get it back to normal before ya leave, right?"

"Yes, we will." I pulled another hundred from my pocket. "Please Steve, don't show up tomorrow."

He snatched the money from my hand. It disappeared into his shorts pocket. As Steve walked away, he shouted into the strengthening wind, "See ya tomorrow"—he caught himself—"see ya day afta tomorrow, lady. And mahalo for da money."

THE NEXT MORNING, I checked with Angel's connections at the Lihue Airport. A private jet, a Gulfstream, had filed a flight plan with the FAA, which detailed travel from Japan to Honolulu to Kauai, estimated to arrive at 10 a.m.

After talking with Sebastian, I had redialed the phone number that Aom had called from. The man grunted. I pictured the giant on the other end. I gave Tamura the same time and location to meet as I had Sebastian. Godzilla grunted again and hung up.

I stood outside and watched two black SUVs pull up in front of the cabin at 11:30 a.m. Even Japanese criminals were on time.

Two men got out from the front seat. Godzilla looked out of place wearing a dark suit and tie among the greenery. The other man, also in a dark suit, carried himself like a mixed martial arts guy with rock-solid muscles, itching for a fight.

The giant opened the left rear door and Tamura-san stepped out into a puddle of mud. The old man's face soured at the sight of his dress shoe coated with mud. Godzilla removed his jacket and placed it across the puddle for his boss to step on. The giant exposed a holstered .357 Smith & Wesson Magnum.

The other guy scurried to the right rear door and yanked Aom from the back seat. Her hands were tied behind, the left side of her face black and blue. Her left eye was half-closed from severe swelling. They'd shaved her head bald. Tamura got part of his revenge. If my plan failed, he would accomplish it entirely and kill her.

Two more of Tamura's gorillas got out of a second SUV. Based on the bulges in their suits, these guys were packing some heavy firepower. Flying by private jet does have its advantages in terms of transporting illegal firearms, but I'd already thought of that.

Tamura and the two guards from the first SUV approached me where I was standing at the edge of the wooden porch. The other two men hung back by their vehicle, their eyes shifting back and forth, scanning the area for any threats to the old man.

Although I'd anticipated the weapons, I hadn't planned for what happened next.

Tamura signaled the two men standing by the second SUV to the cabin. One man palmed a handheld device with an antenna.

He first scanned outside then inside the house checking for microphones and cameras. He nodded to Tamura.

The same two guys then came back with metal detectors. A key part of my plan was about to fall apart. After twenty minutes, one guy came out holding the Glock that I'd hidden among the fireplace logs. He tossed knives from the kitchen onto the muddy ground.

Disappointed but not deterred, I signaled for Tamura to take off Aom's bindings. Tamura grunted a few words in Japanese. Godzilla flicked a butterfly knife open and cut the plastic strap from her wrists. She rubbed her hands together. I could see it in Aom's eyes—she wanted to run. I discretely shook my head, hoping she'd get the signal that something was coming.

Aom said apologetically, "I am sorry, Gena. If I had not told him who had the video, he would have killed me right there."

I nodded, understanding, but thinking ahead to my next move.

A Chevy Camaro rumbled down the muddy road, approached, and pulled in behind the second SUV. Lani jumped out of the front seat and nearly toppled both of us over in the mud as she threw her arms around my neck.

She blurted out, "He told me he had you bound and tied like the pictures, and if I didn't cooperate, he'd call a number and have you killed."

I glared at Sebastian and his flawless complexion. Perhaps the many years of makeup had shielded his skin from UV rays and the resultant aging.

Sebastian's cockiness toward Tamura was apparent. "What the hell is he doing here? Your deal is with me."

Tamura scowled but said nothing.

"He's part of the bidding process," I said.

"Bidding!" Sebastian yelled.

"Yes, whoever is the highest bidder will get the video." I

pretended to be in full control of the situation, knowing that it would take just one screwup for everything to unravel.

"I'll give you a million dollars for the video." Tamura smirked and glared at Sebastian, knowing that he couldn't outbid that amount.

"It's not about money, Tamura-san." Though I despised him, I continued speaking with a level of respect. "It's about bidding on trust."

I received what I expected from both men—confusion. But I knew they would play along because of the famous proverb: curiosity killed the cat.

Tamura signaled for the giant to search Sebastian for weapons. Godzilla violently shoved Sebastian against the Camaro and patted him down. Behind his lower back was a Glock 43, single-stack 9mm with a six-round magazine. The giant slid the gun into his belt. He lifted a knife strapped to Sebastian's ankle and threw it on the wet ground.

Sebastian cockily said to Tamura, "I want those back when this is done."

The old man grunted.

I needed to know, so asked, "How did you get a gun on the inter-island plane and through security?"

"Everything is easier if you know the right people." Sebastian's sneer revealed a hidden dimple. "Now let's get this over with."

I instructed Tamura, "Tell your men to wait outside or there's no deal."

Tamura barked orders. The four men hesitated, but did as they were told.

The five of us entered the cabin's living room. The fire pit in the center was ablaze, light smoke snaking upward to the flue. The rich smell of *kiawe* wood, a sweeter Hawaiian mesquite, permeated the cabin. I waved Tamura to the sofa and Sebastian to the wooden chair. I pointed for Lani and Aom to stand next to me.

Both men watched closely as I strode to the door and threw the bolt on the new lock. Tamura's bodyguards violently jerked the doorhandle. The cabin shook like an earthquake when their bodies slammed into the solid oak door.

"Tell your men to relax. We shouldn't be interrupted, and your men here would give you an unwanted edge." I stared at Sebastian, who nodded with approval.

Tamura shouted, "Hottoite!"

The frantic blows to the door stopped. The heat generated by the flames caused beads of sweat to form on Sebastian's forehead. Tamura retrieved a handkerchief from his suit pocket and wiped his face. I'd purposely made the room uncomfortable by intensifying the fire as a means of gaining a tiny advantage.

Aom couldn't stop staring at Sebastian's tattooed forearm.

I asked her, "Is that it?"

Aom's lips quivered. She avoided Sebastian's glare and hesitantly nodded.

My hatred toward my mother's murderer burned.

Sebastian kept his gaze trained on me. He sneered and said through clenched teeth, "She's a whore. Who's going to believe a prostitute over a famous stage actor like myself?"

If Tamura's men hadn't confiscated the Glock, I would have shot him on the spot. But I held back my rage, remembering Mr. Kapena's voice telling me to *take the hit*.

I bit down my anger and stuck to the plan. "Tamura-san, you have all the money and power any human being could ever dream of. What you want is to live forever. I bet you'd give everything to be twenty-four again."

That got Sebastian's full attention. He straightened in the wooden chair.

"Sir. Why did you go to China for three months?"

Tamura frowned as if he hadn't heard the question.

I answered for him. "The mountain recluse taught you the secrets of Taoist sexual alchemy. The most potent elixir of life, you learned, is the essence that the opposite sex secretes at the height of sexual ecstasy. If you could pluck this essence at the crucial moment, you could nurture your own sexual potency and longevity—perhaps even become immortal."

Sebastian scoffed.

I held up a hand and continued, "In China, during the fourteenth through sixteenth century, the elite performed the ritual of pluck-and-nurture called *tsai-pu*. Emperors and kings got their nutrition from concubines or stables of well-nourished young women kept especially for this purpose. They were treated like pampered milk cows, so that the essences they yielded would be of a superior grade. They'd sought to benefit through an exchange of sexual chi by fondling young girls and drinking their sexual juices. The seekers of immortality believed that the partner should be young and, even better, virginal." I paused and swallowed in disgust. "Your young stable was made up of vulnerable young girls who roamed the streets searching for something that was missing in their lives. Like the emperors of old, you want to beat time."

Sickened, I thought of Sparrow, the chief justice's daughter, and the other countless underage girls who had disappeared from the streets of Harajuku.

I stared at Tamura, trying to read him. "Do you realize how unhinged that sounds?"

Tamara's red face appeared about to explode. But he instantly calmed, perhaps knowing that once he had the video, I would be dead and his secret buried with me.

I stated the obvious. "You having sex with underaged girls obviously hasn't worked out well for you."

Sebastian stifled a laugh.

Tamura's next words awed me. "I'm eighty-two years old."

I couldn't hide the *no shit* look on my face. But I didn't believe him.

I turned to Sebastian because I hated looking at Tamura's smugness. "You have youth, but want power. Are you willing to give up your youth for power?"

Sebastian gave me a look of incredulity, but he continued to listen because of that old proverb.

"If I give Tamura-san the video"—I faced Sebastian— "would you trust him not to kill you?"

Sebastian glanced away, sweat dripping from his forehead and down his cheek.

"If I give Sebastian the video," I said to Tamura, "would you trust him not to blackmail you?"

Tamura shouted, "This is stupid. Now give me the video or you're all dead."

"What you don't know is, if any one of us is killed"—I waved a hand at Lani and Aom— "the video goes viral on the Internet. One copy will go directly to the chief justice, whose daughter you murdered."

Tamura stood quickly and pointed a finger at me. "It was an accident."

I said to Tamura, "The reason you want the video is because you could be found guilty of murder and sent to prison where you'll rot for the rest of your very lonely life. And there are no virgin girls in prison."

Tamura sat back down and huffed out a breath as though saying: *That will be the day.*

"So you might ask"—I nudged my chin toward Sebastian— "why does he want the video?"

Tamura coughed and stared at Sebastian.

"That's right. It's all about power. He wants to be oyabun of your yakuza organization."

Tamura burst out laughing. "Look at him. Oyabun of what? Of men who dress like women?"

Sebastian's fist clenched; his face turned beet red.

"Kiyomi paid someone to call Novak at the bar," I said to Tamura. "I know that Novak owed you money for gambling losses. I wouldn't know the exact words she had told this person to say, but my guess would be that you, Tamura, were collecting on his gambling debt and told him he was dead if he didn't pay up."

"That's where you're wrong." Tamura wiped his face with a handkerchief. "Why kill someone who owes money? Once he's dead there is no more money. But money will continue to flow if he's alive, and when he stops paying, we'll break an arm or a leg or cut his dick off."

"What was said is not important," I said, trying to maintain the upper hand. "What's important is that Kiyomi was waiting for Novak at his apartment. When he returned from the bar, he was drugged and led to bed. I think Misaki was also involved in the scheme. I believe Kiyomi killed Novak while he slept then persuaded Misaki to move closer to the shrine. Kiyomi then stabbed Misaki in her abdomen and made it look like seppuku."

The skin around Sebastian's eyes tightened after hearing that Kiyomi might have killed his mother, but he said, "You're wasting fuckin' time. What does that got to do with all this?"

I answered with confidence, "Novak was blackmailing Kiyomi for free booze and food and girls, and threatened to go public with the fact that Kiyomi was really your mother."

"My mother is Misaki," Sebastian cried out, ignoring what he thought were lies.

Having anticipated Sebastian's reaction, now was the time to drop the bomb, so I pushed on. "Yes, Kiyomi is your mother. She gave you to Misaki because she didn't want a child. But more importantly, she didn't want anyone to know who the real father was."

Tamura and Sebastian leaned forward.

I pointed to Sebastian and nudged my chin toward Tamura. "This man is your son."

Tamura burst out laughing—a hardy, condescending laughter that dug deep into Sebastian's arrogance. Between gags he said, "This guy who likes to dress like a woman . . . my son?" He again cracked up laughing.

Sebastian's face grew redder and redder. His fists clenched tighter.

Tamura continued to ridicule and laugh. "Me, father of this Newhalf. This . . . this *ladyboy*? He—she—can't decide on what sex he wants to be, so he chooses both," the old man criticized spitefully. "And you're telling me that he's, my son." Again, he burst out laughing.

I added fuel to the fire. "Look at him. He does look like you."

Tamura took laughing to another level. "He's a woman with a dick!"

Sebastian went off. He attacked the old man, hitting him with a multitude of punches and elbows. Tamura's body went limp; he'd been knocked unconscious and was bleeding from the mouth and nose. His eyes swelled shut, as if he'd stuffed his head in a beehive.

The banging inside the cabin sparked pounding on the front door. Gunshots were fired. Bullets ricocheted off the new stainless-steel lock. Godzilla scurried to the window and tried to get in from there. The newly installed bars were like those of a jail, but instead of keeping people in, they kept people out. The giant saw the oyabun on the ground and in desperation tried to tear the bars from the window.

The woman who wore the floral muumuu had been right when she said, "You need a jackhammer to get through that puppy."

"Now that we got that settled, where's the damn video?" Sebastian demanded.

"The video is useless to you if he dies."

"He won't die." Sebastian pulled Lani toward him and held her in a headlock. "I'll snap her neck."

"No, wait." My hands shot out. I shuffled over to the pyramid of logs and pulled out the DVD case. "Now let her go."

Sebastian grinned, released her, and said, "Give."

I nodded at Lani. She again stood to my left.

Instead of handing the DVD to Sebastian, I tossed it into the blazing fire and quickly pivoted away. The case, with its powdered magnesium inside, burst into a blinding white flash. Sebastian frantically rubbed his eyes with spread fingers, trying to regain his vision. The bright flash also hit Lani and Aom. Temporarily blinded, they rapidly blinked and squinted. Since they were positioned farther away, their vision should return quicker.

Sebastian stumbled and collided with the wooden railing that encircled the fire pit, trying to get to the kitchen faucet. Before he could wash his eyes, I grabbed the baseball bat by the fireplace and swung it at his head. But I had underestimated his temporary blindness. With speed, quickness, and strength, Sebastian intercepted the bat at the handle and delivered a powerful back-kick to my chest. My body folded over from the impact; the pain intense. I might have cracked a rib.

Sebastian was fighting on instincts, sensing shadows and movements.

I pointed to the back of the cabin and screamed to Aom and Lani, "Lift the board and squeeze out. Run for the taro field and the orange flag. Jump on the mat and hold tight."

Having regained her vision, Aom dashed for the back. She removed the loose board and slipped through the opening. Cool air rushed into the room.

Sebastian delivered a punch to my left ear. I blocked his strike with *tan sao,* then in one continuous motion flowed to his face with an open palm. But my strike bounced off his jaw like a projectile from a Nerf gun.

"Lani, go!" I yelled.

"No!" Lani charged Sebastian with the wooden chair. Sebastian kept blinking non-stop and sensed the movement. He delivered a powerful sidekick to Lani's stomach. Her body jolted to a stop like she'd run into a concrete post. Grabbing her stomach, Lani collapsed to the floor.

I rushed Sebastian. I feigned going for a high tackle, but at the last instant hit him down low at the ankles. His bulk toppled over me. In the melee, I landed on his back. With my short, square fingernails, I furiously dug into his soft eye sockets. He bucked and tried to throw me off, but I held on. My feet came off the ground and my legs wrapped around his waist. My fingers kept digging into his skull. Sebastian screamed, twisted, and reeled from side to side, trying to get me off. Like a rabid animal, I sunk my teeth into his neck, my face contorted with pure hatred. I rode him, screaming like a madwoman.

This beast killed my mother! Shot Mr. Kapena! Kidnapped and threatened my best friend!

I screamed to gain more power, more inner strength.

Sebastian landed two solid punches on my jaw in rapid succession. I staggered backward and fell, my mind blanked out for a second. He stood above me, shaking off the remnants of blindness, and positioned himself to deliver a kick to my skull.

Lani swung the baseball bat at his head. Seeing the shadow and sensing movement, Sebastian shifted. Instead of the middle of his skull, the bat struck his shoulder, and sent him staggering backward.

Delirious, my vision blurred, Lani pulled me to the back of the cabin. We squeezed between the boards. I glimpsed at Aom.

She was hurdling into the taro field. Two of Tamura's men gave chase. Aom was in her element, determined to reach the orange mat, gaining distance from the two men who were flopping and struggling through the mud.

Godzilla surprised me from around the corner of the cabin. He grabbed me by the hair. Lani's fist struck the giant's chest, but it only made the big man laugh. The other man squeezed in between the boards to help his boss.

The giant dragged me to the front of the cabin. Lani bit down on his wrist. He grimaced, let go of my hair, and gave Lani a solid backhand. She flew backwards to the ground.

I picked up a kitchen knife that had been left in the mud. Before he could retreat, I slashed and cut his knee. Then, in a continuous circular motion, I stood up and attacked his neck with a sweeping stroke of the knife. Godzilla raised his hand. The blade sliced his palm. Two knife wounds, and he hadn't made a sound.

Shit.

Lani's mouth was bleeding. She wanted to finish the guy off, but it was pipe dream. He could easily kill us both. Our best chance for survival was to use our speed.

We ran for the forest.

36

Lani and I ran toward the trees and didn't look back.

There were acres of taro filling Hanalei Valley, and I wanted to use this to our advantage, because there was a way, or technique, to walking through knee-deep mud. The trick was to keep your feet flat rather than stepping from heel to toe, then get down on your knees and shins to create extra surface area, bend at the knees, and push forward as much as up with the feet.

Aom grew up in the rice fields of Thailand, so she had that to her advantage. Lani was also a country girl, from the sleepy town of Waimanalo, and had picked pineapple *ratoon* crops as a summer job. I assumed that Tamura's men were city dwellers who spent hours staring at little steel balls amid the clattering noise of pachinko machines in the concrete jungle of Tokyo.

My plans changed when Lani refused to leave me. Yet if it wasn't for her, I'd probably be badly injured or dead.

We continued to sprint toward the trees, a football field's distance away and in the opposite direction from Aom and her pursuers.

Exhausted and dripping with sweat, Tamura's goons struggled

to close the distance with Aom. One bodyguard, dressed in dark suit and tie, got stuck in knee-deep mud just fifty feet from the embankment. Breathing hard, he used a taro plant like a rope to pull himself forward. A second man, also in a dark suit but thinner and built like a street fighter, was also trapped in soft mud twenty yards into the field.

Aom reached the rubber mat at the bottom of the orange flag. In a last-ditch effort, the two men drew their handguns and started shooting at her. The moment she jumped onto the orange mat, a truck engine revved, and a rope leading into the trees, which had been attached to the mat snapped tight like an elastic band. Aom rode the mat like a magic carpet, skidding across the taro field and disappearing into the forest.

Kimo had insisted on helping, so he'd rigged the winch on his truck and connected it to the mat. Although Aom was his only passenger, I exhaled, relieved that she had reached safety.

Beaten, battered, and covered head-to-toe with mud, Tamura's men struggled to pull themselves from the taro field. Sweating profusely, their rumpled coats were draped over sagging shoulders. The two bodyguards dragged themselves onto a partitioned graveled road between taro patches. Barefoot, their dress shoes were buried somewhere in the deep mud. They staggered toward the cabin, breathing heavily, chins down to their chest at failing to re-capture the girl.

I turned back toward the cabin. Lani yanked my arm and screamed, "Forget about them, let's go!"

I ignored her, because I needed to see what transpires in order to defeat the man who killed my mother, and more than likely involved in the disappearance of my father.

Sebastian had regained his vision and balance and, with swiftness, attacked Godzilla, an opponent twice his size, but twice as slow. The mixed martial arts guy had Tamura's arm around his shoulder and half carried him to the SUV.

I glanced skyward for a split second after a crack of thunder exploded overhead like a bomb. Ominous, dark, heavy clouds canopied the sky. Four sudden gunshots rang out. I turned back to Sebastian. Godzilla and the mixed martial arts guy lay on the muddy ground. Sebastian held a gun to Tamura's head, sneering at the oyabun, but didn't pull the trigger.

I shivered at how quickly Sebastian killed.

The two men who'd lost the chase with Aom, their faces drained of energy, scurried toward the two killed bodyguards and the old man lying on the ground.

Sebastian stared at Lani and me, in the opposite direction from which the two men were charging at him. He sprinted toward us, a vengeful scowl on a once feminine face.

The street fighter guy who'd chased after Aom hurried to the semiconscious Tamura and dragged him to the SUV. His partner had another idea. He lifted a handgun and began firing at Sebastian's back as he charged toward us.

Instead of running from the gunfire, Sebastian reversed his course, sprinting and zigzagging toward the man trying to kill him. Glock in hand, Sebastian rapidly fired at the bodyguard shooting at him. A bullet hit Tamura's guard in the belly. The man instantly dropped to his knees. Sebastian vaulted over him, spun around, and fired once. The bullet hit the guy in the back of the head.

Panic filled street fighter's eyes as he witnessed his partner get killed. He slammed the SUV door closed with Tamura crouched in the backseat. Within seconds, the SUV was slipping and careening down the muddy road, away from the cabins.

Sebastian glared at me. I nudged Lani between the shoulder blades and said, "Know my enemy . . . now let's go."

Lani hissed in return. "You're nuts. We could already be in Lihue having a latte at Starbucks."

As we ran, I shouted to her, "Once in the trees, you need to hide, Lan. I need Sebastian to follow me."

"I'm not leaving you, Sista," she yelled from behind. "So shut up and run."

"You're such a hard-headed *potogee*."

"Now you're down to name-calling, huh?"

"I give up," I shouted, but chuckled at her limitless friendship.

The ease with which Sebastian had killed Tamura's body-guards confirmed that I'd made the right decision in applying my father's three-word war strategy.

I headed for the first trap: a steep, fifty-degree mountainous slope, covered with years of accumulated leaves from the canopy of towering trees above. These acted like a lubricant; once you lost your footing, it became impossible to stop. It was like a giant, slippery, two-hundred-foot slide, and you'd end crashing into a row of thorny wild shrubbery at the bottom.

I cried out to Lani, "Hang on to my back when we hit the down slope."

"What?"

I shouted, "I said hold on to my back and don't let go."

Our legs went out from under us at the top of the hill, and we fell on our butts.

Lani yelled, "Oh crap!"

We zoomed down the steep incline.

Lani spun halfway around and tried to grip the ground.

I screamed, "No!" and nudged her with a shoulder to hold on.

She shouted in my ear, "Fuck! Fuck! Fuck!"

From the sounds of Sebastian's footsteps, I sensed he was maybe fifty to a hundred feet behind us. Then it came. Sebastian cried out, "Ugh!"

The rope was where I'd left it, pinched between a wishbone tree branch and pegged to the ground. The other end of the rope was secured to the overhead bough of a giant mango tree that extended high over the slope. I had one chance to grab it. If I missed, we'd be propelled into my own trap.

Getting closer, I clawed at the earth like a boat's rudder, trying to shift a fraction of an inch toward the rope. I reached my arm out to its full extension. I felt the length of rope in my hand. I gripped it with everything I had and hung on. The rough fibers burned my hand, the rope stretched tight. The tree bough flexed with Lani's and my combined weight. My arms felt as if they were being yanked from its sockets, arm ligaments stretching. Lani reached over my head and grabbed on to the rope. Our bodies swung away from the bottom shrubbery.

Sebastian zoomed past us, his legs and heels frantically digging into the loose leaves, but unable to stop. A horrid scream erupted when he crashed into the chest-high wall of thorns and branches.

Spaced apart throughout the shrubbery, we had set up camou-flaged *punji* sticks—bamboo that had been cut and sharpened, the tip hardened with fire and inserted through wooden boards—a primitive weapon used by the Viet Cong.

"Lani—let go," I choked out. She had her arm clamped around my neck.

"Sorry," she shouted into my ear and let go.

I glanced down at the bottom of the slope. Thick, wild thorns and intertwined branches had entangled Sebastian's ankles and legs as though he were caught in a gill net. His face contorted with pain. He fumbled to get up, got up, fumbled again, and fell to the ground.

He screamed. "You're fuckin' dead!"

While on a vacation in Vietnam, my father had talked about using military strategy against a superior opponent. His voice had reverberated during my planning. "It could be self-defeating to attack a superior opponent directly. Commanders gained advan-tage by attacking the corners or exposed strategic points."

From my experience in the abandoned building in Shin Okubo Korean Town, I was prepared for Sebastian's superior fighting skills.

My father had held up three fingers and said, "Weaken and defeat."

Though unsure about the extent of Sebastian's injuries, we kept running and headed for the next trap. Whether he was hurt or simply being more cautious, Sebastian started to drift back.

The narrow trail led to the river. I pointed to the trip wire. Lani was moving as though she were in shock, but still nodded. We stepped over the wire, camouflaged by leaves, which stretched across the trail. It would have worked perfectly at night. I was hoping that Sebastian would be distracted by rage and not see it until it was too late.

Lani: "Where da fuck did you learn this stuff?"

"My dad."

Almost to the riverbank, a hundred yards away, the trip wire snapped behind us. It whooshed, the sound of fast-moving air, a shrieking scream came from behind us. Similar to another kind of booby trap used in Vietnam, the cocked bamboo had whipped foot-long spikes at a hundred miles an hour into whoever triggered the wire. Had the spike hit a homerun, driving into Sebastian's chest, or had it just clipped him?

Out of breath, Lani huffed out, "You think it got him?"

I pulled Lani along by the arm. "I don't know, but let's keep moving. I've got one more about three hundred yards upriver. It's not guerrilla warfare, but electrical warfare."

She frowned in confusion. I didn't have time to explain it to her.

We arrived at what I hoped would finish off my mother's killer.

Because of the many rivers and streams, Kauai had numerous small hydroelectric plants in the mountainous areas. In front of the power plant building stood a substation that transformed the lower voltage of the generator output to the higher voltage of the electrical grid. I had purchased post insulators from the hardware store in Princeville and redone a portion of the surrounding chain-link fence so that it floated above ground.

I instructed Lani, "If this plan fails then stay hidden."

"I'm not going to desert you."

"You're not deserting me, Lan. Once he goes after me, I need you to get back to the cabin and call the police. This is my last chance to defeat him. If this doesn't stop him, he'll kill me."

"When you say defeat, you mean kill him first?"

I didn't answer her.

When Kimo suggested that I call the police, I'd said adamantly, "I seek justice." He'd paused, then nodded in understanding.

Ever since David's death, lightning had fascinated me—nature creating its own electrical phenomenon. It was all about electrical current looking for a grounding point.

I swung the chain-link gate open, stepped into the high voltage substation, closed the gate, and threw the circuit breaker on.

I signaled for her to hide lower in the nearby bush and shushed. "Quiet, I hear footsteps."

37

Although Sebastian was in tiptop physical shape, Gena was like a deer in the wilderness. Even with countless obstacles popping up, her movements were smooth and unobstructed. If not for her friend holding her back, Gena would have been long gone.

One of the bitches cried out, "Oh crap!"

Sebastian grinned and pulled out the gun tucked at the small of his back as he ran. This was his moment; maybe one of them had fallen and broken a leg.

They'd been moving through thick forest, but fifty yards ahead the trail opened up, revealing a backdrop of mountain peaks.

Sebastian skidded to a stop at the top of the steep incline and watched the girls slide down the hilly slope on their butts. He needed to hurry, or the gap between them would grow. With his first step on the incline, Sebastian's feet slipped out from under him and he fell hard on his ass. He let out a noise like someone had punched him in the chest. He was skidding like a runaway sleigh careening down a snowy mountain; these damn leaves were slippery. He dug his heels into the ground, but he couldn't stop or slow down.

When Gena grabbed a rope hanging from a tree and she and Lani swung to the side, he knew it had been planned. But why? The answer came quickly, as he skidded directly toward a wall of thick thorny bushes at the base of the incline. Slipping and sliding, he twisted his body around and clawed at the ground, but he continued to slide.

What the heck, he thought, and let gravity take its course, expecting maybe some minor cuts and scratches from the tangled bushes.

The moment he crashed into the shrubbery; his thigh became ablaze in fire.

Sebastian screamed at the searing pain.

A stick, a fuckin' stick, stuck through his right thigh. The pain was paralyzing, blood dripped from the tip of the sharpened bamboo stick.

A damn trap, a trap—and he'd fallen for it.

Sebastian slammed his fist into the wet ground and screamed, "You're fuckin' dead!"

Hidden among the tangled shrubs were more sharpened bamboo stakes facing the hilled incline. Cringing with pain, he held his breath, then let out a horrific scream as he yanked the stake from his thigh. Blood oozed from the wound. Not enough blood to signal that the femoral artery had been severed, but the injury hurt like hell.

He removed his shirt, tore a large strip from it, and wrapped it tight around his thigh to help suppress the bleeding.

Sebastian braced himself with both hands and pushed off the ground. To test its strength, he started placing more weight on his right leg. He took a step but collapsed back onto the ground. He winced at the pain scorching the right side of his body. He pushed off the ground again, this time with less weight on his leg, and with a cross between a hop and a step, stumbled out of the thorny shrubbery.

I'll make them pay. Make them suffer.

Sebastian then remembered. He quickly scanned around him, searching the thick, tangled bushes for the gun. Sharp thorns poked and slashed his arms like tiny razors. The longer he searched for the gun, the more distance the girls were gaining. He rolled up his left pant cuff and unsheathed a seven-inch, double-edged, carbon-steel combat knife. This should do just fine.

Sebastian limped to where the end of the rope lay on the ground and followed the footprints into the forest. His pace had slowed due to the injury, though he was also taking time to study the terrain for more booby traps. He now understood why she'd picked this shithole place called Hanalei. He should have anticipated trouble, but his mind was focused on two things—one, getting the video, and two, whether to kill her slowly or quickly.

He slowed when he saw a wire covered by leaves, stretching across the narrow path, that only a blind man wouldn't notice. On the other hand, if he had been pushing harder, he might not have seen it. He stopped and ran a finger along its length, while not touching it. The wire led to a bowed, spring-loaded piece of bamboo; sharp wooden spikes embedded along its length.

The primitive booby trap had a cruel nastiness to it. Sebastian used a long branch to trip the wire. The swooshing of fast-moving air caused by the cocked bamboo flew over his head, sounding like multiple arrows shot from multiple bows. He screamed as though he'd been struck by the spikes. But it was more an outburst of fury at the cruelty she had tried to inflict on him.

Rage built on rage; his desire to kill them drove him harder. The trail led to a graveled road with huge potholes filled with rainwater. Sebastian sniffed the air and smelled something electrical up ahead.

He limped and followed the road to a concrete blockhouse.

On the opposite side of a chain-link fence that surrounded a handful of high voltage equipment, Gena stood, valiant and defiant. Where was her friend? Sebastian scanned behind him to check if she stupidly intended to attack him from the rear, but nothing came.

"Well, here I am." Gena's chest heaved. "Come and get me, shit face."

Sebastian faked a laugh. "Shit face, you can be more creative than that."

"Come on," she screamed. "Come here so I can beat the crap out of you."

The only entry into the fenced area was through the chain-link gate. Why would she trap herself inside? Stupid chick.

The Kami studied the gate and relived the movie *Predator*, remembering how the main character, Dutch, had screamed at the alien, "Do it! Come on! Kill me! I'm here!"

Hmm, something was definitely wrong. She was trying too hard to entice him to kill her.

38

Sebastian searched the ground. He calmly strolled to the side of the blockhouse and picked up a discarded, rusted, yard-long, half-inch diameter, galvanized water pipe.

My heart sank. He knew.

With his back to Lani's hiding place, I watched her sneak out from the bushes and dashed down the potholed road, back to the cabin and the police. I could shout out to her and make it two against one, but he could kill us both.

This was my fight, and mine alone.

Sebastian ambled over to the fence, twirling the pipe like a karate *bo* staff. He stood in front of the electrified gate, planted one end of the pipe into the ground, and let the other end pivot with its own weight into the metal. Sparks flew. The circuit breaker snapped open.

He picked up a branch from right next to him and dropped it against the gate and wet ground. No sparks, no nothing. He ridiculed me, laughing. "What're you gonna do now, Gena? Got any more traps?"

Sebastian swung the gate open. I stepped back, but the power plant blocked my retreat. Overconfident with my plan to electrocute this scumbag, I had stupidly trapped myself inside. But screw it, I didn't dwell on my error.

The only way out was through him.

I shuffled left then right, but he mirrored my moves and blocked the gate like a goalie. A sinister grin appeared on his face, and with his cold eyes he looked at me as if I were a caged animal at his mercy.

My only option was to get him talking and work on his fragile ego. Like in the cabin, I projected full control over the situation. I shouted firmly, "I'm going to get the truth out of you."

"Truth?" Sebastian frowned, confused. "It's your mother's fault."

"How—how is this her fault?"

"Because . . ." His voice faded.

"Because what!"

"Justice!" he screamed. "Your mother seduced my father at her bar and left my mother home alone. He'd come home drunk and beat her."

My mind raced, looking for a way out. I tried reasoning. "Listen to yourself, Sebastian. It was your father's choice to visit a bar. It could have been *any* bar. And I'm sorry he hit your mother, but it was no fault of my mom's. None."

"Gena, I know where your father is." His words jerked me back. "You give me the video and I'll take you to him."

More lies.

"I have him held under lock and key."

I knew I shouldn't be talking to this scumbag because I could sense he was a skilled manipulator, but I hurt for the truth. I shouted, "Where's my dad?!"

He took a limping step forward, cringing with pain from his thigh wound. "I knew you were smart, and strong—like me. Everything got complicated when I fell in love with you."

"Love!" I shouted. "Are you fuckin' nuts!"

His eyes first burned at being ridiculed, but then he looked away and avoided eye contact. "You and I are the same, Gena. We're cut from the same cloth."

"No, we're not." I inched two steps away from the building wall. "I don't go around killing people."

Sebastian lowered his gaze to the ground then looked up at me. "Yes, we are. The only difference between you and me is that you *accept and cope*, while I seek justice."

"I feel that my father is already dead." My voice cracked at finally admitting the truth.

"Your father . . . I can take you to him. Just give me the video."

"If he's alive, I'll find him myself." I planted my feet in the soft mud, preparing to run. "But I can feel in my bones that he's dead. Maybe someday the ocean will give him up. As for now, he'll rest in peace in a place he loved. Go to hell."

The sky was a heavy gray; dark, pregnant, ominous clouds loomed overhead as if filled with rainwater and on the verge of pouring their wrath upon the earth. The trees, the valley, and the mountain peaks glided into impenetrable darkness. The heavy drops felt like soft rubber bullets against my skin, spread out in intervals that made each drop visible, quickly building to a crescendo, a violent deluge.

Sebastian's eyes bulged. His scream held me frozen. He covered the six-foot distance in a blink and delivered a powerful punch to my mouth. The impact stunned me; pain shot up to my brain. I stumbled backward and collapsed on the wet ground. He pounced and pinned me with a knee. He hit me again and again, his fist slamming into the side of my head. I tried covering up with my forearms, but his punches came from everywhere, and fast.

He pulled back. His thigh wound oozed blood. He limped

back and tightened the makeshift tourniquet. "Your head games won't work twice."

With blurred vision, I stared up at the treetops, struggling to get up. I stumbled from dizziness and rolled against the chain-link fence. On the edge of blacking out, I shook my head, grabbed a handful of wet mud, and smeared the coolness on my face. My throat contracted and I vomited onto the soft ground.

Although pummeled, I refused to cower, or show any sign of weakness. I ran my tongue along my bleeding gums, spit out a bloody tooth, and shouted at Sebastian, "That the best you got?"

He shrugged with amusement but said nothing.

It wasn't his shouting, threats, or fists that scared me; it was his cold unemotional crazed eyes that held me terrified.

He started talking to himself, almost child-like. First soft, then louder, he counted in Japanese. "Ichi, ni, san, shi, go . . ." The more Sebastian counted, the calmer he got.

The cadence then switched, and he started to count down from ten. "Juu, kyuu, hachi . . ." Each number was like turning a screw tighter. His face muscles tightened; his hands clenched harder into fists.

I stood up, dazed. On wobbly legs I staggered to the left of him like a drunkard. Then, like I did in basketball to get separation from my opponent and position myself for a better jump shot, I slammed a hard right shoulder into his chest. He let out an "oof" and lost his footing on the muddy ground.

I sprinted to the gate, barged through, and ran.

I glanced at the trail leading deeper into the forest and knew that I had a concussion, because I was hallucinating my kid brother standing in the middle of the fork in the trail.

David kept pointing to the right of the trail and he mouthed, "Sugi-sugi-obake." I blinked once and he vanished.

I dashed to the right, where my brother had pointed, knowing something bad was about to happen.

Run! Go Gena! I heard my little brother's tiny voice.

I staggered and weaved, disoriented in the forest and gray darkness. I touched my face; my cheeks were bloody and wet.

"Have to rest . . . to hide, to rest." I pushed myself forward as Sebastian crashed behind me. His voice echoed in the forest. "Gena! Stop right now!"

I can't die here.

"Gena! I'm coming for you!" he hollered into the torrential rain. "It's inevitable, so stop running! Stop—I'll forgive you if you stop."

Keep going. Don't stop.

His footsteps pounded up the steep, muddy hill. He cried out, "I'm right here, Gena! Ready or not, here I come, babe!"

I repeated over and over, "Get stronger, smarter, faster. You're more resourceful than you think you are. You're going to make it! Don't give up. If you give up, you die."

I thought he couldn't get any weirder, but then he started singing above the thrashing rain. "I'm singin' in the rain, just singin' in the rain. What a glorious feeling I'm happy again . . ." He stopped and yelled, "Gene Kelly, 1952. You Americans make fuckin' great movies!"

Lightning flashed. My brother's smile took me out of Sebastian's world of craziness. My mother laughed her infectious laugh. Father and daughter fist-bumped, high-fived, then shouted in unison, "Hooyah!"

An idea popped into my head.

"Gena, stop!" Sebastian screamed from closer behind.

I didn't look back, just kept running. I knew where I had to go, and what I had to do.

"Keep following me, asshole," I mumbled as I ran for the waterfall. "That's it . . . keep following me."

This is where it ends.

39

I led Sebastian to the edge of the waterfall. He wielded a knife in front of me, cutting off any route to escape, though escape was *not* in my plan. The chase through the deluge had washed the blood from Sebastian's face, his scratches and lacerations were now visibly prominent. The puncture wound to his thigh dug deep into tissue layers and dripped blood.

Black clouds swaddled the earth in darkness. Thunder rumbled and cracked overhead. The shock wave vibrated my skin and thumped deep into my chest.

The hate in Sebastian's eyes froze my feet to the uneven, rocky surface. I had no doubt he was going to kill me and toss my body over the fifty-foot cliff into the deep gorge that formed the narrow swimming hole.

The torrential downpour dissolved the rising mist from the falls. My feet slid on the slippery surface. I dug the edge of my foot into a rocky seam for traction.

Sebastian feigned an attack, stabbing at my eyes. I reacted and snapped my head back. The instant I did it, I knew I screwed up. In a single motion, the knife circled and slashed at my midsection.

I automatically reacted, trying to block the attack, but the knife blade sliced my right forearm. I screamed. Wincing with pain, the knife cut deep, blood rolled down my forearm, wrist, and off my fingertips.

Sebastian basked in his imminent victory. I yanked off my tank top and wrapped it around my forearm a couple times to stop the bleeding. I used my teeth to secure a knot.

Mr. Kapena's voice rang repeatedly in my head—*Take the hit. Take the hit.*

I ignored the pain. I ignored the fear of being cut again, of dying. The blood, the pain didn't exist. I readied myself for his next attack.

Large raindrops pelted my face. I repeated softly, "Flow and re-direct . . . flow and re-direct."

I didn't need to see the blade to sense its position in relation to Sebastian's movements. He slashed at my face. This time I didn't react. I followed his momentum, avoided the steel blade, and redirected the knife away from me.

In one continuous motion, my fist shot out at his throat. Knuckles hit soft flesh. His head snapped back. He grabbed his throat, gasping to breathe. I didn't let up. Weakened and slowed, Sebastian again swung the knife, targeting my head. I dropped to one knee and avoided the blade as it swished through the air above me. I delivered a crisp punch to the open *punji* wound.

Sebastian's scream was not human.

He staggered to the edge of the cliff, creating distance between us, like a boxer between rounds trying to regain his strength. His once handsome face was now distorted with pain.

Suki was as interval of vulnerability, of indecisiveness, of rest, and my opening.

This animal murdered my mother. I placed my head down and charged. My shoulder hit Sebastian hard under his ribcage. At the same time, I shoved him outward with my arms for separation, I pumped my legs once. We both catapulted and flipped together over the edge of the cliff, out into space. My stomach floated up into my chest as gravity pulled me down.

Our bodies careened off the cliff.

Falling. Falling.

It was during our family vacations that the local kids had egged me on to jump from the cliff, but they first taught me where to land, and most importantly where *not* to land in the swimming hole.

We hit the brown water in tandem. The icy mountain water stunned me into temporary limbo. Though relieved that I had ended in deeper water, it wasn't over. I struggled to surface. The river turbulence kept pulling me under. I battled the current with every ounce of strength I had, at times swallowing muddy water, and broke through the windblown surface sucking air.

Sebastian's left elbow hung loose from his body, like cut strings from a puppet's arm. I knew the rocks had done its job when I hit the water and heard the sound of breaking wood four feet away from me. If I had pumped my legs too hard or not shoved him far enough away, I too could have met a rocky fate. Sebastian floated on the surface, struggling to tread water with one arm in the building river rapids.

Weaken and defeat.

Kicking off my shoes, I side-stroked to the side of the falls and stood on a shallow underwater ledge. White noise from the waterfall vibrated against my skin. Blood dripped from my wound, creating streaks along my forearm. The air was filled with the thick smell of algae and mud, and the roar of crashing water from the falls next to me.

Though I'd climbed this cliff many times to jump into the swimming hole, that was during the sunny days of summer. The rain had coated the cliff surface in a slippery sheen.

Then I heard it. The heavy thunder, the familiar sound I feared. I heeded my brother's warning. *Sugi-sugi-obake.*

Branches snapped. The earth shook. It rumbled like an approaching freight train, getting louder and louder. Though my heart pounded in my chest, I refused to panic.

David's voice screamed in my head. *Get to higher ground, Gena!*

My fingers clawed at the slippery rock ledges, searching for places to grab, to hold, fighting through the pain. My toes found purchase on ridges no bigger than a fist, lifting my body higher. The rumbling got louder, closer. Water oozed from the slippery face of the cliff. My hands extended, searching for a higher point to grab. Right foot, left foot, one step at a time, don't panic.

"Stay calm . . . stay calm . . . stay focused," I repeated out loud.

Half the distance up the cliff, my right leg jolted downward. Sebastian was gripping my right ankle like a vise with his good hand. His grunts pierced the roar of the falls. The cold, unemotional eyes that once terrified me went from fear to desperation to a wicked leer.

The flash flood rumbled closer, like an avalanche of boulders.

I kicked his hand with my left foot, trying to shake him, but he was still strong. His fingers dug into my ankle. I glanced up and saw a thick, twisted root growing out from the side of the cliff. Rusty water drained from underneath the root, eroding away the earth that could save my life. I stretched, but came up short by six inches.

At first, I thought Sebastian was trying to lift himself up, but realized he was trying to pull me back into the muddy pool and to my certain death.

With anger came strength. I exploded, extending another kick to his hand, then another, and another, until his grip slipped from my ankle to my foot. I stretched the six inches. My fingers grabbed the tree root. I locked my arm around the root and formed a grappling hook.

With tremendous force, like that from a fire hydrant turned on full blast, I got smacked sideways. Water gushed into my face, blinding me. Sebastian's weight increased tenfold, but I held on, praying that the root would hold. It did. Sebastian's hand suddenly slipped from my foot.

I screamed.

The flash flood filled the swimming hole, raising the water from twenty to thirty feet above its normal level in an instant. I clung to the root as if it were a life preserver.

I didn't know how long I'd been hugging onto the exposed root. The dark clouds still hung overhead, but now the downpour had transformed to a heavy drizzle. The chilly water felt refreshing against my face. The dirt-brown river water still raged below, but far less violently than before.

My hands were frozen, locked around the root as though welded to it. I pried my fingers open, needing to get moving. Without the adrenaline burst, fire returned to my wounded arm. Blood dripped from the makeshift bandage.

Pure desperation made me stronger as I worked my way upward like a mountain climber. Fingers, hands, and feet moving in synchrony, higher and higher, until I stood above the cliff looking down at the swimming hole.

The flash flood had left a mass of destruction in its path. Uprooted trees and other debris had washed either to the sides of the riverbed or pushed farther downstream as if an army of bulldozers had plowed through.

I didn't see Sebastian anywhere in the destruction. No one could survive that, no one.

Mind clear. No second thoughts. No pondering of errors or misjudgments.

"Accept and cope my ass." I scoffed, then started walking back to the cabin, loving the coolness of raindrops upon my face. For some unexplainable reason, I began humming the tune in my head then sang out loud, "I'm singin' in the rain . . . what a glorious feeling, I'm happy again . . ."

40

I thought Detective Lau was having a heart attack when his face blossomed red and he said with restrained calmness, "You're telling me to mobilize on the word of a prostitute?"

Lani and I were sitting across from Lau in his office at the main station of the Honolulu Police Department on South Beretania Street.

Lani had fidgeted uncomfortably the whole way in, shading her face with a hand so as not be recognized as we weaved through a throng of uniformed cops.

I glanced at a photograph of a younger Lau and his family at Disneyland, which sat behind him on the wooden hutch. "I know it doesn't look credible, but I trust her. She risked her life to find me and give back my mom's locket."

Still dubious, Lau said, "We could have apprehended the killer earlier if the Thai girl had come forward."

"She doesn't trust cops." I shrugged. "Look, Aom described what happened that night and identified the killer by his tattoo. My dad . . ." I cleared my throat, unable to fill that void in my heart of not having closure.

Lau's eyes narrowed as he fingered his jaw thoughtfully.

I repeated what Aom had said. "Kenji is smuggling underage girls from Thailand, Laos, Cambodia, and Myanmar to make his sex videos. There's a ship arriving from Southeast Asia called the Dhia Malaysia. Kenji will be there because he wants to inspect the merchandise."

Lau puckered his lips and squinted.

"This could be big for your department." I sensed that Lau wasn't politically motivated, but it was worth a try. "Plus, Kenji thinks he owns this island."

He leaned back, the springs on his chair squeaked. His face contorted.

"What if she's right?" I wiggled the bait at Lau's reluctance.

After a long minute, he twisted his head and gave me an indistinct nod.

Since I was on a roll, I pressed on. "I think you should consider having Mr. Kapena at the bust. Kusaka was the prime suspect who set him up by planting bribe money in his house. If it weren't for his wife's condition, he would have fought the allegations. Instead, he retired in disgrace. You guys owe him."

Lau stared blankly forward, tapping a finger on his desk, and nodded again.

"Great." I nearly jumped out of the chair, but settled back and decided to give it one final push. "And one more thing."

Lau creaked his neck back and forth as if trying to get rid of a muscle knot.

I swallowed and said, "Lani and I would like to tag along."

"No." The word fired out like a bullet. His mouth twisted stubbornly in a way I'd seen many times with my dad.

"If it wasn't for me—"

Lau held up a hand. "Still no."

"This guy blackmailed my best friend and made her work at a massage parlor because he threatened her kid brother."

Lau turned to Lani. "We got you on video going in and out of the massage place on King Street after your city job. You lucked out. We were about to raid the place, but someone at the top called it off. But that's been taken care of."

Lani fidgeted in the chair.

"What happened?" I was too curious not to ask.

"A state senator resigned because he got indicted for bribery." Lau paused before saying, "The answer is still no."

I gritted my teeth; I wasn't giving up. "This guy made me strip naked in his office. He's a pig. Please sir, we'd like to see the look on his smug face when he learns he's about to spend the rest of his life in prison."

Lau fingered his jaw again, then glanced out the window at the blue Hawaiian sky. After a moment, he spun back. "On one condition."

"Shoot." Lani straightened in her chair, clearly relieved that Lau had flipped the page on the topic of the massage parlor.

I calmed my friend down and asked, "What condition?"

"You stay in the car." He pointed a stern finger, like a school teacher ordering us to detention. "If either of you get out of the car, I will arrest you—both of you."

"Yes sir." Lani saluted like a storm trooper.

"Very funny." He grinned, then ushered us out of his office. "You're gonna get me fired. Now get out."

As we stood waiting for the elevator, Lani smiled and said, "Touché, Sista."

"What're you talking about?"

"Maybe there's hope for you yet." The elevator door slid open. Lani curtsied and said, "You first, my queen."

"What the heck . . ."

"You never, ever would have done that before."

I shrugged like it was no big deal, but it still felt good hearing it.

· · ·

THREE DAYS LATER, on a full-moon night, an army of HPD and SWAT officers were lying low with night-vision goggles. Everyone was heavily armed with M16s and wearing bulletproof vests. On edge, they waited for the signal from Lau.

It was after ten, and the moon illuminated the surrounding stacks of shipping containers and giant cranes, which cast shadows like prehistoric beasts. The air was thick with the scent of noxious petroleum mixed with seawater.

Lau had reiterated his demand that we stay put, so we sat frozen in the back seat of a black SUV like crash test dummies.

Mr. Kapena sat quietly in the front passenger seat; anticipation written across his face—he had waited years for justice. He lowered the volume on his walkie-talkie to nearly mute so as to not give away our position due to unexpected chatter.

With the ship scheduled to come in at eleven, we had arrived two hours early. To kill time, Lani had been playing with her phone under a thick jacket to hide the glow.

I poked her in the ribs when she started snoring lightly. "If Lau had put us any farther away, we'd be in another time zone."

Detective Lau's SUV was closer to the pending action, but not by much, and was hidden by a shipping container.

"If this is police work, I'd rather be cleaning parks," Lani said.

"With everything going on, I forgot—how'd it go with the lawsuit?"

Lani rubbed her eyes. "Well . . . I decided to call it off."

"Yeah?"

She yawned, croaked, and said, "They agreed to transfer Taguchi the Toad to another department. He must retire in six months or he'll lose his pension."

"So that's it?" I shifted my focus back to the deserted pier.

"Yep." Lani yawned. "All I wanted was fairness."

Mr. Kapena checked his wristwatch for the thousandth time.

His eyes had appeared alert since he'd been released from the hospital. His surgeon went ballistic about him checking himself out, but he eventually relented, as long as Mr. Kapena returned after this was done.

At 11:18 p.m., the cargo ship, stacked with shipping containers, hung low in the water as two tugboats guided it toward the pier.

Mr. Kapena spun around, his eyes dancing with excitement. "You guys wanna get closer?"

I quickly shook my head. "Lau will kill us."

He signaled for us to get out of the SUV. I gripped the door handle and held on like I was being pushed out of a plane at ten thousand feet in the air.

At just that moment, Kenji's truck drove onto the pier. I let out a breath. Although we were in the nosebleed seats, we ducked down and peeked over the dashboard.

Mr. Kapena's binoculars were glued to the pier, which was illuminated by residual light from a tower spotlight. "Don't worry, they can't see us." Lani and I also viewed the area with binoculars.

A large van followed Kenji's truck onto the pier. Two guys exited and met Kenji in front of his truck. Both guys were armed with twelve-gauge shotguns and holstered sidearms. The guy with the cigarette in his mouth must have said something funny to his partner because the other guy burst out laughing. Kenji glared at them to shut up.

Once the ship was secured to the pier, an Asian man in his mid-thirties, bald with a goatee and a Tibetan knit hat with tassels, waved from the ship's deck. The plank lowered and Kenji met him on the port deck. They shook hands as though they were longtime friends. They then climbed a ladder to the topmost shipping container at the stern of the ship.

The guy with the Tibetan hat unlocked the container and

swung the door open. Kenji's body tensed with excitement at the human cargo—a dozen half-naked Asian girls. They all looked to be under the age of eighteen. Their bodies looked weak and undernourished. They were shuffled out of the container, ankles bound together, walking like prisoners in a chain gang.

I was expecting dramatics—Lau announcing something like, "Let's take these mutherfuckers down" on the radio to his men, or something cool like, "Let's go to work, ladies and gentlemen."

Instead, calm and quiet, Lau said into the walkie-talkie, "Go."

Lani gave me a look—*Is that it?*

I shrugged.

Bright floodlights illuminated the area like daylight. The two men in front of the container of girls ran in opposite directions. Within seconds, police and SWAT closed in with guns ready. The moment the two men lifted their weapons, snipers shot both of them in the heart.

Kenji and the guy in the Tibetan hat were soon handcuffed and escorted along the pier to waiting squad cars with flashing blue lights.

Mr. Kapena turned to me. "Mahalo for convincing Lau for me."

I smiled. "You deserve this, Mr. Kapena."

"Kenji will talk in order to get protection." Mr. Kapena grinned with satisfaction. "The yakuza cannot let him live after this bust."

With that smug look of invincibility on his face, Kenji probably figured he'd be free by the end of tomorrow, but things had changed with the indictment of the senator.

Kenji saw us and sneered. "Hey bitches—you still looking for a job?" He forced laughter.

Lani flipped two middle fingers at him. I smiled—justice done.

When I got home, a little after 3 a.m., I walked to the back of the house with a glass of Merlot, sat on the swing, and glanced at the moon. I lifted the glass. "Here's to you, Mom and Dad."

Semi-content, I took a sip. However, the diamonds in their four separate silk pouches kept nagging at me, like a song I couldn't get out of my head. I had already concluded that the existence of the video must just be a rumor.

I drank the rest of the wine and placed the empty glass to the side. I pushed back with my legs and swung forward, waving my arms. As the swing fell back, I turned my body upside down, like I did when little. I had my legs wrapped around the swing's chain like a high-flying trapeze artist, and Mom would push and cry out, "Fly you to the moon."

Something caught my attention.

Being upside down had changed my perspective. I unwrapped my legs from the swing's chain, ran into the house, and retrieved a hand mirror. I held up the mirror to a scribbled mark on one of the swing posts. In the reflection, I saw the number four. I rushed to the other three posts—they all had the number four on them.

The following day, I hired an engineering firm that specialized in ground penetrating radar. A Caucasian man in his fifties named Tom kneeled down on the concrete and rubbed his palm across the surface. "What you got here, little lady?"

"I want to know if there's anything under that."

"Looks like a large part of the concrete pad was extended." I then recalled my dad, a few months ago, having bought few bags of pre-mixed cement and extended a large section of the pad where water always collected after heavy rains.

Tom's co-worker might have been an apprentice based on the way he jumped at instructions to unload the van and set up the equipment.

Within fifteen minutes, Tom had a laptop set up on a folding table, with cables connected to a handheld gizmo. The apprentice was in his mid-twenties, with kneepads pulled over his Levi jeans.

On his hands and knees, he scanned the surface of the concrete pad in systematic grids.

Tom squinted at the laptop, pointing at the screen. "We got something."

I leaned over his shoulder at the dark-shaded, box-like image.

He twisted his head back. "You wanna get it out? That means we gotta bust the concrete, then hire a mason to get it fixed."

"Yes, get it out."

Tom turned to his apprentice. "Bobby, fetch the jackhammer."

After the surface demolition, Bobby used a spaded shovel to clear the pieces of cement.

Tom instructed, "A little more to the left. Yep. Right there."

Bobby dug—*Clink.*

Tom handed him a handheld trowel. Bobby found the edges, dug out a steel box, and handed it to me.

I wiped the box with a wet cloth and started for the house.

Bobby's lips pressed together. "What, you not gonna show us what's inside?"

Tom shot off the knee-high stool. "Bobby my boy, it's not our business."

I shrugged. "Sorry."

I paid Tom, placed the box on the kitchen counter, and retrieved the key that I'd found in my mother's safety deposit box. I tried the lock. It fit. I flipped open the lid.

Inside was a DVD in a Ziploc bag, along with numerous flash memory cards and document hard copies. The majority of them were in Japanese. As I perused the documents, my hand started shaking. This was proof of corruption at the highest level, and not just in the police department. There were ledgers of transactions and payments to government officials.

Since my dad had built the concrete pad extension, he had to know about the lockbox and what was in it. There had to be a reason why he participated in Mom's secret . . . a reason I'll probably never know.

After I reviewed every document and video, I phoned Hanako. "You need to come to Hawaii. I'll pay for your flight and you can stay with me."

Hanako reluctantly said, "Can't you just send what you have through priority mail?"

"No, you need to hand-carry this stuff back to Japan. And don't show it anyone you don't trust. You have to meet with the right people."

Hanako arrived the following night. We went over the documents together, scrolling through the flash drives on my laptop.

I loaded the DVD into the player. "You need to see this."

On the screen, a naked Tamura stood next to the limp body of a teenage girl, the chief justice's daughter. Bound with rope and suspended naked from the ceiling, she wasn't moving. It looked like Tamura had realized what he'd done and slumped on the floor by her dangling feet.

Hanako swore through tight lips, "Kuso."

An envelope was attached to the DVD. I slid the letter out and reread it, out loud to Hanako: *"Kiyomi hid a camera and took this video. She thought I did not see her hide it in the bar. Maybe it was temporary, and she meant to move it later, but I played it and knew people could get killed because of what was on it, so I took it. Kiyomi suspected that I had the video, but I pretend like I didn't. She decided to spread rumors that I had the video and was blackmailing Tamura-san."*

The next morning, I drove Hanako to the airport, her backpack filled with the things I'd found in the steel box.

Hanako exited the truck and leaned in through the passenger window. "I wanted to tell you that they reopened the Novak's murder-suicide case as well. Kiyomi is the prime suspect."

I smiled with approval. "I'm sure the next time I see you, you'll be an inspector, Hanako."

When I got home, the White Whale was parked in the driveway. Lani strolled over and said, "You wanna get some shave ice?"

"Shoot." I hopped into the passenger seat.

With her fingers drumming on the steering wheel to a tune by *Pink* on the radio, she kept glancing back and forth between me and the road.

"What?"

"Hmm . . . do you think Josh has a girlfriend?"

I shrugged. "Tell you what—any man that beautiful must be gay."

"You think?"

"I would be."

"Yeah . . . me too."

We cracked up laughing.

As we drove down the hill with the view of Hawaii Kai below, I felt like I'd gotten better at letting things go. Though I didn't think I would *always* make the right decisions, I could at least try. Perhaps this too was simply a process to be repeated.

Cut-duck.

ABOUT THE AUTHOR

Cless Kai is an emerging author of action thrillers. He was born in Hawaii and now lives between Hawaii and Southeast Asia. After a successful career as an electrical engineer, he decided to pursue his passion in turning years of learning the craft into creative reality. His stories are set in Hawaii and the unique multi-cultural diversity of the Islands, as well as taking readers to exciting locales beyond its Pacific border.